Jeff's Plants

Dedicated to: My dad. I loved you anyway. Still do. Always will. And, to my children. You are the best things I have ever done.

Acknowledgements

Love and thanks to my husband for giving me the time, space, and support to grieve, heal, and write this book. I could not have done this without you.

Thank you to my children, for being the reason I want to heal.

I'm grateful for my friends, starting with Katrina, who planted the "you should write a book about this" seed. Thanks for providing the spark and encouragement. To Toni and Susan, for listening to me drone on endlessly about writing and publishing, and for believing in my story and its power.

Thank you to Kelsi, Tina, Detta, AnneMarie, Katie, Emily, and Jenn B. for beta reading Jeff's Plants, helping me with editing, and giving me amazing feedback. You played a major role in the creation of this book, and I appreciate you all so much.

I am immensely grateful to my editor, Runa Troy, whose patience and commitment brought this book to life in a way I couldn't have done alone. You have a gift for bringing out the best in things. Any success this book experiences will be a result of your insight and dedication.

Big shout out to every person and business that supported the journey of Jeff's Plants – Toni, Main Street Submarines, AnneMarie and Brad, Jennifer Fox, Hilton Garden Inn, and Hertz Rental Cars. *Hey Hertz, that Jeep may have saved my life.*

To everyone who inspired the characters in *Jeff's Plants*, thank you for being a part of my story. I hope you appreciate how you have been depicted. If you do not, that is nobody's fault but your own.

Jeff's Plants

A Tale of Loss, Legacy, and The Long Road Home

By Korva Keddie

"If you listen to my music and you see me, you're not getting anything out of it. If you listen to my music and you see yourself, it'll probably make you cry, and you'll learn something about yourself. And now you're getting something out of it, you know?"

Joni Mitchell

The End

Youtube.com
Steve Windwood (Blind Faith)
"Can't Find My Way Home"

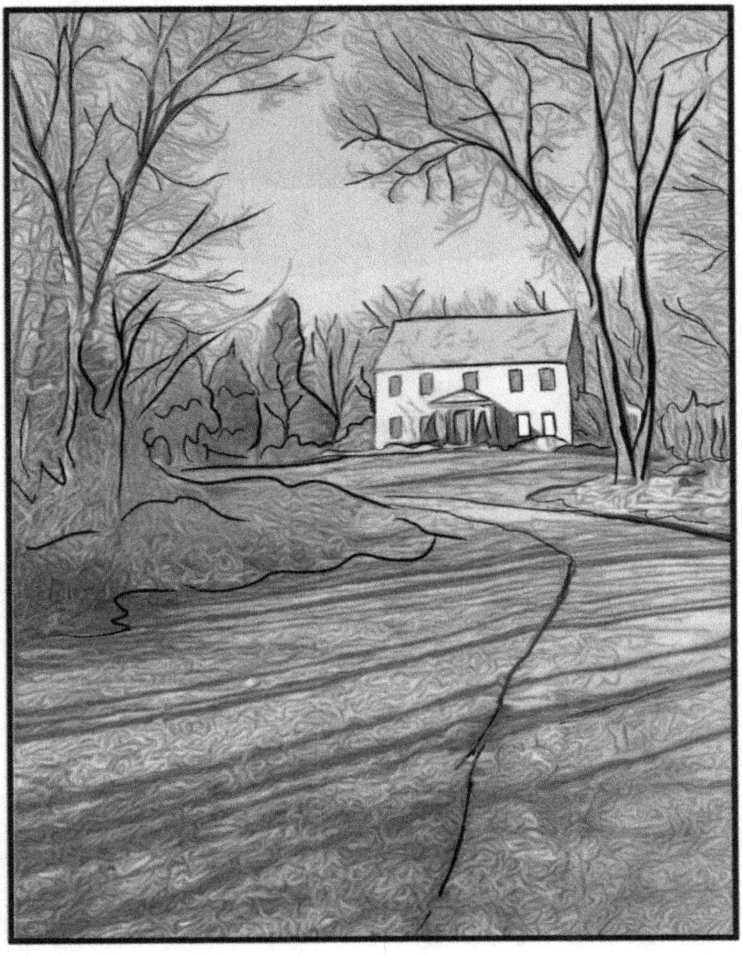

Chapter One

I would never have imagined that I could travel more than five hundred miles per hour and still be going too slow. There were thousands of miles to go, my father was dying, and our time was running out.

I arrived at Logan International Airport around 5:30 p.m. on Wednesday, December 22, 2021. The airport was a mess, as had the airport in Seattle been that morning. This was the first winter holiday season after more than a year and a half of lockdown, and people were traveling in hoards. At the same time, the pandemic brought on by COVID-19 was still running rampant and wreaking havoc. The understaffed airlines and airports would attest to that.

The lines were long and moved at a snail's pace. The man I stood behind for the better part of thirty minutes received a text message that made his face fall. He tapped the shoulder of his partner. She had an infant strapped to her front who she bounced to pacify, all while trying to keep her two other toddler children from running off. She read the text, mouthed the word "fuck" and began dragging their luggage and their children out of line.

Similar stranded families filled the corridors with piles of luggage, impatient children, and parents wrought with anxiety, desperate to find new ways to reach their holiday destinations. I could relate to the anxiety. My chest was tight, and my heart palpitated. I felt so much angst I could have crawled out of my skin. However, it wasn't my airport experience that weighed heavily on me. In fact, for me, everything went well. I had arrived at the airport with plenty of time to spare, so the long lines and delays didn't impact me. I even had time for a sit-down meal. But it wasn't enough to give me ease. I needed to be in Boston yesterday. Hell, I needed to be there two weeks ago.

I flew first class. It was not something I would do under normal circumstances but given the state of things, the idea of sitting in such close quarters with other people skeeved me out. I'd become a bit of a germaphobe over the previous couple of years. I was also so raw with emotion that I couldn't stand the idea of a stranger touching me. I was too vulnerable to be here with all these people. I needed as much space as I could carve out and was willing to pay the price for it.

As a result of my flight status, I was one of the first passengers to arrive at baggage claim. A gentleman approached me. I wouldn't say he was short, but he was below average height. He looked to be in his late sixties. His outfit, which could have come straight from an LL Bean catalog, was a pair of dark denim jeans, a classic scotch plaid flannel shirt, dark blue fleece vest, and rubber Moc Bean Boots. He reminded me a bit of my father. At least I know Jeff would approve of his fashion choices. He asked, "Are you in from Seattle?"

"Uh, yes. Yes, I am," I said looking back to see I was one of the few Seattle passengers ready to pick up their luggage. "I got a bit ahead of the crowd, but I'm sure they'll catch up pretty quick."

"Oh, good," he said, "my daughter and her kids are on that flight."

I felt myself hit with a wave of sadness, the likes of which I've never before felt. I remembered a time when my father had come to this airport to pick me and my children up. I knew that would never happen again.

We chatted for a couple of minutes. We talked about his daughter, where she lived in Seattle, and how long she'd been there. He told me about their Christmas plans. Then came the dreaded question, "What brings you to town?" he asked.

Through a tightened throat I said, "I'm here to visit my... dad... He's been put in hospice care."

By "visit him" I meant spend his last days with him. I had been holding back a river of tears for the better part of the last eight hours, and I couldn't stop them anymore. The dam broke. I began to cry what would have been an ugly cry if not for the face mask I was wearing. I put on a pair of sunglasses to hide my state from the rest of the crowd.

"I'm so sorry," he said. While the furrow in his brow showed concern for me, his sudden fidgeting suggested he was uncomfortable. I think he regretted asking. To his relief, his daughter and grandchildren arrived just before things got too awkward. "Merry Chris-," he stopped himself and said, "take care of yourself."

"Thanks," I said with teary eyes and a smile he couldn't see.

The kind man behind the Hertz rental car desk provided a similar experience. There had been a problem with my reservation. At first, I was told that it was something that couldn't be fixed after regular business hours and that I would have to come back the next day to pick up my car. But when he found out why I was there, he went above and beyond to get me a car straight away. He stumbled over what to say to me as I left. Happy Holidays did not feel appropriate. He settled on, "Take care," as well.

As awkward as those two interactions were, I felt so relieved to be able to tell someone what I was going through. I just spent the day with so many people, yet I don't think I'd ever felt so alone.

The drive out to Boxborough felt both too long and too short. Too long in that, all I wanted to do was be with my father and know how he was. I hadn't talked to him in months or heard from him by text in days. I didn't know how sick he was or wasn't. I wondered if I'd make it to see him alive. Even though he received his cancer diagnosis three years prior, and even though I knew this day wasn't long off, I believed that he was doing well. He and Joni made sure of that. Now I'm rushing across the country because all of a sudden, the time is now. All day I felt this push to hurry up and get there, but getting closer did nothing to relieve my sense of anxiety.

Thanks to the damn pandemic, I hadn't seen my dad in nearly two years. I was afraid of what he would look like after all that time. The last thing I wanted to do was burst into tears the second I saw him. Sick people don't need to be reminded that they are sick. But in his case, there was no "getting well" again, and I didn't want to remind him of that either. There was also the issue of me not knowing what I was walking into, given that just a couple of short months ago I was told to stay away. Now, as I tried to loosen my grip on the steering wheel of my rental car, only a few short miles stood between me and the truth.

My stepmother, Joni, called on October 5, 2021. We had made plans for a family get-together to celebrate Christmas later that year. My sister Jennifer and I were bringing our families back east to meet up with my parents and our brother James in New Hampshire. Joni said that my father started a new round of chemotherapy, and it wasn't going well. He was slated to continue through December, and he would not be up for traveling.

I asked, "Why is he back on chemo? Last I heard, everything was going well."

"Oh, ya know, it's just a maintenance thing. He'll just have to do this for… ya know… here on…," she said with an unsteady voice.

I didn't believe her. I didn't believe much of anything I was being told about his cancer.

At the end of the conversation with Joni, I said, "Listen, I need you to promise me something."

"Ok…," she said with reluctance. Her tone was shaky and suggested that she wasn't comfortable making that agreement until she knew what I was going to ask.

"Please tell me if things get bad. Ya know, like… if he is going to die. I need to say goodbye." I would have expected her to respond with "Of course" or "I promise" or something that acknowledged the importance of my request. That isn't what I got.

Instead, she responded with, "Well, chemo never killed anyone, Korva." The way she said it gave me the impression that she thought I was being too dramatic. I also took that as a decline to make my requested promise.

She said that Jeff didn't want to talk, he wasn't feeling up for it, so I emailed him:

> *Joni called today. I'm so sorry you aren't feeling well. Chemo sucks. I'm thinking of you. Please let me know if there is anything I can do. I know Christmas is cancelled. If you're up for it, maybe I could come visit during one of your off-chemo weeks. I'd love to see you, no matter what your situation is.*
>
> *Love you tons, Beans*

Beans was my childhood nickname. It fell out of favor at some point. Either I had outgrown it, or he stopped using it when I fell out of favor. I was the black sheep. I had been labeled a troubled teen and never quite shook the reputation. Even as an adult, no matter how well I was doing, the stain of my youth would not relent.

He sent a brief response later that evening:

> *Yes, I know you guys spoke. I'll give you a call when I have a lucid moment. Seems like I perk up after 6 or 7 days (Fri/Sat). For reasons I don't quite understand, I seemed to have gotten*

more than I bargained for this time. Maybe I thought I was a Chemo veteran of some sort.

Love J

I didn't hear from him "6 or 7 days" later. Either he still wasn't feeling well enough to call me or he didn't want to talk to me. Both options sucked. I let go of that and decided to reach out to him again. This was a risk for me. My father and I had a complicated relationship. Other than a few years during my adolescence, things were never easy between us. I hated it. I mustered up some courage and emailed:

I didn't hear from you, so I'll assume you still aren't up for it. I'm so sorry.

I'm writing to let you know that I want to come out there. I know this is not a good time for company, so I can redirect the money we're saving by not flying six people to NH towards getting a room at the beautiful Boxborough Regency for a couple weeks. And I can get my own car. I just want to see how you're doing and be of service - drives to appointments, or grocery store trips, or doing dishes, walking dogs, whatever. I'm fine with short visits and taking covid precautions. Whatever it takes.

It sounds like this last month has been challenging for all y'all and I want to help. Even if you don't need it, I need to do it. Ya gotta give me this.

If there is a time when I can be most useful, let me know. Otherwise, I'm thinking 10/21-11/4.

Get back to me when you can. I love you and you're in my thoughts always.

Love, Beans

His response to my email confirmed my fears.

Korva, this is a bad idea. The last thing I need right now is a guilt trip. I've got enough on my mind as it is. I don't need more stress from company. I'd like what privacy I get.

I'll let you know when it'll be most useful. I've got appointments this week that could improve the situation, so just wait.

I'm not trying to be mean, but if you show up, I'll be pissed. I'm just trying to be honest and save heartache for everyone.

Sorry, Jeff

Dammit all to hell. What the hell is all that? What guilt trip is he talking about!? I asked for what I wanted and emphasized its importance, and that's a damn guilt trip? And whose heart is he trying to save from aching? Because he's breaking mine.

I so desperately needed to be with my father. I wanted to make a few more memories or to have one more conversation. I wanted to know him just a little bit more. I felt confused and rejected. I wanted to beg and plead with him. I wanted to lash out in hurt and anger at him. But I stayed quiet. For the first time in my whole life, I decided not to respond to my father. At all. He said he'd be in touch, so I dropped it.

On November 21st, nearly a month and a half after our last email exchange, I sent:

Just checking in to say I'm thinking of ya and hope you're feeling better. Send an update when you can.

To which he responded:

I'll call you when I have a lucid moment. Not much new, still dealing with the ravages of this ill-conceived Chemo torture.

Then on November 25th he sent:

>*Haven't been really up to conversation these last few days. They dragged me down to the hospital for another lung CT scan on Tuesday…no new findings. Still saying radiation damage and back up to 40 mgs prednisone. I'll call when I can. Happy Thanksgiving.*

The part of me that gives everyone the benefit of the doubt wanted to think that it was thoughtful of him to reach out. The jaded part of me that has been around the block a time or two with this man, thought this was a bullshit email written as a preemptive strike to make sure I didn't call. It was hard not to be cynical.

Worry, however, superseded cynicism now. Nearly two months had gone by, and he still wasn't up for talking on the phone. I know he didn't like talking on the phone, but come on. I wondered if he was afraid that if I heard his voice, I would know how bad it was and make a bigger issue of seeing him. Maybe he knew I would hear through his bullshit. Maybe he couldn't lie out loud to me. Of course, there's the part of me that was afraid he didn't want to talk to me because he didn't like me. All things I had to keep letting go of, and often not so gracefully.

On December 13th, my stepmother called to let me know Jeff was in the hospital. He had asked to be taken to the ER in the middle of the night. He was in crippling pain. The idea of it made me nauseous. My father was as stubborn as they came, and for him to give in to pain was not a good sign. I asked what the source of the pain was. She gave me some blurry answer about the doctors thinking maybe he had a cyst in his liver erupt.

I remember thinking, "Are erupting liver cysts a thing? Shit."

That afternoon, when talking to my sister, the language changed to them finding "spots" on his liver. The next morning the truth came out.

One of two tumors in his liver had burst. That was the source of his pain. I didn't know what to think.

I said, "Did they not see these tumors on his last scan?! His cancer is gastroesophageal. When did he start having liver cancer? Last I was told things were 'looking good'."

"No, they saw them. Yeah, I don't know what to say, Korva," Joni said matter-of-factly.

I was speechless. In that moment, so much became clear. The cancer had metastasized, and they knew it. I felt an overwhelming surge of anger because this truth revealed so many other untruths. They knew when they canceled our Christmas plans. They've been lying to me for who knows how long. I don't think they had ever been completely honest about the extent or the prognosis of this cancer. But why?

He called me on February 10, 2019, to tell me about his diagnosis. As soon as he said the word cancer the questions came pouring out of me. What kind of cancer? Gastroesophageal. How big? He didn't know. How many? He didn't know. What stage? He said, "They don't tell you that kinda stuff anymore."

I thought, "Hmm. Bullshit." From that point on, the reports were short, non-specific, and focused on the side-effect issues he was having rather than the state of his cancer.

They had been lying to me for the last three years. What was I supposed to do about it now? My father was dying. Joni's husband was dying. This wasn't the time to pick a fight, so I didn't press matters further. Plus, I was afraid if I did push the matter, I may never see or talk to my father again.

He went home from the hospital on Thursday the 16th of December. At this point, he wasn't eating. He was heavily medicated and slept most of the time. On December 18th, he was hospitalized again. This time for vomiting blood. One of the esophageal tumors was bleeding. Not a good sign. I talked to Joni on Sunday the 19th, chomping at the bit to book a flight. This was the second time in a week he had been hospitalized and my anxiety about what was really happening to Jeff was through the roof. Joni asked me to wait until Monday when she spoke to the oncologist about ongoing treatment. On Monday the 20th, my stepmother, my half-siblings Jennifer and James, and I had a conference call.

Joni said Jeff was being brought home and would be put in hospice care. My first reaction was anger, and I mean full-blown rage. *Hospice care?* He went from being fine, to having erupting and bleeding metastasized tumors, to being in hospice care all in the course of a week. This was happening too fast, and I felt like I was being robbed. I've been trying to get my family to deal honestly with the reality of Jeff's impending end since his diagnosis. Now here I am, too far away, needing to travel the week before Christmas in the middle of a goddamn pandemic. I was ready to lose my mind. *My father is dying, dammit.*

I didn't know who I was madder at. I was mad at Jeff for lying to me and using his anger to manipulate me. I was mad at Joni for also lying to me and enabling all of this bullshit. And I was mad at myself for letting them get away with this garbage. I had been stonewalled and gaslit. Again. I knew what was up. I knew this whole time they were lying. I went along with the goddamn program, and it had cost me.

I was asked again to wait to book my flight until they got hospice worked out. I didn't wait. I booked my flight, a hotel room, and a car that night. I got the last first-class seat. Tuesday the 21st, after waiting eight days, I got the official "book your flight" text from Joni. A text that should have come much, much sooner.

Chapter Two

I was full to the brim with dread as I pulled into my parents' driveway. Joni came through the garage to meet me. She was already crying. *Crap. She isn't a crier; this can't be good.* We whimpered hellos, hugged, and dragged my things inside. Then came the obligatory greetings to the dogs and cat. My brother, James, was there. It was good to see him.

He looked much older than I remembered. He had a couple more wrinkles around his eyes and a couple fewer hairs on his head. He was looking more and more like a taller, lankier version of Jeff every day. I'm sure this has been hard on him. James lived with our parents and had to watch Jeff's disease unfold. While that would be hard on any person, James is on the autism spectrum. I couldn't say exactly where on the spectrum because it's a taboo subject in my family, but I worried that it would impact his ability to process what was happening with our father.

I kicked myself for not reaching out to him more over the last couple of years. There was twenty years and not enough track record between James and me. We weren't close. However, his greeting that night was especially warm and welcoming, and he felt more comfortable and familiar than ever before.

After we got settled, Joni went to check on Jeff. They had a hospital bed and other hospice gear set up in his office. It seemed right given how much time he spent there. She asked if I wanted to see him. I couldn't. I felt like I had chickened out, but the ground underneath me wasn't solid enough yet. We small-talked for another fifteen minutes or so until we heard noise coming from his direction. Joni went in for a moment and then popped her head out and said, "He says come on in."

Well, shit. Here it was. A moment that I have both wanted and dreaded with every ounce of my being. I wasn't ready, and that didn't matter. I crept into his office. The first thing I noticed was the smell. It wasn't bad, but it wasn't right. It was institutional and felt out of place. The lights were dim and hazy. My eyes searched until I found him. *Fuck.*

I had to steel myself to keep from a full breakdown. His eyes were still his, but everything else looked unfamiliar. His face was puffy; a probable result of the steroids he had been taking to assist with the inflammation he had in his lungs. His mouth looked like it was foreign even to him, like he couldn't find a comfortable way to hold an expression. I'm sure it was the result of the fentanyl patch and oxycodone cocktail he was on. His words came out in soft, short, labored sentences. His breath came in a struggled pant. I wondered for a moment if he was crying. I couldn't tell. After a few minutes, his breathing leveled, and we were left sitting in silence.

Because I didn't know what else to do, I went into service/survival mode. "Do something. Do anything!" I thought. I asked if he was comfortable or needed anything.

He said, through some effort, to me and Joni, "The two of you… are going to… have to… embrace… inaction."

I wanted to cry but instead gave a soft chuckle and said, "Right… So seriously, what do you need? Are you comfortable?" That's when I noticed his hard-brimmed ball cap.

Jeff was a "buttoned up" guy looks-wise. His signature outfit would have included a pair of nice - perfectly aged, to show wear but not distress - real denim, jeans. In the 1980s they would have been ironed with a crease down the front. He'd wear a crisp, white oxford shirt. Ironed meticulously with one button undone at the top and sleeves rolled cleanly and exactly to his mid-forearm. He would wear soft leather loafers in an orange-ish brown-ish tone that were the same color as the backside of his guitar. And for the last decade or so, he'd wear a hard-brimmed ball cap. My favorite was the classic New York Yankees one.

His hair had been thinning for a long time. Not like regular male pattern baldness. His was all over and more diffuse. It bothered him. And I understood. I, myself, have been struggling with hair loss on and off since my mid-twenties. It's the worst. So, I empathize. And there he was, on his deathbed, wearing that damn hat. I asked if he wanted something else for his head, like a beanie or something. He said, "Yeah, you got one?"

As a matter of fact, I did. The day before, in preparation for being away from home for an undetermined length of time, I decided to put away *all* the clean laundry (even that one basket that only gets emptied once every six to nine months). I came across one of my husband's thin cotton beanies. He has them to keep his bald head warm at night. Something made me pack it for this trip.

I dug it out of my suitcase and brought it to my dad. I knew there was no way he was going to let me help him with that, so I handed it to him and told him I'd keep my eyes closed. He gave a little laugh and said, "Close your eyes AND turn around. No peeking." It was a sweet moment. He was being… playful. I didn't expect that.

I didn't know what to do or say. I just sat there, trying not to bawl like a baby. I asked if I could hold his hand. He said yes. He seemed to drift in and out of consciousness. During one of his more "lucid moments" he said, "It's good to see you." I can still hear it in my mind. I didn't know it at the time, but that would be the last real thing I would remember him saying to me. It healed a million things. It was a gift, but at that moment it broke me.

Tears and anguish erupted from me but only for a second. I reeled it back in because I didn't want to remind him that he was dying and that I was devastated. Through a tight throat, I managed to get out, "It's good to see you, too."

I stayed up as late as I could that night, making sure he took his pain medication and drank as many fluids as possible. There were reports that he was being a difficult patient, but he was good with me. He took all the medication he was given. He put on a brave face when he had to swallow through pain that had made its way through several medications. A couple of times, as he slept, I would notice him grimacing. I would reach over and hold his hand. He'd wake up for a moment, see me, and fall back to sleep, seeming to be more comfortable. At least I like to think so.

Crazy as it sounds, it was exactly what I needed. All I ever wanted was to love and express caring for my dad, and in these small moments in the darkest hours of a Thursday morning, I got the chance.

Joni had hired someone to help overnight so that we could get rest. At around 3 a.m., I caved and went to bed. I wanted to go get a pillow and blanket and sleep in the recliner next to him, but it had been a long, hard day of travel, and I needed a few hours in a soft bed. I thought I'd take the late shift again tomorrow since I was already on Pacific time.

By the time I got up the next morning, the hospice nurse had already been in to see Jeff, and his medication had been changed to morphine. He was sleeping more soundly. The grimaces that had broken his rest the night before had stopped, and I was grateful for that.

My sister's flight got into Boston around 2 p.m. that afternoon. Even though it hadn't been a full twenty four hours since I had made the trek from Logan International, I offered to go pick her up. I figured I could use the ride back from the airport to prepare her for what she was walking into.

"He's been sleeping most of the day," I said to Jennifer as we made our way back out to Boxborough. "Maybe he'll wake up when we get back."

"Yeah, maybe…" she said. "I don't know if… I'm just not good at this stuff. I don't know… if I want him to wake up. I mean, what do I say?"

"Yeah, I don't know," I said. I felt for her. I didn't know what to say either.

"What does he look like?" she asked with hesitation. I was sure she didn't really want to know.

"Well," I searched my mind for the right words, "he… doesn't look like himself. I don't know how to describe it. Just be ready to be surprised. I mean, I was a little shocked by how far along he is. It's hasn't even been two weeks since the first ER visit and he… he… is just further along than I was expecting."

"Huh…ok," Jennifer said as she stared out the window. She seemed distracted, as though her mind was somewhere other than the car.

"Ya know, Jennifer, they were lying to us," I said changing the subject.

"Huh?" she asked, now perked up and present. "What do you mean?"

"Well, that was bullshit about his chemo being par-for-the-course treatment activity. No, his cancer has spread. That's why he went back on chemo. They lied to us."

She let out a deep sigh and said, "What is wrong with these people?"

"Beats me," I said with a shrug. There was no figuring them out. Changing the subject again, I said, "So what do you think your mother will do… ya know… after he's gone?"

"Oh, huh, I have no idea," she said as if she'd never considered it.

"Ya think she'll move out to Indiana?" I asked.

"Yeah, um, I don't know," she said with a shrug.

"My guess is that she would. Why would she stay here?"

Again, she said, "Yeah, I-I don't know."

Jennifer had the same experience of anxiety coming down the driveway as I did. I was glad that at minimum she had an idea of what she was walking into. She had the same initial difficulty going in to see him but got up the nerve faster than I had. He hadn't been conscious all day and still wasn't awake. Maybe that made it easier for her.

We ordered dinner from a local Italian restaurant. When it arrived, Joni poured us all glasses of wine, we dished up our food and started catching up on everyday life things. It was nice. I felt lulled by the comfort and normalcy of our conversation. For a good fifteen minutes, the stress of the previous few days felt lessened. It was a welcome relief. Until I remembered something Joni had mentioned during our conference call earlier that week.

Joni recounted a dream that Jeff had shared with her during one of his hospital stays. In the dream, he was in bed in a hospital room, and the door to the room was closed. He said he could hear us all on the other side of the door and that we were partying.

That broke my heart. My father and I had a turbulent relationship. Many times, I have felt dejected and angry. Many times, I wanted him to experience the cost of the way he had treated me. I'm sure at some point in my life, the idea of my father dying alone in a hospital bed while we partied outside his room would have occurred like just desserts. Yet here we were and the last thing I wanted was for him to pay for anything.

I don't know what compelled him to share this dream with my stepmother or what made her share it with us. I do believe that it was through divine intervention. "What if this is that moment?" I thought. Here we are partying, in relative terms, while he lay in his hospital bed out of sight. I put down my food and checked on him.

His breathing wasn't right. He was inhaling and exhaling sharply and then took long pauses between breaths. I got Joni. She came in, listened, and said it was probably "just part of the process." I didn't know what that was supposed to mean but decided that I was going to sit with him. I ran upstairs, got my portable speaker, went to his bedside, and started up one of his favorite albums, "Veedon Fleece" by Van Morrison. I had brought the speaker with the intention of playing this album and enjoying it with Jeff, but that's not how things would play out.

In my father's dim office, the music seemed louder than it should have. I tried to turn it down but couldn't see through the tears in my eyes and my hands trembled too much, so I left it. *Maybe Jeff wanted it that way.* Joni stood at the head of the bed. She leaned in close to him, stroked his face, and spoke softly in his ear. The music muffled anything she was saying to him, giving her the space to have privacy with her words. I sat to his left, holding his hand. I tried to center myself and get grounded, but I couldn't. My head was buzzing. Part of it came from my own sense of panic, but I could also sense the panic in the room. And I could have sworn I could hear my sister in my head saying with spite, "Why does she get to hold his hand?"

I shook that off. Even if it weren't a figment of my imagination, I wouldn't have been able to do anything about it. Instead, I listened to Jeff's breaths as they came fewer and further between. I looked at my siblings. Their faces were wet with tears. My sister's expression screamed to me, "Is this really happening!?" It was. I couldn't believe it. *This is too fast.* With every part of me, I willed him to take one more breath. *Oh please, just one more.* This couldn't be it.

I could hear Van Morrison singing "Fair Play" and it filled my entire head. "Fair play" is a colloquial Irish saying that means "congratulation" or "well done." The song speaks to me of the courage it takes to follow your true path and dare to dream. It suggests that whether we like it or not, sometimes there is only one way we can go, and we must leap into that unknown but fated future with faith and trust. It made me think of my father right now. There was only one way he could go, and it was into the greatest unknow there is. *Fair Play to you, Jeff.*

His last breath was louder than the others, and it came out of him with force and finality.

No, no, no, no, no. Please don't leave! I thought about what to do, but there was nothing. *How is this even happening?* We hadn't even listened to one full song! Seeing how Joni responded made it all real. The first thing she said loud enough for us all to hear was, "Fuck."

She sank to the floor and sat with her head in her hands, bawling. In the forty years I have known her I can say I've seen her cry twice, maybe three times. She sat there sobbing like a child. It had happened. He was gone.

My father's empty shell lay there, looking small and slack. At a glance, he appeared to be sleeping, and the child in me wanted to shake him and wake him up. I wanted my dad back. But his body was so still and so silent that I couldn't be in denial of its vacancy.

Time seemed to slow and, in a way, stop. The air around me felt different. Charged, like there was built-up static energy. The lights held a more golden sparkle. Somewhere, hidden behind my despair, I sensed a familiar warmth and comfort. It felt like him, and he felt elated. Amid this shock and sorrow, somehow there was a faint sense of bliss. How was there space for such a feeling right now?

Chapter Three

The gentlemen from the funeral home arrived sometime between 10 and 11 p.m. They looked quite spiffy given the time. I was impressed. My stepmother chose Dee Funeral Services out of Concord because they had unknowingly played a quirky role in my parents' life story.

Jeff and Joni lived for a couple of years in a home in Concord that sat on a hill above the funeral home. On regular occasions, they would look down and see their cat, Pesky Louie, mingling with the funeral goers. As Joni was relaying this as the reason she had picked them to care for Jeff, said cat came up and rubbed his head on one of the men's legs.

He looked and said, "Is this the cat?" He leaned down and gave Pesky a scritch. "I remember him. We used to call him our therapy cat." He was glad to see that the cat was alive and well. After his disappearance in 2014, they had assumed the worst. My father would have thought this whole connection was a hoot. Being cared for in the afterlife by people who knew his nomadic cat is a story Jeff would have loved to tell over cocktails.

That night, after they took his body and there was nothing left to do, I lay in bed, desperate to sleep. But it evaded me. How was I supposed to sleep now that I was pulled up by the roots?

I felt like I was in a scene straight out of *Avatar – The Last Airbender* (animated version because it's better). Some of the show's special characters are able to manipulate and utilize the four elements. They are called - Earth, Air, Water, and Fire – "Benders." When Earth Benders do their work, they dislodge rocks and other earthen matter with abrupt and shocking blows using either their fists or feet. Then, for a moment, the rocks that were just unearthed hovered above the ground, suspended and waiting for instruction. That's how I felt. Like reality was shattered and in suspension all around me.

When I was young, my father saved me. It wasn't like he was a hero or a saint. He was fulfilling his minimum parental obligation, but it still showed up as salvation for me. My earliest life, from birth through to about five years old, was spent with my mother. She suffered from serious drug addiction. My life with her was scary and disturbing. I was a feral child in a confusing and dangerous world. When she could no longer pretend to parent me, she sent me to live with Jeff.

On February 5, 1978, I was twenty-three days shy of being five years old. My mother put me on a plane, alone, to travel three thousand miles across the country. I know the date, not because I remember it but because it was the date of a historic weather event. It marked the beginning of a three-day blizzard that would shut down New York, New Jersey, and most of New England. "The Blizzard of '78." My father, whose birthday was smack dab in the middle of this blizzard, was stuck in Connecticut on a ski trip and couldn't get home to receive me. My mother put her four-year-old on a plane alone, to travel thousands of miles into a blizzard, without a parent to receive her. That sums up my toddler years.

My Aunt Lizza picked me up from Newark International Airport with her then boyfriend and one day ex-husband, Ed. They were both so welcoming and comforting to me. I don't recall feeling scared. Being on my own and counting on the kindness of strangers was what I had been used to.

My relationship with Jeff was a little awkward at first. He had no idea what to do with me. I didn't know who he was and had already developed complex trust issues where adults were concerned. But we worked it out. He made sure I ate well. I slept in a clean, comfortable room. I felt relieved and happy. He was my first experience of safety, and he became a sort of lifeline for me. Now he was gone, and I felt set adrift and lost. My only anchor was the faint smell of him in the air of a home we never shared together.

I remember seeing the light of day brimming just before dozing off, and I would awaken too soon and unrested.

Every time I wake up, I go through what occurs as dimensional realignment. It goes something like, "Who am I? Where am I? What's today? What am I supposed to be doing? What time is it?" Beginning on December 24th, a mere two days after touching ground in Boston, the realignment procedure included, "oh yeah, Jeff isn't on the planet anymore." The first wakeup without Jeff was the hardest. Before the end of my third conscious breath, I was crying.

I got myself cleaned up and pulled together. I then joined my family downstairs and poured a cup of coffee. My sister came into the kitchen. She was wide awake. There had already been calls made to the funeral home and the hospice people. We needed them to get the hospital gear out of my dad's office ASAP. It was a difficult room to avoid and seeing that bed only brought back seeing his lifeless body lying there. And the smell… it was just wrong. Jennifer let me know there would be a delay in picking up the equipment. She said the hospice company was short-staffed due to illness and the holiday.

Jennifer then recounted how the fire in the fireplace re-stoked itself, without aid, earlier that morning. She seemed touched by it and happy to tell me. Of anyone in the house, I would be the one to believe that it had been Jeff. My father was the ultimate fire builder. He made an art of it, with his meticulously folded and tied newspaper fire starters. They looked like origami creatures, and he swore by their efficiency. It was an expression of Jeff's magic. It wasn't a stretch for me to believe that he was with us, making sure the fire was lit for Christmas Eve morning.

After I got caught up on whatever info there was to relay, we were each assigned people to call. I got my father's BFF Greg and my Aunt Barbara. I called Greg first. Greg was my dad's bestie since junior high. I have known him my whole life. When I moved back in with Jeff in 1978, on the weekends we would hang out at Greg's with a handful of their other friends. Sure, they would drink beer and smoke weed and whatnot. And while I'm sure that doesn't sound like an ideal situation for a young kid, they didn't do it in front of me, and they made sure I was entertained and well-fed. I felt safe, which may be more of a testament to how fucked up my life was before my dad.

Greg is good with people. His smile is his calling card. His voice is deep and soothing. He's empathetic and genuine. I think Greg brought out some of my dad's brighter and more jovial parts. He was always happier when Greg was around.

Greg answered and I could barely get the words out. All he said was, "No." He couldn't believe it. I understood. He did his best to muster kind words of reassurance sprinkled between exclamations of disbelief. We ended our conversation with a promise to be in touch again later that day. We needed to make plans for Greg to come over for dinner before Jennifer and I went back to our respective homes. One of my favorite things about my trips to Massachusetts was spending time with Greg, but this time seeing him would be bittersweet.

My next call was to my Aunt Barbara, my dad's last remaining sister. His youngest sister, Lizza, passed away in 2016. When he was diagnosed, I told him he needed to talk to Barbara about it. "Yeah, yeah, I know. I will," he'd say. After a year of that, I told her. She asked me how he was, and what was I supposed to say about a guy dying of cancer? That he's fine? I'll keep secrets, but don't ask me to lie for you. At least not to someone that I love. The next time I saw him, which would have been in February of 2020, I told him that she knew and a month or so later they discussed it.

I kept in closer contact with Barbara after Jeff went back into chemotherapy. She was helpful to me. Her husband died of cancer and much of his response to his illness and his imminent death was like Jeff's. While I still didn't get it, knowing this helped me understand that his behavior wasn't about me. And it was healing to have her empathy.

She couldn't believe it either. How did this happen so fast? We spoke for just five minutes or so. She promised to pass on the word to our extended family. Her voice cracked from sadness as we hung up. It was a real punch to the gut. As promised, she got the word out. Within no time, messages from cousins and other family members came rolling in.

I joined Joni and Jennifer back downstairs and shared condolences from Greg and Barbara. They shared updates for the calls they made. And, at least for that day, that was all we could do. Joni and Jennifer went on to discuss dinner plans and what they would try to do that day. Everything seemed quite business as usual, and it made me uncomfortable. They even commented on watching their caloric intake. Meanwhile, all I wanted was shots of whiskey and to bury myself in chocolate anything. Now I felt guilty like I should be exercising or something. Ugh. I hate the fat-girl triggers. Between that, the crappy night's sleep, and the coffee, I was fidgety and anxious. I couldn't keep my body still.

I took a walk around the house. Their replica colonial home featured a good loop of walkable space that centered around the main staircase. Part of said loop took me into the dining room and living room. They were on the south side of the home, so the sun shone warmly there for most of the day. That was where Jeff kept many of his plants. Out of the corner of my eye, I caught glimpse of a peace lily that looked dead and appeared beyond saving. I felt a sudden, and understandable desire to bring his plant back to life. I couldn't make my father take another breath but, dammit, I was going to revive this plant.

I picked her up and took her to the kitchen sink. Joni was standing at the counter. She looked over and said, "Oh no, that one seems done for."

I said, "Maybe. These peace lilies can be a little dramatic. Perhaps we're due for a Christmas miracle." I let the water run through the plant for a solid minute or more.

"Too bad you can't take these plants with you, Korva. I will probably let a lot of them die. There's just too many," she said and shrugged. "Plants were your father's thing. Not mine."

That's when I heard a voice in my head say, "Take my plants home, Beans."

I said, "Hmmm. Maybe I could keep my rental car and drive them home…."

She said, "The plants? That's nuts. But… I mean… they're yours if you want them."

"Yeah," I said, "that would be nuts. Never mind." But the thought of her letting my father's plants die made me sick. My father loved those plants. I suppose I was being too sentimental. Driving across the country in January was not an option I should entertain. It would take too long, cost too much, and be potentially dangerous. I supposed I'd have to be satisfied with, hopefully, saving this little peace lily. For now.

All the false normalcy was racking my nerves, so I felt relieved when Jennifer told me she was sneaking off to talk to her therapist. She made a point to tell me not to mention anything to her mother about it. I thought that was strange, considering that Jennifer is a mental health professional, and she had experienced what many people would consider a mental-health crisis. Why hide that from your mother? *Maybe there was something going on.*

I would have loved to have a therapist to talk to that afternoon, so I didn't blame her one bit. Even if she had to be sneaky about it. I wanted to talk about how I felt, and I didn't feel like I could. Everyone was acting so… normal. I didn't want to be the one who kept bringing up the sad stuff. I also held my tongue because so much of my grief was flavored with anger. They lied to me, and I did not like it. But what was I going to do? He's gone…

But she isn't. And she lied to me. I was in this vulnerable state, with a person who I didn't trust. It didn't matter why she lied to me. If a person can convince themselves that it's ok to lie to you once, they can do it a thousand times. Plus, Joni and I endured a long, rocky history together. There were so many unresolved issues, all of which seemed to be present today. But it was not the time to address them. Today was for giving compassion. After all, she and my father somehow made it through thirty-eight years of marriage. I chose to respect that.

Chapter Four

I remember the first time I met Joni. It was in the spring of 1982. I didn't realize the significance of this meeting at the time. And I was too young to understand the questionable nature of the circumstance.

I was in third grade. Jeff and I were living in Connecticut with his fiancé, Charlotte. I'm not sure when Jeff and Charlotte began dating, but I met her several months before we all moved in together, which would have been in the summer of 1980. Jeff and Charlotte would only stay together for a couple of years. All I can do is speculate as to why, both because I was young at the time and because the ending of their relationship was yet another taboo subject. The party line was that the breakup was due to incompatibilities that were irreconcilable, but I know there were other "situations" that factored in.

It was true that Jeff and Charlotte were very different. He came from a middle-class family that was fun and easy going. Charlotte came from a stricter and more structured family, although they were quite fun as well. She ate in places where it mattered what order the forks were in. Jeff's folks drank beer from the bottle. She possessed ideas about how my upbringing should go and since Jeff didn't have a clue what else to do, he let her take over. He made her be the bad guy over parenting and discipline on more than one occasion, and as a result, Charlotte and I experienced some rough spots in the beginning.

I was a very head-strong and defensive kid. That stemmed from the time I spent with my mother. She was addicted to heroin. We went from home to home, from man to man. My spotty memory of the time recalls very little interaction with her. What I do remember included her being unconscious or incoherent. I remember roaming around the streets of Reseda, California with a pack of six- to eight-year-old kids hoping their parents would give me snacks. I was three and four years old at the time. There was no actual, functioning adult to care for me. It was bad… but more on that later.

The stability and normalcy that Charlotte represented made me feel shameful and vulnerable. It highlighted all the ways I felt broken and, as a result, Charlotte's strictness and structure read more like punishment and disapproval. I responded defensively at first. I was a kid, and I didn't want to do whatever thing she was making me do. But Charlotte persisted in getting through to me. Charlotte loved me. She took care of me. She made sure that I wore clean, well-fitting clothing. She took me to get my hair cut. She took me to the dentist. She made sure I was learning how to take care of myself and my belongings. She taught me manners. She modeled self-respect and dignity to me. She made me believe that I was worthy.

She showed up over and over as someone who was willing to do the work. She was willing to have the conversations that helped me understand where she was coming from and the importance of why she made demands of me. She didn't just tell me what to do with the threat of "or else." That said, I wouldn't mess with her. She had a sharp tongue when pushed far enough. She showed me decency and respect, and she asked for the same in return. That made me start to soften into this new and stable life. I started to experience the benefits of being "normal."

When I first returned from life with my mother, I was shocked by how the children of Madison, New Jersey lived. These kids had two parents, nice homes, three square meals a day, and went to church. None of them could relate to where I had been. They wouldn't believe the things I had seen. In comparison to them, I felt freakish and ashamed of the life I led up to that point. But now, with Charlotte, I was one of them. I was normal.

My life made a complete 180-degree turn from my days in Reseda, and it was because of Charlotte. Where there was no parent in sight for too long when I was too young, now I lived in a routine that included a mother figure who did my hair before school every morning and took me to my Brownie meetings. I was doing very well in school. Charlotte made sure that my homework, which needed to be done each night before she and Jeff got home from work, was graded and corrected. She was already talking to me about college and about what amazing things I would grow up to do.

In late winter of '82, at the age of nine, I was told we would be moving to Florida. On our first trip down there to look for housing, Jeff ended his relationship with Charlotte. We were staying in a hotel, and they went downstairs to have dinner, leaving me to watch TV in the room. It was no big deal; at that point, I had been a latchkey kid for two years. When they returned, I was asleep and awakened by the sound of her crying. I'm not sure how long she stayed up in the bathroom, but I stayed quiet with my head under the blanket until I somehow managed to get back to sleep.

Jeff told me what happened the next day. He broke off their engagement. He assured me that we would be ok. The next few months were a mix of emotions. I was sad and confused. The last thing I needed was to have more instability. While Jeff made me feel safe, Charlotte made me feel stable. But there was also a part of me that was relieved. I could go back to being feral. It was easier. It was familiar. And at least I still had Jeff. We made it work before; we'd make it work again.

To Charlotte's credit, she seemed to handle this situation respectfully. If she was taking any anger out on Jeff, I didn't see it. That said, they didn't see much of each other after the breakup, even though I lived with her for the remainder of the school year. My father was working in Florida. The original plan was that he would go down there first, and then Charlotte and I would move after the school year. She kept that agreement for me so that I wouldn't have to change schools that late in the year. For about three months she took care of me. She continued to treat me like someone she loved, and never once took her upset with my father out on me. That takes a kind of integrity that few people have.

Jeff would come home on weekends, but not every weekend. When he did, Charlotte would drive down to stay with her parents in New Jersey. It was on one of these weekends that I met my future stepmother. She came over under the guise of being a friend from work, which while not a complete lie, was also not the complete truth.

I liked her. She was engaging. I remember she showed me how she could twirl a baton. I thought that was cool. She looked like many women did in the late 1970s. She had dark brown hair that was wavy and just past shoulder length. It was cut in layers. She had bangs that were feathered back at the edges. She had brown eyes, and I remember her beautiful acrylic nails. They made her fingers look like long, spindly spider's legs.

She was about five feet seven inches tall, the same as Jeff. *Huh, the same as Charlotte.* And the same as my mother. As a matter of fact, they all looked rather similar, his height, brown hair, and brown eyes. Of course, my mother was the fairest of the three. Charlotte, I thought, was far prettier than Joni. Maybe that was why the thought that this woman could one day marry my father was the furthest thing from my mind.

But that's what was on Joni's mind. Sometime in the early '90s, she recalled to my aunt one night over drinks, that once she set sights on him, she was going to have him no matter what. In a relationship? Didn't matter. Had a kid? Didn't matter. Hurting people to get what she wanted? They'll get over it. How this impacted Charlotte and me was not a factor in Joni's decision-making process, but for me the effects of her actions would be long felt and, in many ways, devastating.

Charlotte and I said goodbye when the school was over. She dropped me off in New Jersey at my grandmother's house. I don't remember much about that parting or how I felt at the time. Around my fortieth birthday, I tracked Charlotte down and got in touch. She was doing well and had created what sounded like a happy and successful life for herself. She sent me a box of things that she carried around with her for more than thirty years. It was full of old-school assignments and artwork of mine from the time we were together.

It also contained letters from my grandmother, Ginny. In them, Ginny made pleas to Charlotte to spend time with me while I was visiting New Jersey for the summer. The letters were dated two years after Jeff and Charlotte broke up, and one year after Jeff and Joni got married. I am sure my grandmother knew that I needed Charlotte, and I'm equally sure she didn't want my father to know she had reached out to her.

At first, being alone with Jeff in Florida was nice. The pressure I thought Charlotte was putting on me was off, but I kept doing a good job anyway. I had a long list of chores to do around the house each week. It kept me busy after school and earned me a hefty allowance. It felt good to contribute and to have responsibilities. Jeff and I got along well, so home life was quiet and comfortable.

Joni started visiting that fall. He and I traveled once to visit her after we moved. It quickly became obvious that she was not just "a friend from work." I was fine with her, and she was nice enough. At first, it was fun. She'd take me to aerobics class with her, or she'd take me down to the neighborhood pool. But that didn't even last a year. I don't know how or why it started, but our relationship began to sour.

She moved in at the beginning of 1983. They got engaged soon after. She was quick to start expressing upset with me. She just didn't like the way I was being raised. I was given too much freedom. I was offered too many choices. I had too much say in the decision-making process. I earned too much allowance. Jeff wasn't doing it right. He should be more involved and more in control. She wasn't wrong about that part, but the rest I would argue against. Maybe it didn't look normal, but normal rules couldn't apply. I was a good kid, and we were doing our best. That should have been enough. It needed to be enough. That was a battle I never won. And from Joni's perspective, it wasn't even a battle I had the right to start.

I didn't understand. Things didn't seem broken. I didn't know why we fought over fixing it. She started insisting on change. After three years of being a latchkey kid, she put me in daycare. They put me in an afterschool program with babies and toddlers. I was in fifth grade, and I was the oldest aged child they would accept. There was one other kid from my class, and I was sure she didn't like me. It was the worst. It was boring as hell. My friends all made fun of me. It was humiliating. I was often the last kid picked up, or Jeff was late, because he and Joni went out for cocktails after work. That just furthered said humiliation. It felt like punishment. I didn't understand what I had done wrong.

The honeymoon was over by the time they married in July of 1983. I spent the summer, as I had for the last five years, with my grandmother in New Jersey. The wedding was in Connecticut. After, I returned to New Jersey while Jeff and Joni went on their honeymoon. I was with my grandma Ginny for two months that summer. I loved it. When I returned to Florida for the school year to start, everything changed.

Our townhouse was in the process of remodeling. The dishware in the cabinets was moved around. When Jeff and I moved into our townhome, he gave me the bigger of the two bedrooms. Not to be nice. He wanted the smaller room's private and more scenic deck. After the wedding, I came home to find out that our rooms had been swapped without discussion. I was a child, and I should have no say. And that's how the trend would continue.

Now, I understand these things more as an adult. It wasn't the content of the message; it was the delivery. More and more I got situations handed to me with increasing disregard for the impact it had on me or my feelings. The arguments got louder. The contempt grew uglier. What was good for me mattered less and less. It became all about the power struggle. Not just between her and me, but between the two of them. I seemed to be paying for both.

Jeff's response was crap. His tendency to avoid confrontation really left me hanging. At first, he tried to mediate, but that was doomed to failure. I remember about two years in, he broke down and asked me to "be the bigger person" about it and "take one for the team."

Umm… what? I was eleven or twelve years old. He wanted me to just fall in line and get with the program of someone who obviously didn't like me. That's a lot to expect. It occurred as an impossible request. Even if it wasn't, it would have made no difference.

I began to feel more and more unwelcome. The fighting stopped and the unfettered contempt began. She spoke to me only when necessary. When she did, her tone suggested that I was the last person on earth she wanted to talk to. She would either avoid looking at me or her glance would relay disgust. I felt crippling anxiety every time I walked in the front door. I had nowhere else to go. I had no other family in Florida. I was trapped.

Every time we'd argue over some meaningless thing, I would say, "It just feels like you don't like me". To which she would reply, "I like you just fine. I just don't like how you behave." But she didn't like me.

Nothing about her treatment said that she cared one iota about me. I was sure she hated me. And now, so did I. I was told that if I wanted them to be nice to me or to show me love, I had best start acting better. What I heard was that I had to earn their love. I had already determined that I wasn't worth it and that was never going to happen.

The year after the wedding my grades began to drop. I went from being a straight-A student to barely breaking the C mark. By the time I was in seventh grade, I was experimenting with drugs. I became sexually active not long after. I thought it was what I must do to make someone love me. By the time I was in high school, I was a party girl. I still shudder to think of the risks I was taking at such a young age.

In May of 1988, my sister was born. Six months later we moved back to New Jersey. I was excited and hopeful. There was a new baby in the house, and we were going to be closer to extended family. Maybe this would be the turning point, and we would become a "real family." But nope. Things got worse.

Jeff and Joni engaged with me even less now, which was hard to believe possible. My sister was the new center of the universe. Joni's contempt remained unwavering, but my father was changing. He seemed to be more and more checked out. If I caught him at the right level of buzzed/drunk, he'd engage, and it would be nice. But other than that, he was in his world and not to be disturbed. I found out the hard way not to cross that line.

One day in the spring of 1989, my friend, Tara, was over to hang out. That wasn't a common occurrence as Jeff and Joni didn't like me having people over. I asked Jeff if he would give us a ride to the mall, which took a ton of courage considering I didn't feel comfortable asking my parents for anything. I couldn't tell you how many years it had been since either of them had driven me anywhere. Hell, I tried to do team sports, but I couldn't, because at thirteen years old I had to find my own rides. I was too embarrassed to ask anyone's parents, so I had to drop out of soccer after I got stranded at an away game and had to walk eight miles home. I was lucky it was a close game.

I asked him for a ride to the mall, and he said no. I, like every normal asshole teenager, rolled my eyes and said "fine" and walked away. Welp, that went over like a turd in a punchbowl. He lost his mind. He gave me the ole, "You roll your eyes at me, and I'll roll your head down that hallway" speech.

Then I said it, the thing that made him go nuclear. I said, "I rolled my eyes because I never ask anything from you and the one time I do, you say no."

He looked at me and I swear I could see the heat waves roll off him. He went on a verbal rampage that ended with him calling me, "an ungrateful little cunt."

And I said, "You need to shut the fuck up."

He cleared the space of ten feet in a microsecond, grabbed me, threw me to the floor, and with my head between his knees he started punching me on the ear. Hard. It hurt. I somehow wiggled out of his grasp and landed on my back. He stood, straddled over me about to hit me again, when I managed to get my two feet up under his groin and launched him off me. He fell back several feet.

Meanwhile, my friend, Tara, is standing there witnessing this. Jeff turns to her, tells her to leave, and she does so with haste. She walked straight home, and her mother called the police.

Maybe an hour later, Officer Ed walked into my room. I was very familiar with him. Not because I got in trouble though. It was because I worked at Olde Town Deli on Main Street in Boonton. Best Taylor Ham, egg, and cheese in the state. This job would prove to be the best thing in my life and the owner, John Leone, was an angel sent from God. I only wish I had realized it then. It was John's policy to give the "town's finest" free coffee. Officer Ed's order was a large coffee, light and sweet.

"What the hell is going on, kid?" he asked and took a seat next to me to look at my head. My ear was swollen, hot, and purple.

"I asked my old man for a ride to the mall, and he said, 'No.' I rolled my eyes, he called me an ungrateful cunt, I told him to shut the fuck up, and he beat my ass."

"Ya know, he says that he didn't touch you," Officer Ed said. His voice sounded hesitant, not knowing how that would land.

"Well then explain my head," I said.

He grimaced as he looked at my ear and said, "Yeah, he says you must have done that to yourself. And your stepmother says she's afraid you're going to hurt someone or burn down the house or something."

"What!? No! Oh my god. I just asked for a fucking ride to the mall. You can't think I did this to myself," I said, still in disbelief at how this situation had escalated so out of control.

"No, kid, of course not. Look, do you have any family close by or somewhere to go?"

"I don't know. Maybe. I… don't know. Where the hell am I going to go? Shit."

"Your friend's mom, the lady that called this in, said you could stay there if you needed a place for a few nights. Pack a bag and I'll give you a ride."

I went and stayed with Tara. I hoped to only be there a night or two, thinking I could live with a relative. The next day I called my grandma Ginny, Jeff's mom, and asked if I could stay with her.

"Your father already called, Korva. He says he threw you out because you told him to shut the fuck up and kicked him in the balls."

"What!? No. That isn't what happened." I relayed my side of the story to her.

"Korva, listen, I don't know what to say. Your father told me not to get involved. I'm sorry." Wow. My father lied to my grandmother. There was one less person to whom I could turn.

I called my mother's mother and asked to stay with her. But she said no because my grandfather couldn't handle a teenage kid around.

After about three weeks the New Jersey Division of Youth and Family Services set up a meeting with my father and me. In the meeting, I was asked what I wanted. I said, through restrained tears, that I wanted to go home and that I wanted to be with my father.

Jeff turned to me and asked why.

I broke down. *Why? What do you mean why?* I said, "Because I love you. And I have no one else."

What could he say? He let me come home. There was no welcome home from Joni. She resumed her usual routine of either ignoring me or looking at me like I was a pebble in her shoe.

As this was all happening, my social life turned into a train wreck. I'd churned through a series of friendships that didn't work out. I had a habit of falling hard for guys who were happy to use me but just weren't all that into me. My attendance in school was becoming spottier and my concern for my grades was non-existent. I lived like a person with no future, no hope, no self-respect, and shame for having none of the above.

I hit rock bottom the winter before I turned eighteen. My parents were planning to move to Delaware. They took my sister, who was just a toddler at the time, to look for homes one weekend. I invited some friends over while they were gone. Yes, I know I wasn't supposed to, but it was nice to feel a sense of freedom at home for a change. I always felt so unwelcome that I never was given the chance to enjoy it.

It snowed that weekend and the prints in the snow made it look like I threw a huge party when in fact there were only six people. Plus, the neighbors ratted me out for having people over. Jeff and Joni were pissed. They stopped talking to me. I could walk into a room and be treated like I wasn't there. For weeks. It ended when Joni's parents came to visit. I happened to be home that evening, where I'd normally be working, so my dad asked if I wanted to eat with them. I know that it was just for a show and that they wouldn't be speaking to me if Joni's folks weren't there, but it still felt relieving.

Joni's mother asked if I was ready to move. I said no. She was surprised because as it turned out, we were moving the next weekend. I held back my rage and my devastated sadness until after they left. Then I confronted Jeff and Joni about it. Why didn't they tell me that we were moving next weekend!? They didn't want me to go, and if that was the case, I wasn't going to go. What was I going to do? I didn't know for sure. I was just done living with people who didn't want me.

I ended up moving in for a couple of months with my then on-again-off-again boyfriend. His mom liked me, but he was one of the guys that wasn't all that into me. I was cramping his style, evidence by him avoiding being home when I was there, which just further reminded me how unwanted I was. When that didn't work out, I moved in with a friend and her parents. I knew that wasn't going to last forever and I was sinking into depression. I felt there was nowhere to go. There was nothing in my future calling me to life. I was so tired.

One night, I got very drunk and took my car for a drive through an area of Boonton Township known for being dangerous. The narrow roads are full of blind twists and turns. There are no streetlights and visibility is short. I drove fast. I drove recklessly, accelerating through tight curves in a way that pushed the limitations of physics. I hoped for death. I can't count the number of times I tried to turn my hands to move that wheel, and steer into a tree or ravine, but I couldn't do it. I couldn't make my body hurt itself. I didn't want to kill myself, but I didn't want to live anymore either. I begged God to take me. *Please, please, please.* But he didn't.

I'd like to say I woke up the next day with a new sense of meaning, purpose, and gratitude. I didn't. I did have a newfound sense of resolve, stemming from a strange space. You see, now I knew I didn't have what it took to end my own life. If I couldn't do it drunk, I couldn't do it sober. I was stuck here living this life. I had to turn things around.

I swallowed my pride, called my father, and asked him if I could come home. He said yes, but with condition. If I wanted to come home, I needed to call both of my grandmothers and tell them that the story I told about my father calling me an ungrateful cunt and then beating me upside the head was a lie. I was forced to tell them that I had indeed given him attitude, told him to shut the fuck up, and kicked him in the balls.

I still don't know how to unpack how fucked-up this made me feel, but I had nowhere to go. I accepted his terms. I called both of my grandmothers and did as he instructed. Both of my grandmothers said that they knew I told the truth before but understood that I must say what I said in order to go home.

From the moment I moved to Delaware, my goal was singular: prove them wrong. I would be successful in spite of them. Yes, perhaps motivation not worthy of a TED Talk, but I needed something to propel me. I got my GED, because all this was happening in what would have been my senior year of high school. I started attending community college, maintained a 3.8 GPA, held down multiple jobs, and got my overall shit together in a matter of a few months. There wasn't a whole lot left to hold against me, and Joni still didn't like me.

One time, when I was working two jobs and going to school full-time, I stopped home for a quick lunch. I left a small plate, a utensil, and a cup in the sink. I would have taken care of it when I got home later, but when I came home the dishes were gone. I thought that it was nice of Joni to take care of them. I then walked up to my third-floor room to find those dishes sitting on my bed. Joni, who suffered at the time with chronic foot pain, would rather have walked up two flights of stairs than put my three items in the dishwasher for me.

Another time, at one of our rare Sunday dinners, I mentioned that I wanted to start working out and asked if our YMCA membership was a family one. Joni said it was. I verified with her that I was listed as a member, and she assured me that I was. When I went down to the Dover branch with my friend, Jessica, to sign up, I was told the only people on the account were Joni, Jeff, and Jennifer.

I said under my breath to Jessica, "Of course, I'm not listed. That bitch doesn't think I'm family."

Well, the nosy front desk lady told Joni what I said. At the end of the day, I pulled up to the house to find my father sitting on the back porch. As I approached, he said, in an amused tone, "I don't know what you did, but she's pissed. Something about the YMCA."

I went inside and she went off on me. "How dare you talk about me like that in front of people I know?! Did you think she wouldn't tell me?!"

"Well, I wasn't talking to her, so I'm not sure why she would. But it doesn't matter, I wasn't lying. You don't treat me like a member of this family. No matter what I've done you just can't accept me. Why? Why can't you accept me as part of this family."

"Because I just don't like you," she said. There it was. She finally told the truth.

"You don't have to like me," I spat back at her. It was one of the most liberating moments of my life. I knew when I was ten years old that she didn't like me, and she finally admitted it. Now we could stop pretending that she "liked me but didn't like my behavior." I could have done everything right and it wouldn't have changed that she just didn't like me.

Fortunately, I had too much to focus on to be hung up on Joni anymore. I was busy with school and work. She was busy with Jennifer. I moved out about a year or so later, to California to live with my mother. Six months later, Jeff and Joni moved to California. They lived about an hour away from me. I would visit on weekends and do my laundry or wash my car, just like a normal kid would after moving out of their parent's home. I worked hard and was self-sufficient. She still didn't like me. Every interaction she had with me occurred like something she had to endure.

I moved to Seattle in 1993, a year and a half after moving to California. I would call home once every week or two. She would talk to me for five or ten minutes and then inform me that Jeff didn't feel like talking on the phone. Most of the time she wouldn't even try to get him on the line. I wish I knew what "gatekeeping" was back then. She still didn't like me. I'm not sure when she started to treat me like someone she could stand. Perhaps when I got married or after I became a mother myself? Maybe it was when she realized she could control me if I thought she cared about me? The latter has a ring of truth.

Somewhere along the line, we developed a relationship. It was pleasant enough. I appreciated it, but I've never known where I stood with her. I'm not one of her children and that was clear. She always sounded reluctant and uncomfortable if she was ever in a position where I was referred to as her daughter. But, all things considered, I thought that we came a long way and made some silent amends. She came out to visit us in Washington a couple of times without Jeff. Joni, Jennifer, and I went on a girl's trip together. Things seemed ok, and I allowed all the past's bullshit to be swept under the rug. I had to leave it under the rug so I could have a relationship with Jeff.

Now, she was all that was left of the people who I saw as "parents" and I felt insecure and uncertain. I already knew she could lie to me. I felt there was much more that I didn't know. But it was just a feeling. There was nothing I could do or say about it. It added to an already overwhelming sense of anxiety and grief.

Chapter Five

I woke up crying Christmas morning from my first lucid, post-mortem dream about my father. In the dream I was living with my parents in the home that my ex-husband and I lived in together. I don't know how old I was, but I know that I was in college and had a paper due that day. I had done all the work but had forgotten to write it out. I tried frantically to get the paper complete but was writing by hand and kept making mistakes. I'd get frustrated, throw out what was written, and start all over. This went on until I had to make myself stop because it was almost time to leave for school. I was headed upstairs to take a shower when I walked past Joni and Jeff.

As I passed them, I found myself struck by reality. I looked at my father, who looked much younger in this dream, and said, "Oh my god, you're not here anymore." He looked at me with confusion. "I can't talk to you anymore. Don't you understand? You're not here anymore." Now he looked worried but kept moving away as my stepmother dragged him past me and into the kitchen.

She said, "I don't know why she's making such a big deal. She can still talk to everyone else. Why does she always have to be so dramatic? See, now you're all upset and it's because of her...."

I turned and screamed, "I do not want to talk to anyone else! No! That is not what I'm doing! That is not me! I just want my father!" My breath caught me, and I woke up mid-sob.

Technically speaking, I don't know if it's a "lucid dream," but I've experienced similar dreams before. In them, there is always a contradiction between what is happening in the dream and what I know to be real. In this case, realizing that my father, who appeared to be alive in my dream, was dead. I often have dreams like this about my grandmother, his mother.

The first dream about her was a year after she died. I was with her in her living room watching TV when I became aware that in waking life, she was dead. I asked her where her brain cancer originated from. She told me it was the microwave. She lived in a mother-in-law's apartment in a house she shared with my aunt. The kitchenette counter, where the microwave was kept, was level to her head and within three to four feet. I've been leery of microwaves since.

I continue to have dreams of my grandmother and each time, whilst dreaming, I'm aware that she is no longer amongst the living. I consider these dreams, even if they're just in my head, to be gifts. I hoped that I could have that experience with Jeff. But this morning, rather than feeling grateful, I felt perplexed. I kept thinking back to how confused he looked, and I felt guilty for having forced him to contemplate that he was dead. It's ironic considering that in real life I hadn't forced him to look at the fact that he was dying and instead went along with the business-as-usual ruse. I regret it.

Christmas morning felt surreal. It looked like Christmas. The decorated tree was well lit, and the fireplace crackled with sparks of warmth, but the coldness of loss overshadowed whatever Christmas joy there may have normally been.

My husband sent a couple of little things with me to open. He knew that my parents didn't give me gifts. Once I became a mother, I just stopped getting gifts for any occasion. No explanation until several years later at which time I was told that, "Your kids get the gifts now." I'm glad Bryan thought to send something along. I opened those alone in my room.

Watching my stepmother and brother open gifts from my deceased father was more than a little strange. I tried not to pay attention but made note of a bottle of Port he left for Joni. I hoped she would open it while I was there. James opened the gift from me, Star Wars-themed Dr. Squatch soap. James was a Star Wars fan, and who doesn't like a nice-smelling soap?

I made more of an effort to have a relationship with my brother over the last few years. We've never been close. I was twenty years old when my brother was born and moved to Seattle four months later. While I lived at home when my sister was young, I didn't have time like that with him. Our relationship wasn't encouraged either. It would have been all my doing and in the face of the same gatekeeping Joni did with Jeff. I didn't get the impression that Joni liked the fact that my sister looked up to me as a young girl. She had no control over that, but she seemed to do her best to make sure that didn't happen with my brother.

I was also afraid he wouldn't like me. I'm sure he heard plenty of Korva-related propaganda and I know I've behaved like an idiot around him. My father had a way of bringing out my inner "acting-out fifteen-year-old" and James got to witness it without any context. I didn't know how to explain myself to James. I didn't know how to have a relationship with him. The best I could do was talk to him about the things I knew he liked and hope we'd eventually bridge the gap.

In September of 2021, three months before dying, my father reached out to me to help James with a project. While Jennifer would have said I was Jeff's favorite, I knew it was James. I think that Jeff wanted this last chance to do something to help James lead a fulfilling life. James had expressed interest in creating a podcast, which is something I have experience with. So, Jeff reached out and asked if I could give James advice. We met on Zoom, and I gave him as much introductory information as I could. It felt good to think that I could be a positive influence on him. I like to think that this was Jeff's attempt to connect us, maybe. That could be the wishful thinking of my inner child.

My sister gave me Christmas goodies, a pair of soft socks, a cardigan, and a blanket. I felt bad, I hadn't gotten her anything. The month of December was more than I bargained for. I dismantled my kitchen to do a partial remodel, and my home was an upside-down disaster, plus dealing with the ongoing escalation of Jeff's situation. It was more than I could handle. While James' gift was an easy choice, I didn't have a clue what to get for her, and I didn't have the energy to figure it out. I apologized for it and promised to make it up to her.

I noticed Jennifer was quiet and more distant this morning. I started noticing the day before. At first, it occurred to me that she was distracted, which of course made sense given her father just died. But there was more to it. It was like there was a certain vigilance to her distraction as if she were looking out for something or trying to figure something out. I also got the increasing sense that she was feeling resentful toward me.

I know this may sound a little crazy, but I felt a distinct sensation about my sister when my father was dying. Again, my stepmother was on his right side as he passed, and I was holding his left hand. In my head, I could hear my sister saying, "Why does she get to hold his hand?"

I felt a ton of resentment coming from her and I wanted to believe I was wrong. Before falling asleep on Christmas Eve, I sent her a text asking for time to talk. Late morning, Christmas morning, we got a moment alone.

"Hey, Jennifer," I said quietly, feeling awkward about needing to have this conversation. "Are you, like, mad at me?"

"No. Why would you think that?", she asked, seeming surprised.

"I don't know. Just a feeling," I said. I was certain something was off, and I was hoping she'd be forthcoming.

"Nope. I'm fine. Ya know… if anything, I guess, I'm feeling a little protective of my mother but… no, I'm fine."

Well, that seemed an odd thing to say. What's to protect? And from whom? Me?

"Oh, well… yeah. Must be me," I said. "I'm just feeling insecure. You know… with Jeff gone. I just…" I hesitated to finish the sentence but decided to let it out. "I just don't feel like I belong anymore."

She seemed to shrug this concern off and said "Oh, well, I don't feel that way." Just then, Joni walked up, and Jennifer said, "Do you, mom?"

"Do I what?" Joni asked.

Jennifer looked at me to answer that question. *Fuck.* "Well, I was just telling Jennifer about how I feel… kinda… lost. I mean, Jeff was my anchor, and I feel… set adrift." Then I said with reluctance, "And I don't feel like I belong here anymore…" My voice trailed as I started to cry. There was something deep inside of me that wanted to belong here, and it felt desperate.

"That's how I felt when my father died, too," Joni said. "It's totally normal."

Was it? Once again, I received a response that didn't assure me that I was loved or wanted. Was she normalizing my experience to get me to shut up, or was she sincere? I couldn't tell. I dropped it. I felt ashamed of having even said the words.

Somewhere in the back of my mind, there was a voice screaming at me to run, to get as far away from this house, these people, and this life as I could. I felt a fundamental sensation of being a mouse in a den of vipers. All I had to go on was a feeling. Everything was *fine*. Same as always. But it didn't matter, even if something was going on under the surface or behind my back, as much as I wanted to run, I couldn't leave yet. I wasn't done being in my dad's house.

On Sunday the 26th, my sister's husband Josh joined us. Her children were with their biological father, so Josh was free to travel. He's very much the cliché of a girl marrying her father. Buttoned up looks wise, nice clothing, tailored to fit him. He's successful and career-driven. I mean, he even looks like Jeff.

I drove Jennifer out to the airport to pick him up around mid-day. This drive to and from the airport was becoming more familiar, and as a result, more comfortable. But the tension with Jennifer negated that peaceful, easy feeling. I knew there was something wrong, but I couldn't press her. Instead, I'll make small talk about a subject that makes me feel at home. Astrology.

"So, I did some astrological chart comparisons. Found some interesting stuff. You wanna hear?" I asked. Although we hadn't been raised with any spiritual foundations, Jennifer was metaphysically curious enough.

"Sure", she said and sounded half sincere, which seemed understandable given the intensity of the last few days.

"Well, Joni and Jeff have interesting synastry."

"What's that? she asked.

"Synastry is the term for comparing two charts. In this case, I compared Joni and Jeff's natal charts. Natal charts are the ones created the moment of your birth. Jeff and Joni have this mutually receptive synastry type thingy. Her natal sun in Capricorn is conjunct, like… in the same spot… as Jeff's natal Venus. And Jeff's natal sun in Aquarius is conjunct Joni's natal Venus. It's like a visa-versa situation with the same two planets and that's not all that common."

"How 'bout In English this time?" Jennifer said.

"Heh, oh yeah right. So, your sun sign is associated with your birthday. It is the one everyone knows and reads horoscopes for. The sun sign is associated with the ego and identity. Venus rules relationships, which seems a given because it's linked to love, but it also rules income, possessions, value systems, sense of self-worth, things of the like. So far so good?" I paused and gave her a raised eyebrow.

"Yup", she said.

"When one person's sun and another person's Venus maintain the same space in the sky, and are conjunct, it's a good thing. Normally. This alignment is one of partnership and cooperation, but there tends to be a leader in this duo. It's usually the Sun person because of the sun's connection to both ego and leadership. Since they both have their Sun conjunct with the other's natal Venus, this is prime for power struggles. Like… of biblical proportions."

"Huh," she said. "That tracks."

"What's even more interesting is that Jeff and I have a similar gig going on."

"How so?" she asked and seemed more interested than when we began this conversation. I was happy to be in my element for this moment.

"Well, it's the same except instead of the Sun and Venus, it's our North Nodes and Venus. Way heavier vibe. The nodes of the moon are about our soul's journey. The south node is our karma. It's both the gifts we've been given as well as any debts we haven't paid that we drag into this life with us. The north node is our dharma, what we're here to learn and become."

I stopped and glanced her way to see if she was with me. She gave me the nod to continue.

"So, Jeff and I have our dharma's conjunct each other's Venus, the planet of relationships. This often indicates fated relationships; relationships meant to test us. In other words, me and Jeff... that was never going to be easy or fun." The thought brought tears to my eyes.

"It pisses me off. I didn't want this to be so hard. And yet somehow, I couldn't stop it. Fuckin fate. And you know what's crazier, my north node was conjunct Jeff's natal Venus which means...."

"Um.... no idea..." she said.

"Oh yeah, well, it means that it was conjunct your mother's sun. Her identity is meant to test me and make me stronger... and we have past life connections for sure. I mean, she used to hate me on an illogical level. Like she hated me before I could do anything for her to hate. That's the kinda shit that comes from unresolved karma."

"Hmm," was all Jennifer said to that. I stopped talking about it. I knew Jennifer didn't want to talk about my past with her mother. She either didn't believe me or didn't want to. "What about me and dad? Have you looked at our charts?" she asked in a hopeful tone.

"I pulled them up but didn't do any analysis yet. I did notice one thing."

"What's that?", she asked.

"It was your moons. They're both in Cancer. I don't have his exact birth time… dammit… but they may even be conjunct."

"What does that mean?"

"Well, our moon sign reflects our emotional selves, how we experience, express, and process emotions. Moon in Cancer folks tend to be very nurturing, loving… almost motherly."

"And Dad had a moon in Cancer?"

"Yup," I said.

"That doesn't track," she said.

"Yeah, it does. The dark side of the moon in Cancer is that when you get hurt, you get mean. He was hurt, so he was mean. He hurt so long that he didn't know how to do anything else. Hence the booze. But he was nurturing in his way. He was always concerned with our food and nutrition. Cancer rules the stomach and sustenance. He loved cooking for us."

"Huh, yeah," she said and seemed to drift off into a memory.

"Yeah, interesting, right? It would also mean that the two of you handle your emotions in similar manners."

"Yeah, we both have avoidant attachment styles…," she said, "but beyond that… yeah, I don't know."

"Just a perspective to consider. I'll look closer at the charts later."

That trip to the airport flew by, and other than driving into the wrong pick-up lane at Logan International, it all went well. When we returned, we started making various plans for the week. Josh would take care of some phone calls on Monday. An appointment at the funeral home to finalize things was needed. There were a couple of dinners to schedule as well. One with Greg and one with my cousin Lindsay, who lived in the area. I'd take care of both of those.

That afternoon, I received a call from my dad's friend, Gary. He was a part of the crew of dudes Jeff grew up with in Madison, New Jersey. I hadn't seen him since 1992 when I moved to California. I made a stop at his place in Scottsdale, Arizona on my way to Los Angeles. It's funny how familiar his voice sounded, even after all these years.

He called with condolences. He also told me that he had a copy of a CD that my father made. Back around 2007-8ish, my father went through a songwriting phase, and he recorded and produced a CD. It's called "Ethereal Days," and includes songs named "Home in the Sky," and "Avalon is Burning." It was quite confusing to me that the man who could come up with these song titles never wanted to have a deep conversation. Gary said that I needed to have Jeff's CD, and he would send it to me. I couldn't imagine when I would have what it takes to listen to it.

December 27th rolled in like any other Monday. But it wasn't. It was my first Monday without Jeff. It was hard to believe I had been in Boston only five days. As promised, Josh was on the phone several times with the hospice caregivers trying to get the equipment out of the house. My stepmother was in touch with the funeral home and planned to meet with them the next day. She mentioned that we would need an obituary, but she figured the funeral folks would do that for us. However, that was a task I was up to, so I got to work.

I knew it must be succinct. My father was a man of few words. I intended to highlight the things that meant the most to him. I guessed that his career topped that chart. I don't think that family was less important, I just think he knew how to function and succeed in the business world. I don't think that family and fatherhood felt as easy. I know that my sister and I both experienced the heartache of what seemed like a lack of interest from our father. It was a source of commiseration for us.

Something else that meant the world to him was music. He played guitar for over fifty years. I think his guitars were friends to him. Something he could express himself through without the need to explain himself. It was a simple and reliable relationship and warranted mention in his obituary.

After sorting out some dates, I threw this together:

George Jeffrey "Jeff" Rafter, of Boxborough passed away peacefully on December 23, 2021, in his home surrounded by family.

Born in February of 1952, Jeff was raised in Madison, NJ as the son of George "Jukie" and Virginia "Ginny" along with his sisters Barbara and Lizza. He had a large, loving extended family and a group of what would become lifelong friends. He married young and, while that marriage didn't last, it produced his daughter Korva. In 1983, he married the love of his life, Joni, and together they raised their children, Jennifer and James.

He graduated from Fairleigh Dickinson University in 1979 and began his career in telecommunications. This career would move him all over the country. His business acumen brought him many achievements and much success.

He was a man that enjoyed good food, drink, and music. He was a natural musician and an epic storyteller. His sense of humor and his deep belly laughs will not soon be forgotten.

He is survived by his wife, Joni, three children, sister Barbara, and grandchildren William, Annie, Alex, Jessie, and Jax. He is preceded in passing by his mother, father, and sister Lizza.

As per Jeff's wishes, the family will be having a small, private memorial service.

I supposed that fit the bill as far as obituaries go, but it wasn't enough. What a strange exercise to sum up a life in such few words. *What will my life's words be?*

Greg came for dinner that night. It was a welcome distraction to what felt like increasing but unspoken tension from Jennifer. She just seemed so agitated, and I had no idea why. She wasn't expressing anything verbally, but something was building in her. Joni, on the other hand, was as cool as a cucumber. Maybe she was saving her breakdowns for behind closed doors, but as far as I could tell she was even keel and moving forward.

Seeing Greg without Jeff was harder than I thought it would be. They were besties. It was one of those relationships that didn't require communication to achieve understanding. Greg just got Jeff. I was so grateful for it. My father moved around so much in his adult life, and he hadn't seemed to make many close friends along the way. Jeff was an introvert and didn't need much socialization. I get that. I don't have a ton of friends, but the few I have are golden and add so much to my life. Knowing he didn't have that was worrisome to me. So, when he ended up in Massachusetts, where Greg lived for many years, I was happy about it.

My stepmother made lamb for dinner, and it was delicious. We drank wine and shared Jeff's stories. Greg filled in some long-standing blanks. He told us about how they met when they were in junior high school through mutual friends. He told us about the origins of Jeff's nickname, "The Glove." I had always thought it was because they played softball back in the day. Turns out he got the moniker around the age of fifteen when he proved slick at being able to catch stolen beers, tossed over the hedges at the neighborhood block parties. The fact that I had not known this story sooner just pointed out how much I did not know about Jeff. My heart broke a little more.

We listened to music. My sister and I belted out a pretty good rendition of Van Morrison's "Into the Mystic". It was a lovely evening of reminiscing. Things wrapped up sometime between 10 and 11 p.m. Greg hugged each of us goodbye. He got to me last. He held out his arms and said, "Beans, you've always been my favorite." I didn't think anything of it. Of course I was, he and I went way, way back. I was sad to see him go. The uncertainty I was feeling about the future left me wondering if I would ever see Greg again. I hoped that I would.

On Tuesday the 28th we went to Dee Funeral Services in Concord to discuss what was next. They informed us that Jeff was still in their care. "Holy shit," I thought to myself, "He was still here?" I was sure cremation happened right away, and I was super creeped out that his body was still there in the building with us. Feeling quite ridiculous, I worried that he may be lonely or uncomfortable. Perhaps that's why they used phrases like "taking care of" when referring to the treatment of his remains.

The gentleman who worked with us was John, and he was amazing. His voice was soft and sturdy. He validated our experience and normalized the process of grief. He asked us about who may want keepsake portions of Jeff's remains. I wanted some for sure. Based on the response of Joni and Jennifer, I felt like they thought that was weird. He assured me that it was not and that it was natural to want to keep a part of our loved ones with us.

Joni wasn't planning on a traditional funeral. Between this damn pandemic and the fact that Jeff would not have wanted a traditional service, Joni had decided she would plan something in the spring or fall for the family. Though, as the days went by it seemed more and more like lip service. *Could she be future faking? No, why would she?* I was a little disappointed about the prospects of no memorial service, for selfish reasons. It was my job to deliver eulogies for the family. Public speaking was one of the few things my father expressly told me he was proud of me for. I'd have to find another way to honor him.

Jennifer seemed off at the funeral home. It was like she was there but somewhere else far, far away. It was hard to tell if it was grief, shock, or something else. I sensed that same resentment toward me. I couldn't imagine what I did to deserve it. She was behaving uncharacteristically, and the more I spent time with this side of Jennifer, the more I began to wonder how well I knew her.

I was fifteen when my sister was born. I was excited to have a sibling, but afraid at the same time. I already felt like a second-class citizen. Her birth was about to downgrade me to third. But the moment I saw her I fell in love. She was cute as a button, and as much as I wanted to resent her, I just couldn't. It wasn't her fault.

I remember when she was a teeny, tiny baby. We were still in Florida, so she was just a couple of months old. I was walking past her room, and she was just waking up from a nap. Joni was in the shower. I didn't know what to do. I was afraid to go anywhere near my sister because of Joni. God forbid I rub off on her, so I didn't dare pick her up. But she was waking up alone, and I was afraid she'd get scared and start to cry.

I went into her room and knelt next to her crib, so I was at eye level with her, and I talked to her. I told her that she was safe and that I was sorry, but I was afraid to pick her up. I told her that no matter what happened, I would never let my insecurity get in the way of my love for her. I told her that I would never take my upset out on her and that none of this was her fault. Even so, it was hard to watch her grow up with the life I wanted. She got attention. She did extracurricular activities. She got rides to the mall without being called an ungrateful cunt. They took her to the dentist and put braces on her teeth. She had privilege. They didn't hate her.

I know that she had her challenges. She was a highly sensitive and emotional being in a home that didn't validate feelings, and that is not a trivial challenge. Because I was older than her, I tried to help her. I know she loved me, but I often wondered what the Korva-related propaganda was like in the home she grew up in. I wondered how much she participated in activities that furthered my separation. Did she feed into my black sheep status? How many lies has she told, or truths has she omitted? I realized that underneath the love, I didn't trust her. I didn't like it.

By Wednesday, the restlessness was palpable. I was fine, but my sister needed to get out of the house. In the morning, she and my stepmother went for a walk on the wooded trails by my parents' house. Since the hospital bed and hospice equipment was removed, I took the opportunity to cleanse my father's office, spiritually speaking, with smoke.

I brought a bundle of sage, mugwort, lavender, and basil that I had grown in my garden. I opened the windows and burned as much as I could without setting off the smoke detector. I loved the smell of this particular blend. I also burned a white candle, dressed in palo santo infused oil and rolled in the same herbal mixture, as a way to help clean and clear residual negative or traumatic energy. He died in that space, but he also spent many, many hours in the space. I'm sure some of those hours in recent months were less than happy times.

It felt good to do something that expressed my spiritual nature. Also, sad that I must hide it. I wasn't raised in a religious or spiritual home. My father's family was Catholic, and I'm not sure about Joni, but our household had zero talk of spirit or God. Spiritism in many forms was mocked as illogical or irrational. My own spiritual inclinations have been something I have felt shameful about where my family is concerned. I guess with my father's passing, while I still felt the need to hide, I cared a lot less about the mockery.

Thursday the 30th, was another business-as-usual kind of day. Joni made a point to tell me that she was meeting with her accountant to go over taxes and it "just couldn't wait until next week." I knew that wasn't true, but it wasn't mine to make issue of. Jennifer and Josh spent an hour or so in the basement working out, and of course there was more talk of calorie counting.

That night, my cousin Lindsay was slated to have dinner with us. She is my father's youngest sister, Lizza's, daughter. Jeff and Lizza had a strained relationship. When their mother Ginny died, there were issues with assets and inheritance. My father had been the executor of the estate, but I'd bet dollars to donuts that Joni was handling the financial matters though. He always let her take care of the money. Hearsay suggested that there were unaccounted-for funds or missing checks. It was a mess and there was a lot of animosity, but I'm not privy to the full story. That said, I would speculate Jeff and Lizza's division happened much longer ago than my grandmother's estate issues. Like my sister and I, from early on, one sibling had a good relationship with one parent and the other with the other parent. My guess is that they resented each other for it and, unfortunately, were never able to resolve that rift. I would like to think Jennifer and I are beyond harboring the resentment of sibling rivalry, but I suppose when our parents' multi-million-dollar estate is being distributed, we will know for sure.

Lindsay was Lizza's only daughter and next to the oldest, after me, of our first cousins. She lost her mother to cancer in 2016. Like Jeff, there is a question as to whether or not she knew more than she said about the extent of her illnesses, so Lindsay understood the feelings of shock and betrayal I was experiencing. Lindsay also knew my history with Joni and wasn't surprised when I asked her to meet, just her and I, for coffee before dinner.

I was hoping to be able to drive my father's Porsche to meet up with her. It was a one-year-old Carrera 911. Not sure what drove my father to buy it. I guess it was one last extravagance. Since his first trip to the hospital, it sat in the garage and Joni mentioned multiple times that Jennifer and I should drive it. Jennifer had taken it out a couple of days ago, so I figured it was my turn.

I told them, "I think I'll take the Porsche to meet Lindsay, if that's ok."

Joni said, "Yeah, I don't care."

Jennifer on the other hand, looked miffed. "Oh, I guess. I was thinking about driving it to the mall. But that's fine. Whatever."

I had forgotten that she planned to go with Josh to some high-end mall. I'm sure she wanted to pull into valet parking in a brand-new Porsche. I mulled that over for a moment in my head and said, "No, you go ahead and take it. It's not important to me." In hindsight, I should have taken the damn car. I should have taken that car and driven far away and fast. Instead, I drove my rental Toyota Camry to the Acton Coffee House to meet Lindsay. This had become a regular meeting spot for her and I ever since I had been visiting my parents in Massachusetts.

We found a cozy two-top table in the corner, and I got her caught up on the events since I arrived. She wasn't surprised by the bad vibes I was getting. My father's family weren't too fond of Joni, but Lindsay didn't know Jennifer very well. After Jeff and Joni moved to California and my grandmother died, they stopped making efforts to stay in touch with Jeff's family. Jennifer's only experience of extended family was Joni's family. It's too bad, she missed out.

The plan was to go back to the house for dinner around 4 p.m. Lindsay and I were there, but Jennifer didn't return from the mall until right around 6 p.m. We ate a low-key dinner of spaghetti and meatballs. We shared some stories and laughs. When it was time for Lindsay to go, I felt a similar sadness to when Greg left, except I knew I'd see her again.

Chapter Six

That night, sleep was hard to come by. I was uncomfortable and anxious. My heart beat loud and heavy. A few times I got myself good and worked up, thinking I was dying or something. Deep breathing helped, but not enough. I could still hear the relentless pounding in my ears.

It was Thursday, December 30th, one week of Thursdays since Jeff's death. I was planning on leaving the next day. I wanted to drive down to New Jersey while I was already on the east coast so that I could see my Aunt Barbara and my good friend, Toni. It was just a short three-and-a-half-hour drive, way easier than a flight across the country with all the extra hours of airport time, etc. But leaving was scary. It wasn't like the times before. He was gone and I didn't know how I fit in. *Could I ever come back here?*

Also, there were the lies. I couldn't help but think that there was some explaining to do. The lies and omissions well predated my father's cancer. I was having severe trust issues, both with my stepmother and now with my sister. They both had a history of choosing to keep things from me.

Four Thanksgivings ago, in 2018, I called home to wish my parents a Happy Holiday. I called Joni's phone, because my father never answered his. So, I was surprised when he answered hers. It sounded like he was in a restaurant. I said I could let him go if they were out somewhere. He said, "Um, no, we've just got a full house over here."

Excuse me? I felt instant pain. I wanted to say, "What the fuck?" but instead I choked back tears and said, "Oh, really? Who's there?" I already knew at least part of the answer.

"Ah, let's see, Jennifer and her family, Joni's parents… and um… Joni's sister and her kids, and her brother. Didn't anyone mention this to you?"

"Um, yeah, no."

"Oh, well, It's for Joni's dad anyway. Ya know, his health is on the decline and uh… she wanted to get the gang together."

"Yeah, of course," I said, barely keeping my grip. I wanted to both burst into tears and fits of rage. "Um. That's cool. Um… ya know, I'm gonna let you go. Ya know, I can't hear you over all that noise."

"Oh, ok. Well, I'll be in touch."

"K," I said as I hung up.

Damn, that hurt. The whole family got together, without me. After thirty six years, I still wasn't a part of Joni's family. I could only imagine how the planning went with Joni and Jennifer. "Should we invite Korva?" "Nah, that's too complicated, let's just not say anything about it – what Korva doesn't know won't hurt her." I think "What Korva doesn't know won't hurt her" was an ingrained part of the culture of my family. They would do things without inviting me or telling me, and when I found out they would say something like, "We didn't tell you because we didn't want to hurt your feelings" or "we figured you wouldn't want to come." Of course, if I was hurt and expressed those feelings, I was turned into the "dramatic one" to top it off. All reasons to lie or omit and make that the normal way to handle me.

I knew I should just let it go. I knew that if I responded, it would not go well. I would be made into the bad guy for reacting. But I just could not resist. I was hurt. This felt unjust. And I was so tired of the way they treated me. I had hit the point where I didn't care anymore. I couldn't keep subjecting myself to people who didn't want me. I sent the following text to Jeff, Joni, and Jennifer:

I was debating not saying anything, but I have to address the elephant in the room. I want relationships in my life based on trust, honesty, and respect which makes sweeping this under the rug a non-option.

First, I totally understand the rationale behind my not being included for the Thanksgiving holiday. I get it. It was about Jim and I'm not close to him and my presence would have only lent itself to more chaos. It did hurt for a quick minute, but I was able to process it and find peace.

My problem is not with the fact that I wasn't invited. My problem is with the fact that I'm relatively certain that if I hadn't called, y'all just wouldn't have told me anything and it would have become something to hide from me. And it wouldn't be the first time. Plenty of times something has slipped in conversation and things get super awkward for a minute as we all realize that I wasn't invited to something, and it was kept hidden from me.

I get that it may seem like the thing to do to avoid hurting my feelings. But there's two problems with that:

For one, we're working under an assumption that avoids reality. We're assuming that I don't know my position in this family. I do know. I know that I'm a secondary member. I'm not as close knit as y'all are with each other. I know Jennifer and her family are going to get priority over mine because of it. I accepted that many years ago. If we're telling ourselves anything different then we're only deluding ourselves. And please don't dispute this. The evidence is this: I have never been privy to something that was hidden from Jennifer, and I'm certain that she cannot say the same of me. Now, understanding that I understand my place means you have nothing to protect me from.

Second problem, how am I supposed to have a relationship with people that hide shit from me? The truth always comes out. Every time there's an awkward slip, I get to wonder how many other things are being hidden from me. That hurts more than the truth. No feelings spared there. How am I supposed to trust you?

I think I have proven to y'all that I have an endless ability to forgive. Please, moving forward, don't hide things from me. Be proactive and just tell me what and why and trust that I can handle it. And trust that I'm going to love you no matter what.

As a related aside, when we were in San Francisco and your will got brought up, things got super awkward. That shit was palpable. Is there something around the administration of your estate that you are concerned will be a conflict? I realize that this is a bit direct, but it has been gnawing at me ever since. Wouldn't it be better to deal with things like this by being forthright and honest? Let's just deal with reality.

I know y'all have a different way of dealing with things. But I like to have clear air in my relationships, so I have to speak my mind. I apologize if this causes you discomfort.

Several hours later, my sister called. I realize now that this was a classic case of being "handled." She said that they weren't hiding it from me, they just hadn't gotten around to telling me. She said that I wasn't intentionally left out, it just hadn't occurred to them to invite me. After all, this was an event for "Joni's family." Also, she said, I shouldn't take it personally, and if I wanted to feel like I belonged, I should just start acting like I do, and then…poof! Like magic, I would belong.

I wish I had a greater understanding of gaslighting that day. Back then, I was clueless and would instead walk away from one of these "unfortunate events" confused and feeling shamed. I let them convince me that I had made them treat me this way. It was all my fault, and I was lucky they tolerated me. It was a pattern I fell into with ease. I've spent the years following this "Thanksgiving Incident" immersed in therapy and my spirituality, healing and growing, so I suppose on some level I am thankful for how things unfolded.

Joni called a couple of weeks later. By then I was over it. It was just another one of those things that happened. Jeff never responded. After Christmas that year, I decided that I would go no contact with my parents, other than text or emails for birthdays and holidays. My family of origin has been the greatest source of ongoing pain for me. I was tired. I needed to heal and that wasn't going to happen if I didn't stop the pain at its source. That lasted for all of six weeks. The call about the cancer diagnosis that came early in February 2019 put an end to that. I had to get back into the dysfunction because I knew I wouldn't forgive myself if I let my father die without trying to… I don't know… maybe make things better?

My sister said that when my father was gone, he'd take the dysfunction with him. She believed that my father was an addict, and our whole family structure was built around it. Her mother was the enabler, I was the scapegoat, and she was the golden child. I supposed that left my brother to be a lost child, but I think Jeff would have said he was the hero. And she believed that all the bad things would stop when he was dead. She was wrong. For me, it was worse than ever. I felt unsafe and I had no idea why or what to do about it. Tomorrow I am leaving for New Jersey. There was no time to resolve this, and what's worse is that I didn't even know what to resolve.

I lay in my parent's guest bed, begging for sleep, stressed beyond any stress I've felt before or since. My chest hurt and my heart pounded. I seriously considered calling 911 but was too tired to move. It occurred to me that I may be so tired that I might simply just lie there and let myself die. That's when I heard him.

"Beans, you gotta get outta here."

It was Jeff's voice. It was the only sound that drowned out the pounding of my heart in my head.

In my mind's eyes, I could see him. He stood at the window of the guestroom. He looked good. He looked to be about 40, wearing his signature outfit – crisp denim jeans, white oxford shirt, rust-colored loafers. No hard-brimmed hat anymore. He had a lush, dense head of hair. He stood with his arms crossed, gazing out into the dark woods of his backyard.

"Is that you? "I asked.

With a wise-ass grin, he asked, "Who else would it be?"

I let loose with the questions: "Are you ok? Am I ok? What do I do now? What the hell is going on here? Can I trust these people? Am I crazy? Is that you? Will you stay with me?"

Jeff said, "Woah, Woah, woah, settle down over there…. First of all, don't do anything. You've done enough." His arms were crossed, then he reached up to his face with his right hand and smoothed out his mustache. It was what he did when he had something serious to say. "You try too hard, Beans. Stop." He paused, reviewing the list of questions I hurled at him. "And no, you can't trust them. Let them do what they do. You'll see who they are. You'll know what to do." He turned and looked at me and said, "You're gonna be good, Beans. Better than good. Of course, it's me and… of course, I'll stay with you. Now get some rest. Ya look like hell."

Somehow this little mental exercise was all I needed to finally succumb to sleep. *Or maybe it was with the help of my father.* I could only be grateful for what little rest I got. The next day, it was time to go. I'd been at my parents' house for nine days. That was the longest stay since I moved out in 1992. I processed as much as I could there, and in some ways, I found new and exciting things that I must work through.

While I didn't run out the door, I wasted no time getting ready to go. I fought hard to keep myself together. Somewhere inside of me, I knew I'd never be there again, and it hurt. I spent a moment in Jeff's office. The walls were lined with built-in shelves, and those shelves were full of pieces of my dad's history. *The Rolling Stone Book of Comedy*, with Robin Williams on the cover, had been on his bookshelves since it was published in 1991. There was a framed print of a steam train painted in watercolors. My stepmother said it was a Homer painting. He also had a shelf or two full of ceramics I made him some twenty years ago and there were two large acrylic paintings I made for them around 2004 or so. Let's say that my artistic skills have improved dramatically since I gifted these things to Jeff. That didn't get in the way of the fact that it felt good to see them on his shelves. Joni would likely throw them out now.

I said goodbye to that space, and to what remained there of Jeff. At this point, if I could have snuck out of the house unnoticed, I would have but it was time to face the goodbyes. I choked back all the feelings, all the confusion and sadness and rage. I gave Joni a quick hug, careful not to look her in the eyes too long. Then I hugged Jennifer. My intention was another quick hug with as little contact as possible, but instead, I found myself locked in an unwelcome and strangely long embrace. "What the hell is she doing?" I thought. It felt like more of a power play than an act of love.

Pulling out of the driveway felt incredibly significant. Adios, to whatever bullshit I could sense and not explain. As the distance between me and it increased, I felt my tension ease. I could finally breathe again.

Take me Home

Youtube.com
Peter Gabrial
"Solsbury Hill"

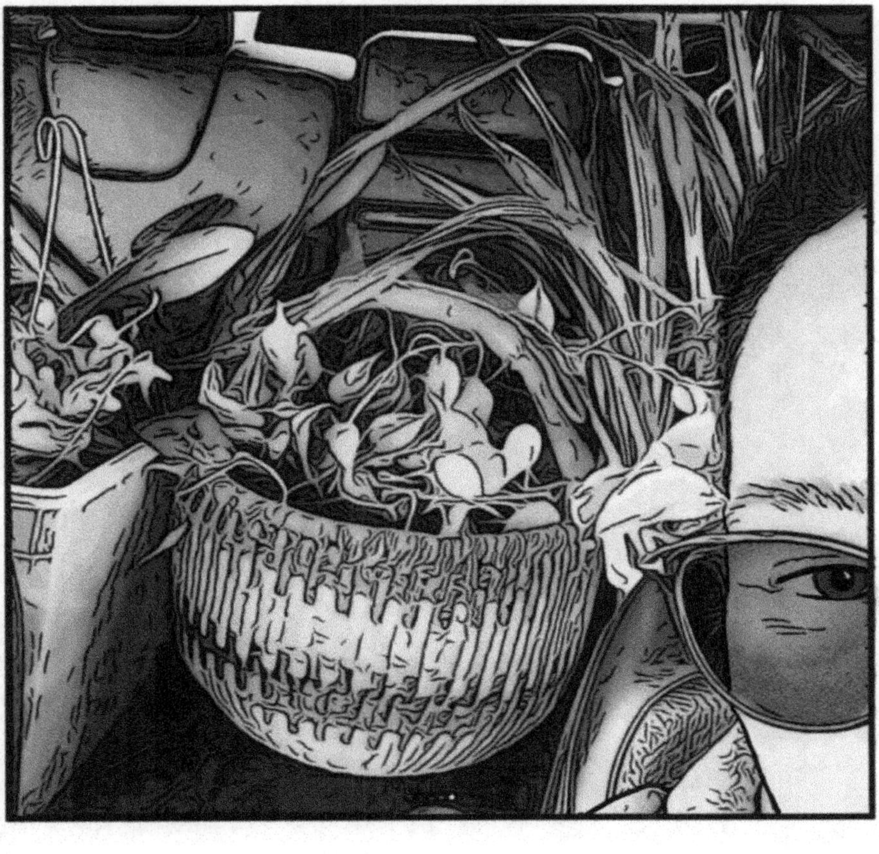

Chapter Seven

The road to New Jersey was smooth and uneventful. I happened to miss all the traffic, which was incredible given the number of traffic-prone cities I drove through. My only complaint was that my left eye would not stop hurting. It had been watering non-stop since I woke up. And my nostrils were running right along with it. As the evening sky began to darken, I found myself having difficulty seeing due to extreme haloing around the oncoming headlights. It was stress I could have done without.

I arrived at Toni's house in Lincoln Park, New Jersey around 5:30 p.m. Toni is a friend from the two years of time I did at Boonton High School. Her apartment was situated in a sprawling complex of brick buildings. Looking to have been built sometime in the mid-twentieth century, these buildings each housed at least ten to twelve apartments, and there was a whole sea of them to drive through before finding Toni's quiet little corner.

Getting settled in at Toni's felt like taking off the world's most uncomfortable bra that had been holding up my whole soul for entirely too long. I've known Toni since my sophomore year of high school and being with her is like going home. For the first time in too many days, I did not have to hold anything in. I got to express my most authentic self fully. I was able to relate my experience in spiritual terms without the worry that people were rolling their mind's eyes at my woo-woo crap. I felt the weight come off me and I was so grateful for the space Toni created.

Before heading to Lincoln Park, I stopped at Dee's Funeral Home to pick up my keepsake portion of Jeff's remains. They gave him to me in a gift bag. Inside was a white box with a label that read, "George Jeffrey Rafter." Nothing else. It seemed surprisingly plain for it being such a significant artifact. My father's body was in that box. Even so, I think Jeff would have appreciated its simplicity.

We placed the box on a small, freestanding bar that served as Toni's altar. It was about counter height and not quite three feet wide, with drop-down shelves that created more room for mixing things up. It was all decked for Yuletide celebrations. What stood out was the mini tree covered in lights and ornaments that represented the many stages of Toni's life. Beside it was a huge cement bust of her spirit familiar, the wolf, sporting a fluffy Santa hat. Because it was a bar, its contents were things that you would expect, like bottles of liquor in the cabinets and wine on the racks. But this was also an altar and was where Toni kept some of her more sacred things, like her crystals, jewelry, and photos of loved ones passed. Her mother, Freda, who died in 1979, was prominent amongst her ancestral photographs. I was honored she had carved out a space for Jeff. It was hard to believe it, but he was amongst my ancestors now. *God, I miss him.*

I began spewing all the feelings I had contained for days. Disbelief, anguish, rage, fear, sadness, regret, hope, relief, peace, confusion, desperation. All of the feelings. I got to express them as they showed up without worrying how they would affect the listener. And Toni listened. She validated me and empathized with my grief.

It was New Year's Eve. I had been away from home for ten days now. It was strange to be gone that long and through two major holidays, Christmas and now New Years. I missed my family and wished I could enjoy that time with them, but I knew that's not how things would go if I were home. I wouldn't be able to be present, never mind enjoy a happy New Year's Eve with them.

This night was a very appropriate time to be going through a sort of mourning ritual. NYE is an annual practice in endings. For me, it is a time of acknowledgment, accounting, gratitude, and completion, which was exactly what I needed. This night was about acceptance and honoring the end. It was also about acknowledging that there was more to come. More to sort out and work toward ending, but also more abundance and reward for said work. Tonight, I would just enjoy the space between what was and what will be, and let it heal me.

New Year's morning I awoke light and fresh after a good night of catharsis. I had a plan for the day ahead. Toni and I would go on a pilgrimage and there was much to do. We were going to take Jeff home. Back to his family, his ancestors, and his roots.

It was mid-day and there were only one or two other people at Saint Vincent the Martyr's Cemetery. I parked along the side of the narrow road that meandered through the park-like setting. I couldn't remember where my grandparent's actual grave was for the life of me. I had been there as a child with my grandmother to visit my grandfather many times. I had been there when my grandmother was buried back in 1995. After that, I had only visited New Jersey three or maybe four times and didn't make it out to the cemetery during those trips, other than to drive by.

I had a vague idea of the section they were in, so I figured we would just wander until we found something. I was able to look up a photo of the headstone on Ancestry.com to get an idea of what shape and color we were looking for. I felt guilty the whole time, treading on people's resting places. Toni continually crossed herself murmuring sweet Catholic things under her breath. I just kept up with the awkward, "excuse me, pardon me. So sorry. Excuse me," like someone walking in front of you at the movie theater.

After about fifteen minutes of roaming, we found them. The bright red and gold of the Fireman's Flag, which stood for my grandfather's service with Madison's Volunteer Fire Department, beckoned me from the end of a row. Their headstone was small and nearly identical to all the stones around them, except for the flags and the small plaque at the foot of the plot placed in honor of my grandfather's service in the United States Army. The stone reads "Gin + Juke," nicknames for my grandmother and grandfather, and below that the word "Peace." My Aunt Lizza's cremated remains were interred there as well. While I was not sure what would happen with the largest portion of Jeff's remains, I did want to make sure that some of them made it here too.

That morning, I had opened the box from the funeral home. The first thing I saw was a sweet tuft of light blue tissue paper. Beneath the wrapping, a sandwich baggy sealed off with a twist tie. I chuckled. It was even less ceremonious than I was expecting. I asked Toni for a small but solid container for stashing some ashes. I wanted something that would be easy and discreet when sprinkling. I'm sure there are all kinds of laws around scattering remains. I didn't know about the state of New Jersey's laws, and I didn't look them up so that I could claim plausible deniability after the fact. I was not going down for this, so the container had to be stealthy.

Looking at the remains was hard but, and in a strange way, healing. The ash was a very fashionable light gray. It looked… clean. There were bone fragments, and that took me aback. Those were his bones. They had been a part of what animated him for almost seventy years. They had traveled. They had been injured. They had carried him well. Those bones knew more about my father than I ever could, even under the best of circumstances. I'd never considered bones with such deep reverence. I felt more grateful for my own.

Toni gave me a small, cylindrical, aqua blue container that had once held "Hello" brand toothpaste tablets in peppermint flavor. In my mind I could see my dad take a deep inhale through flared nostrils and say in his baritone voice, "Mmmm, minty."

I stood over my grandparents' grave with the little container in my hand. I had no idea what I was doing.

"You should say something," Toni said, giving me a nudge. Toni is good at making impromptu speeches. I'm more the type to write out and practice a speech 40 times before delivering it.

"Yeah, uh, ok…" I said with reluctance. "So… um… hey." Dammit this felt awkward. "So… I hope that you are all doing well and that the… umm… afterlife is… uhhh… enjoyable?" *Listen, what do you say to dead people?*

"Grandpa Juke, I'm sorry I don't remember meeting you, but I've heard good things. I hope to make your acquaintance down the road… I mean, like waaaay down the road… And Ginny…"

The moment I said her name it was like she was there with me, and I could feel her love. I started to cry and talking became much harder. "Ginny… I miss you so much," I said through sobs. "There's no one on earth like you… You were just… the best. I'm so grateful that I got to be your granddaughter."

"Aunt Liz, thanks for believing me. Thanks for having my back and speaking up. I love and miss you tons."

"And Jeff…" I stood there bawling with his little minty fresh tin in hand. "Jeff… I hope you feel better now. I hope that you're happy to be home, with your mom and dad. I… I miss you… and… I'm so sorry. For like, everything. I'll never forget you and um… I promise to do my best and uh… ya know, make you proud and all. I'll do the work for us, ya know, to heal our generational trauma and stuff. Ummm… yeah. So, I love you all… and ahhh… please take care of each other."

I looked around to make sure no one was watching and then emptied the contents of the little tin over the top of the grave. The ground was wet, and the ashes seemed to dissolve on contact.

I once again dried my tear-soaked face, took a few deep breaths, and bid my ancestor's farewell. As we headed back to the car, I said, "Hey Toni, let's stop and get something to eat. There's a little place by my grandmother's old house that used to be owned by the Chipoletti family. Chippy's Deli had the best Sloppy Joes. I hope that it's still there."

Toni said, "Stop. Look!"

I stopped, looked to my right, and saw that the plot I stood on belonged to Michael Chipoletti, passed away in 2016. "Holy Crap! Maybe this is Chippy!! What are the odds?" *Well, you don't have to twist my arm, Universe.*

The new name of Chippy's Deli is Main Street Submarines. I'm happy to say that the Sloppy Joe's were as bomb as ever. In most U.S. states, a Sloppy Joe is a mixture of ground beef in a tangy tomato-based sauce heaped on a hamburger bun. For the record, that's a Manwich. A Sloppy Joe in Madison, New Jersey is a triple-decker sandwich on rye bread, with any meat of your choice (mine was roast beef), cheese (often Swiss, but I prefer Havarti), coleslaw, and thousand island dressing. It is to die for.

We chose to eat there as I was not going to attempt eating a Sloppy Joe in the rental car. We placed our order and I found the restroom, which if I'm being honest was half the reason I had to stop for food. As I walked back past the checkout counter to our table, I walked by a woman and heard her say, "I'm picking up for Jeff." I thought, "Huh, what are the odds? I was there for Jeff, in a roundabout way." It gave me a chuckle as I felt that familiar tickle synchronicity gives me. Then, as Toni and I were devouring our sandwiches, the young lady behind the counter called out, "order for George." Again, with George being Jeff's first name, I wish I had the skill to calculate the probability of this.

I told Toni about the woman picking up for Jeff and now this lady has an order for George.

"Well, George Jeffrey Rafter is most certainly here with us," Toni said, confirming my feelings. I was glad I had a witness.

We began the walk down memory lane by stopping at my father's childhood home. My grandmother kept it for a little more than a decade after my grandfather passed in 1976. In the late '80s she moved into a split-level home that she shared with my Aunt Lizza, leaving that Kings Road house behind.

The house was modest and cute, built in 1929. Back in the day, it was a light yellow, if I recall right, but the current tenants had painted it a darker olive-ish color. They had also removed the screens that enclosed the front porch. I can't imagine the rationale behind that move. The screened-in porch was a highlight of that house. I remember many summer evenings out there cooling off, safe from the swarms of Jersey insects.

I wondered if that house was still as creepy as I remember it being. From the outside, it looked like an average, almost boring, house, but it held a dark past. It was something that I felt as a child, especially in the attic. Previous owners had converted the attic into two bedrooms and a bonus space, which was where I slept when I was young. I remember having more than a few disturbing experiences in that space. I would be playing in my Aunt Barbara's room and then out of nowhere, I would get scared and have to run out of the room and down the stairs as quickly as my little feet could take me. I would be terrified but for no obvious reason.

Twice, however, my experience was more tangible. I was lying in bed, getting ready to doze off, and I got the distinct physical impression of someone sitting on the bed next to me. I'd feel a weight depressing the bed and the sensation of force against the side of my leg. I remember being afraid, pulling the covers over my head, and closing my eyes. In my mind, I could see a person sitting next to me. He was a teenage boy, and he was fighting with someone. The second time this happened was the last time I slept upstairs in my grandmother's attic.

I found out in the early '90s, a few years after my grandmother moved, that a teenage boy had hung himself in that attic before my grandparents owned the house. I wish I could find information about him so that I could pay my respects. And I wish I had known about him when I was a child. They didn't tell me because they didn't want to scare me. Instead, my experience got downplayed and I walked away questioning my sanity.

Aside from being a little bit creepy, my memories of the house were blessings. The summers I spent with my grandmother, hanging out at the neighbor's pool. Running through piles of autumn leaves with my coat buttoned around my neck like a superhero's cape, free and hopeful. My grandmother napping in her favorite chair. All the times we laughed at ourselves breathlessly over the dumbest things. That house has beautiful energy because of all that goodness, and I am hoping it helped that young man's soul find peace.

It was midafternoon by the time we drove by my mother's childhood home. I needed to see it. I have dreams about this house with annoying regularity. I want that house. I want to own it and build a farm there. Not because it belonged to my family, but because that house had a soul, and I loved it deeply.

From as early as I could remember, my grandparents' house felt like magic. It was a large home of almost 5,200 square feet. For a five-year-old, that's a castle. Built in 1908, it had the smell of history. Some good, and some not. The servant's stairwell in the main lobby of the home never sat well with me. While it was fun for hide and seek, when I found out it was built to hide the comings and goings of people deemed lesser, it lost its luster. Even still, that house calls to me in my sleep, more than thirty years since I last stepped foot in it.

It's funny to me that I feel more connection to that house than I do to my mother's family. My relationship with all of them was expert-level dysfunctional and storybook tragic.

My mother got pregnant with me out of wedlock. She was nineteen and Jeff was twenty. The course of action they chose was to keep me and get married. They eloped in the summer of 1972; I was born the following February. My mother's father was old school and got quite angry about it. All of it. Hearsay suggests that there was a significant rift between my mother and her parents for a while, but I only have a few, fragmented pieces of information from that time. It was another part of my past no one wanted to discuss.

Marriage and parenthood didn't look the way either Jeff or my mother had hoped. She was not responding well to being a mother. From what I know, she was neglectful and preoccupied with her growing drug habit. He worked as a roofer and was trying to provide. Reports from my Aunt Barbara would say they were not living in a shotgun shack, but they weren't living with the comforts that my mother had been used to. After all, she had grown up with a bedroom that I'm sure was comparable in size to their entire apartment.

Things would begin to fall apart for them in the fall of 1974 when my mother miscarried her second child. I don't know the whole truth of this story, but I know this miscarriage ended with my mother needing a partial hysterectomy. She would not be able to have any more children. She was only twenty-two years old. She was never the same after that. My parents split up before my second birthday.

At a little over two years old my mother "absconded" with me to California. Absconded is the word my father always used. It was accurate and, under today's standards, I would have been an Amber Alert. He tried to fight it in court, but in 1975 fathers didn't have much say concerning custodial matters. Given that he didn't know exactly where she was, there was little he could do.

Once in California, my mother lied to me about who my father was. I was at an age where it had been long enough since I had seen Jeff, I had forgotten him. She told me that my father was the man we had moved to California with, Roger. I found out he was not my father after she left him for the nudist man who lived in the apartment downstairs. I was hungry one night, and couldn't find my mother, so I went upstairs and asked Roger for some dinner. He said, "Go ask your mom. I'm not your father." *Um. What?*

I remember regularly finding my mother passed out on the floor in the bathroom. I remember when she wanted me to go back to sleep in the morning, she would make me lay in bed with her naked boyfriend. I remember sleeping in the bathtub of a roach-infested motel that we stayed in with some guy after things didn't work out with the naked guy. I remember all that and more horrible shit. I don't know how Baby Korva managed what I can't imagine dealing with now.

I moved in with my dad just before I turned five years old. My relationship with my mother was non-existent after that. She would call sometimes around my birthday, not necessary on my birthday, all strung out, and say things like, "How come you don't call me?"

"Because I'm a child. That's why," is what adult Korva would have said. Young Korva just said, "Sorry."

At the same time, I had a good relationship with her mother, my grandmother, Peggy. She was just as magical as her house when I was young. She was fun. She felt safe. We had a special relationship. But that wouldn't last into my adulthood.

When I moved out of my father's home in Dover, Delaware in 1992, I moved in with my mother, back to California. The idea was that I could go to college inexpensively because she was a California resident. It was my first solo trip of any distance, never mind across the country. I was full of hope. I finally had the chance to get to know my mother, and from what I could tell, she had gotten her act together. Or at the least, had her addiction in check enough to hold a decent paying job. My hope was that I would fit in with her and that I would finally feel like I had a family.

She took me out to dinner the night I arrived in Reseda. She told me that she was just recently diagnosed as HIV positive and likely had been so for a couple of years. She had contracted it both sharing needles and being intimate with a man who had died from it. I wasn't even sure what all of this meant. It was the early 1990s and, while HIV/AIDS had been in the spotlight for around a decade at that point, there was so much I didn't know or understand about it. Should I be worried and, if so, about what? Did this mean she was going to die? Was I safe living with her? Were there things I should or shouldn't do? I didn't know. All I knew was that it felt like a cloud had obscured whatever rainbows and sunshine I had conjured up in my head about my new life with my mother.

She lived in a one-bedroom apartment, half filled with bicycle and computer parts, with two cats, overflowing litter boxes, and a dog. I wouldn't say she was a full blown hoarder, but she was well on her way. I slept on the fold out couch and kept my clothing in one small cabinet. Within about four months I had gotten myself two jobs and was making good and predictable money. I asked her if we could move into a bigger apartment so that I could have a bedroom. I thought I had shown I was responsible and could be counted on. She refused. She didn't want to.

She asked me to help with the bills, and I did. I knew I was making more than my fair share of long-distance calls, and I had no qualms with paying for it. One day she asked me for seventy-five dollars to pay for the charges I had incurred. I wrote her a check on the spot. Shortly after I overheard her asking her father for seventy-five dollars to pay that same bill because I was not paying her and she couldn't afford it. I can only imagine how many times this happened. That is what addiction looks like.

This living situation ended when I came home at 11 p.m. after working two jobs since 9 a.m. She was there with a friend. They were sitting on my bed, also known as the fold out couch. They were high. This lady starts in on me for being too clean. She said all my cleaning up and changing things was stressing my mom out. She said I must have thought I was too good for them. She kept at me in a way that was trying to evoke a response. My mother sat there letting this forty-something-year-old woman pick a fight with her eighteen-year-old daughter. I was ready to give her one. I asked her if she'd like to step outside, and that was when my mother intervened. My mother was furious with me. She had let her friend berate me in an inflammatory way for being a "too-clean bitch" (no, that's not a thing), and I got in trouble when I told her high ass to come with it.

I was done. I moved out immediately. I stayed with a co-worker for a couple of nights, found an apartment, and cleaned my stuff out of her house in less than a week. For my grandparents, she spun the tale into me abandoning her for being poor and HIV positive.

After I moved out, our relationship took on a different feel. I was mad at my mother for how she treated me. She had the chance to be my parent. Instead used me as an excuse to lie for money and treated me like I was a stuck-up bitch for refusing to live in filth. When I moved to Seattle in 1993, we returned to having a non-existent relationship. That seemed to be fine by her until I didn't invite her to my wedding in 1999.

She was mad. My grandparents were mad. It was a whole shit show. I just didn't think that it was right to have her there. My mother had abandoned me. She did not bring anything to my life other than a whole lot of heartbreak. Her being there would have made that day uncomfortable for me, and likely for Jeff and Joni. That was not going to happen. I was willing to pay the price for this choice.

After the birth of my oldest son, William, in 2000, we began to mend our relationship. I had paid for her to fly up to Seattle, but she canceled at the last minute. I think the anxiety of it all was too much. I visited her a couple of times and was able to get pictures of her with William. I would later find one tucked in the pages of her missals after she passed.

In 2002, she was bitten by a neighbor's dog and the wound never healed. She sued their homeowner's insurance and with that money she bought herself a condominium and a car. At this point she had been sober-ish for about eight years, thanks in large part to her conversion to Catholicism. She even kept her condo clean. It took two years before her body finally gave in to the infection of her dog-bite wound. The downturn in her health happened fast, and no one told me. She died on February 18, 2004, ten days before my thirty-first birthday.

I learned about her passing the night before her funeral. My aunt, my mother's only sister, had a stranger call to tell me. I barely had time to make it to her service, but I did. Later I learned that my aunt had forged my mother's will, making herself executor and beneficiary, taking away the last opportunity for my mother to contribute to my life and the life of my children. It wouldn't have been much, but it would have been something.

My grandparents found out that I had put all the pieces together and knew what my aunt had done. They called me, threatening that if I took this matter to court, they would testify about what a terrible daughter I was and that my mother didn't want me to receive a penny of her money. It broke my heart. I didn't care about the money, I just couldn't bear how heartless and cruel my grandparents were to me. *How could they hate me so much?* I couldn't pursue any legal action over forgery, fraud, or theft because the cost seemed too great. I didn't want to prolong my pain any further. I would not find out until many years later, when my grandfather passed in 2018, that I was expressly written out of his will. I thought perhaps it happened after the whole will-forging incident in 2004. But no, it happened in 1993, when my mother told him I had abandoned her by moving out.

I've made peace with all of this. She was an addict, and it governed her behavior. Her parents, I believe, were riddled with guilt and regret, and were in deep denial. This is where my spiritual beliefs come in handy. I believe that when people pass, they immediately gain access to the truth. I believe that in death, whatever misconceptions we may have had in life get washed away. The filters created by our egos, and the egos of others, melt away to reveal pure and shameless truth. They were wrong about me in a way I could not talk them out of in life, but when they passed, they could see the true me and know that all I have ever wanted was to love them. And I forgave them.

Chapter Eight

Toni and I drove past Kings Road Elementary School, where Jeff and I had both attended. He for the totality of his elementary school years, and me, twenty-one years later, for kindergarten and first grade. Then we drove by the "hippy house." It was across the street from Drew University in an old mansion that had been converted into multiple apartments. It was where Greg lived back in the day. We drove by Fairleigh Dickinson University, where Jeff had received his bachelor's degree, and where he met Charlotte.

We drove by the apartment he and I lived in while he finished school and started his first real career-oriented job for Morris Cablevision. It was a cute two-bedroom, two-story apartment in a red-brick building behind Morristown Memorial Hospital. I liked my room. It was the first time I had my own official bedroom. It was an apartment, full of odds and ends furniture, likely handed down, but it was a beautiful little home. My father was good at making the best of what was available to him.

The rest of the Madison tour included St. Vincent's church where my grandmother attended, and St. Elizabeth's, where she had worked as a telephone operator. We cruised down Main Street where I pointed out what used to be the Woolworth's where I would spend all my allowance. I have so many memories in Madison, and I loved it so much. *Maybe one day I'll come back here and live for a while.*

We were headed north on Interstate 287, back to Lincoln Park, when Toni asked, "You wanna go through Boonton?" Her tone was hesitant because she knew that I did not remember much of my time there fondly. That was where my father called me an ungrateful cunt and beat the side of my head purple.

"Nope," I said, sounding somewhere between a stubborn adult and a petulant child.

"You sure? The exit is coming up."

"Yes, I know, and yes, I'm sure." I said firmly.

"Really? I mean, maybe it would be good for you."

The exit came into view and while I was sure I didn't want to go, at the very last minute the voice in my head, my voice this time, said "do it." I took the exit that led to Margaretta Road, where Jeff, Joni, Jennifer, and I lived for just about three years in the late 1980s and early '90s. It was a nice two-story, four-bedroom home on a cul-de-sac street, up on a hill with a beautiful view. I remember when we moved into that house in November of 1988 thinking it would change everything. This is the kind of house normal people live in. We would become a real family. Well, that didn't happen. I thought seeing the house would bring back a whole host of unwanted memories but, to my surprise, it did not. Instead, it brought up something far more welcome.

I almost drove right past the house, that's how different it looked. The structure itself was the same, except that they had changed the exterior color. But the biggest difference was the growth in the landscape plants. They were mature and beautiful. It was a sight that made me happy, because it reminded me that I too had grown, matured, and was more beautiful.

After Margaretta Road we decided to trek out into the back roads of Boonton Township. I think people who haven't visited New Jersey have the idea that it's urban and dirty. After all, it has gained itself the moniker, "The Armpit of America." But people tend to see only a small portion of New Jersey depicted in media, and often parts that are on the outskirts of New York or Philadelphia. While it does have some grungy bits, as do all places, New Jersey is a predominately beautiful state. It's the Garden State, and Boonton Township has some of the loveliest roads I've ever driven.

For Toni and me, these roads were a walk down memory lane. But given that it had been thirty-odd years since I'd driven them, I had forgotten the way around. Toni had to direct me. She led me all over hell's half an acre, for a good sixty minutes. We traveled through country roads that served as time machines as we passed one- and two-hundred-year-old homes and farms that looked like relics in the modern world.

We listened to Jeff's music (Van Morrison, Steely Dan, Joni Mitchell, Little Feet, The Rolling Stones, etc.), sprinkled in with music from our youth. Occasionally, the memories would flood back, and I would clearly remember where I was. That was especially so when we made that hard right onto Kingsland Road.

Something about the narrowness and sharp turns in the road brought back the memory. This was the road I had driven on the night I tried to kill myself. I completed the loop that went through Boonton Township which led to this winding road more than once that night. Toni and I had been talking about this failed suicide attempt just the night before.

I said, "This is the road, Toni. The one I tried to die on."

She paused for a moment and said, through held-back tears, "Don't ever do that again."

"I won't."

Any sense of sadness I had when I realized what road we were on was quickly overridden by a sense of gratitude. What a beautiful life I had grown into having. I had worked so hard to be a better, healthier person. I was in a stable, happy marriage. I have three beautiful, healthy children, and I am proud of them. I had a warm, welcoming home with a gorgeous garden. I had friends that loved me. I wished I could go back and whisper in that seventeen-year-old girl's ear, "It's going to be ok. Better than ok." Maybe that did travel back through time because somehow, I survived that night. And everything changed.

It had been an eventful day, and I was happy to get back to the sanctuary of Toni's cozy apartment. We immediately changed into PJs. I put on my favorite bathrobe, which is referred to as "Robey" amongst my close friends and family. It's a wearable security blanket and it may be my favorite article of clothing. We mixed cocktails and prepared for another healing night of reminiscing and expressing grief. The candles were lit. The mood was set. I put some music on the portable speaker I had packed. The same one I used when Jeff passed. We continued the music mix from the car. *Jeff's music.*

Van Morrison's "Into the Mystic" came on. Even though I'd heard this song a million times, there was something different about the way it sounded. The song had a crispness, a newness as if I'd never heard it before. I closed my eyes and was whisked away to a space in my mind that felt very real and very much otherworldly.

In my mind, I saw my father. Not in the way I usually see things in my head. Often when I try to visualize something or someone, I can't hold a steady or constant image. It's spotty like the reception won't hold. This time it was like an HDTV. I saw him with crystal clarity. He was sitting on a short stool, playing guitar. He was wearing his signature outfit; perfectly aged denim, a crisp white oxford shirt, and orangish-brown loafers. He was outdoors on a stone patio, dimly lit by hanging string lights and a firepit. Behind him was a grassy knoll that created a little amphitheater. I felt like I could reach out and touch him.

Toni saw the tears streaming down my face and tried to distract me. She gestured in a way that suggested we get up and dance. I closed my eyes again and whispered, "Let me see this. I need to see this."

He was glowing. He sang along, bigger and louder than he had ever in life. I could see fleeting and transparent images of other musicians, drummers and horn players, projected like holograms on the knoll behind him. It was as if I could see what he was imagining in his mind. At one point he looked directly at me. His eyes were wide, and his expression said, "How cool is this? Can you believe this?" as though he could not be happier. It was blissful, wild, and intense. I will never forget it.

The song ended and I came back to consciousness. I felt so remarkably happy. Happy for him. He was at peace and all things were possible. He was released, relieved, and full of hope. All I could say was, "Oh my god, that was a gift. What an incredible gift." I recounted what happened to Toni.

"Wow," she said. "I could tell something big was happening. I just couldn't imagine what. Yes, that was a gift."

That whole day had been a gift. I got to time-travel through my father's life. I've no doubt he was there with me. I was sure he was in the backseat, wearing his gold-framed aviators, smoothing out his mustache, and going over all his memories along the streets of Madison, New Jersey. And I got to revisit my own youth in a way that made me more grateful for being alive.

Chapter Nine

The next couple of days with Toni was a long string of resting, lounging, and processing. We ordered a variety of delicious New Jersey delicacies, pizza, more sloppy joes, and a couple of Taylor Ham with egg and cheese sandwiches. *It's Taylor Ham, not pork roll!* We watched, or more accurately rewatched, our favorite TV shows, like *Outlander, Ozarks,* and *The Witcher*. We had very little on the agenda and that suited me fine. I was just happy to be with someone who wasn't constantly talking about how many calories they had consumed like Joni and Jennifer the day after Jeff died.

Sunday the 2nd was the first new moon of the year. *I can't believe I had been gone from home for only eleven days. So much had happened in such a short time.* I have been using Jan Spiller's New Moon Astrology once a month, on the new moon, to set intentions for the last few years. This new moon was in Capricorn. Capricorn represents the zodiacal father and authority figures. New Moons are about new beginnings, planting new seeds. It seemed a perfect moon to set intentions for grieving and healing regarding Jeff.

We smoke cleansed the heck out of Toni's house. We used sage grown in my garden, along with a blend of purification herbs that I had made. The same ones I used in Jeff's office. Then, I meditated on my new moon wishes. They are as follows:

1. I want to easily find myself in a new and healing relationship with my father.

2. I want to easily find myself listening to and expressing my own inner authority.

3. I want to talk to Dave Matthews.

That last one finds its way into my new moon wishes on a regular basis. I believe wishes should include both tangible things to work toward and things that would require a miracle. That Dave Matthews wish would require a little divine intervention, I am sure. Either way, throwing in there creates what I call balance.

That afternoon, I thought about Jeff's plants. It saddened me to think of them dying. How wasteful. They had meant something to him. And plants had been a source of bonding for us once upon a time.

Back in the late 1990s, we both kept orchids. I had been given my first orchid in 1996 by an ex-boyfriend's mother. It was a phalaenopsis. It was love at first sight. On the next visit to my dad's, I noticed that not only was he keeping orchids, but he had a whole orchidarium. He was totally into it. As I got older, my attention would focus more on outdoor plants, but during the pandemic, my love of house plant tending was rekindled.

When I said to Joni that I should drive home and take the plants with me, I wasn't serious, but the idea began to make more sense. The situation in the world made air travel look like a first-class pain in my ass. The Omicron variant of the Coronavirus had taken off and droves of people were getting sick. I had already seen the effects of staffing shortages on my trip out to Boston, and it had only gotten worse. On top of it, it had been snowing and cold in Seattle for most of the holiday week, causing even more cancelled flights.

I had a ticket home booked for Tuesday the 4th, but it seemed too soon. I wasn't ready. If I went home now, I would get sucked back into regular daily life and not take the time to process this experience. I had made that cross-country trek from Delaware to California back in 1992 and it was life changing. Perhaps I was ready to do it again. Then I could take home Jeff's plants.

These plants were more than just organic matter soaking up water and sunlight. They were a meaningful and important part of his life. He had cared for them, and not half-assedly. I think that when we tend things, living things like people or plants, we imbue them with our essence. To me, these plants were a part of Jeff. They were a living part of his legacy, just like me. I wanted to keep them alive.

I started to formulate a potential plan, trying to decide if this was even doable. I knew I needed to talk to Bryan about whether or not this would work for our family, but I was going to wait until I was sure I was up to the task before we worked out the logistics back home.

My trip in 1992 was across the southern United States. I followed Interstate 95 to I-40 to I-10. It was a nice trip, and I was leaning towards doing it again, minus the I-10 portion which was too far south. I was concerned about the northern routes because of winter weather. Driving in snowstorms or icy conditions was stressful and I wasn't sure it was worth the risk. If I took I-40 all the way across, I would have to finish my trip driving up the West Coast. This would be a long trip.

I hemmed and hawed for a good, solid twenty-four hours, checking distances and driving times for various points to points. I figured the minimum was seven days on the road, but that did not include visits with people along the way. I was going to get my money's worth out of this adventure and see as many people as I could without taking weeks to get home.

Time away was a struggle. *I should get home.* I had been gone for two weeks at this point. I had departed in the middle of a partial kitchen remodel and my house was a disaster. My husband most often worked with people overseas and early in the morning. Having to take the kids to their respective schools would cut into a huge portion of his working day. I felt like I was shirking my duties and that I did not deserve the luxury of taking this time. To be clear, Bryan did not make me feel like that, I did. I had to get over that.

In the twenty-one years since my oldest son was born, I had not been away from my children for more than ten days, with the average being closer to four days. My youngest was now thirteen. They would be fine without me for a little while longer. My chores and projects weren't going anywhere and the only person I answered to about them was myself. But these days would pass in the blink of an eye. These days were most prime for healing. I had to make the most of them. I had lived forever with the trauma that my relationship with my father generated. I needed to be done. I needed this time to do that.

I called Bryan and ran the idea past him. Of course, as usual, he was supportive. He said he would rather I come home but he agreed that this was for my best and was one hundred percent on board. He understood that this placed burden on him, but he had already worked out an alternative work schedule with his boss when I had left for Boston, not knowing how long I'd be gone. Nothing was changing.

I was worried about my kids. I know that they're old enough to take on more responsibility and that my husband can take care of them fine. I was just feeling guilty. And then I received a message from my daughter:

> *I heard that you might not be home on Tuesday, I just wanted to let you know that there's no pressure in coming home. I actually would prefer that you do what you think you need to do; I think you deserve this time to yourself. Whatever plans you go with, I don't mind, and I'm sure Alex doesn't mind either. I just*

want you to know that we all love you so much, and hope this time genuinely helps you. Hopefully, your plans for the orchids work, if I remember the flower properly. :) love you so much, stay safe ♥

What a good, kind, and compassionate kid I have. I felt fortunate and grateful. I felt relieved. I could just *be* with this experience.

I cancelled my airline ticket, but I would still have to drive back to Boston on January 4th to exchange my rental car. I had prepaid to save money and, as a result, my contract was with the branch of Hertz that was specific to Boston Logan Airport rather than any branch of the Hertz Corporation. I would have been more put out by it, but I had to get back to the area to get Jeff's plants anyway. I arranged the plant pickup with Joni after the car exchange.

I began plotting my cross-country course but felt very non-committal. I could start off heading south, that way I could stop in Charlottesville, VA. I have friends there that I'd like to see. Also, I'm a huge Dave Matthews fan, perhaps a wee bit obsessed. Even though he lives in Seattle, the band got its start in Charlottesville, and I think he still spends plenty of time there. You know, I could run into him at the grocery store or something. I wanted to see the bar where he worked when he got his start. That kind of fan-girl stuff. Don't judge. Or do. Whatever. Then, if I decided to continue the southern route, I could stop in Roebuck, South Carolina to see my astrologer friend, Jennifer Fox aka Foxy. This idea was gaining appeal.

After that, I wasn't sure. I figured I could wait until I got to South Carolina and see what the weather looked like. If I stuck to the main interstates, the roads would be clear, even in the north. Or at minimum, they would be kept as clear as possible. My concern was more with active weather systems. If there were no new weather events (snow, etc.), I could head north to shorten the trip. If there was, I would continue across the south. It was incredibly unnerving. Cross-country driving in January is a real wild card for weather and safety over much of the land between me and home. There were too many unknowns. *This could go very wrong.*

Chapter Ten

Tuesday, January 4th rolled around and ready or not, it was time to hit the road. I had to make it to Logan International by 1:30 p.m. to return my current car and pick up the one that would carry me across the United States. This pick-up time allowed me to get there, do whatever with the cars, get to my parents'- I mean, *Joni's house* - pick up the plants, and get back to New Jersey around sundown. I planned to stay with Toni one more day and then head out on Thursday, January 6th.

The drive to Logan is about three hours forty-five minutes if the stars align. I have heard instances of this drive taking eights hours. I planned to get an early start but not too early. The morning wasn't rushed, and it helped that I was able to just hop in the car and go without having to pack and load up luggage.

The car I was driving was a gray Toyota Camry. I liked it. I had gotten used to how it drove. This contributed to the trip back to Boston feeling more comfortable. I felt more familiar with the area too. I thought back to my drive to Toni's days prior and noted the difference in my state of being. I left my parents'- *Joni's* - house devastated and full of doubt. I'm returning calmer and more certain. Staying with Toni had allowed me to blow off some grief steam. I was much better off for it.

I got on the road somewhere between 8:30 and 9 a.m. It was a beautiful day. Crisp but not cold. It was the first sunny day I had seen in what felt like forever. It was as if I had dragged the Seattle weather along with me. Truth be told, that suited me fine. I loved the weather in Seattle. Almost half of my youth was spent in Florida. The rest of my pre-Washington life was spent in areas that got a lot of sun, so the move to Seattle's five solid months of gray was an adjustment. Not only had I adjusted, but I had become rewired to love it. Come September 21ˢᵗ each year, I'm begging for the cool, clouds, and rain.

The route I chose took me across the Tappan Zee Bridge, or what used to be called that (I will always call it Tappan Zee, because it is fabulous to say). This way I was able to avoid driving through New York City. My chosen route took me through northern New Jersey, just a little piece of New York around White Plains, a large diagonal cut through Connecticut on Interstate 84, and then into Massachusetts.

So much about this route felt familiar. Between the ages of seven and nine years old, when Jeff and I lived in Connecticut, we made the drive across Tappan Zee Bridge at least once a month to visit family in New Jersey. We would take short trips all over New England to ski in the winter. The man I took those trips with and the man that died in his office in Boxborough, Massachusetts were two different men. I realized that I spent so much of my life with Jeff trying to go back to New England in 1979, when he was young, hopeful, and happy.

I thought a lot about my dad. Every time I felt the urge to resist thinking about him, I'd remind myself that was the point of this trip: to think about my dad. To have as many thoughts and feelings as I could. I mean, isn't that the way we work through things?

I passed a sign in Connecticut for the Southport exits. That was where Jeff and I had lived when we first left New Jersey. That would be the first of many job-opportunity-related moves we/he would make. That was where we lived in a small two-bedroom townhouse with Charlotte. I couldn't help but feel sad to think that Jeff, Charlotte, and I never got to be a family. I don't think I had ever mourned that loss before. I wasn't supposed to talk about it. I had to pretend like nothing ever happened. To do anything else would be disloyal to Jeff. But now he was gone, and I had the freedom to grieve the loss of Charlotte. I felt overwhelmed with deep-seeded sadness and empathy for a little girl who had to live her life without a mother.

Wait, I am that little girl who had to live her life without a mother. I am that little girl who cried herself to sleep night after night because no one cared. I am that girl whose life was pulled this way and that way, at the whim of people who could not see past their own selfish noses. I am that girl who was abandoned, neglected, bullied, and scapegoat by the very people who should have nourished and protected her. I am that little girl who was treated like trash and chastised when I acted like it. I am that little girl who only ever wanted to feel love and acceptance and, for the life of her, could not get it. I do not know how to heal that little girl in me, but I could start by acknowledging her and giving her the love, acceptance, and protection she always deserved. When I pulled off the highway to get gas some twenty miles later, my face was soaked with tears and my nose ran like a sieve.

One of the best things about this route is the full-service rest stops. Being able to get gas, coffee, and use the bathroom all in one convenient location is a gift. The west coast lacks, at least in my experience, good rest stops on interstates. There was no traffic to speak of, so I made it to the airport with time to spare. It took about thirty minutes to get my old car turned in and my new car picked up. The Hertz attendant directed me to the row of available SUVs and told me I could take my pick but recommended the charcoal gray Jeep Grand Cherokee. I'm glad she did because it proved to be a solid, reliable ride.

This was my fourth trip from the airport to Boxborough, since arriving on December 22nd. This would be the last time for the foreseeable future. Possibly the last time ever. While the route had become easy and familiar, pulling up the driveway was still hard. I glanced at the windows of Jeff's office, just to the right of the front door. It was dark and he was gone. Nothing about this place was the same.

I did my best to stay focused on why I was there. I still had to drive back to New Jersey, and preferably with as much daylight as possible. Joni seemed to understand that, so we got to work quickly. There were a lot of plants. She had already determined which ones she wanted to keep, so I gathered up and took the ones that made sense. Some plants were just too big or maybe wouldn't travel well.

The back of the SUV filled up quickly. I felt like I had ransacked the joint and had to make sure that it wasn't too much. She said no, she had what she wanted. I picked up a couple of other things too. Since I had the car, I might as well. One was a small guitar I had given Jeff. In my mid-thirties, I tried taking guitar lessons. I was playing drums in a band at the time and thought I should learn what my father would call "a real instrument." I bought a cute little Martin LX1. It wasn't super fancy but sounded nice. As it turns, guitar playing wasn't my jam. Since it was just collecting dust, I gave it to my dad, who I knew would put it to good use. However, it came with the caveat that when he was done with it, I wanted it back. He was done with it.

The other thing I picked up was a fiddle my grandfather had given me when we lived in Southport. It was with the intention that I would start violin lessons. That didn't happen, but this fiddle got dragged around with us ever since. I could have sworn Jeff said that he couldn't find it and thought they had likely gotten rid of it. But Joni found it without a problem and now I could take it home, too.

I don't know what I'll do with it, as it's in rough shape. I'll likely just keep it for posterity rather than having it refurbished. My grandfather had been an amazing bluegrass fiddler. He played with some big artists, like Leon Russell, Bill Monroe, and even Jerry Garcia when he was in the band "Old and in the Way." He played the Grand Ole Opry multiple times. My grandmother had their family room plastered with the Playbills. He even wrote a Christmas song which has been recorded by a few famous artists. While my relationship with my grandfather ended on a sour note, I was proud of his accomplishments, and this little fiddle can embody that.

I was glad that I had a reason to go back to my parents' - *Joni's* - house. My brother, James, had already gone to work when I left last time. Thankfully, he had the day off and was home when I came for the plants. He seemed happy to see me and said that he had felt bad for leaving without saying goodbye. Now, at least, we had that chance.

I was sure that Joni was ready to have space to herself again. But was she? Last time I left, my sister was still with her. I think they were both looking forward to that time together. But this time, she was going to be without the distraction of company. She would be home alone, a widow in the house her husband died in. I wondered how that would feel for her because it was hard to tell.

Even with the history we had, I had spent much of the last few years trying to find the good in her. My inner child still longed for a mom and dad, but it is that longing that had betrayed me more in this life than any other one thing. It makes me overlook mistreatment and settle for less than what I deserve. Even knowing this, I could not seem to stop hoping that one day she would love me, and that then I would belong. But now, things are different. Jeff was gone and I think that I had been lied to for the last time. Something had to change, but that was tomorrow's problem.

The visit was short. All of twenty minutes actually, and very business-like. Get in, get the plants, and get out. Leaving, I gave James the proper goodbye that we missed and gave Joni a hug. She asked for updates on my trip home, but I wondered if she was asking to seem nice. As I left the driveway, I took one final glance at my father's office. I hoped whatever part of him that may have remained there would find peace.

That night heading back to New Jersey, I witnessed my first sunset of this adventure. Once again, I imagined my father with me. He was sitting in the front seat, in his signature outfit, with the seat pushed back as far as it would go and halfway reclined. He had his knees bent and his loafered feet on the dash. He smoothed out his mustache and stared out the window, smiling at the beautiful picture that nature was painting for us.

"Beans, that's what I'm talking about."

He stretched out as much as he could, placed his hands, fingers entwined, atop his not-balding head and let out a deep, satisfied sigh. It left me feeling like everything was going to be alright.

Chapter Eleven

Toni and I got a late start on Wednesday the 5th. It was exceptionally cold that morning and there had been freezing rain overnight. The top local news headlines revolved around the multitude of accidents that had happened during the morning commute and the closure of several roads and freeways. We did have errands to run that day, but there was no point in hurrying. We enjoyed our coffee at a leisurely pace.

By noon, the temperatures had risen and the concerns about ice on the roads had passed. We began our day's excursions at Toni's favorite apothecary, Mayernik Kitchen in Pompton Plains. The main drag through Pompton Plains has a quaint, small town feel to it. The road is lined with shops, mostly two-story brick structures. While the buildings, looking to have been built in the mid-1900s, were on the older side, this strip of road felt lively and in renewal. That was especially so for Mayernik Kitchen.

The apothecary looked fresh, clean, and very much inviting. The exterior of the store was a crisp white with rich black accents. The windows were still decorated for the holidays, or maybe for the season of winter, with paintings of pine boughs and cones sprinkled with snow. It was well done and tasteful. Inside, a bold, dark-stained, rustic, wooden counter played anchor for the store's many, well-kept nooks and shelves of herbal goodness.

Part of today's mission was to look for containers to make transporting Jeff's plants easier. I found a beautiful, colorful woven basket. It was large and had a sturdy, leather-wrapped handle across the top. It would be perfect for the plant we nicknamed "Rapunzel." She is a  philodendron and has lots of long, luxurious vines. I felt bad spending forty dollars on a basket to safely haul one plant around, but it was something I was certain I would use again.

Since that only guaranteed safe transport for one plant, I had to get something for the rest. There were fourteen plants in total. I knew because of the cold temperatures along the way, I would be taking these plants in and out of wherever I was staying at night. I figured large, clear Rubbermaid totes would work. Clear would let light through and allow me to see if any plants were being damaged. Plastic would be sturdy enough to move without concern, and I could water the plants in place. I knew I'd put the containers to good use when I got home as well.

I also needed snacks for the road. I probably wouldn't "need" them. I didn't want to snack my way across the country, but I picked up chips, chocolate-covered pretzels, and trail mix anyway, just in case. I also grabbed a pair new yoga pants. I had either jeans or PJs, I needed something in between that was comfortable enough to wear for eight hours of driving, but presentable enough for filling up at the gas station. Put like that, I realize the bar here was pretty low. I found a pair of soft, velvety leggings that fit the bill. They would need to be washed before I left. As would the rest of my clothes.

I hadn't necessarily run out of clean things, but all my favorite clothes were dirty. We used the laundry room at Toni's apartment complex. Part of me misses using laundry mats. The ability to wash more than one load at a time seems magical to a mother who once ran a five-person household. Plus, these machines are so fast. My clothes were washed and dried before my washing machine alone would have finished.

I spent the rest of the afternoon getting organized, checking routes, and generally obsessing over what I should do and what could go wrong. Always with the question of "Have I lost my mind?" lingering in the back of my thoughts. I downloaded a couple of road trip apps, one of which would prove to be incredibly useful. I got the plants ready, too. It had been 14 days since my father's passing but it had been almost a month since he had been hospitalized the first time. It had been at least that long since these plants had any real tending and they needed some love.

I took them into Toni's bathroom and got to work. There were dead leaves that needed to be clipped off. Then they all got a good, deep watering in the tub. After about an hour of draining, I took them all out and placed them on the sill, the sink, and the floor and took a long hot shower myself. Toni said to take my time, and I knew that the plants needed the humidity, so take my time I did. When I was done, Jeff's plants all looked noticeably greener, plumper, and happier.

I had picked out the perfect containers and the plants tucked into them with ease. Rapunzel looked especially pretty in her vibrant basket. I took a couple of clippings from her and my father's peperomia for Toni. They were the only ones of the bunch that could be propagated from cuttings. Toni said she'd call them both Jeff - Jeff A and Jeff B – which is almost as creative as Dave Matthews naming his band the Dave Matthews Band, so of course, I approved.

With everything ready to go, we settled in for a chill evening. We ate take-out leftovers that we had gotten from a local Italian restaurant. For me it was manicotti, and it was even more delicious on night two. We exchanged gifts that day for Little Christmas, and this evening we made burnt offerings and toasts to La Befana. It's an Italian thing, and Toni is Italian.

Toni is the quintessential New Jersey Italian woman. She went to catholic school, she knows the proper pronunciations of all the good Italian deli meats, and she has a superstition for every occasion. Personally, I prefer to remain oblivious to superstitions. Not because I'm beyond believing in them, but because I think they only work if you know them. It's the ole ignorance is bliss defense. Now, thanks to Toni, I can't put my purse on the floor and it's a pain in the ass.

I was struggling a little with leaving the next day. I had gotten very comfortable at Toni's. It was peaceful and welcoming. It had become a sanctuary for healing. Plus, I had finally gotten Toni's cat, Ruby, to let me pet her. She hid all of day one, by the end of day two she came out of hiding, day three she stopped running away every time I moved, day four she got within six feet of me, and day five she finally let me pet her. But now it was time to go. I missed my own cats.

The next morning, I was up early, bright-eyed and bushy tailed. I had the good sense to go to bed early the night before, which always makes me feel extra adulty. I didn't want to leave Toni. I wished every day that she lived closer to me. *Maybe one day.* But there was no more putting off going home. I got into my rental Jeep and buckled up. I thought of Jeff. In my mind, I pictured him leaning forward in the seat next to me, looking out the front window, with a giant grin on my face, and rubbing his hands together. He said, "Let's roll."

Without Love
where would you be now?

Youtube.com
Doobie Brothers
"Long Train Running"

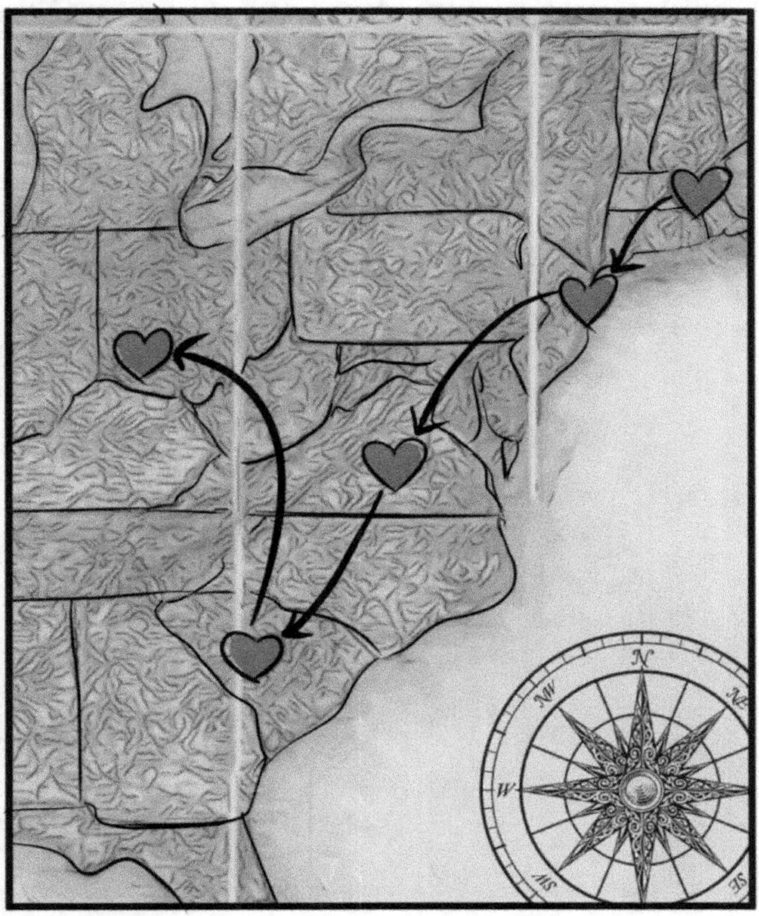

Chapter Twelve

The first leg of this trip would take me to Charlottesville, Virginia. I'd be staying with my friends, Brad and AnneMarie. I probably would have gone there even if I didn't have friends in Charlottesville. It is one of a few Dave Matthews fan meccas and, as previously mentioned, I'm a giant fan. I also think I may have met him before, but I'm not sure. It's the greatest mystery of my life.

Even though I had been hearing the Dave Matthews Band (DMB) on the radio since the mid-1990s, I hadn't given them much notice until 2002. For Christmas 2001, I was given a new car stereo by my now ex-husband, Tony. I had it installed a couple of weeks later, in early January. That day, I decided to take a drive into Seattle to see my good friend, Melody. Tony and I had moved out to the suburbs of south Snohomish County a little over six months prior and it still felt very foreign to me. I used any excuse I could to get back to the city. Melody, or "Mel", was a frequent excuse to do so.

I met Melody in 1994 at work. We became fast friends, which was odd considering she was a year older than my mother, and very much like her. While she wasn't addicted to heroin, she did have my mother's disdain for being responsible. That said, she was a gem of a friend. She knew me very well. And most importantly, she accepted me completely. She passed away in 2018, suddenly of a heart attack. I loved her dearly. I would put her in the top three of my closest friends in this life.

While heading into Seattle to see my friend Mel, I tried to find the perfect CD to christen the new player but none of the ones I had would do. I realized I had been listening to the same fifteen CDs for the better part of the last dozen years. I needed something new. I switched on the radio to 103.7, which at the time was "The Mountain." They played "adult contemporary" music, whatever that is. I told myself that if I heard a song that caught my ear, I'd go buy that album straight away. Halfway to Seattle they played "Stay" by DMB from the live album *Listener Supported*. It was good. That night, whilst running errands with Melody, I picked it up.

I put it on play as soon as we were back in the car, ran a few more errands, and then took Melody home. As she got out of the car, she turned and said, "Hey, I really like this Dave Matthews guy." By the time I drove the twenty-five miles home, I was in love. I continued adding to my DMB CD collection. So did Melody. She kept pushing me to listen to one CD in particular, Dave Matthews and Tim Reynolds *Live at Luther College*. I kept passing. It's an acoustic album, which didn't have a lot of appeal to me at the time. My big draw to DMB was the drummer, Mr. Carter Beauford. Finally, one rainy spring afternoon, she twisted my arm just right and I gave in.

Live at Luther College played in the background as we caught up and ran errands. It was good, but I wasn't writing home about it. Again, no Carter Beauford on the drums. At some point, whilst out and about, we decided it would be fun for Melody to come out to my place overnight. That way we could hang out and have cocktails and such without the worry of getting her home. We stopped by her apartment, so she could feed her cats and pack a bag. I was left alone in my car, in the rain, with Dave and Tim.

 The song that came on was Little Thing. It began with a few short, soft, somewhat off key, but beautifully sorrowful sounding guitar phrases. Then, this ghostly sounding music is accompanied by a short story of an encounter with a stranger, a small woman, who had given Dave directions. When he began describing the way she spoke to him, the way she gave him directions, I was immediately transported back in time.

In July of 1994, I was working as a caterer and barista for a company that is now called Dan's Belltown Grocery in Seattle. One sunny afternoon, I think it was a Friday, I was outside taking a smoke break (don't judge, everyone smoked in 1994). I noticed a young man get off the bus. Something about him caught my eye and I watched as he walked down the street, headed south and away from me. Then he stopped, stood still for a long moment, turned around, and started walking north, back towards me. He squinted his eyes, and I realized he was trying to see something behind me more clearly, perhaps the street sign. He stopped, paused, turned, and walked away from me again, only to turn back toward me a few paces later. Then, I watched him return to the bus stop. It looked like he was trying to make sense of the downtown map posted there. He was lost. Now all of that made sense.

I walked up to him and said, "Hey, you look lost."

He turned around, startled, and looked at me as though I might be trying to mug him. He said, "Uhhh, yeahhh.".

I said, "Well, where are you going?"

He stuttered, "The… ahh… Pike Place Market. I'm… ah… meeting friends for coffee."

I laughed and said something like, "You must not be from around here." I wasn't laughing at him for being lost. I thought he looked like he was from here, so it threw me off that he was a tourist. Anyway, I gave him directions. "Go down there until you get to this street or that street (I can never remember which comes first, Pike or Pine), then go that way (west) for a couple/few blocks, and either street you take will end with a big ass neon sign that says you're there, and then you're there."

We talked for a couple of minutes.

He asked, somewhat sheepishly, "Do you know who I am?"

I looked at him puzzled and said, "Umm, no. Should I?" *Why would he think I would know him?* My mind's eye I took a screenshot of his face and scanned my memory bank. *Did I know this guy?*

He was all like, "Oh. Um. No. Nope. Ah. I just… thought… ya know…"

While that seemed weird, I dropped it and moved on. "Since you're clearly not from here, where are you from?"

At first, he said, "Well, that's complicated."

So, I said, "How about… where do you live now?"

I cannot remember what he said, but I do remember that he lived in a state I had driven through when I moved from Delaware to LA. I was able to make small talk about it – pretty place, nice people, etc. It was somewhere on the Atlantic Coast. I want to say it was Virginia, but there is too much room for wishful thinking there.

I am reasonably sure it was 1994, but I had forgotten about this encounter until that night in the rain, in my car, waiting for Melody to pack a bag. It was 2002. At that point, it was a foggy memory at best. I do seem to remember talking about the fact that I had been in Seattle for a year, and he asked about what I thought of it. I think it was summertime because it was a warm and sunny day. I remember he said something like, "I thought it always rained in Seattle." I said that it didn't really. I mean, it does rain a fair bit, but truthfully it looks like it is going to rain more often than it actually does.

From what I remember, the young man looked a lot like Dave Matthews, but it was so long ago. He had short dark hair, was clean(ish) shaven, and had distinctive eyebrows. And he was tall. I think I may have even said something like, "Damn, you're tall." *Good god, I hope not. I mean really, that's not smooth at all.*

I know that it is a one in seven billion chance that this young man was Dave Matthews, making it highly unlikely, but I cannot shake wanting to know. This has become one of those mysteries in life that I will be pissed if I die and never solve. And while I am not *actually* obsessed, the potential of running into Dave at the gas station in Charlottesville was enough to get me there. I mean, a girl can dream, right?

The sign reads, "Welcome to Virginia. Virginia is for Lovers." I remember thinking as a kid that this slogan was a little too risqué. I've since looked it up and the original campaign was "Virginia is for History Lovers." It then branched out to mountain lovers, beach lovers, sports lovers, and so on. It eventually became shorten to just "for lovers."

To honor having reached my fifth and final state of the day, I asked Siri to play DMB's "Virginia in the Rain." The lyrics of the song refer to being naked in the rain.

I laughed to myself thinking about how much tequila it would take for me to be naked in the rain. I had put on more than my fair share of weight during this pandemic. But even before that, I've had a long struggle with my weight. Especially since I started having kids in my late twenties.

I had taken up running when I was thirty-one to try to maintain a healthy size. After my mother died in 2004, a woman I knew happened to be organizing a training group to run the Honolulu Marathon as a fundraiser for the AIDS Foundation. Me, having zero athletic background, signed up, moved by the idea of helping people like my mom. To say it was more than I had bargained for is an understatement, but I completed that marathon, and it was miraculous. It was the spark that started a more than decade's long love affair with running.

Running was the source of many things for me, especially the long-distance runs. It taught me how to make, set, and achieve goals. Running taught me that I had more endurance and wherewithal than I had ever known. Through a mom's group I helped organize, I found a handful of running buddies that would become lifelong friends. So many positive things came from being a runner, but it didn't make me skinny. Even though I ran a lot. Nine marathons, close to three dozen half marathons, 5ks, 10k, 15ks, extreme relay races… I ran a lot and, for the life of me, I could not get my weight down. Of course, now that I've put on all this Covid weight, I would pay to be the size I was back in my marathon days. *Ain't that the way.*

Being overweight has been a real source of shame for me, and in many ways that went back to Jeff. Jeff was a fit man, who valued being skinny. He was known for his disdain of obesity. Once I came home from a summer with my grandmother. As it happens, it was the same summer I had started my period. Between hormones and too much sugar in my diet, I had gained weight. The first thing my father said when he saw me at the airport was, "Wow. Ate a few too many cookies this summer, did ya?" Yes, I did. Chocolate chip Entenmann's, and it was totally worth it. But his attitude was that it was something to fix and from that point on, I only felt truly comfortable around my father if I was skinny.

Now I understand that being a healthy weight is important, but I have spent so much time and energy focused on losing weight and dieting that I'm simply tired of caring about it. I'm burnt out. I hate admitting it but, in some ways, I am relieved that I'll never again feel the stress of being judged by my father for being his fat daughter. Even with that stress removed, it would still take a long time, and a lot of therapy to get me naked in the rain.

The roads in Charlottesville were wet, but not with rain. It had snowed the day before, and while the roads were clear, AnneMarie had to shovel a spot on the front curb so I could have a place to park. It was around 6:30 p.m., it was cold as hell, and there was more snow on the way. Brad and AnneMarie helped me haul my stuff in, which would include one giant suitcase, one duffle bag, two plastic bins, and one bright woven basket overflowing with vines.

Then, AnneMarie and I bundled up, grabbed a couple of drinks, and found a cozy spot on her covered porch to watch the wintery scene and catch up.

AnneMarie is a fantastic conversationalist. She has this way of drawing people out of themselves. Not in a prodding or intrusive way. I think she can see who people are, and see what they love, and she's able to point it out beautifully in conversation. It really is lovely, as is she. AnneMarie couldn't look bad if she tried. I don't think she's aged either. She is a fashion genius, with a look that leans toward what I would call retro 1960s (non-hippy variety). She has a whole room of her home dedicated to her fashion collection and it is a collection to behold. There isn't an occasion AnneMarie couldn't dress for.

She had been dealing with parent-related pain as well. Her father had passed away in August of 2021, three months before Jeff, and the loss was still very fresh. On top of this mourning, her mother was having significant health issues and AnneMarie was getting ready to spend an undetermined amount of time in St. Louis helping care for her. It was clearly stressful.

It felt relieving to be with someone who was also mourning. Even though everyone I was in communication with understood what I was going through, I felt like I had to limit how much I talked about it. Death is not exactly the most uplifting topic, and I didn't want to be a drag. But, with AnneMarie I could say it all. I felt free and understood.

I can't remember exactly when I met Brad and AnneMarie, but I can tell you when I met their sister-in-law, Katrina. In 2008, when my daughter was just one year old and I was pregnant with my youngest, I started a mom's group. I needed to socialize and so did my kids. I tried preexisting mom's groups in my area, but they weren't fun. Meeting once or twice a month seemed lame. It was going to take forever to get to know people like that. Plus, I needed regular activities. So, I started my own group through Meetup.com.

We were "The Real Moms of Snohomish County" and that group was a blast. We had daily play dates, running groups, moms' nights out, and more. Many friendships were formed with the ladies in this group, and one of them was my friendship with Katrina.

Katrina likes to tell the story of our meeting in a way that makes me feel good. She says she remembers the first mom's group outing we did was a walk at a nearby trail. The idea was to have the kids in strollers and try to get some exercise, but on this day, Katrina's daughter was not having it, and she was letting us all know. I was fairly unphased with what was happening. Kids get upset and have fits; it's what they do. I just kept walking with her, talking about whatever we could, and taking it all in stride. She later told me how good it felt to not have the experience of being judged or disapproved of. I'm glad that was how I occurred to her.

I wouldn't say we were fast friends. As a matter of fact, we ran into some snags getting to know each other. However, once we got past them, we were left with a deep and loving friendship that I am so grateful for. She had sent a care package to me at my - *Joni's* - house after my father passed. It included all the ingredients for my favorite cup of coffee with comfort snacks. She said it broke her heart to think that I was going through this loss and might not be able to drink coffee the way I like it. She has a heart of gold. Find yourself friends like Katrina.

Brad and AnneMarie are Katrina's husband, Phil's, brother and sister-in-law. They have been coming to visit their family in my neck of the woods annually for as long as I've known Katrina. I make a point of seeing them every time I can, but often those visits are far too short. This trip to Charlottesville gave me the opportunity to spend more one-on-one, quality time with Brad and AnneMarie. It would be a gift to get to know them both better.

I got to sleep late the next day. When I woke, I could tell it was well into morning by the angle of the light though the window. I'll admit to being disoriented. This was the third place I had slept in under three weeks and it took a moment to place myself. The room I stayed in was Brad's office. It did double duty as guest room. The bed was soft and comfortable. Across from me was Brad's desk; neat, tidy, and covered with various nerdy, fan guy things such as a Star Wars AT-AT Walker model and some Boba Fett art . The walls were decorated with more than a dozen ornate skate decks, some painted by Brad himself. They were good, and I was impressed. I had not pegged Brad as an artist, what as he is a scientist by trade. I like when adults have hobbies and are unashamed fans, it doesn't matter what of. It reminds me that we all have playful children inside of us.

It was nice to not feel compelled to get out of bed. I had nowhere to go and nothing to do. Plus, Brad and AnneMarie had to work, so there was no hurry. While it felt relaxing, it simultaneously felt unnerving. It was strange for me to consider in the midst of this nebulous life I was living, other people's regular lives moved on. It added to my sense of feeling set adrift and lost.

That afternoon, AnneMarie and I went to the Downtown Mall. It is a roughly four-block section of road, closed to traffic, lined with unique shops and restaurants. We ate lunch at Otto Turkish Street Food. I had doner kebab for the first time. It was quite good.

The real reason for our mall excursion was to see Millers. It's the bar Dave Matthews worked in when the band formed. It wasn't due to be open until 5 p.m., and unfortunately, we did not have the time to wait. AnneMarie had plans that couldn't be changed and we needed to get back to her house so she could get ready. She promised to take me to Miller's after her commitment, which would likely be around 9 p.m.

It was just me and Brad for dinner. We ordered an Indian takeout. Chicken tikka masala had become my most recent comfort food favorite. I could not eat enough of it. Brad and I binge watched the sci-fi show *The Expanse* on Amazon Prime and enjoyed some good eats. When 8:30 p.m. rolled around, AnneMarie messaged to see if I was ready for Miller's. I had to laugh. It was official. I was too old to go out to a bar in a college town at 9 p.m. Not even my Dave Matthews obsession could get me out the door. *Good lord, when did I become so boring?*

In planning for the next day's drive, I ran my proposed route by Brad. He is a car enthusiast. He enjoys rebuilding cars and put his focus on BMWs from the 1970s. He often goes road tripping and knows a bit about long-distance travel. He agreed that, barring any new weather patterns, the interstates west should remain clear. I checked the upcoming weather forecasts, and from what I could see, no new precipitation was due on the northern route. I also consulted the app *DriveWeather* which will forecast the weather specific to the route you choose. According to it, everything looked good to go.

I liked Charlottesville, and one day was not enough. I made a mental note to come back here one day in the springtime. I bet it's gorgeous. But now I had to get moving. Arguably, dipping down south into Virginia hadn't gotten me that much closer to home. Dipping further down into South Carolina wasn't making any homeward progress either. However, if I sat down and ran the numbers, making these detours made more financial sense than planning separate trips later. *Look at me justifying.*

I was able to enjoy breakfast with Brad and AnneMarie before hitting the road. Next stop, Roebuck, South Carolina and my good friend, Jennifer Fox (aka Foxy or the Fox). Foxy had just moved to South Carolina in August of 2021, and I was happy for the opportunity to visit her and her new home.

I met Foxy in the spring of 2003. We were both attending the Brenneke School of Massage in Seattle. At the time, there were three massage schools in the area to choose from. One was a budget school with a substandard reputation. The other two both had reputations as being academically good schools and, of those two, Brenneke was the most holistic. The elective courses included various energetic practices, like reiki and craniosacral therapy. It was, as they say, very woo-woo. I liked it.

It was an odd time in my life. I had been a mother for two and a half years and was struggling with one doozy of an identity crisis. So much of my own childhood trauma came to the surface because of having a child of my own. I clearly remember the day, the exact moment, that the dam broke. The flood of repressed pain it had been holding back for most of my twenty-nine years of life came and took me down.

William was about eighteen months old at the time. It was a sunny afternoon in late spring. He had just gotten up from a nap and was sitting on the floor with his blanket and sippy cup, playing with a toy. I was on the couch watching him. The sun shining through the window lit up all the fussy blonde hairs that stuck out in all directions on William's sweet little head. I remember feeling so in love with this little boy, and at the same time so sad and so guilty. I was so tired. I was so lost. I was not the mother that this baby deserved, and did not know how to be.

As I watched him play, I remember thinking, "Where was I when I was William's age?" The answer to that question broke the levee. Flashes of brief scenes, dark and scary scenes, rolled through my mind. Along with them came intense sensations of loneliness, fear, rejection, desperation, and panic. I felt like I was drowning in a sea of trauma. Once I had pulled that cap off, there was no putting those images and feelings back in. While I would like to report that this release made my life better, it absolutely made it worse. Now the genie was out of the bottle, and I had no control over how it made me react and respond to life.

This mess I had unearthed was just one layer of the hot mess that I was. Leaving the workforce had taken away my greatest source external validation. I had no support from family and no suburban friends. I was a mess emotionally and mentally. My sense of self-loathing was at an all-time high. While I wouldn't realize this when enrolling in massage school, it ended up being instrumental in putting me on the road to healing. I would say it changed the trajectory of my life, and I'm thankful for that. I am also grateful that it brough me The Fox.

Foxy and I became good friends over the course of that year. As we are both astrologers, we would credit our shared compatible aspects in Pisces and Capricorn. I think what drew me most to Foxy was that she was straightforward and wholly uninterested in dramatic bullshit. After graduation, we opened up a small massage practice together, Solstice Healing Arts. The business was short-lived. Within the first year of practice, Foxy was diagnosed with ovarian cancer and needed to focus on her health. At the same time, my first marriage had begun to disintegrate, and I had to redirect my focus as well.

In 2007, Foxy moved back to her home state of Indiana. We kept in touch here and there for several years until our lives came back together around 2018. She was the one that inspired me to deepen my understanding of astrology. I had always understood the astrological archetypes but seeing her read a chart changed my world. Astrology was a language I had to learn. The charts told stories, and they did not lie. Foxy told me a long time ago, because of the placement of my lunar nodes on the Cancer/Capricorn axis, that my parents would be the source of both my undoing and rebirth. I am here in this life to resolve my karma with them, and with Joni, so that I can become myself. No lies detected.

The day I drove to Roebuck was sunny and dry. So far, I'd been lucky with the weather. I rolled into Charlottesville between two snowstorms, but while I was there the roads were clear and safe. The day before I left New Jersey they had had issues with iced over roadways, and shortly after I left, they had snow. All I could do was hope that this luck continued. I kept telling myself that my father was with me. We were on a mission that was sacred and there was no way harm would come to me. I was protected. True or not, the thought helped care for my nerves. There is no room for anxiety when you are on a mission. My father would be proud, yet I am left to wonder if my "go get 'em" attitude isn't really a survival mechanism and a product of trauma. Perhaps not something to be proud of, but it's gotten me through hell more than once.

I spent much of the trip to Foxy's on U.S. Route 29. The highway is two lanes in each direction, separated by a wide forested median. The road meandered through rolling hills and countryside that was surprisingly beautiful. The communities I passed through were small and spaced out. From the road I could see old but well-kept homes perched on hills above farmlands. Many of the gas stations along the way played double duty as mechanic shops, farming implement depots, or feed stores. There were lots and lots of churches. In my romanticized version of this world, these were kind people who were devoted to God and community, and life here was good.

For a moment, I felt envious. There was something simple about this scene before me. Not stupid simple, but simple sweet. Simple being slower and maybe more meaningful. For my whole life, the furthest I had lived from a major city was when I lived in Dover, Delaware. And it's not very far from several major cities. But even there, life seemed less complicated and more enjoyable.

I arrived at Foxy's sometime around 5:30 p.m. She was already cooking dinner, which I was thankful for. I hadn't had a real meal since breakfast and tried to avoid snacking. She made her signature "buffalo pie". It was like shepherd's pie, but with buffalo meat, green beans, and corn rather than ground beef, carrots, and onions. It was damn good. The rest of the evening we spent chatting, in between Foxy's preparation for the next day's astrology class.

I slept fabulously that night. Foxy, who has superb taste and is a skilled host, had the most comfortable and chic guest room in which I have ever stayed. Mid-morning the next day Foxy, her husband, Joel, and I had breakfast at their favorite crepe restaurant, Mon Ami. It was adorable. I got a smoked salmon crepe with cream cheese and green onions. It was incredible. The salmon, which was the perfect level of smokey, was also fresh, and not too fishy. The cream cheese was whipped to perfection, light and airy, and the green onions were perfectly ripe and in peak flavor. The crepe was thin and delicate with a slight crispness around the edges. Ten out of ten, would recommend; Chef's kiss.

That afternoon, I was able to attend Foxy's astrology class live rather than through Zoom as usual. She taught about the lunar nodes' shift into Taurus and Scorpio that would happen on January 18, 2022. It would mark the beginning of an eighteen-month period when deep-seeded patterns and secrets are revealed, and the collective will have its values tested. After that, we cozied up in her family room with her sweet pups, Thoth and Jimmy Chew. We watched the *Harry Potter Twenty-Year Reunion Special* and binged the entire first season of *Discovery of Witches*. We took breaks to snack and chat. If there was a better way to spend a Sunday, I could not think of it.

That night I checked the weather. The northern route home looked pretty clear. I decided, in the spirit of making this trip quicker, I would start heading that way now. This would put my sister's home in Indiana in the direct line of travel. I had messaged her previously and mentioned that there was a possibility I may head her way. Now that I was sure, I sent her a message asking her if I could spend the night. She said that would be fine and that she was excited. I wondered if her excitement was genuine, given how stressful things had been in Boxborough.

I got up reasonably early on Monday, January 10th. I wanted to make sure I had time to shower before I left, less because I was dirty and more because the plants needed that dose of humidity before getting back on the road. I wasn't sure if I'd have time to steam the plants at my sister's. I wasn't planning to be there for very long. As awkward as things were with Jennifer, I did not know how comfortable either of us would be with this visit. I didn't want to wear out my welcome just to steam the plants.

Chapter Thirteen

The trip to Jennifer's was the longest leg I had driven thus far, at roughly five hundred and thirty miles. I figured in nine hours of driving, at least. I chose to go north from Roebuck to Lafayette, KY, then west to Evansville, Indiana. The route took me through the Great Smoky Mountains National Park in Appalachia. Being one of the oldest mountain ranges in the world, the peaks and forests looked weathered, soft, and peaceful in comparison to the jagged rockiness of the Cascades out where I lived. The upward pass climb was scenic, leisurely, and uneventful. Unfortunately, I had grossly underestimated the backside of that pass.

Driving down mountain passes gives me anxiety. I knew that going into this drive, but these mountains are half the elevation of the mountain passes I'm used to driving through. *How bad could they be?* The sudden drop in grade, as well as the quickness and curviness of the road surprised and unnerved me. Even the camber of the road worked against me, as it seemed to be pulling me into the median divider. There also was an inordinate number of semi-trucks on the road. We have very few eighteen-wheeled vehicles on the interstate in western Washington, so it was something I wasn't accustomed to. I did not like it.

I could feel my stomach tighten and my knuckles whiten from the tension. I wished I could slow way the hell down and not make myself a hazard, but that wasn't an option. I'm a big chicken when it comes to downhill anything; skiing, bicycling, and driving (not running though; I'd run like the devil out of church down a hill). I realized that I had no idea how long this would go on for and that did nothing to ease my stress.

"Beans, ya gotta relax." His voice broke the stressful silence and startled me. I saw Jeff in my mind, sitting in the passenger's seat looking totally at ease. He said it again, "You gotta relax. Downhills. You have to relax into them."

"Ugh, now is not the time for an overactive imagination, Korva," I said out loud. Then I gave in, thinking of how I would respond if my dad really was there with me and trying to help.

"I'll try," I said through clenched teeth.

I took a few deep, loud, cleansing breaths. I stayed focused on keeping my abdomen soft and breathing for the next ninety minutes. It did help. When the road flattened out for good, I was able to relax enough to realize I was starving. It had now been a good five hours since I had last eaten and I'm sure that mountain pass burned more than a few calories. I pulled off to get food. Cracker Barrel biscuits and gravy. For the record, it did not live up to the hype, but the little country store attached to the restaurant had some cute things.

Once I was back onto the road… the nice, flat, boring road… I realized that the stress of the mountain pass had done me a favor. It had distracted me from the low-grade dread I was feeling about seeing my sister. There was something wrong with our relationship. I could feel it, but I could not put my finger on it. It ate at me but what could I do? There was nothing tangible to address. It was just my gut, which is the world's easiest thing to gaslight. I would have to ride this out and see how it went.

The sunset driving through Indiana was awe inspiring. The horizon line was low and highlighted with a bright, radiant band of red that faded upward into a gem like aqua, and finally into a deep navy blue.

It reminded me of the coloration of a Pendleton blanket. I imagined Jeff next to me. He always had an appreciation for good, ambient scenery… and Pendleton blankets. I wondered what Jeff's spirit would think about going back to Indiana.

My family moved to Indiana in 2002. I had been living in Washington State since 1993, and they had been living in Orange County, California since 1992. As far as I knew, things were good from them in California; he had a good job, my stepmother was a partial owner in a small business that she loved, my sister and brother were getting a good education. The only thing I could gather is that their money would go further in Indiana, and the taxes were better. I don't know.

My father took another job working in telecommunications, specifically cable television. Cable TV had been the bread and butter for as long as I could remember. It was a career that had its perks. We always had the newest and coolest channels. This also meant I watched too many movies at too young an age; "A Clockwork Orange" may have been a bit much for a nine-year-old. Over the years we enjoyed tons of "cable loot" which was what we called the promotional goods that Jeff got to bring home. I even had an original 1980s black satin MTV logo jacket.

About two years after moving to Indiana, he lost his job. Downside of working in cable TV? There tends to be only one or two companies in any given area. Which means there were few to no executive level jobs available at any given time. He couldn't find work and his stretch of unemployment went on for too long. Jeff's self-worth was inextricably attached to his job and income. The longer he went without lucrative work, the deeper he fell into depression. His marriage and relationships of all sorts suffered. Being an expert in self-destruction, I saw him heading down a dark path of alcoholism and loneliness. So, I called him out on some things I thought would contribute to further decline. Was I being completely judgmental and self-righteous? Yes, absolutely. Did I handle the situation well? Nope. And that's ok. I know my intentions were good. I wanted my father to be happy and healthy, and that's not where he was headed. Regardless, calling him out on his destructive behavior got me shunned from our family.

From the fall of 2008 to Christmas of 2012, my father and I didn't speak. I served as an example of what happens to people who call my father out on anything. My sister and stepmother were both aware of what was happening. They knew he was drinking too much, way too much, and falling into a deep, dark depression. Rather than stand up for his health and wellbeing, or for me, they stayed silent. During that time, I felt so ashamed of myself for having made a mess of things, again, and for making my father withhold his love and alienate me. But in hindsight, I'm beginning to see that the real problem was them all along, him included. My intention was health, theirs was avoidance. Their cowardice was very costly.

Sometime in 2012, Joni, Jeff, and James moved to Boston, while Jennifer chose to stay in Indiana. A new job opportunity had finally presented itself and things were looking up for Jeff. He was back in a familiar position with the potential to provide for a very comfortable retirement. He was back in New England, a place I knew he was fond of, and his best friend, Greg, was less than an hour's drive away. Unfortunately, something this move could not fix was his alcoholism. Even in the face of this new job, new home, and new hope, he continued to drink more and more. It broke my heart.

I got to my sister's house minutes before dinner time. She had fixed a taco salad. After dinner, I got to spend time with my niece and nephew. We played a G-rated version of *Cards Against Humanity*. It was fun. My niece is a good kid. She reminded me of her mother at that age.

She's smart, well-spoken, and well behaved. She is also seemingly perceptive and intuitive. My nephew is a firecracker. He's fun, bright, and energetic. I enjoyed engaging with them and was sorry when bedtime came around.

It was a school/work night, so an early bedtime was on the agenda for everyone. It was for the best. Once the distraction of playing with the kids was gone, we were left with the uneasy awkwardness I had dreaded. Every conversation I tried to start went nowhere. She was especially disinterested in talking about her mom and anything related to her mom. I asked how Joni was doing and the answer I got was "Fine." That was it. Usually, Jennifer would have something to share from the perspective of a mental health professional as to how her mom was managing her grief and/or suppressing her emotions. Nope. All I got was "She's fine."

It felt like no matter how many words were being shared, there were a hundred that were being held back. It created more tension than I had the bandwidth for. I was not used to this kind of dynamic with Jennifer. Normally our relationship was easy. Something had changed and I felt powerless over it. I wondered how long it would go on and what I would take to put an end to it.

The next morning, my sister and her family were up and gone before I was out of bed. My alarm went off at 7:30 and I was on the road within thirty minutes. I did not feel comfortable in her house alone. I skipped the shower and opted to get food along the way. My next stop, Salina, Kansas, was a long six hundred and fourteen miles away and I needed to get going. I booked a room at the Hilton Garden Inn. They would be my hotel chain of choice for the remainder of this trip. No more fun visits to look forward to. From here on out, this drive was all business.

Travelin' So Long

Chapter Fourteen

My adventure had taken on a whole new feel. Not knowing how far away the next friendly face would be unnerved me. There were still 1,850 miles to home and there was nothing to anchor me between here and there. There were so many things that could go wrong, and I was alone. But what was I going to do? I had an SUV full of plants and failure was not an option. *"Failure was not an option." What a very Jeff thing to think.*

I took Interstate-64 through Indiana to meet up with I-70 in St. Louis. It was an uneventful stretch of road. The pace was leisurely, the roads were clear, and I was grateful. The landscape was… flat and brown. I'm sure in the summer months, much of what I saw would have been thick with produce crops, but now there were only bare and open fields. It was kind of boring, and it made me antsy.

I had downloaded a book that I tried to listen to on and off, but I couldn't focus on it. I couldn't listen to music without crying so I ended up in silence. I couldn't focus enough to process my own thoughts, or the noise from the world around me, or the landscape in front of me. I felt maxed out. I wasn't even halfway home, and I already wanted to quit. I was so sick of this. All of it. The stress, my feelings, the damn color of the freeway, moving at 70 mph. Whatever part of me thought this was a good idea, had vanished. It reminded me of my experience with running marathons.

The process was always the same. Get super excited and sign up for a race. That excitement would get me through the first half of training, which would usually last four to six months in total. Then halfway through training, I would plateau and want to give up. Once I finally broke through the rut, I would be excited again and couldn't wait until race day. Race day would be more of the same, working off the energy of excitement for the first thirteen miles and then spending the next thirteen talking myself out of quitting, just to feel the relief and pride of the last one thousand feet. I had hit that halfway slump. I just didn't want to do this anymore. *What had I been thinking?*

The Hilton Garden Inn at Salina was a welcome sight that night. I wanted a cocktail and a place to sit that wasn't going 70 mph. The luggage carts were smaller than the ones I was used to, so I needed to take two trips to get all the stuff up to my room. It was unseasonally warm (I refuse to use the word unseasonally, it's weather not steak), so I contemplated leaving the plants in the car overnight. Thankfully, I thought better of that, as it dipped well below freezing that night.

My first trip through the lobby, after collecting my room key, was with a cart full of greenery. I got a funny look or two and a couple of comments, but no questions. It was a good thing, too, because I couldn't share the reason for these plants without crying and I wasn't in the mood.

I had booked a king bed deluxe. It was only twenty dollars more expensive than the regular king room, so why not? I was a big fan of the bathroom. It was spacious and fully tiled. The shower was large, and its glass doors were clean and rolled smoothly. All steamed up and full of plants, it was like a tropical vacation. I took a longer-than-usual shower, both for myself and the plants.

After that, I put on *Antman and the Wasp*, which I've seen a million times, and allowed the familiarity of it to lull me into a surprisingly restful night's sleep. When the alarm went off the next morning, I did not have the same sense of regret I felt the previous day about choosing this journey. Instead, I awoke feeling rested and hopeful.

I got out of bed around 7 a.m. and pulled back the shades to reveal sunny, blue skies, and a thick layer of frost covering everything as far as I could see. It did not make me want to hurry up and go. I figured since I had time, I'd make myself a cup of mediocre hotel coffee and get back in bed to do some social media scrolling. My friend Toni sent me a TikTok video to watch. I can't remember the content, but the song playing in the background was Dan Fogelberg's "Leader of the Band." In the lyrics, he references his father's eyes growing old.

I instantly remembered my father's eyes as he lay dying in that hospital bed in his dimly lit office. They were tired. They broke my heart. I miss them so much. I exploded into tears, sobbing like he had died again at that moment. *Shit.* I couldn't stay in bed scrolling any longer. I had to get up and get moving or I was going to be stuck there crying for hours and risk driving in the dark. Instead, I got packed up and was out the door around 8 a.m. That would prove to be a huge blessing.

As I stood in line waiting to place my breakfast order at a local coffee shop, trying to keep "Leader of the Band" out of my head, I decided that this day would be all about the music. I would listen to all the songs that made me cry. As many as I could think of until I was all cried out.

Always at the top of the list is Van Morrison. In Jeff's world, Van Morrison was all the things. Had a problem? Van lyrics. Need a metaphor? Van lyrics. Need a reason for living? Van lyrics. Meaning of life? Well, you know. Some songs have more significance.

"Caravan." During the days Jeff and I would hang out at Greg's house on the weekends, way back in '78, Jeff and I would duet this song. My father wasn't good with kids. He didn't play games or go to theme parks or any of that kid stuff. But he loved to sing, and so do I. Singing

Caravan together was the place where our interests could meet, and we could interact playfully.

 "Saint Dominic's Preview." The first line of the song refers to cleaning windows with shammies, and every time I hear it, my inner child cringes. I was an industrious kid. I liked making money. My father was good at creating ways for me to earn it, and one of them was washing his car. He was a very particular man, especially when it came to washing his 1979 BMW 325i in Topaz Brown. Shammies only. He'd hover over me pointing out every spot I missed. I would shammy that car until not a speck of dirt or droplet of water remained. It was instrumental in the development of my work ethic, even if I hated it at the time. To this day, I can detail the heck out of a car.

I think "Saint Dominic's Preview" feels like a hopeful song. I listened to it many times during my move from Los Angeles to Seattle, which was another long and transformational drive. "Saint Dominic's Preview" conjures a vision of opening large, heavy wooden doors, like the ones depicted on the album cover, to expose a view of the rising sun and a bright new day.

I couldn't pick one song off the album *Veedon Fleece*, even if I wanted to. The album is an entire work, which broken into pieces doesn't necessarily have equal parts. I love it as a whole. I was one year old when *Veedon Fleece* came out, so it's been a part of my soundtrack for as long as I could remember. The image that most comes to mind when I listen to it is Jeff, kicked back on the couch, gazing at a fire he had spent all night tending, smoothing his mustache, and lost in thought a million miles away. I spent so much of my life wondering where he would go in those moments.

Joni's Mitchell's *River* always brings on the waterworks. These were lyrics that I felt deep in my soul. I had spent more than my fair share of Christmases feeling like I wished I could skate away on a river. As a kid, I had a love/hate relationship with Christmas. I  loved it because it was one of the only days of the year when I was almost guaranteed that my stepmother would not be a bitch to me. Ironically, it was the same reason I hated it. One day a year of false hope can break a heart for life. Now, being that my father died so close to Christmas, this song would take on even greater sadness for me.

Court and Spark – the whole album. It's less than thirty-seven minutes in total and I just couldn't choose one song. This album reminds me of the brief time I spent in Delaware and the amazing bedroom I had. The house in Delaware was built in 1930. It was big and beautiful. My room was on the third floor. It had what I called "Amityville windows", two quarter-circular windows that open out on a vertical hinge. Outside my room was a huge, old magnolia tree. It was magical and peaceful. For me, it was the healing sanctuary where I finally saw a glimpse of my worth.

 I spent hours up in the room listening to and singing along with Joni Mitchell. One song in particular always caused a lump in my throat, "Trouble Child." For the first time in my life, I finally knew that the things that they said about me were not true. Like Joni says, they may talk like they know me, but they do not.

Steely Dan's *Gaucho*, another short album that I had to listen to all of. I think Jeff's love of Van Morrison and Joni Mitchell came from my father's more bohemian self, his inner hippy. Steely Dan was sleeker, more modern. I think it spoke to the part of Jeff that loved the perks of affluence, good food and liquor, expensive cigars, and tailored suits.

Aja is another fabulous Steely Dan Album. There is not one bad song on it, but "Black Cow" may be my favorite. My attachment to it and it's meaning to me is one hundred percent made up in my head. It is complete fiction. But it makes me think of my father's relationship with my mother. From what I can gather, it is a song written from the perspective of a person experiencing the impact of someone else's addiction and finally giving up.

From all accounts, my father truly loved my mother. Both of his sisters declared her the clear love of his life. He "adored her." I used to think that people would say that to make me feel better, but the story never changed even as I aged. He had to watch my mother as she fell further and further into her addiction, and there was nothing he could do. Or maybe there was, and he couldn't do it, or chose not to. We never talked about it, but I always wondered how he really felt. Did he have regrets? Did it make him sad?

Little Feat's "Time Loves a Hero" will forever make me think of Jeff. My favorite version is from the *Waiting for Columbus* live album because of that intro. Drums only *ga-dugga dugga daka, ga-dugga dugga dakadak, ga-dugga dugga daka, ga-dugga dugga dak dak dak.* It hits hard.

Arguably, this is one messed-up song. It's about a dude who decides one day to leave his wife and family to become a beach bum in Puerto Rico. Jeff loved this song, and it made me sad. I think Jeff liked this song because he felt burdened by his own family and could relate to this guy wanting bailing out. The guy in the song was free, and Jeff wanted that too. I just wish he had realized that he was trapped by something besides his family and that we could have been the source of something very different for him. But even though I acknowledge it's one messed-up song, I still like "Time Loves a Hero."

My second favorite song off *Waiting for Columbus* is "Spanish Moon" but the whole album fantastic. It reminds me of cleaning house when I was a kid. My dad liked a clean house, and he was good at making that happen. On Saturdays, he'd open the

windows, crank the tunes, and get to work either cleaning the house or taking care of the yard. Little Feat was often a headliner. So was Bob Marley, with *Exodus* making the playlist most often. It made the whole thing fun.

Neil Young's "Old Man." I've been crying over this song for too long to remember. As an adult, when things got difficult between us, I would wonder if the source of my problems with Jeff was how alike we were. It's not uncommon to be challenged by people that we see ourselves in. These reflections can spotlight things we don't like about ourselves, things that we regret, or things we're afraid of. But, if we did have similarities, they were hard to see. And now, I'll never know what really got in our way. Maybe one day I'll shake the need to know. In the meantime, I'll keep digging the music that keeps Jeff on my mind and in my heart.

The drive from Salina to the Colorado border was seamless and perfect for this emotional, musical memory lane. The weather was clear and in the mid-fifties, warmer than normal. The rest stops (bathrooms only) were spaced perfectly. As soon as I started to think that I needed to go, a rest stop magically appeared.

The road through Kansas seemed flat, but the way the sky started to look gave me the impression I was gaining altitude. I crossed the state line into Colorado and at the first obvious town, Burlington, asked Siri for the elevation. He replied in his Irish accent, "Burlington, Colorado is 4,170 above sea level." Then I asked for the elevation of Salina, Kansas. It was 1,227 feet. How had that happened? The elevation kept climbing, one foot at a time, all while keeping the illusion of being flat.

Traffic moved without issue through the Denver area as I connected to Interstate 25 North, and I was grateful for it. The day seemed to be going off without a hitch. Right around Fort Collins, my GPS changed the preset route. Instead of staying on the main freeway, it directed me toward U.S. Route 287. I didn't know what triggered the change. It was faster, but not by much. And I assumed that weather wouldn't be an issue regardless of which route I took, so I went with it.

The first stretch of road was flat and straight. It led through large acre properties and beautiful homesteads. Several miles in, the road took a hard turn to the north and became curvier and hillier, and the land more rugged in appearance. A few more miles in, and the small, rural town I had just been in seemed a whole world away. The land, stricken by strange, peach colored light, was unlike anything I had ever seen. It looked extraterrestrial, like a Martian sunset.

To the east the land formations occurred as desert canyon-like, tall walls cut into layers of clay in vibrant colors of yellow, orange, and red. The sage brush became dense and looked healthy and green for this time of year. To the west there were large, gray, jagged rocky formations coming from the ground about a mile or so away. Maybe more, it was hard to tell. They jutted upward like shark fins. I'm pretty sure it was the top of the Rocky Mountains. It was crazy to think I had spent all day driving on a road that looked flat, yet here I was on the top of the Rocky

Mountains. I couldn't wrap my head around that or what I was seeing in the world around me. I don't think I'd ever been so awestruck.

The wind began to pick up, but it wasn't too bad. As I drove, the road ran closer and closer to the jagged, shark fin rocks to the west. As it did, the wind continued to pick up more and more. Still not too bad. The sun had started to set, and it was meeting a horizon line that seemed strangely close to me. The edge of the world looked like it was perhaps half a mile away. The sun looked so much larger than usual. It cast a golden glow over the snow-covered ground and made the terracotta-colored striation of the rocks to my right look even brighter and more intense.

Right as I found myself consumed by this gift nature was bestowing upon me, I rounded a corner and was hit hard by the wind. I mean hard. It stole my breath. The steering wheel jerked, and I felt every muscle in my body tighten in response.

"Shit," I said out loud. "It's just a little windy. I'm only thirty miles or so away. I'll be fine. It's fine. Just a little breezy. Easy Breezy, right?" But I wasn't buying my own bullshit.

The wind continued to pick up and I drove by the first of what would be several semi-trucks pushed off the road. *That can't be good.* The snow, which was powdery like glitter, began to blow across the black asphalt before me. First, it was just a translucent covering across a short section of road, maybe ten yards or so. It was stressful but still doable. Then, the wind blew snow across longer stretches of road and it got more and more opaque. Finally, sections of the road that were much longer than I was comfortable with were completely whited out. There was no road at all, only sparkling snow as far as I could see.

I looked down at the GPS. I had twenty-six miles to go. *Surely this wouldn't last twenty-six miles.* Five miles later, when traffic was stopped so that an overturned car could be cleared from the road, I was Lamaze breathing. I was not okay. I noticed the sun was almost beneath the horizon line. We needed to get these cars moving as soon as possible. I did not want to do this in the dark for twenty-one more miles.

They got the accident cleared fast. Once we got going again, I had to try to stay as close as I could to the car in front of me, and they were travelling much faster than I would have liked. But I had no choice. They were clearing the snow so I could see the road. I also had to make sure to stay far enough away that I wouldn't hit them in the event of sudden stops. It was a fine line, and it was intense. For the next fifteen miles and twice as many minutes, the wind kept up and the road stayed white. My abdominal muscles cramped under the tension. I was terrified. I wanted to just stop the car in the middle of the road, get out, throw up, and cry.

I pictured Jeff in the seat next to me. He sat all the way forward in his seat, eyes wide.

"I can't… I can't do this. I have to stop," I said, panicky, shaking, and on the brink of sobbing.

"Nope. You got this, Beans. I'm with ya. Remember?? Divine mission. Protected. Just breathe. Stay calm. You got this." His voice was sure. I had to believe him. I was divinely protected. My father was with me. I would be okay.

About five miles out of town, the wind died down enough to leave the snow in place. Now I was only being pushed around by the gusts every few minutes or so. I couldn't believe that I had made it. I was still shaking when I checked in for my room key. I mentioned something about the trip up US-287 and the man at the front desk confirmed the weather could be extreme along that stretch of highway. That felt like a mild summation.

The Hilton Garden Inn at Laramie had those same, small luggage carts, so it took two trips to get my stuff to the room. Afterwards, I headed downstairs to get a cocktail. I'd earned it. I made small talk with a couple of ladies at the bar while I was waiting for my drink. They were Wyoming residents and when I recounted my experience, they said it was normal for the area. *Now I know why nobody friggin' lived here.* I asked about the stretch of Interstate 80 I would be driving the next day. She said it got windy too but would not say how it compared. I was already stressed about tomorrow's drive. *Thanks, lady.*

I went back to my room, dragged the plants into the bathroom, and took a long, hot, steamy shower while drinking my double Manhattan. It was a solid two hours before my muscles relaxed. That was one hundred percent the most stressful driving experience of my life. I'd later look up local road conditions and the warnings for that stretch of highway while I was on it were the highest they could be before closure. "Extreme Blow-over Risk" they call it, meaning the wind gusts were sixty miles per hour or faster. A quick google search would have told me that that thirty-five-mile stretch of US-287 is one of the most dangerous roads in America. I had not done my homework.

That night I considered the next leg of my trip with greater scrutiny. I looked up weather reports and checked highway cameras. The *DriveWeather* app was the best. It could predict all kinds of weather for your specific route; precipitation, temperature, windspeed, and more. I found that it updated every few hours, so I had to check in for changes, but overall it was spot on. The next leg of the trip would be to Twin Falls, Idaho. All signs point to clear, sunny skies, and smooth sailing.

I slept like the dead that night, feeling like I had shaved years off my life. But it was an epic tale of survival and triumph. Jeff would have loved it.

Chapter Fifteen

There was no pressing snooze the next morning. The *DriveWeather* app suggested getting out by 9 a.m. latest to ensure calmer winds. It would be easy for me to pack up and get out of there, so I aimed for 8 a.m. I got up, made a cup of coffee, and showered. The plants liked these hotel bathroom steams. I got breakfast at a coffee shop on the way out of town.

Interstate 80 proved to be kinder than US-287. There were reader boards every few miles on the side of the road with information about conditions. Today, forty mile per hour gusts were expected and there were areas of reduced speed. And it was easy peasy, lemon squeezy. Thank heavens, because my nerves couldn't handle another experience like last night.

I headed to Twin Falls, Idaho by way of Salt Lake City, Utah. Five hundred sixty-five miles and more than eight hours in the car. It was one of my longer days of driving. Old age put limits on how long I could be in the driver's seat before my spine protested. It's hard for me to believe I could once upon a time drive twenty-four hours straight through.

In 1993, I took a road trip that changed the course of my life. I was living in Hollywood, California working for an answer service, Proxy Message Center. We answered phone calls for various high-profile doctors, lawyers, production companies, talent scouts, and actors. I was the swing shift supervisor, so I got to deliver messages to our VIP clients. Every night at 5:30 p.m., I got to talk to Alan Alda to relay his daily messages. When Elizabeth Montgomery called in for her messages, she came directly to my desk (I was instructed to never call her Lizzy, no matter how many of her callers did). I was 19 years old, and I thought it was the coolest.

 In early May 1993, my newly found love for Alice in Chains made me watch the movie "Singles" and it was like the hand of fate knocked on my door. It was set in Seattle, and it looked amazing! I did not enjoy southern California. While I loved my awesome, old Hollywood apartment, it consumed most of my income. I could barely afford my car and there was too much ramen in my diet. It seemed to me that in southern California, at that time, you were either rich or poor, and I wasn't rich. I didn't see a happy medium and a good life felt too far away. Plus, it was so dry and dusty. I wasn't a fan.

I decided to take a couple extra days off around my already long Memorial Day weekend. The plan was to drive up and check out Seattle. Like, no big deal. Just hop in the car, drive twenty-four hours straight through, check out the area for two and a half days, and drive twenty-four hours straight home. My back would need be put in traction if I even gave this consideration nowadays. Plus, I was dirt broke, so this meant sleeping in the car for at least one of those nights, perhaps two. I'm glad I did those things while I was still young and able.

I fell in love with Washington. I went back to Hollywood and gave my two-week notice. I sold whatever I did not need and packed what was left into my Tornado Red '88 Volkswagen Fox and the smallest, cheapest U-Haul trailer I could rent. I have been in Washington ever since and couldn't imagine living anywhere else. Well, except maybe Madison, New Jersey.

Once I was on the road and was comfortable with the idea that I could manage the weather situation, I started to consider how I was going to pass the time. I could not do another cryfest today. I'm glad that I had that experience, it left me feeling lighter in my heart, but I wasn't up for it again. I had an audible book to listen to, but I did not like it. I wanted to, but I didn't. I had enjoyed a lot of silence on the road so far, but I thought too much of it today would make the drive to Twin Falls feel even longer than it was.

I had gotten a text from my friend, Emily, the day before. She was just checking in to make sure I was doing well on my trip. It had been a while since we had connected, and who knew when I would see her next? I decided to call.

I met Emily in the summer of 2008, around the same time I met Katrina, and also through my mom's group. Emily and I would become running partners. We began walking, because I was seven months pregnant with my youngest son, Alex, and it hurt to run. Emily was adamant that she was not a runner. But, when Alex was about three months old, and it was time to start running again, she joined me.

Over the next five years, Emily and I would track more miles together than I could ever count. She had to take a couple of breaks to have babies, but other than that, we were running. We mostly trained for longer distance runs, half or full marathons, which meant a lot of hours together pounding pavement. Having a partner helped distract me from the desire to stop running. We would talk about everything, and as a result, Emily and I knew so many of each other's life stories.

We started our conversation with a recount of the time before, during, and after Jeff's passing. At this point, I had told the story enough times that I was able to get through it with fewer tears. I noticed that the more I shared the story, the less certain parts hurt. I think this is the same as the mechanics of talk therapy. Keep saying the words until they hurt less.

Then she shared what she had going on. She had tested positive for the BRCA1 gene and had been looking at dealing with some scary health issues. Once I was caught up on her health stuff, we talked about all the other things; husbands, kids, school, friggin' COVID-19. We talked for three hours and forty-five minutes. It was great. By the time we hung up, I had only two hours left to drive. It was funny to me that, under these circumstances, two hours felt like no time at all. Any other day I'd be whining about it.

The Hilton Garden Inn at Twin Falls is right around the corner from the tall bridge that spans the Snake River. It also had luggage carts that were too small. I suppose after all that sitting, taking two trips with my bags and plants wasn't the worst thing that could happen. I got things settled into my room and went down to the bar to order food and an adult beverage. This time I was toasting to an uneventful trip. There was just one day of driving left. I was sure the worst of it was behind me.

The bartender greeted me with a smile. She introduced herself as Sharon and let me know it was her first night of work. She had been training with the day crew, but tonight she was on her own. She poured me a Chardonnay, it was a generous pour, and I pulled up a seat at the bar to wait for my food. She asked what I was doing in town. I got most of my reason out without crying. Then, we talked about plants. She too fancied herself an indoor gardener. I love having things in common with random strangers.

I got my drinks, two because I was having happy hour with my girls, and I headed up to my room for a Facetime chat with Toni, our good friend, Susan, and Susan's sister, Wendy.

Toni and Susan met in 2015 in a *Supernatural* (TV series) fan chat room. I met Susan in 2017 when she and Toni came out west to attend a *Supernatural* fan convention in Vancouver, BC. During the pandemic, Susan, Toni, and I spent many hours on Facetime sorting through all the troubles of the world, hashing out plans for the future, daydreaming, and day drinking. Susan usually plays the voice of reason out of the three of us, somebody has to do it, but tonight she and her sister, Wendy, were buzzed and goofy. Just the entertainment I needed.

We got all caught up with each other's lives. I shared the harrowing tale of wind and snow that had been my trip the night before. I could have stayed on the line with them until the wee hours, but I had to make it an early night. I needed to shower, review the next day's route, and get to bed. I wanted to get an early start the next morning.

Six hundred forty-one miles to home. It translated into more than nine hours of driving. I would be crossing another time zone, so I didn't have to factor in as much time for stops. I figured I should count on ten hours to be safe. It would be the longest leg of the trip, but it was the last which made that an easier pill to swallow. The *DriveWeather* app showed a promising day. Very little wind and mostly sunny with a few foggy patches. I wasn't worried. I was pretty sure I had already driven straight through frozen hell. I was certain I could handle anything.

I was on the road by 8:30 a.m. That would get me home around 6:30 p.m. I would be driving after dark, but those roads would be familiar, so I was fine with that. I stopped for my now usual breakfast; a bacon and egg sandwich with a sixteen ounce *care-ah-mel* latte. It was hard to believe that this would be my last morning doing this.

It had been twenty-three days since the last time I had been home, and it felt like forever. A lot had happened in that time, and it had changed me. I was surprised by how impacted I felt by Jeff's passing. I had expected it for three years. I knew this was coming. But the moment I watched him take his dying breath it felt like a black hole opened and took away a part of me with him.

Even though I wanted to go home, I still didn't feel quite ready. This trip had three goals: 1) get the plants home safe, 2) process grief, and 3) figure out where to go now. How was I doing with those things? Well, the plants were doing well. They got the spa treatment every night and were looking way healthier than they had on day one. But what about the other things?

I think that I had processed as much grief as I could, and I knew I was nowhere near done. I still felt too many things to pin down one feeling at a time, but I think the easiest one to get hold of was my anger. I was mad. I was mad at my father for stealing the experience of spending his final days with him. Once again, I had asked for what I needed, and once again it made no difference. The last goddamn thing he could have done for me, and he chose not to. I know I must sound like a spoiled brat, but the reality is that I was extremely neglected, and I resented the hell out of it.

I was mad at him and Joni. I don't know if he asked her to lie or if she told him to lie. I don't even know how much she knew about the true state of his health. I do know that she chose to lie to me that day when she called to cancel our Christmas plans. Choosing to support that lie meant my father spent too many of his last days alone, or in the hospital with strangers. From what I know, Joni didn't spend much time with him during either of his stays. Maybe he said that was what he wanted, but if he wanted to die alone it was for unhealthy reasons like avoidance, guilt, shame, or embarrassment. She let him die like that. I was livid and it was a good thing.

This anger of mine was white hot like the sun. I could feel it burning through the dense, sharp bramble of gaslight and scapegoating they had planted all around me. Was it them? Or was it just her? Did he calculate like her too? Or had she planted that thicket, one poisonous vine at a time, over a long forty years, all while convincing me that she loved me? Is there something more heinous you could do to a person? Now, this fire shed light on reality in a way I could not deny. I knew this fire would serve me, so I let it burn.

"FUCK!" I growled through clenched teeth and hit the steering wheel with the percussive side of my fist. Jeff's face flashed through my mind, but I blocked it out. I could never stay mad at Jeff, and I wanted to be mad. It wasn't my favorite feeling, but it was necessary. I needed to feel it to work through it. For nearly fifty years, I had been living a life where I believed that I did not deserve to be angry. Whatever situation had made me angry must have been my fault, so I stuffed it down.

My abandonment issues ran deep. Ingrained in my subconscious was the belief that if I were angry at them and expressed it, they would leave me. If I became a burden by being mad at them without right, like the ungrateful cunt that I was, then I risked losing the only safety net I thought I had. But now, things are different. With Jeff gone, I felt more and more like I had nothing to lose. I could express all this anger and be done with it for good.

The last goal of this trip was figuring out where to go now. That was going to take more than the remainder of this car ride to work out. I knew my grief would be complex and difficult. But in some ways, my life ahead had gotten easier. I'm sorry to say but the bright side of Jeff's passing is that it in many ways lightened my load. His approval had meant too much to me. It colored too many of the decisions and in many ways paralyzed me. It kept me from honoring my truest self, as I attempted to make myself into someone they could love. There were no number of marathons I could run, groups I could start, plants I could grow, projects

I could do, things I could build, or art I could make that would amount to him or her being proud of me.

When he died, the weight of all that failure was lifted. Metaphorically speaking, I no longer had to tend to a plant that would never blossom, no matter what I did. That wasn't a burden Jeff had put on me. I had, and it took him being gone to realize it. Now I could give myself permission to stop. I could appreciate my life more. I felt more comfortable in my own skin. There was no one left to impress, and I felt free. *God, what I would have given to have both this freedom and Jeff still here with me.*

"We're gonna do this different next time, right? I'm going to do all this work, and next time it will be good, right?" I asked the empty Jeep, half laughing and half crying.

Jeff came to mind, in the seat next to me, watching the scenery.

"Yep, Beans. For sure, next time." He said, gazing off in the distance, smiling.

"Okay. Next time it is," I said, feeling more hopeful as he vanished from my mind's sight. My thoughts returned to the present, to the task before me. What is there to do now?

As for Joni and Jennifer, I had no idea what was going on with those two, but I couldn't ignore that something was off. I also had no idea how to address it. We've never talked about conflict or worked anything out. We always swept everything under the lumpy-ass rug. It felt like there was always something there, dark and looming, like the elephant has been in the room so long it's up and died.

Even if I worked that out, there was still the issue that I simply felt like I didn't belong there. I had struggled for years with feeling like that was my fault. If I could just impress them enough, they would treat me like I belonged. Or if I let go of not belonging, would things suddenly change? Like, I just start thinking I belong and then, like magic, I would. But I don't think that's how it works. If people don't want you in their club, it won't help to pretend that you're in it.

The situation with my sister perplexed me. Our relationship has always been good. But I'm sure that she has participated in her mother's lies and omissions. My only question is, how many times and to what extent? I would bet she has a million justifications for it, like actual millions in cash money, and they were still lies and omissions. But what's most hurtful to me is the fact that, of all the people who could have changed the culture of our family, she had the best chance. She had the favor of being able to sway how I was treated. She did nothing.

She did nothing, because she gained from my scapegoat status. My sister is our family's golden child. If I'm the bad guy, it's easier for her to maintain her status. Her status earns her privilege. How can I have a relationship with someone who benefits from my second-class status? I was beginning to see that she was not who I thought she was.

I kept going back to that last night at my- Joni's house. I was sick with anxiety over my distrust of Joni and Jennifer. I was gaslighting myself and full of doubt, and sorrow. Nothing was the same. I didn't know how to navigate it. Jeff said to me that night, "Don't do anything. You've done enough."

Had I done enough? I had tried so hard, too hard even. I had stifled myself and set aside my emotional needs for so many years just to still not fit in. I had to stop. I deserved more than scraps. I deserve relationships with people who are honest with me. I deserve relationships with people who are willing to communicate. And I needed to make sure I did not settle for less.

I spent about three hours driving in silence, pondering these things. Around Baker City, Oregon, I noticed my first patch of fog. I remembered that the *DriveWeather* app had shown a few patches through Oregon and Washington and thought that it should not be a problem. And it wasn't for a total of five minutes.

I rounded the corner that heads up the Wallowa Mountain pass at about seventy-five miles per hour when I ran headlong into a wall of white. The car in front of me vanished, except for two tiny, dim, red lights the size of fireflies. I could only see clearly about two to three car lengths in front of me.

I felt tension and anxiety ripple through every single muscle in my body. I sat up straighter, gripped the wheel as tight as I could, and leaned forward with squinted eyes trying to see better. I turned off the radio. I slowed down to fifty-five miles per hour and put on my hazards. People were flying past me on the left. Fine by me. I would have looked to see who these brave people were or shot them an incredulous glance, but I couldn't take my eyes off the road. I couldn't see beyond twenty to twenty-five feet in front of me. At fifty-five miles per hour those feet flew by in a fraction of a moment.

"How was this road not closed!?" I said out loud, thinking there was no way this could last for long. *Oh, silly me.* It went on like that for forty-five minutes. My muscles ached and my chest hurt. After that, the fog thinned enough that I could see the two cars ahead of me, vague exit signs, and the guard rail. For the first time since hitting that white wall, I could take a full breath. "Phew," I was through it. Or so I thought.

That lasted about fifteen minutes until I hit another white wall.

"No! Fuck!" I shouted. *This can't be happening.* I spent the next five hours driving in and out of whiteout conditions until I finally stopped in Ellensburg, Washington for a coffee (*because that was the last thing I needed*). The fact that I went that long without urinating is a testament to the fact that I could not take my hands off the wheel long enough to drink a sip of water.

I sat in the coffee shop's parking lot and cried and swore… a lot. I was so tired. I thought that Wyoming wind had taken first place in the most stressful drives, but lo and behold… six hours of pea soup fog is the champion. I've never felt so nerve-shot in my life. I considered looking for a hotel room. Jeff was in the passenger's seat. He shifted around like he had all his muscles contracted for the last six hours too.

He said, "Whooooof. Damn, Beans."

"Yeah, I can't do it," I said shakily through sobs. "I think, as soon as I can stand, I'm gonna check into that hotel." I motioned to the hotel across the parking lot.

"Whaaaat?", he said with astonishment. "No. What happened to my Beans? The one who didn't give up. We're just over two hours from home, and you're a goddamn legend. You're goin' and you're goin' to make it."

"Goin' and goin' to make it" was a shout-out to my childhood. One time, my dad and Greg took me out cross-country skiing. I was seven years old. About halfway through the day, I started whining about wanting to stop.

My father said, "If ya wanted to eat, ya better keep up."

And then he left me, in the middle of the woods. I stood there crying until something in me switched on, or snapped, or both. I was pissed and I was gonna show him. I was going to get out of those damn woods and get my damn lunch. I stood up taller, set my brow with determination, and got back to skiing.

"I was goin', and I was goin' to make it," is what little Korva said.

"Shit, you always knew how to get me to do stuff," grown me said with a reluctant laugh as I put the Jeep into drive. I was thankful he had pushed me, it gave me the confidence I needed to accomplish the mission. I wanted to be home. I adjusted myself to sit taller in my seat, set my brow with determination, and put the car in drive before I could change my mind.

The fog cleared when I hit The Summit at Snoqualmie and started making my way down the west side of the Cascades. The air was clear, I was driving on familiar roads, and I felt safe. My body still hurt from the tension, but I'd be home soon. Even the forty-five minute backup I found myself in on Interstate 405 didn't take away from my relief.

I pulled into our driveway just after 8 p.m., January 14th. I had been away from home twenty-three long, sad, strange, transformative, frightening, and liberating days. I was dead-ass tired. My chest was tight, my muscles ached, and my head pounded.

I sat in the car for a long while, looking at my house. I needed a minute of stillness and quiet. I could see the lights in my kids' windows and imagined them in their rooms, gaming online with their friends. I know one day they will return to their homes after I die. I hope it will be less complicated for them. I hope when I'm gone, my kids will only have to miss me.

Talks to Angels

Youtube.com
Black Crowes
"She Talks to Angels"

Chapter Sixteen

I have read in countless articles about grief and mourning that nighttime was supposed to be the most challenging time of day. All that quiet and stillness brings up a lot of thoughts and emotions. While I cried myself to sleep more than a time or two, I had the hardest time with mornings. I was often sobbing within the first few seconds of being awake.

I had left the curtains open slightly the night before. I wanted the sun to wake me up, and it did. The view out of my window reminded me of why I love our home. Our house is perched up on a hill and looking out my window I could see the treetops, made golden by the sun's first rays. I had the window open so I could hear the birds singing. It may have been the middle of January, but I was perimenopausal. I could've slept in a refrigerated box and still been too warm.

I went through the usual checklist in my head, *"Where am I? What is today? Am I supposed to be doing anything?"* Followed by, *"Oh yeah....Jeff's gone."* It was like reliving his death with the dawn of every day. I wondered how long that would go on.

I had been told many times that the first year after a significant loss was the worst. First holidays and birthdays hit hard. I had braced myself for a year of adjustments and grief. What I had not wrapped my head around is that one year is bigger than it sounds. One year is twelve months, fifty-two weeks, 365.25 days, 8,765.82 hours, 525,949.2 minutes, or 31,556,952 seconds. I think grief highlights the seconds. From that perspective a year somehow seems much longer.

The first few days at home were about settling in and returning to some semblance of normalcy. I had left in the middle of a kitchen renovation. While I had made a point to get things back to being livable before I left for Boston, it had been weeks since I had been home and there was quite a mess to catch up on. I was not ready to tackle the remainder of the kitchen project, but I had to get a handle on the chaos. And of course, there was all the unpacking. Ugh. However, I was excited about getting the plants unboxed and put on display. They looked good and had weathered the trip well.

Monday, January 17th, would bring the return of early mornings and trips to schools. It had been over a month since I'd last made these rounds. My children had been bus riders before the pandemic. The bus stop was right in front of our house. It just made sense. But post-pandemic, the school bus occurred to me as a high-risk science experiment, so I have been driving them to and from school since they resumed in-person instruction in 2021. Between the various back-and-forth trips to the kids' schools, I kept myself as busy as I could. I needed the sensation of moving forward. Plus, I had to keep moving, literally.

I began experiencing all the physical symptoms of prolonged anxiety. The near-constant ache, weight, and heaviness in my chest had me using our blood pressure cuff whenever I sat down for a minute to watch TV or social media doom scroll. Sometimes, when I doubted its accuracy, I would stop and check it at the local pharmacy. My blood pressure read as elevated two or three times but other than that it was normal. I was just so antsy. I couldn't sit still. Lucky for me, finding things to do is a specialty of mine.

I got back to work on the kitchen renovation in early February. The old kitchen design was pretty on point for the year the house was built, 1999. It's a split-level home and its design predates the popularity of the open-concept floor plan. Jeff hated that architectural description. He'd say, "there was no 'concept' about it, it *is* an open-floor plan."

Our main living space includes our living room, dining room, and kitchen. It would have been a large, open, and lofty space were it not for the monolith of a pantry that sat in the middle of my house, keeping the kitchen closed off from the rest of the space.

We hemmed and hawed about whether to pay for a full remodel or figure out a less expensive way to renovate. A full remodel would have been nice, but we had so many other household projects that we wanted to do. The house was more than twenty years old, and updates were coming due. We could either put a ton of money into the kitchen or spread it out to smaller improvements throughout. We chose the latter.

I had figured out a way to remove the top portion of the pantry and turn it into an island. The floor plan would be… different… but we were planning to be in the house for at least another decade, so the deciding factor is what would work for us and not resale value. Bryan and I had demolished most of the old pantry, and I was in the process of installing the new cabinets when I had to leave for Boston. The plan now was to finish building the new island, paint the cabinets, and have new countertops installed. This would keep me busy at least through the end of the month, and I needed that.

February hosts several important dates. My father, my brother, James, and I have birthdays in February. The 10th marked the anniversary of the deaths of both Jeff's father and grandmother. It's what he called "The Rafter Family Curse Day." I wondered if he had realized it was February 10th when he called to tell me he had cancer in 2019. Also, the anniversary of my mother's death is the 18th. February is rough.

I reached out to James on his birthday. I've never gotten the impression that he wanted to talk on the phone, so I sent him a text message saying happy birthday and asking if he had any plans.

He responded with, "Thanks. And no, not really."

I said, "Well, I hope it's a good day." After I sent it, I wondered if that was insensitive. Jeff had only been gone five or six weeks at this point. I had no idea how James was feeling. Was having a "good day" a weird thing to wish him?

Jeff's birthday on the 7th was hard in a way I hadn't expected. For the first time in my life, I saw the wholeness of my dad, not just the parts I experienced. He had been someone's newborn baby, born with endless potential and millions of paths to follow. He had been someone's adolescent child who found out that Santa did not exist and that his father wasn't Superman. He had gone through the ol' awkward teenage phase. He had his heart broken. I felt like I was mourning all the things that had never become real for that baby born seventy years ago to the day. I mourned all his wounds that went unhealed and all his dreams that were left unfulfilled.

Of course, I mourned for myself, too. I missed him. Or maybe more accurately, I missed the hope that Jeff and I could one day have a close relationship. It was all I ever wanted, to have a real and close relationship with my father. For the life of me, I could not make that happen. Now, it is no longer possible. In addition to all the things that would never happen with Jeff, I was becoming more aware of the truckload of other losses I had to mourn.

From the time that my father and stepmother got married, the attitude towards me was, "Yeah, you had a tough childhood, but that's not what's happening now; so, stop whining about it."

I was never given the space to process and heal the trauma I had experienced being a very young child living with a heroin addict. I was never able to acknowledge the abandonment and fear I experienced. I was just expected to be strong and get over it.

I too had been a baby born with endless potential. Now, I was pissed about how many of those things had been taken from me by the choices of others. My mother's choice to do drugs, and later to take me away from my family to some foreign place, exposing me to things grown-ass people shouldn't be exposed to. And Jeff's choice to leave Charlotte for my stepmother. A choice that may have robbed me of the chance for a normal and loving family. Perhaps nothing with him was slated to be normal.

I hated to consider how different my life would have been had Jeff and Charlotte gotten married. I felt guilty because I knew that would mean I wouldn't have the life I have now. My kids wouldn't exist and that's a reality that I wouldn't wish for. But I wished I could have gotten here without the abuse I had to endure because of Jeff marrying Joni. Her role in my life would whittle away what little sense of self I had been able to conjure and would send me into a cycle of self-loathing and self-destruction that I'd have to work all too hard to get out of.

I also couldn't help but think that Jeff marrying Joni is half the reason he died just shy of seventy years old. Joni just watched his downward spiral into alcoholism, appearing to have never made a peep about it. Now, I know plenty of situations where a woman may feel afraid to say something, but Joni was tough as nails. If anyone in that house was afraid, it was Jeff. There's a part of me that believes Joni hoped Jeff would drink himself to death. Charlotte would never have sat on the sidelines and watched Jeff kill himself. She was a fighter, especially for the wellbeing of the people she loved. I'm also sure she would have called me on Jeff's first postmortem birthday to see if I was ok. Joni, however, did not.

I hadn't spoken to Joni since I left Boxborough on January 4th, a little over a month ago. We exchanged a couple of texts during my drive back to Washington. More accurately, I sent texts, and she responded to half of them. When I visited with my sister on the way home, she mentioned she was planning to drive back to Boston with her kids to spend Jeff's birthday with her mom. She didn't want Joni to spend it alone. Jennifer was also planning to help Joni go through Jeff's belongings and would be driving in the event there were things she wanted to take home.

I knew that they were together for his birthday. While I also knew I could have reached out to them and asked for support, I didn't.

Jeff's words were with me, *"Let them do what they do. You'll see who they are. You'll know what to do."*

I had expressed my insecurity to my sister. I told her that I no longer felt like I belonged. She said she didn't feel that way, but her actions were saying otherwise. I guess I wanted their behavior to prove me wrong. It didn't. I wouldn't hear from either of them until my birthday at the end of the month.

I was on my way back from a girls' weekend trip to Lake Chelan when Joni called. I happened to be in a car full of people heading through a mountain pass with spotty reception. I opted not to answer. She didn't leave a message or text. I thought that was odd. In the past, if she tried to call and I didn't answer, she'd do one or the other. But not this time. Had I not sent her a message when I got home, she would not have wished me a happy birthday at all.

I struggled with whether this was me being too sensitive. I thought maybe she was too busy to text or message. Perhaps I was reading too much into her behavior. But I kept coming back to the fact that she had done the bare minimum to reach out to me, that fulfilled whatever sense of obligation she might have had, but didn't relay any real love or concern.

I didn't hear from my brother at all. I wasn't hurt by that though. I guessed that for the last few years, he had sent me birthday texts because he was reminded by Jeff, which made me feel good. I supposed Joni was not going to take up that mantle. Fostering a relationship between my brother and I did not appear to be a priority of hers.

My sister called me at what seemed like the last possible minute. Sometime around 7:30 p.m. my time, bedtime for her. She called, sounding tired, distracted, and disinterested. It was a short and uneventful conversation. I thought it seemed strange. In previous years, she would have texted me earlier in the day, but today it was like she put it off as long as she could. What the hell was going on? Why was she being this way to me?

Chapter Seventeen

With all the uncertainties in the world, at least I can count on home improvement projects always costing more than anticipated and requiring twice as many trips to the store for supplies as planned. The paint I had chosen for the kitchen cabinets could only be purchased from specialty stores, often vintage or antique shops selling to people who intend to refinish or repaint furniture. The closest of these stores was Home Inspirations on First Avenue in downtown Snohomish.

Downtown sits on the banks of the Snohomish River and once served as an important trade post in the late nineteen and early twentieth centuries. It is a quaint strip, maybe half to three-quarters a mile long, lined with antique shops, clothing boutiques, restaurants, and bakeries. Some of the best beef stroganoff on the planet is made at The Cabbage Patch. I like Snohomish quite a bit and I try to go there whenever I have an excuse. I took Jeff there when he and Joni visited, which is why the many trips to and from Home Inspirations for supplies made me think of him.

One morning, while on the way home from buying the last of too many expensive, but worth it, pints of paint, I had a realization. My father would not see my new kitchen. Or the finished retention walls that I had started the year he was diagnosed. Or any of the feats my children would accomplish. Or anything about our lives ever again. I mean, I already knew this, but for whatever reason I was experiencing it in a new way, a deeper way.

It felt like a chasm had opened up and swallowed parts of my future reality that I hadn't even realized I had already created. He was supposed to still be here. He was supposed to see my new kitchen. He was supposed to watch his grandchildren graduate. He's supposed to be there when they get married. We were supposed to sit on my front porch, sippin' whiskey, yelling at the kids to get off the lawn. We were supposed to have our time. The time that I was robbed of some forty years ago.

It hit me hard. I erupted into tears. It was one of those gut-wrenching cries that steals your breath like a punch to the chest. It knocked the wind out of me - all the way out. I could not get my breath back no matter how hard I tried to gasp. In hindsight I think I should have pulled over.

"Breathe," Jeff said from the passenger's seat.

He started to take deep breaths himself, loudly, in through the nose and out through the mouth, like he was coaching me on staying alive.

I took my next breath in hard. It hurt. It was like the air I swallowed had been a solid and not a gas. I don't think my lungs have ever been that empty. I imagined the sensation I was having was much like drowning. I thought of Jeff again, sitting in the passenger's seat making sure I didn't stop breathing again. He sat like that for several minutes, taking audible breaths to remind me to calm down.

When I did, I said through belabored sobs, "I wish you were here, Jeff... I wish you could see my kitchen." Tears and snot flowing down my face.

"I can see your kitchen," he said.

"No. I mean for real. Like, I want you to see it, ya know... like, with your eyeballs... Ah feck, you know what I mean. I want to make you Thanksgiving dinner. You still hadn't had my thanksgiving dinner, or my Christmas prime rib. There's just so many things that still hadn't happened in real life," I said, feeling devastated with sadness, tinged with anger.

"I'm sorry, Beans. I know you wanted those things but that wasn't the trajectory. I mean, it's not your fault, but even if I hadn't gotten cancer, that wouldn't have happened."

My sobbing came to a sudden halt, and I turned cold as the words sunk in. *"That wasn't the trajectory."*

No, it was not. And a trajectory would assume a plan. I knew who did all the planning. Joni.

"Yeah, I suppose not," I said, with an ounce of venom. "And, speaking of trajectory, where am I supposed to go with her?"

"I don't know, Beans," Jeff said with a heavy sigh knowing exactly who I meant. "But I'm tellin' ya, there's nothing good for you there."

"What the hell does that even mean, Jeff?" I could still feel the residual pain in my chest from when I swallowed the solid air.

"I don't know how else to put it. You can keep going back to her… to the two of them… for the rest of your life, but there ain't nothing good for you there. The result in the end will be the same: you being disappointed."

"Why though? Why?"

He let out a long *haaaaaaa,* and then said, "I can't say."

"What do you mean you can't say!!?? Why not?" I was pissed.

"Because this needs to play out, Korva." I could sense what occurred as a combination of regret and frustration in his tone. "Look, I'm sorry, Beans. Just… I need you to be patient and let things unfold. I need you to stay quiet and watch. For one year. Wait until I've been gone for one year. Just wait. Can ya do that?"

Everything in me wanted to call Joni and Jennifer out on their bullshit, like right this second. Waiting a year was a big ask. But in the past, reacting too quickly had been my downfall. Every time. There was always a reason, always an excuse for the way I was being treated. My behavior would then be labeled as an overreaction and would be used to justify their treatment of me. It was a cyclical and dysfunctional beast that I seemed to feed every damn time.

"Ok, fine," I agreed, with reluctance, to be quiet and watch.

That agreement, however, didn't take my mind off the situation. I knew something was going on. Something shady. I could feel it. I'm sure it had something to do with money. My father had just retired four months before he died. He had been part owner of a company, and it had just sold. He made multiple millions. I'm talkin' lotsa money.

My stepmother was a self-proclaimed "rich widow." She tells me this just days after Jeff died, sitting across from me in her living room, practically flaunting it in my face. She declared it as though she had earned a badge of honor. She played the long game and now she has the bank account to show her strategic prowess. She had won her millions fair and square. I'm sure she had big plans for them too.

I knew that Joni would make sure that my sister and her family received as much benefit as they could from the Rafter family estate. Not so much that it risks her own comfort, but she's going to be generous. Especially if there's any tax write-offs involved. I didn't think that would be the same for my family. Or at least there was no evidence that it would be. I didn't care about that though, at least not about the money part of it. What I didn't like was that my sister was going to receive benefits that I wouldn't. It just furthered my sense of feeling rejected and abandoned. I didn't belong. I didn't deserve equal treatment. I wasn't worthy of her money.

My desire for truth and justice would have to sit back and try to relax. I had to trust that inaction would prove fruitful. I can still hear Jeff's words, said to me from his deathbed, I would have to "embrace inaction." Those words now held more meaning and gravity now. I had to trust him. I had to trust that the truth would reveal itself to me in good time. In the meanwhile, I'd get back to being busy.

Monday, March 2nd marked the beginning of Lent. I'm not a practicing Christian and I wasn't raised in a religious home. My grandmother Ginny (my father's mother), on the other hand, was a good Irish Catholic girl. She went to church every Sunday plus all the church-going holidays. She prayed the rosary daily and slept with her beads under her pillow. I loved her expression of religion. She did not force her beliefs on me nor shame me for not sharing them. She just showed me the peace she experienced because of her faith. It moved me.

In 2002, I received the unexpected inspiration to start observing Lent. It had been a difficult time in my life. My oldest son was a little over a year old, and I was in the midst of a major identity crisis. I had no idea how to be a mother, and my life's first and biggest wound was being abandoned by my own. I needed help, so I reached out to the only mother figure I knew, Ginny. Although she had passed away in 1995, she was still very much with me. My choice to begin observing Lent was an expression of my love for her, an offering to her in the hopes that she would guide me in turbulent times.

Every year since, I've given up something for Lent. For me, the purpose is not to suffer, but to see how specific things in my life affect or control me. One year I gave up coffee and started drinking black tea instead. It felt like cheating since I had just swapped one caffeine source for another. The impact of this sacrifice seemed minimal, I hardly noticed a difference. But, at the end of the seven weeks of Lent, that first cup of coffee I drank hit me like a freight train. Coffee was having a more substantial impact than I knew, I had just gotten used to it. Now, while this didn't make me give up coffee for good, it did give me the power to make more informed decisions.

For the last few years, I've given up alcohol. I think it is part of why I've seen a steady decline in how much alcohol I consume. That and old age. I've also given up social media a couple of times, with the same result. Every year, post-Lent, I consume less and less of it. This year I would give up social media and alcohol. I also switched to a plant-based diet, which proved to be harder than giving up the other two things combined. I felt like I needed deep cleansing. I hoped it would help bring me some clarity. Maybe then I would see whatever it was I was waiting to see.

Waiting is not my strong suit, for more reasons than I can count. I am often embarrassed by my lack of patience because I've too many times become obsessive, wanting to understand, express, or fix something. I had no idea how not to do those things. Every day that passed without me reaching out to Joni and Jennifer felt like a major victory. The only thing that made this possible was the endless list of to-dos I had to distract me.

I finished with the kitchen around the third week of March. I was pleased with the way it turned out. The cabinets were painted two tones of blue, dark marine blue on the bottom cabinets and a light, creamy teal on top. The new counters were white quartz with a subtle marbling and small copperish golden flecks throughout. I also installed new copper door handles and knobs that my son Alex said gave it a subtle steampunk feel, which I like.

The window that had always been above the kitchen sink somehow felt twice the size and, with the removal of the pantry, the whole living space seemed lighter and more cheerful. I felt proud and accomplished. It wasn't perfect, but it was light years better and more enjoyable. With the kitchen project complete, it would be time to move to the next thing… building a series of retaining walls on the slope behind my house. It was tall, steep slope, covered with blackberries and bramble, and impossible to manage. It was a project Bryan and I both dreaded because it required labor that would push both of us to our limits, but we could put it off no longer.

We bought our house in February 2007. Bryan had hoped for a newer, more modern home on a smaller lot, but I pushed for the house with land. One of my most important criteria in buying a home was the view from my kitchen sink. I hate doing dishes. I really hate it. And if I must do it, for like friggin 'ever, I want at minimum to have a good view from the sink. Most new homes on small lots have kitchens that look straight into their neighbor's kitchen. I know there are ways to mitigate that, but I didn't want mitigation. I wanted a good view.

The view from my kitchen sink is like that of being in a treehouse in the middle of a forest. There are treetops as far as the eye can see, with little to no evidence of other people, except for the sparkle of distant house lights through the trees at night. When you get up close to the windows on the back of the house, you can look down onto an acre sized meadow that is shared property with my neighbor. Then, on the far side of the meadow there is a tree line that hides Little Bear Creek which serves as our property line. It's peaceful. Looking back there I could easily forget that I live half a mile from division after division of small lot, single family homes.

Our house is split-level with the main living quarters on the top floor. In addition to that, immediately behind our house is a slope that drops roughly twenty feet over about the same number of feet in distance.

It is a steep slope contained around its edges with a three-foot tall wall. It was woefully inadequate. The steepness of the slope made it difficult to traverse and impossible to maintain. In the years we've been here, a dense thicket of blackberries took over the space, which is no bueno, friends. A bramble close to the home encourages critters to burrow and nest. I'm a hard pass on inviting rodents as close neighbors.

The plan was to pay to have the blackberries and bramble cleared and then build a series of terraced retaining walls. In total there would be five walls, each on average four feet high. Each terrace would be about four to five feet wide. It would require about 1,200 sixty-five-pound retaining wall blocks, three cubic yards of one-and-a-half-inch drain rock, six cubic yards of 5/8 minus crushed rock, and a shit-ton of calories, which was good because I had some serious comfort eating to do.

It was a massive undertaking. I started it in the spring 2019, the year that Jeff was diagnosed. For us to be able to do any of this work, I needed to create an access ramp. When I began the build process, I thought I could use project updates as a way to stay in more consistent contact with Jeff. I began making videos to show him the work I was doing, as well as talk to him about what the kids were up to.

I sent him several of these over the course of 2019 but stopped after about nine months because he never responded or commented. It broke my heart. In the last video I shared some very vulnerable things with Jeff, things I didn't share with anyone else. I was going through a rough patch with one of my kids and had worries and was afraid. When he didn't respond to that, I figured he either didn't watch them or didn't care. I was done. I wanted so badly to go back to the no contact strategy. But I couldn't.

My father had cancer and no matter how his treatment went, the hourglass was running out faster. It scared me. I wanted to connect with him. I wanted him to know me, out of some desperation for him to approve of or accept me. But he didn't respond. At all. I felt pathetic. When was I going to get that he was just not that into me? Or was that even the truth?

I got to work on the wall project in mid-March. I'd make small, daily goals. Sometimes it would be moving and placing as many blocks as I could while the weather permitted. On easier days I would shovel as much dirt as I could in two hours or complete a few feet of base layer. I took my time working. I took a lot of breaks, too. And I cried a river. I didn't know I could cry that much. I'd be out there shoveling and bawling. It was exactly what I wanted and needed to do.

I often wondered if indulging in these emotions was a good idea. I was not moving on. It seemed as though I was upsetting myself on purpose. I should know better than to listen to certain songs, but I did it anyway. Sometimes the songs took me back to sweet places that brought out happy tears, and sometimes they would sing to my deepest sorrows. That said, there were also times when I  would work in dead silence and still end up a hot friggin' mess. Sitting, smelly and sweaty, on the damp dirt ground, sobbing like a baby.

Jeff often joined me for my workdays. He'd sit, feet dangling off the side of a wall. He'd be sparkling clean despite how dirty everything was. I'd work in silence and imagine him seeing and appreciating my backyard. It is a magical space. I imagined that it was a nice place for Jeff to be.

Our property is home to a variety of wildlife. We've seen coyotes, deer, fox, and bobcats strolling through, and we have tons of birds. There are a couple of dark-eyed juncos that make nests on my front porch every spring. They make a whole lot of noise when we use our front door because they don't like us being so close. You'd think they would choose another building site, but they've been making their nests there for years.

They hatched two sets of babies this year and it was fun to watch them grow up.

This spring we also had a little crow family take up home in a tree behind our house. There appeared to be four adolescent crows that were using our property as safe space for exploration. When I'd take work breaks, I'd watch them climb trees, hopping up from branch to branch, testing their wings, and learning to fly. I was both envious and empathetic. I'd imagine it wasn't an easy skill to gain. When they weren't practicing flight, they were pecking around in the grass for bugs or fighting with each other. I'd yell at them like I imagined their mother would. "Knock it off, you kids!!"

I also noticed that whenever I went outside, a little robin would appear within minutes. It seemed like it was waiting for me to come outside. It would just watch me and follow me around from afar. I kept feeling like it expected something from me, like perhaps other people were feeding it so that's what it wanted from me? But I didn't feed it, and it kept showing up. I decided to name it Georgie, and I'd talk to him.

Jeff liked my little robin friend, too. He had been a bird watcher in life. I was glad to have him here with me, enjoying the birds and this space. This was a healing space, and I think he needed it. I know I did.

One afternoon while working on the wall project, I sat down to take a break. And, as per the new norm, I did a little communing with my dad. "Jeff, what's happening? Like, what the hell is going on with Joni and Jennifer? Or is it just me? Am I being too sensitive?"

He said, "No, you aren't being too sensitive, but that's all I can say."

"What?! Whudda you mean?" I whined in my best New Jersey accent.

"I just can't tell ya, Beans," he reiterated with a guilty shrug.

"Well, isn't that just friggin dandy?" I threw my hands up. "You leave me with this mess, and you can't even tell me what I'm dealing with."

He said, "I can't tell you because words aren't enough. There's just too much. But I can show you." That's when things got weird.

I closed my eyes, and when I opened them again, I was seeing through someone else's vision. I was walking through my parents' kitchen, from the refrigerator around to the dining side of the kitchen island. I was looking across the island at my stepmother. She was doing dishes or cleaning something at the sink. The only thing clear was her face. The periphery was blurred, but I could hear the water running.

She was angry and flushed. She said, "No, I don't want her here. You know how I feel about this. There's just too much going on, and I don't need her here. You know I don't need to deal with that." It was clear that this was not negotiable. Her attitude expressed disgust that she was even made to answer whatever question she had just said no to.

The more I tried to focus and figure out what I was seeing, the more garbled and muffled the words became, and the image of my very agitated stepmother faded just as she had shut off the faucet and turned to walk away. I came back to reality and found myself sobbing. Again. My eyes were shot. Ever since the drive to New Jersey on New Year's Eve, my eyes had become increasingly dry and irritated. Crying, apparently, does not aid in the lubrication of the eye. On the contrary, tears serve to dilute whatever natural friction barrier your eyes make. My dependence on eye drops would only continue to grow from here.

"What the fuck… was that?" I was shaking. My heart pounded in my chest, which was so tight that it was hard to breathe. What just happened? One minute I'm sitting on a retaining wall in my backyard and the next I was in my parent's kitchen. It was so real, I swear I could have reached out and touched her. "What… was that? "I asked between panting breaths.

"It's just what you saw. I mean, I can't say anything about it. I can only show you."

"What do you mean, you can't say anything about it?" I asked, feeling more than miffed.

"You've gotta make sense of this yourself, Beans. I'm not supposed to interfere… too much. It's… complicated."

"Interfere? What do you… I can't… uh… ah, shit. That's… great," I said. "I give up." I dropped my chin to my chest and slouched my back, resigned to the fact that I may never make sense of any of this.

I sat there bewildered for a solid thirty minutes, waiting for my heart to slow. Even after I calmed down, I didn't know what to make of what just happened. Maybe I had worked too hard and was experiencing oxygen deprivation and passed out for a moment. No, I knew Jeff had shown me something. But what and why?

This would happen two more times under very similar circumstances during the month of April, which in hindsight makes astrological sense. On April 12, 2022, transit Jupiter, the planet of expansion and growth, was conjunct transit Neptune, which rules the subconscious mind and connection to spirit. For everyone, this would usher in a time of heightened spiritual growth and psychic awareness. This conjunction could also cause an increase in lucid dreaming and/or sleep disturbances. For me, this was happening in conjunction with my natal Mercury placement. Mercury rules your conscious mind. From this perspective, having psychic visions seemed par for the course and that helped me validate them, but not completely. There's always that inner skeptic.

The second vision, which arrived a couple of weeks later, focused on my sister. I was in the backseat of an SUV. The engine was running, and it was warm inside, but I got the impression that it was cold and wet outside. The view out the front window was that of a lush green tree line, and it was obscured by droplets of water on the windshield. I saw my sister approach the car with a person I could not quite make out. She got in the passenger's side door, sat down, and gave a good shiver. She was bundled up, wearing boots and a scarf.

Although I couldn't see, I got the feeling her husband got into the driver's seat. My visual focus was on the side of her left shoulder and the back of her head. As she adjusted herself and buckled her seatbelt, she answered a question that I hadn't quite heard with, "Welp… I don't like it, but what am I gonna do?" Her pseudo-southern-Midwest accent stood out. I could hear it as though she was right there with me.

That was all I saw. Why had I seen that? *"Well, I don't like it, but what am I gonna do?"* In my mind, it translates into "I know it's wrong but I'm not giving up my privilege for it." Was that who my sister was? The answer yes seemed more and more likely.

The third vision was of Joni. She appeared to be in a professional office. My perspective was that I was sitting on her left-hand side. Someone was sitting past her, on her right-hand side. I got the impression it was my sister, but they were unclear. I could see the edge of a large, dark wooden desk in front of her, covered in piles of paperwork.

She sat leaning forward, staring at the paperwork in front of her. She clutched her purse on her lap so tightly that her knuckles were white with tension. I could see the agitation on her face. There was chattering all around her. Something was being debated, and it made her angry. She pursed her lips and waved her hand like an axe, as if to say she had heard enough. The room fell silent, and she said, "She'll get over it. Move on." Her tone was authoritarian, and her words were final. She had her eyes fixed on the papers in front of her. Whatever was written on them was all that mattered. No sad-eyed puppy was going to rock her resolve.

Nothing about what I saw in that vision surprised me, which then made me begin to doubt what I was seeing. Was I conjuring this up in my head? *Is grief-psychosis a thing?* Maybe this relationship I have in my head with my father wasn't healthy after all. Maybe it kept me stuck in grief. I hadn't made any progress since he passed. I was only feeling worse and worse by the day. My anxiety levels were through the roof. I started wearing a Fitbit just to make sure that my heart wasn't racing all the time, because it felt like it was. And now I'm having weird visions, or hallucinations. I decided to just sit with these things. Maybe it was crazy. Maybe it wasn't. I had to trust time would tell.

Chapter Eighteen

The end of April had me busy with a vegetable garden redesign that had been on the to-do list for the past few years. I had a rabbit problem. I had been losing the war against the cutest enemy on earth. We had been battling for five years. My first attempt at defense was to install a fence. I had the entirety of the garden, a thirty foot by thirty-foot space, surrounded by what I thought was sufficient fencing. I planted my first crops of brussels sprouts and cabbage. About six weeks later, just when they were beginning to take off, a rabbit got in and ate twelve of eighteen plants.

I spent the next month patrolling the perimeter of the fence, filling in any holes or shoring up areas that looked pushed in or passable. I planted again, and guess what? They got in again. My little crops were being decimated! I couldn't tell for the life of me how these rabbits were getting in. Then, one warm spring evening, I was sitting outside, sipping a cold Corona, resting after a hard day's work. Out of the bramble of my neighbor's yard hopped a wee rabbit. It hopped upon my garden wall and then hopped straight through that damn fence like it didn't exist. *Well shoot.*

I swapped out that fencing for one with a smaller grid and for the rest of the season things were safe. Early the next spring I went out to do some clean up and uncovered the sweetest little nest of baby rabbits – smack dab in the middle of my damn garden. They mocked me, those fluffy little balls of joy.

I had tried doubling up the fence or burying parts of it. I tried covering crops with row covers and hoop houses. I tried scent deterrents like onion and garlic juice. By the fifth year, I had given up growing any crops rabbits would eat. That leaves a lot to grow because there are plenty of things they don't eat, like tomatoes and squash of all sorts. While they are my favorites, a good kitchen garden needs things like leafy greens, carrots, and peas. I had to get this bunny problem under control.

After overthinking about it for way too long, I was sure I knew what strategy to use. Rather than one fence around the entire garden, I had to find a way to protect just the crops that the rabbits eat, and I had to protect each of them separately. Multiple smaller spaces seemed easier to protect than one big one.

I was talking to my son Alex about it, and he said, "Excellent strategy, Mom. That way if your perimeter is broken, you'll have limited assets exposed." *He was thirteen.*

I laughed and said, "Where on earth did you come up with that?"

"Minecraft," he said. It was this moment that let me feel a little better about all the video games he plays.

My new rabbit barriers needed to be small, strong, and adaptable. I change my garden through crop rotation often and any investment in structures needed to be in ones that could be moved or work double duty. I was also going to build support structures to try new growing techniques for my tomatoes and cucumbers.

This project was long overdue, and I was excited about it. I enjoy designing and building things that solve problems. I like working with my hands. And except for table saws, which I'm afraid of thanks to several bad horror movie tropes, I like working with power tools. It took about two weeks to get everything built, painted and in place. Unlike the wall project, this work required concentration and seemed to result in fewer tears. It was a welcome break.

I was out in the garden when Joni called on May 4th. This was the first time I had spoken with her since leaving Boxborough on January 4th, now four months ago. The beginning of the conversation looked like any other conversation we'd had over the last decade or so - what everyone was up to and what the weather was doing. I asked Joni how her mother was. She said she was fine. I asked If she had any travel plans. She answered vaguely about maybe seeing her mom and then changed the subject.

After about twenty minutes of meaningless small talk, she says "Oh, I have news!" like it nearly slipped her mind, "I'm moving to Indiana."

I said, "Oh, that's not news."

"Oh, did someone tell you?" She sounded surprised.

I said, "No, I just knew that you'd end up there."

Joni said she and Jeff were planning on moving to Indiana but put things on hold because of his health. She said she had purchased thirty acres of land. She said it was mostly wooded with trails that she could use for walking her dogs and that her grandson Jax could take his four-wheeler out on. The property also had a barn that Jennifer could fix up for her horse if she wanted. She was having a house custom-built. She said she finally got to have the house of her dreams.

I told her I thought that sounded wonderful, and I did. I think that being close to my sister and her kids would be a blessing for them all. I asked her what my brother thought of the move. I know he hadn't liked Indiana when they had lived there previously, and he seemed to enjoy his life now. I wondered if this move would be upsetting to him. She did not say one way or the other how he felt about it, but she did say, "He's either moving with me or I'm cutting him off." I'm assuming that meant she would stop any financial support she was giving him.

It made me wince. I mean, I had been led to believe that James was not capable of living on his own due to the autism that no one talked about. What I observed about him told a different story. Yes, he seemed naiver than most people his age, but he held a job for a decade and had managed some financial responsibilities, albeit minor. What if he could live on his own with a little help? Why not support that? I don't know. This was not my place, so I let it go.

I asked when she was planning to move.

"Oh, you know… we'll have to see how the market looks. Maybe we could move there and rent a place for a while… um... I don't know."

"When will the house start being built?" I asked.

"Well, these things take time. Who knows? And ya know with all these supply chain issues… well, there's just no saying."

"You mean they haven't given you any time frames?" I was starting to get annoyed with her vagueness.

"Yes and no, it's complicated."

She was stonewalling me. When that strategy wasn't deterring me, she derailed the conversation by telling me the story of a near-miss coyote attack that happened to her and her dogs on the trail by her house.

I walked through my garden pulling weeds, only paying half attention. I knew that she was using this story to distract me. Coyote is the archetype of trickster. My stepmother was using a story about a trickster to deflect me from seeking the truth, and the symbolism was not lost on me. I sent an energetic shout out to that coyote. And the darkest part of me got a little chuckle at the visual of my stepmother scared to death by something that could see right through her bullshit. 

We had reached the end of our awkward conversation. I said "Ok, love you."

Either she didn't hear it or ignored it and went straight for "Bye." There was something in that "bye" that sounded final. The way she drew out the long I and E sound seemed to say, "Fuck you." And then we were done.

I pulled my earbud out and kept weeding. I felt surprisingly unaffected considering how much bullshit I'd just heard. Waiting over twenty minutes to tell me the headline news and acting like "oh yeah" about it. *Bullshit*. Refusing to answer questions about the timing of her move. *Also bullshit*. The deflection and misdirection, obvious signs of stonewalling, stood out in a way that I could not even gaslight myself out of seeing. Deep inside I could feel a stirring of anger, but overall, I felt calm and non-reactionary. It was unfamiliar.

The craziest thing of all was I was acting like Jeff. The way I was walking through my garden felt like the way my father would walk through a garden. As I listened to my stepmother talk, I experienced a level of disengagement that only my father could pull off. I am horrible at even feigning disinterest, but during this conversation – especially the coyote story – I was so far elsewhere that she could have been giving me the PIN to the family millions, and I would have missed it. This wasn't natural behavior to me, but I saw my father in it. I felt like I had been body snatched.

"Jeff, what the hell? Did you just, like, possess me or something?"

He said, "I wouldn't call it *possession*. I just asserted some influence over you. You have no poker face, and I wanted to be sure that you gave her nothing."

"Um… boundaries dude!" I said, annoyed with the intrusion.

"Ok but…" he said. "What was it like?"

"What was *what* like? Possession?" I asked in response.

In my mind, I could see him walking in a thoughtful and meditative way around the circular path that surrounds my little tomato greenhouse. His steps were slow and steady. He looked at the ground as if plotting exactly where each part of his foot would meet it. Without looking up, he said, "Everything sticks to you, Beans. People toss their nonsense garbage at you, their bullshit biases and opinions, and they stick to you as if they were your own. What was it like to be like Teflon? How did it feel to let that crap slide right off you? You weren't part of the bullshit either. You were an observer. What did you see?"

I had indeed felt like an observer. I had seen more clearly than ever before. I saw the stonewalling. No, I had not made that up in my head and I did not doubt that for the first time. Three times I asked the same question, and three times I was denied. She was hiding something from me, and she wasn't going to give it up. I am sure if I pushed hard enough, she would have claimed her house was on fire to get off the phone with me before she'd fess up to whatever she was hiding.

Normally, this knowledge would have enraged me. I would have been hurt, angry, and sad. This time was different. I felt… less. I felt all the things I expected to feel, it was just less intense. It was manageable. I was being lied to and there was nothing I could do about it, and I felt okay. Those other feelings still existed, but my experience in the present was of calm and acceptance.

"It feels damn good," I said, "but you can't just body snatch me."

"Of course, I can," he said, "I'm your father, I have rights." He gave a chuckle, in a way that acknowledged that response wouldn't go over well with me. "Anyway, have you noticed how active you have been? You know, all productive and stuff?"

I said, "Yes."

He said, "That's me. I'm whispering in your ear to keep moving, to pick up that pile of clothes off the floor, to go ahead and put that dish in the dishwasher or straighten up the greenhouse because you have an extra couple of minutes. I want you to focus on nurturing this life you're creating and not on whatever other people are doing. I'm teaching you skills I failed to teach you in your youth. I'm teaching you how to feed your self-worth through the joy of maintenance," he said. "All that energy? Yeah, that's all me."

It did make sense. I had been staying super busy and had an abundance of excessive energy. He was right, my relationship to maintenance was changing. I'm more of a project planner and implementer. Upkeep is not my strong suit. This showed in the way I gardened. My favorite part of gardening is planning and seed planting. Once the garden gets going, and the weather starts getting too hot, I lose interest. Maintenance has always occurred to me as boring. Because of that, by the end of the season, my garden is a bit of a shit show. But that's ok because I also enjoy wiping the slate clean. So basically, I like the beginning and the end, but the middle is where I'm lacking interest and skill. Well, my father had those skills.

Jeff made maintenance look like an act of love. At least the things he wanted to maintain, like his plants. My father had whole rituals designed and devoted to his house plants. Each Saturday he would carve out a chunk of time to give each of them, and he had quite a few, love and attention. He had expensive taste and would buy only the finest clothes, shoes, and cars. He also did the work necessary to care for those things so that they maintained their value. He considered his care an investment. His relationships were a different story.

My inner 10-year-old hates that my father paid more attention to his goddamn plants than he did to his children (sorry plants, I know it's not your fault). In a house full of orchids, I had to be a cactus. I had to suck every ounce of love and care I could out of the air, and I lived in the desert. He straight-up neglected me. He spent more time shining his loafers than he spent engaged with me in any given week. When it was just him and I, I could deal with it. But his neglect and her contempt were too much.

I had spent so much time thinking I deserved to be neglected. Thinking I had not earned their love or care. Thinking I was fucking garbage. And none of that had to happen. So many years of self-loathing and self-destruction. Trauma that I was sure I had already passed on to my children. None of it had to happen. And he took better care of his goddamn car.

"I know, Beans."

His words broke through the rage I had just gotten in touch with.

"Listen, you gotta get over it. Yeah, I know, I'm an asshole. Hear me out." He paused as if waiting for my agreement before he would proceed.

"Get on with it," I said. I was fuming with anger but realized that his words rang true. I did not like it.

"Look, you're right, ok? I should have taken care of you. But I didn't. I have a million excuses, but no good reason. And here's the thing, so fuckin what?" He paused so that those words could sink in. I did not like them. "There's nothing I can do about what I didn't do. I'm an ethereal being, not a time traveler. I can say sorry until I'm blue in the face, and it changes nothing. What I want now is to do what I couldn't or wouldn't or didn't do then. I can teach you things. Let me help you. But… ya gotta get over it first. This is what's happening now and what is happening now is so much better than that bullshit past."

He was right. If I wanted to have a new relationship with him, I had to get over it. I couldn't do it while he was alive. I wish I could have, but I simply could not.

"How do I get over it?" I asked.

"You gotta give it up. You want acknowledgement. You want justice and fairness. And you aren't going to get them. Ever. It's fucked up, but true. Joni will never own her cruelty towards you. She believes you deserved it. Nothing will change that. Holding onto your sense of victimhood only keeps her winning. You gotta get out of the game, Beans. Give it up," he said.

Damnit, that was not what I wanted to hear. "Can't you use your non-corporeal status to, like, haunt her into doing the right thing?"

He laughed and said, "No, but she did break a promise to me and for that, I spend a lot of time sitting in the chair across from her while she reads her newspaper. I stare holes in her, reminding her of her broken oath. Drives her nuts. It's like having an itch she can't scratch. But no, I can't make her do anything. She's been set on this course for as long as I'd been ill. Likely longer. I should have known."

"Bullshit," I said, "you knew. You knew exactly what she'd do and how she would treat me. You chose to believe her words though because it was easier."

"You're damn right it was easier, Korva. I was dying." But I could tell as soon as he said that he knew it was a cop out. The whole time he was "dying" he wanted us to pretend he wasn't. I hated that. I thought it was a denial that wasted time for all of us. So now, he doesn't get to use it as an excuse for, once again, failing to protect me.

"Ok, fine. I didn't want to deal with it, and I made a fuckin mess," he said with a frustration and regret that was palpable, "I'm sorry. I want to make it right, and I need you to get over it. Not for me. I'll say sorry a million times if need be, but you must choose to let go."

"I don't know how to let go," I said.

He said, "I'll show you. You let go the same way you build, every day, one piece at a time. I will help you."

All of this was too good to be true. All I'd ever wanted was to have a loving and supportive parent/child relationship with my father and now I was having it… in my head. Part of me was well inclined to believe I was interacting with his spirit. It seemed so real. I could see him in my mind when we interacted in a way I couldn't visualize anything else. I had physical symptoms when I interacted with Jeff. My heart rate increased, and I felt… amped. I would lose track of space and time when we talked and would experience "coming out of it" when our interactions were over. Still, I had to accept that perhaps this was all one big psychological breakdown, and my symptoms may simply be a product of the anxiety I couldn't shake.

I've always had doubts when it comes to spiritual things. My natal sun, Mercury, and Venus placements are all in Pisces, which rules our connection to spirit. The sun is my ego, Mercury is my mind, and Venus is my heart. I crave spirit with my whole being. My childhood home life was atheist and spiritism was borderline mocked. Jeff, a logical Aquarius sun, and Joni, a practical Capricorn sun, both preferred things that were tangible and physical. If it couldn't be proven, it didn't exist. But religion and spirituality had always been of the utmost importance to me. I didn't know what god was, but I knew god was something. Something in the space between holding us together, connecting us, bringing us life, and taking it away. I had felt it, but I was programmed by my family to feel foolish for it. I had to fight doubt every step of the way.

So once again, I had to ask, what if it weren't real? Was I just having imaginary Jeff tell me things I want to hear? And if so, was that so bad? I'd been struggling with this since that last night I spent in Boxborough, when he first told me that I wasn't in good company with Joni and Jennifer. And once again, I chose to believe in the powerful healing nature of this experience.

What a gift. I could have a relationship, real or imaginary, with my father and let him parent me now. I was allowing my imaginary father to be the father that I always wanted. The trick now was to let him. I had to get over it and I needed to listen to his guidance. *Who could I become if I had a father that showed me love?*

"So, whaddaya say?" he said, rubbing his hands together in anticipation, "Wanna give this a shot?"

I was moved by his enthusiasm. I needed that. I had always needed it. I was afraid. It seemed so risky to invest in something that could in fact be high-level delusion. But I needed it. I needed my father. Maybe I was crazy, but I could feel the gratitude for having this experience permeating through every cell in my body. Real or not, it was calming, comforting, and healing. I was touched, deeply.

I said, "Ok, let's do this". After a long pause and through choked-back tears, I said, "Thanks, Papa."

"Papa? Huh, you've never called me that before," Jeff said.

It's true. I had always called my father by his first name. Familial relations were confusing to me when I moved in with Jeff in 1978. I mean, my mother had told me that another man, Roger, was my father. I found out he wasn't shortly after she broke up with him. Then, three nights before I flew out to live with Jeff, my mother put me on the phone with a stranger and said, "This is your dad." Calling him Jeff was easier. I think it made him more comfortable, too.

I said, "I know, but that's what I want to call you now. Ya know, sometimes."

He said, "Alright, I'll try on 'Papa' and see if I like it. You try listening to me and see if it helps. Ok?"

I smiled and said, "Ok, Papa."

Chapter Nineteen

I've never been a fan of Mother's Day. I spent my first twenty-eight years not knowing who, how, or why I'd celebrate. Then I became a mother and felt unworthy of celebration. Honestly, it was a day I dreaded. But this year was different.

I spent most of Mother's Day weekend with my friends Emily and Katie at Quinault Beach Resort and Casino on the Washington coast (not far from every *Twilight* fan's favorite, Forks, Washington). We arrived late in the evening on Friday and opted to grab a bite to eat at the restaurant and go up to our room to play card games. Saturday, we took a drive down the coast to look around and stopped for a little stroll on the beach. The Pacific Northwest coast in May isn't what most people consider a lovely trip to the beach, but that day I loved it.

The weather oscillated between sunny and stormy with average temperatures in the mid-fifties. There was a substantive breeze and the windchill made it feel much colder. The seas were rough and the sky above me was spotted with patches of brilliant golden rays shining through heavy black clouds. Looking at it made me think Mother Nature was reflecting outward what I felt on my insides. I was holding two very different feelings, similar to the dichotomy of the sky above me.

Like the darkened clouds, full to the brim, I was heavy with anger. I had been abused. Not just as a child, too. I was still being abused through lies and exclusion. I had finally seen through forty years of gaslighting and stonewalling, and it made me want to unleash a whole storm of rage. But I knew it wouldn't do anything more than fuel the narrative that I was overly sensitive, emotional, and dramatic. So, the storm in me churned with no clear outlet.

At the same time, I was beginning to see a new light in my life. Since Jeff's death, I was becoming more able to differentiate the life that I was given versus the life that I had made. Jeff, my stepmother, my sister, my mother, her parents, and whatever heartache I associated with them were from the life I was given. They were things that I had to survive. But the life that I had created was one worth surviving for.

My friends were true. My husband loved and supported me. My children were good people with kind hearts, and I had faith in my relationship with them. My life looked more and more like a gift. No, more like a reward for not only having survived the life I was given but for making a good life despite the cards I had been dealt. More than one person has noted how normal I seem given my tumultuous background. I was becoming proud of myself and my life. Perhaps this too contributed to my desire to do a better job maintaining it.

Emily and Katie reflected a part of my life that I was proud of. Emily is the friend I talked to for a major portion of my drive from Wyoming to Idaho. I met her in my mom's group. That's where I met Katie as well. The three of us ladies have tracked a lot of time and miles together. And I mean that literally. The mom's group that I started back in 2008 had many subsets to it, one of which was a tight-knit group of runners. That's where Emily, Katie, and I would find our bond. We trained together and traveled to running events together. It was fun and they were much-needed friendships.

These were two of the few women I have ever felt truly and freely myself with. My experience in early life with women had made me very leery of having relationships with them. My mother had proven herself untrustworthy when she abandoned me. I know it's more complicated than that, but that was how I experienced it. It occurred to me that my stepmother was always trying to compete with me for my father's love. I think she pitted him against me, and I think she enjoyed it like a game of chess.

These core relationships set up a pattern of attracting female friends that mimic my mother and stepmother. Any time I found a girlfriend with similar tastes and interests, we would end up in competition with one another. It was maddening. I do not like to compete. That's not to say that I don't do it, but I'd prefer not to. I don't like what it brings out in me. Plus, I'd prefer having company in my interests. Emily and Katie were good company and good friends.

Those days at the beach were refreshing. It was leisurely and fun, and it eased the tension that had been building in me since my call with Joni the week before. We headed home on Sunday, made a stop on the way for lunch, and were back in time to enjoy Mother's Day dinner. We ordered pizza from my favorite Mediterranean restaurant. It wasn't fancy but I loved it just the same.

When I was young, Mother's Day was just another day to loathe. I had never had anyone to pick me up and brush me off when I fell. Mother's Day reminded me of that, every year until I gave birth. I spent every Mother's Day after that feeling unworthy and shameful of myself as a mother. Until this year. Yes, those two things were still there. But growing in me, just like the rays of gold breaking through the blackened sky, was gratitude for the life I had created and the gift of the people in it.

I had my garden planted by mid-May. It was a little late for some of the crops, but I was confident it would all work out. I was still amped up and full of can-do energy. I seemed to be working non-stop on either home improvements or everyday maintenance. I had never been so on top of my chores. I felt good about it, but I had to be honest with myself about the fact that this was not sustainable. All this activity was being fueled by crippling anxiety. The only thing that kept my angst manageable was if I kept working. "Just keep making it better," was what the voice in my head would say on repeat. So, I did.

My sister's birthday is in the middle of May. We had not spoken since the end of March, when she had called me looking for plant recommendations. We started that conversation talking about everyday life stuff. We shared how the kids were and how work was going. She mentioned something about being excited to be having new California Closets installed soon. I wondered where she was getting the money for that. Perhaps her business was doing better than she was letting on. *Perhaps her mother is paying for it.*

Then, things became more serious. She acknowledged that she had been "off" and was starting to understand why. She opened up about how she had regretted her handling of Jeff's last years and that she may have been envious or resentful of the way I had dealt with it.

I remember the first conversation Jennifer and I had after Jeff shared his diagnosis. We had both expressed morbid hopefulness at the idea that being faced with his mortality might make our father more interested in fostering relationships with us. Where Jennifer and I differed in response was that I reached out to him, while she waited for him to reach out to her. Neither approach bore the fruit either of us had hoped for. My approach had created a slight change in my relationship with Jeff, but it was too little too late. At least I knew that the actions I took would not leave me with the regret of inaction. I think that was what she was feeling.

She also mentioned something that had happened while we were in Boxborough that had been bothering her. She said the night Greg came for dinner, as he was leaving, he hugged me and said, "Beans, you were always my favorite." She was upset by this. I didn't know what to say. While it may have been a little insensitive of him to say, I don't think he was trying to be mean. Greg had been like a father to me when I was young. She had interacted with him a little more than half a dozen times, and mostly in the last eight to ten years.

I felt both empathetic and annoyed. She was hurt and I understood, but really, did she always have to be the favorite? Couldn't I win this one? But I let it go. I had been dealing with real issues, and this seemed petty in comparison. But to Jennifer this must have been a big deal. The last thing she said about it was, "Well, at least I'll never have to see him again." While I wanted to know more about what that meant, she was clearly distraught, so I did not push the matter.

Even with the tension around being "Greg's Favorite," this felt like the most normal conversation we'd had in a long time. We would exchange a text every couple of weeks after that and things seemed more normal, but the conflict I had felt didn't resolve. Something was going on and I knew it. The more time passed, the more I began to see that conversation in March as a ruse. I think she was being vulnerable to get me to open up and share my real thoughts with her. She's very intuitive, so I'm sure she knew I was being guarded and keeping my true feelings close to the vest.

When I woke up the morning of her birthday, I remembered how she hadn't reached out to wish me a happy birthday until the last possible moment and then was tired and disinterested when we spoke. I thought about doing the same. *I should make her wait for my well wishes.* I should treat her just like she's treating me. But I decided against it. That's just not the person I wanted to be, and I still loved my sister. I sent her a message as soon as I had thought to, which was 6:40 a.m. "Happy Birthday! I hope you have a great day! Let me know when is a good time to chat."

She responded that night at seven o'clock pacific time with, "Thank you!! Sorry… serious delays over here today. What do you have going on Sunday?"

Call me petty but it took twelve hours to send that response? Now, I know my sister has her phone in her hand every waking hour of her day and I am supposed to believe that that was the first time in twelve hours that she could respond with three pathetic sentences. I'm sure she sent at least twenty personal texts that day. *At least.* She was making the choice not to respond. I had started to notice in the few weeks before Jeff's death and since, her response to my texts have been getting slower and slower. Hell, sometimes she straight-up ghosted me which was an all-new and annoying behavior. It was difficult to *not* read anything into it.

I responded to her right away and said, "Yes, I have work to do but I'll be able to make time." I did have a ton of work to do.

Those messages were exchanged on Thursday. Saturday, I sent another message trying to pinpoint a time. We settled on eleven o'clock, her time, on Sunday. That was two hours earlier in my time zone, perfect for talking and still being able to get to work at a reasonable hour.

Sunday came along and I tried calling shortly after nine o'clock my time and my call went straight to voicemail. She then sent a text saying that her kids made her take them to IHOP and that she would call me from the car when she was done. As promised, about an hour later she called from her noisy car, obviously distracted. I told her to wait and call me when she got home. It sounded like she did not like that but agreed to it anyway.

I was already feeling like I was getting the runaround. She made plans on top of our plans and did not bother to tell me until I was trying to call. Then she calls from a car full of people knowing damn well that would be an awful time and place to catch up. These occurred as avoidance tactics, but what was she avoiding?

She called me from home about thirty minutes later. She was sniffly and stuffy, sounding like she was either sick or had been crying. I hadn't noticed it when she called from the car. I asked if she was all right.

"Oh… yeah," she said in a shrugging-it-off sort of way. She asked me how I was.

"How am I with what?" I said with a chuckle, "With regular life, or grief, or existential crisis?"

She said, "Let's start easy. Regular life."

I told her regular life was good. I had a ton of energy and was getting a lot of work done. I told her about my garden remodel. The kids were well. Everything was… good. I asked about her regular life. She told me she had been very busy with the kids and work and… everything. According to her, she was either running around in a frenzy or sitting catatonic on the couch. It was relatable.

She asked how I was doing with grief. I instantly broke down crying. At this stage in mourning, I was always a heartbeat away from crying. In many ways, my grief had gotten worse in the last couple of months.

I said, "I'm a mess. I cry every day. It… it just hurts." I couldn't say any more. Besides, there wasn't anything else to say.

She said, "Oh honey, I'm so sorry."

Not gonna lie, my first thought was "Bitch, I'm not your honey." I don't know why, but damn, that rubbed me the wrong way. After taking a brief pause to compose myself, I asked how she was doing with her grief.

She said, "I'm fine, really. I barely think about him."

I felt gutted by those words. I pictured Jeff in the seat next to me. He was slouched slightly in his chair, arms folded across the front of him, head hung heavy. I could see the hurt and regret on his face and had to fight back a wave of crying that would have been messy. I just said, "Oh."

After about twenty minutes of conversation full of starts and stops and palpable awkwardness, I finally said, "We may as well discuss the elephant in the room. Your mother told me about the move to Indiana."

"I wasn't avoiding anything, we just hadn't gotten there yet," she snapped.

I thought, "Uh-huh. Let me get this straight, this big thing happening that will change your everyday life, substantially, wasn't the headliner? I wonder why?" I shrugged it off and moved on.

I asked what she thought and felt about it. Her answers went something like "Oh, yeah, it's ok." Any question I asked about the move or the property, she avoided answering and changed the subject. I wasn't asking for information that her hairstylist didn't already have, but she wouldn't give me even the slightest detail about this move. More stonewalling. What in the fuck? It was infuriating but I had to move on.

I asked how our brother was doing and what he thought of the move. Again, I didn't get the impression that he was a fan of Indiana.

She said she didn't know. She hadn't talked to him. She said, "As far as I know, they (being Joni and James) had only had one five-minute long conversation about the move."

I said, "What the fuck? That's weird."

She said, "Why? They're both avoidant. He probably prefers it that way."

And I said, "Or he doesn't know how to talk about it… or is afraid to talk about it." Then I abruptly cut myself off and said, "But ya know what? That's not my business." Jeff had warned me to stay out of the situation with my brother and stepmother because it had too much scapegoat potential. I didn't need any more blame put on me, and it wouldn't help James anyway.

I tried to lighten the mood and ask about something fun. "Hey, you got any good plans coming up? Ya know, something you're looking forward to?"

She said, "Yeah, I'm going to California next month. This year marks the twentieth anniversary of us leaving there and I thought I would make the pilgrimage back. We'll stay in Orange County for a few days and then meet… um… them… in… uhh… San Diego and ah… be there a couple of days…." She just stopped talking.

"Oh. That sounds nice. I hope you have a good trip," I said and dropped it. Whatever just happened was so awkward. It occurred to me that there was more about my sister's current life that she could not share with me than she could. I made an excuse to cut the conversation short.

Prior to hanging up, she said, "Love you."

"Do you?" I thought. I held my tongue and considered the long-term impacts of my next words. "I love you, too," I said.

We hung up and I exhaled like I had been holding my breath underwater for the last thirty minutes. I was hurt. I was angry. I had to keep that to myself. What if I was wrong? I did not doubt who my stepmother was. I saw who she was a long time ago. I simply had to remember. But my sister was different. I did not want to believe she could hurt me. I loved her. I was invested in her. I had trusted her. The risk of loss clouded my judgment.

As I sat processing our call, I remembered what she had said about Jeff. Her words went through my mind. *"I'm fine, really. I barely think about him."* While I could tell she wanted to come across as cool and nonchalant, she seemed cold and smug. She reminded me of her mother. I didn't know whether she was lying about how she truly felt. How could she have moved on so quickly?

My mind returned to Jeff in the seat next to me. He had changed his position, in that his feet were up on the chair across from him and he had slouched deeper into his seat. His arms still crossed in front of him, but now his chin rested upon his chest. Without moving his head, he looked at me from the corner of his eye. He looked shameful and embarrassed. He said, "You can't blame her."

He paused for a long while. I sat waiting. I could tell he was trying to boil down a lot of information and I had no idea what to say.

He said, "You kids got stuck in the middle of an epic power struggle, a real-life *War of the Roses*." He pursed his lip, and his eyes took on a fierceness that was hard to read. I could also see the glint of a tear forming. It looked like a combination of rage and regret. "You and your sister just experienced it differently, but it was the same damn battle."

"It started with you, Beans, but not because of you. When Joni and I got together, she said she didn't want children, and she agreed to leave raising you to me. It wasn't long into living with us that she changed her tune. She started having issues with my parenting… methods." I could see waves of realization rolling across the expression on his face. He exhaled sharply out his nose and continued, "Shit, I didn't have a method. You and I were just doing our thing, and it seemed to work. We got along well. Your grades were good, your chores got done, and you were a nice person. Wasn't that enough? I mean, I know there was a ton of shit I should have been doing that I wasn't, and I've got no good excuse for it, but things weren't bad."

He looked over at me, as if searching for confirmation. I said nothing. He continued, "Well, in her mind, they were bad. Shameful even. You didn't fit the mold, and the more she tried to shove you into it, the worse things got. But I did not see that. I just saw you doing exactly what she predicted you would do."

I said, "Yeah, that's how narcissistic abuse works."

He paused as if debating whether that tangent was worthwhile. I'm assuming it was not because he continued with, "Yeah, I don't know about that, but I do know this… you were used as a pawn to make one person right and one person wrong. It was a power struggle that fucked you up. I'm sorry."

While I never expected an apology, I had always wanted one. My father had made choices that led to my suffering. Yes, I didn't make anything better with the way I behaved, but I honestly thought there was no real path to redemption for me. My stepmother wanted me to be a different person. She didn't like me, and she wanted to control me. It was his choices that forced me into that situation. This apology acknowledged that it wasn't all my fault, and he knew it. This is an acknowledgment I'll never get from my stepmother.

Joni had told me a couple of times after Jeff's diagnosis that I should not expect any deathbed confessions or apologies from my father and if I go seeking them it will just make him angry with me. I wondered why someone would say such a thing. Was she looking out for me, or was there another reason?

As if he was reading my mind, Jeff said, "It's because she was afraid of it. She wanted to make sure you didn't get any closer to me."

"What do you mean? Why?" I asked.

He exhaled hard through his nose again, "Ack, I can't… that's for another day. Let's get back to your sister."

He shook off the brief derailment and got back into storyteller mode. "So, about four years into our marriage, she got pregnant. She says she wants kids now… and I'm like what the fuck? She'd been harping on me for a good few years about what a shitty parent I am, and now she wants to have kids with me…. Why?" He stopped, looking off to somewhere in his past and shaking his head. "What was I supposed to do? I don't know if she meant to get pregnant or not. But the next thing I knew, she was. I couldn't ask her to get an abortion, but I didn't like it. I mean, she keeps telling me what a shitty parent I am. Now I'm going to do it with her and hear shit about it for the next eighteen years. It was a mess, Beans. And the whole time she's still harping on me about you."

"I'm sorry," I said but added, "I mean, I'm sorry that you went through that. I'm sure it sucked."

"Yeah, it did," he said, "But you're right, you shouldn't be sorry. Those were my choices." He continued, "Well, that first pregnancy miscarried, and she was devastated. She said she wanted to try again and this time I gave in and agreed. Again, what was I supposed to do? She was so sad, and I wanted her to be happy." He shook his head, "Fuck." I could feel his regret. Not for agreeing to have a child, but for a million other things.

"Anyway, then came your sister and, for a while, things were good between Joni and me. She was happy. I mean, she still harped on me about you, but at least she had a distraction. Then, as your sister grew up into such a "good girl" it only served to prove how bad you were, Beans, and further, how bad I was as a parent. By the time your sister was old enough to require complex parenting, I had been fully disqualified, and my attitude was like, 'Oh yeah, if I suck so bad at this then do it yourself.'

Which ironically is exactly what she wanted. I got cut out and I let it happen," he said, that last sentence bringing up a choke of tears.

"She hates me. She's hated me for a long time," he said.

"Who?" I asked.

"Your sister," he said with a sigh, slumping deeper into his chair.

"She doesn't hate you," I said.

"Oh yes, she does," he said and there was no arguing with him about it. "The power struggle between Joni and I used you kids to prove which one of us was better, which one of us was right. You and your sister responded to it differently. You tried desperately to connect with me, and she disconnected. I'm sure she got plenty of commiseration and agreement for her stance," he stopped and gave me a slight side-eyed glare as if to say he knew I was one of her commiserates.

And I gave a look back that said, "Yeah, and….??" He moved on.

"Anyway, her mother didn't do anything to help the situation. I think she encouraged it. Your sister has one side of the story. I would have told her my side, but she had to ask."

I cut him off there. "That's bullshit, she was a kid. How was she supposed to ask?"

"How was I supposed to tell her?"

"Tell her what?" I said with the tone showing increased annoyance.

"Tell her that her mother was the reason I drank," he said.

I said, "Say what?" and gave him the ol' gimme a break look.

He said, "Well, she wasn't *the* reason, but don't think you're the only one that got abused by her. She knew all my vulnerabilities and used every one of them against me. But nobody saw it. Meanwhile, I wore my dysfunction like a merit badge. It was an easy job though… getting people to hate me."

He was right. As far as I could see, she had painted herself as his victim, his enabler. But what if that weren't true? What if he was the victim, or her enabler, or another scapegoat?

He said, "Your sister hating me gave Joni more control."

"Control of what?" I asked.

"The narrative," he said. "She wants to control people's perspectives, and ultimately their behavior. She's in a constant state of calculating and making moves. It's why she loves chess. As long as I was the bad guy, she was the good guy. Just like as long as you were the bad kid, I was the bad parent… your sister was a good kid, and she was a good parent. Et cetera and so on. It was all part of her-"

He stopped abruptly, paused, sat more upright in his chair, and said, "Look, I'm not going to confess anyone else's sins. This is a woman that I loved and that I banked a whole lot of time with. Her sins are hers and I will leave them. What matters here is this…," he took a deep breath and exhaled it forcefully, "…I failed you girls. I should have protected you and didn't. And I should have shown your sister more love. It was what she wanted. I knew it, but I just didn't give it to her."

"Why the hell not?" I asked.

"The same reason she didn't give it to me. We're a lot alike, your sister and I," he said.

That's their Cancer moons at play. Jennifer and I had discussed this very dynamic while driving to the airport to pick up Josh. The moon rules our emotions and how we express and manage them. Jeff and Jennifer had the same avoidant attachment styles, and when they get hurt, they get mean.

Changing the subject, I asked, "What do I do now?" His issues with Jennifer were his and I was done hearing about it. "There's obviously something going on with those two and I want to know what."

He said, "I can't get involved."

"What the fuck do you mean you can't get involved?! This is all your goddamn fault!" I said with a fury that surprised even me. The stress of knowing that something was afoot had taken its toll on me.

He let me calm down a moment and said, "I have commitments, Beans. And loyalties. Unfortunately, I have competing loyalties. I'm doing my best. I'll do everything I can to guide and help you, but I can't outright tell you things that I've promised not to tell. If the tables were turned, it's what you would want, too."

He was right. Dammit.

He continued, "Listen, you'll figure it out without me telling you. There are answers out there. And if I know you, Beans, I know you'll find them. Truth always finds its way to you, or you to it. I've always thought that was interesting about you. Inconvenient at times, but always interesting."

He was not wrong. But the truth does not exactly "find me." It was more like little subconscious whispers lead me to *it*. I see the clues and hear the hints. My gut always knows when lies are told. Sometimes it just takes me a while to put the pieces together. My gut said that there was something about this property transaction that was making everyone act shady. But what? I mean, she bought a property and is moving. What's the big deal? Why all the stonewalling? To find the truth, I had to find that property.

The Pieces

Chapter Twenty

I would have made an excellent stalker if I wasn't so afraid of being called crazy. But the truth is when it comes to finding information, especially forbidden information, I am relentless. To me, the only things we can truly hide are the things we keep locked up in our heads. As soon as action is taken or words are spoken, it leaves a mark in the world and that mark can be found. There was a real property transaction out there that could be seen, and I was going to find it.

Step one of the unofficial stalker's guide to uncovering some bullshit: assess what you already know. What did I know about this property? I knew it was in Indiana and reasonably close to my sister. I knew the property was 30 acres. I knew it was wooded, that there were no homes built on it, but there was a barn. That, my friends, is a lot of information.

I started with a quick search on the tax assessor's site for the counties surrounding Jennifer's home. No properties were listed under either Jeff or Joni's name. Then I searched Zillow for properties sold since January of 2022, the month after Jeff died. I figured that was likely a little too soon, but it didn't hurt to check. I found no thirty-acre property bought in 2022 in the entire southern half of Indiana. I conducted searches in as many ways as I could think of given what I knew and found nothing. I had hit a dead end and had to walk away for a while. At least until inspiration would tell me where to look next.

Several days later, I was out in my garden and remembered the conversation I had with my sister after the now-infamous Thanksgiving Incident of 2018. It was the one I wasn't invited to. In the message I sent to my sister, father, and stepmother confronting them about excluding me, I wrote:

"...when we (Jennifer, Joni, and I) were in San Francisco and your (my parents') will got brought up, things got super awkward. That shit was palpable. Is there something around the administration of your estate that you are concerned will be a conflict?"

In the post-incident conversation that followed, the one where Jennifer played handler to her overly sensitive sister, she mentioned that it was coincidental I brought up the will. *More like synchronistic if you ask me.* Jennifer said that Joni and Jeff had seen a lawyer to have one written up the Tuesday before Thanksgiving. She said that she was the executor and trustee. Jennifer and I were both slated for thirty percent, and my brother for forty percent of the estate's worth once my stepmother and father had both passed. James was getting a higher percentage because he had greater need. I understood that.

I remember I laughed and said, "I'm not getting any of that money."

She said, "Of course you will! You'll never be written out."

But I knew, if Jeff went first, there was no way I'd get a dime. Especially since, after the Thanksgiving Incident, I had intended to go no contact with Jeff and Joni, maybe even with Jennifer, too. I was so tired of feeling left out, lied to, and misunderstood. The only reason I resumed a relationship with them was because of Jeff's cancer diagnosis.

I look back now and wonder, how they happened to draw up a will just a couple of months before my father was diagnosed as terminally ill. Did they know in November of 2018 and wait to tell me for three months? *Maybe they didn't want to "ruin my holidays."* My parents have lied to me or kept things from me under the guise of "not hurting my feelings" so many times. I doubted everything they said. Never mind the toll it takes on a person to be repeatedly lied to by the two people on earth you are supposed to be able to trust the most.

The memory of the conversation with Jennifer about Jeff and Joni's estate dislodged a block in my investigation. If they had a trustee, Jennifer, that means that they had put the property in a trust. Just two weeks before Jeff died, Bryan and I had finalized our will and created a trust for our property. Our property is no longer in our names, it's in our trust's name.

I dropped my shovel and ran into the house. I grabbed my laptop and pulled up the land manager's link for the county where Boxborough is located. I entered my parents' address. Boom! There it was. Not only did I find the name of the trust, I also got to see the document that named my sister sole trustee.

I hate to admit this, but it stung. Tradition would suggest that the oldest child gets to be executor and trustee. To hear my sister talk, it's a job she doesn't want. Maybe she's lying. I don't know. I do know it was a job I would have been honored to have. But I wasn't *her* oldest daughter, and that hurt. Forty years with Joni and she still didn't consider me her family, never mind her daughter. I hated that a part of me even wanted her to want me. *Ick!* I shook that feeling off and got back to business.

I had what I needed to find the property now. I went back to the county records in Indiana, put in the name, and boom… there it was. But something didn't add up. There were three property listings with two addresses. I pulled up the one at the top of the list. The first thing I saw was the transfer of ownership date: August 11, 2021.

Um, you wanna say what? They bought this property last year? My stepmother had said that she and Jeff were planning to move to Indiana, but it was just a plan. Now I knew it was much more. And I knew that they had *both* straight-up lied to me. So did my sister.

I spoke with Jeff in September of 2021, a month after his retirement (and the purchase of this property, it would appear) and three months prior to his death. I asked him what his plans were for his non-working life. He said he did not know and awkwardly brushed it off. I now know that he was also hiding the truth about his health from me, too. He was about to start chemotherapy again. I wish I had known then that this conversation was the last one we would have.

And he fucking lied to me. Twice.

I pictured Jeff sitting on the couch by my window.

"How fucking dare you?" I stared daggers at him. "How fucking DARE YOU!?" Those last words left my throat burning and raw. The anger I felt was nuclear, like I could have gone off and wiped out all living things within a twenty-mile radius. But instead, I cried. Again. And it was wretched. The kind of cry that rocks your whole body and leaves you tired.

When I regained my calm, what felt like a very long time later, I asked him why. "Why lie to me about this? You knew that I knew you'd move to Indiana. Why lie to me?"

He said, "You know that answer, Beans."

I took several deep breaths and sat for a minute. I did know. "Joni told you to. She said it was for James. She didn't think he could handle it. Or that's what she said…"

He said, "Bingo. Yeah, she didn't want him to know yet, and so you couldn't know either."

Many years ago, I made a choice, and it impacted how "in the know" I was allowed to be. In May of 2002, during a visit with them, my parents told me they would be moving from California to Indiana over the summer. When I asked what my sister thought of it, Joni responded with, "Oh, she doesn't know yet. We'll tell her a couple of weeks before the move. Don't say anything." I was told that they didn't want to upset her prematurely, but I think it was more like they didn't want to deal said upset prematurely.

Well, I'm sure that there are plenty of people who would agree with my parents' handling of the situation, but I did not. I thought that my sister, who was fourteen at the time, deserved to know about this move in real time. To me, that is a respectful way to treat a member of your family. And I told them so. I said that I would not tell Jennifer, but that I would not lie to her. If she asked me outright, I'd tell her to go talk to her parents about it. I was not going to lie to my sister.

Now Joni uses that as the reason to lie to me and hide things from me. I won't lie for her, and that equals disloyalty in Joni's mind. I'm okay with that. My stepmother didn't want my brother to know about the move, and she used that as her excuse to lie to me. She'd say that it was in his best interest. That he shouldn't have to deal with his father passing *and* know she was going to drag him back to Indiana.

"She knows that he's a thirty-year-old man, right? Not a fourteen-year-old girl," I said through clenched teeth. "But I still wouldn't have gone out of my way to tell him if you had been FUCKING HONEST WITH ME!!" I stopped and took a couple of breaths to regain my cool. "I didn't tell Jennifer, and I wouldn't have told James either. You knew that. What the fuck, Jeff?"

He got squirmy. "Yeah… I dunno, Beans," he rubbed the back of his head as he spoke. "She said don't tell you. Do you have any idea what kinda shit show I'd have dealt with if I had told ya?" He squirmed some more. "I didn't want to lie, but… I just…eh… you know, it's… ah." With that *ah* he exhaled, emptying his lungs completely, and sank into his seat. All the squirming stopped. He sat very still for a few moments.

"I got no reason," he said. "I just… didn't want to deal with it. And…" He paused, his eyes welling with tears, guilt, and shame, "…it was easier. It was easier to lie to you. Even though I knew you would figure it out. Even though I knew it would hurt you. It was just… easier. I knew you would keep loving me no matter what kinda bullshit I put you through. So, it was… just… easier.”

Every part of me wanted to scream, *“Fuck you! Fuck you, you fucking fuck!”* I wanted to kick him and keep kicking him. But he sat there, sad and pathetic, slouched in his seat looking like a weak and wounded animal. He was right. I could not hate him. And I hated myself for that. I did not want to be someone who was easy to hurt. I did not want to be expendable.

I took a deep, cleansing breath, wiped off my tear-soaked face, and looked at him. “I can’t,” I said, shaking with rage. “I can’t do this right now.”

I turned and went downstairs to Bryan’s office. “You will never believe this bullshit,” I said.

He looked up from his computer wide eyed. My husband loves gossip. “What bullshit?” he asked, hoping for some good dirt.

“The property my parents bought in Indiana closed last fucking August. They all fucking lied to me. Jeff lied when I asked about what he was doing after retirement. Joni lied to me when I asked her what she might do now that Jeff was gone. And my fucking sister lied to me when I asked her if she knew what her mother would do now that her father was dead. The whole fuckin lot of them, liars.”

“Wait, what are you talking about?” he asked, clearly confused.

“Oh, this whole property purchase situation has been eating at me, so I did a bunch of fishing and found the property purchase online. She fuckin lied.”

“How did you find it?” he asked, still looking puzzled.

"Stalker skills. Anyway, that's beside the point. What the hell am I supposed to do with this?" I was angry and paced back and forth. "My friggin 'sister, Bryan… my friggin *half-sister*… lied to my goddamn face. I can only imagine the depths of this."

"How do you know your sister knew? Maybe she didn't," he said.

"*Half. My half-sister,*" I hissed at him. "Oh, come on. Joni isn't the kind of idiot to purchase thirty acres of land twenty minutes from her daughter without making sure said daughter was planning to stay there. Jennifer knew," I said, the disgust in my voice was clear. *How could she do this to me?*

"Why?" I asked him, sounding more sorrowful than I had when I walked into the room. "Why do they do this to me?" I asked as my head fell, and I began to sob.

He got up and came over to me. He asked if I wanted a hug. I appreciated him asking because often when I am upset, I don't want to be touched. But this time I did. He held me while I ugly cried. I just could not understand what I had done to deserve this treatment. Especially from my sister – strike that, my *half-sister*. She lied to me. She participated in hiding something from me. She knew while I was there, while my father was dying, and after. How could she do that and then claim to be someone who loved me?

The anger began to override my ability to be touched, and I think Bryan could pick up on that. He let go and I began pacing. "Goddamnit, I'm just so fucking mad. What should I do? I can't just let them get away with this shit."

"What can you do?" he said. I couldn't tell by his tone if that was a real question or a statement of resignation.

"Umm… fuck… I don't know," I said with sharpness, wanting to pick up the nearest computer monitor and throw it against the wall.

What could I do? I had no legal grounds to do anything. Just because something is unjust, does not make it illegal. I could confront Joni and Jennifer. I could tell them that I knew they were lying to me, but to what avail? I knew that they would turn it around and it would all be my fault. I would be told that they lied to me because they had to. I said that I wouldn't lie for them, so now they had no choice but to stop telling me things.

What a fucked-up thing to do, asking your kids to lie for you. I can see asking someone to not repeat information, sure. I wouldn't share another person's secrets, but I can't commit to lying for another person. And I would never ask my kids to lie to a loved one for me. Damn. It's dirty. But I had to get over it.

"Get over it" played on repeat for several moments in my mind. Then something clicked. I flashed back to the vision I had earlier this spring about my stepmother clutching her bag and waving off someone's concerns, as she sat across from the big wooden desk, saying, "She'll get over it." Was this it? Was this the thing I'd get over?

I went back to staying busy around the house to keep my mind off them. It rarely worked though. I could not stop thinking about them and what they were doing. Then, about a week after my first revelation, while once again working out in the yard, I remembered something. There were three property listings, and I had only looked at one. What was that all about?

While I didn't drop my shovel and run inside this time, the next opportunity I had, I pulled up the county website to take a look-see. The first property I pulled up had a closing date of August 11, 2021, the same as the one I had seen a few days prior. The second property listing closed on February 2, 2022. That's weird. Why make two separate purchases for this property?

These tax assessor documents didn't have the descriptive information I wanted about these properties, so I checked Zillow. The first property I pulled up was the one sold on or about August 11th. It was as she described it, wooded with trails perfect for horseback riding or four-wheeling. Except, it was just twenty acres. She said she had purchased thirty. I scrolled down further to see that that property was under contract on June 16, 2021. So, they had lied to me for almost a year.

The second and third properties listed with the county were sold as one plot. I could also tell by the description that both properties were being sold by the same people and had been on the market for the same amount of time. This one was ten acres, and it had a barn on it. The barn that Joni said that Jennifer could "fix up if she wanted." Hmmm. I scrolled down further. The transaction history was… interesting.

The ten-acre property was listed for sale in September of 2020. It was removed from the market a couple of times and showed many price changes, but there had been no pending contracts until December 22, 2021. The day after my father was put in hospice care. On this date, Zillow showed a "pending sale." The day before he died. After fifteen months on the market, somebody out of the clear fucking blue put an offer on this property adjacent to the property they had already bought. Unbelievable. The history then shows the property was relisted and put under contract again on January 10th, with a closing date of January 21st.

It looked shady to me. What are the odds that someone else offered to buy that property the day after he was put in hospice care and pretty much given a death sentence? What are the fucking odds? This can't be real. Did my stepmother reach out about buying this land as soon as she found out he was as good as dead?

Oh, no, no, no, no, no. Oh no! My heart beat like a Taiko drummer was wailing on my chest. I thought that perhaps someone could have made an offer on the house, and maybe it fell through, and then she made the January offer. But that wouldn't matter. Given the timing of the purchase, either way this played out, my stepmother and sister were discussing this while I was there. My father had just died, and they were scheming behind my back in the next fucking room.

I thought of conjuring up imaginary Jeff to answer for this but remembered that he couldn't rat her out. Fine time to get a moral compass, Dad. So, I stormed down to Bryan's office.

"Oh my god, Bryan, you're never gonna believe this *shit*," I said. This time he didn't look up with as much hopeful curiosity as last time. He seemed to know instinctively that it was bad news. "She bought ten of that thirty acres of land the day before Jeff friggin' died. Or within a few days of him dying. Or some shady shit. But it's the property with the barn. Why did she need a barn? Why wait to buy that property? What the hell is going on?"

I was ranting like a rabid lunatic. Bryan just listened. And again, I asked him what I was supposed to do.

He was calm in his response, "Korva, I'm struggling to be a grown-up and give you useful advice here, because what I want to do is go curb-stomp some folks for you. But that's not your style. So, I'll say this… something I think may help you or inspire you… sometimes the best revenge is a life well lived."

I gave him a look that expressed being impressed and he quickly added, "Yeah, I didn't make that up. I heard it somewhere. Doesn't matter though because it fits. Go live a good life. That'll show 'em."

I'll give Bryan a ton of credit, for there were too many times he watched me willingly walk into certain heartache with my family. He would do his best to discourage the actions he knew would not give me what I wanted. He knew calling them out on lies or mistreatment would get me nowhere. He knew no matter how hard I tried to make things work, that my efforts would not be matched. And, when I inevitably did what I did and got hurt, he was there to support me. He never once said I told you so.

He was able to see the situation and what it brought out in me in a way I simply could not. He could see the desperation. He would say that it only came out when my parents were involved.

In his words, "Your family throws you scraps, and you thank them because you're starving."

He's an Aries, he doesn't mince words. And he was 100% right. Deep down, that was exactly how I felt. He also knew what I needed to hear. I could aspire to live a good life as a means of seeking revenge. I had done it before back in Delaware, many moons ago, and I would do it again.

An image of Jeff crossed my mind. His facial expression suggested that he liked this advice. I did not want to deal with him right now, plus I didn't want to get lost in that conversation with Bryan right there. He had no idea that I was having an imaginary relationship with my dad. I didn't know how on earth I'd explain it.

Go live your best life. It was solid advice. I guess that's what I had been doing since I'd gotten home from Boxborough. Being active and getting work done felt good. My overall attitude toward my life, aside from this bullshit with Joni and Jennifer, was optimistic. I was feeling more and more grateful for the life I had. I could see how that would seem like getting revenge on someone who wished you ill. It was a thought I would ponder for days to come.

Good advice aside, this still didn't help me figure out what to do with them. I knew I had to at least wait until I was less angry to talk to them, but I wondered what good that would do. I couldn't believe a word they said. They have shown a consistent willingness to lie to me; so, why would that ever change? This shit's been going on for forty years. Why stop now?

The words "forty years" ran through my head for the next week. Sometimes I'd have clear thoughts like, "After forty years she still couldn't love me, or respect me, or care about me." But other times I would just have the words *"forty years forty years forty years"* running like a chant in the back of my head. Then, once again, while working out in my garden, I was struck by another vision.

It was Joni. She was in a restaurant or formal dining space. It was daytime. A bank of tall windows was behind her, and her image was strongly backlit. The tables were large and round with white table clothes. She had just taken a sip of her wine and was placing her glass very intentionally back on the table in front of her. She pursed her lips and said, "I've been forced to have a relationship with her for the last forty years, I just don't think I want to do it anymore. I'm not even sure I like her."

Then the image changed, and she was somewhere else. This time it was in a more casual environment, likely someone's home. The lights were dim, and she was once again drinking wine. She said, "Look. I just don't like her. I've been dealing with her shit for forty years and I don't want to do it anymore." The image then changed to standing in someone's kitchen, with her saying similar words. In the last scene I saw, she referred to me as the "forty-year-stain on her life."

When I came to, I was sitting on the retaining wall of my garden. My breath heavy and my heart beating hard. These experiences wiped me out. I had to steady myself. I focused on the sounds around me. I could hear birds in the trees, my chickens scratching around, and the juvenile crows in the backyard fighting.

"She doesn't intend to have a relationship with you." Jeff's voice startled me. "As soon as my days were numbered, she was done with you." He was standing, leaning on the wall that I was sitting on. His gaze was fixed on a stone that he absent-mindedly rolled around with his right foot. His arms were crossed on his chest in front of him. "But she kept up appearances... she had me fooled."

I said, "Well, that's fuckin grand." I started to get up and walk away.

"I'm sorry. I didn't know. I thought.... I don't know... that maybe things really were... different..." his voice trailed.

I nearly sprained my eyes rolling them and said, "How could you not know? Even Greg knew."

I had spoken with my father's best friend, Greg, a couple of weeks prior. I had sent him a text to let him know I was thinking of him, and he said, "Give me a call, Beans." So, I did. It was before I knew the specifics about the property sales history, but after I had spoken to my sister. All I could do was catch him up with the fact that Joni was moving to Indiana, which he had already known since August of 2021, and that Jennifer and Joni were acting weird.

During that conversation he asked if Jeff had made sure I was taken care of. I assumed he meant financially. I said, "No, not that I know of. I mean, supposedly I'm still in the will, but everything goes to her first. And now that he's gone, she can change who it goes to next."

He was put off by that. He said, "Did he really trust her to take care of you?"

He also suggested that Jeff not wanting me to come around in his last months may have been because Joni would be mad to have me there. I figured he knew something I didn't know, but if he wasn't offering up specifics, I wasn't pushing it. I didn't want to ask him to breach some kind of confidence he may have had with my father. But Greg expressing distrust alone spoke volumes.

"Look," Jeff said, back in the garden. "She said she would be fair."

Just then, I flashed into a vision very similar to the one I had of my sister a while back. I was in the backseat of an SUV. It was dark and raining. My father got into the passenger's side door. This time I could see the driver. It was Joni. Jeff had his seat pushed back far enough to rest his right foot on his left knee. His left arm crossed his chest, and he smoothed his mustache, as usual, with his right hand. He was pensive and nervous. And he looked tired and weak.

They sat in silence for what felt like forever as she drove. He gazed out the window, deep in thought. He finally took a deep breath and released it with anxious force. He took another softer breath and exhaled out of his nose. "Just..." another deep breath, "Just… promise me you won't fuck her over."

She responded with, "How could I fuck her over? Come on, she'll get her fair share."

I snapped out of it, this time because I wanted to. I felt a little ill though.

"Damnit, Jeff, it would be easier if you could just tell me this shit."

To which he responded, "I can't. I already told you that."

I mulled over what I had seen a couple of times. "You mean to tell me that was enough for you to trust her? She didn't even fucking promise!"

I was on fire. I thought back to that conversation I had with her a couple of months prior to my father's death. She was calling to tell me he was back on chemo, and we had to cancel our Christmas plans. I had asked her to promise to tell me if Jeff's cancer had become terminal. She said some bullshit like, "Chemo never killed anyone, Korva." *I hated the way she said my name, always with a hint of disgust.* And what the hell kind of answer is that?

"She was stonewalling you. Just like she did to me. *Fuuuuuuck*," I said, "How could you have trusted her to take care of me? You knew she didn't like me. You knew she was a greedy bitch. You knew, as soon as I gave her a reason, she'd write me out. You knew she didn't need a reason. You had to know it! How could you do that?

"Wait a minute," he said, in a smugness that reminded me of who he had been in life, "I thought you didn't care about the money."

I could have gotten whiplash from the speed with which my head turned around for my eyes to meet his. I stared at him long and hard with a face that said, "Fuck around and find out."

"It is *not* about the money," I said, slowly, emphasizing each syllable. "I do not need your fucking money. It is about justice." I paused to calm myself and made a note to check my blood pressure when I went back inside (spoiler alert: it was fine). "It's about justice, and equity. Those multi-millions that my stepmother now has were bought and paid for by every member of our family. I didn't contribute to it being earned, but I goddamn paid for it. You two dragged me all over hell's half acre in your pursuit of money… and hers… never once having my needs taken into consideration. Taxation without representation. I paid for my share by surviving neglect and abuse. And now I'll be written off like the piece of trash she always thought I was. Fuck."

I had to stop. I felt pathetic. There was a faint voice in my head telling me, "Stop whining. Stop being the victim. None of that is true. You're crazy. It's all your fault."

I tilted my head back as far as I could to stretch out my neck. It was tense and achy. I took note of the blueness of the sky. It was mid-June, and while the weather had been cold and wet, this day was sunny and warm. I allowed that moment of feeling the sun and watching the clouds roll by to bring me back to being grounded and centered.

"It wasn't, isn't, and will never be about the money," I said calmly. "It's about justice."

"Welp, you ain't gonna get it," he said. I couldn't tell from his tone if he meant to be an asshole or not, but it didn't land well.

"You think I don't fucking know that?! Of course, I know I'll never get it. Thanks for the reminder though. Really needed that." I was so frustrated. "How could you do this to me?"

"Korva. What the hell was I supposed to do?" he said with a tone he hadn't yet taken with me. He was pissed. "How was I supposed to do anything just for you? She had our money so buttoned up… If I did anything, and I mean anything, with our money, she would have seen it. And then what? 'Sorry Dear, but I think you'll be a greedy and treacherous cunt when it comes to my daughter.' It would have opened up a Pandora's box of hate and contempt. It would have hurt people. What was I supposed to do?"

"No, so instead you hurt me! Again! What the fuck, man?" I said, having lost whatever cool I had been able to conjure, "because it was easier." I practically spat those last words out.

This interaction felt familiar, my father and I locked in some kind of pointless standoff. While we stood there in stubborn silence, I mulled over what he had said. What was he supposed to do?

"Look, Beans" he said, sounding calm and focused, "I can't emphasize this to you more. You can't change anything that has happened. These interactions don't change what is done. I want you to move on. Not because I don't want to deal with it, because I have forever to deal with this, but because I want you to live a good life. Listen to me, you have to be done with them. There isn't anything good for you there."

I had mixed feelings about the idea of "being done with them." On the one hand, they were people whom I had considered family, and I don't take that lightly. Family is forever, or so I thought. I had never considered life without them. I had considered going no contact before, but there still would have been some contact during holidays, birthdays, etc.… But now I was contemplating severing ties entirely.

As if reading my mind, he said, "Give it time. You'll know what to do. In the meantime, get revenge by living your best life. That was sage wisdom that your husband gave you. He knows you well." He smiled contemplating that thought and continued, "Listen, Beans, I know I let you down, but I'm here now. I can still be your father now. We good?"

He stood in front of me with a sincerity that was unfamiliar. A brief moment of fear racked me as I considered that this could all be the onset of schizophrenia or dementia, and perhaps I should be speaking to a professional about these episodes. I shook it off. I was fine. I was more confronted by the idea of my father looking me straight in the eyes.

"Yeah, we're good, Papa," I said. I couldn't stay mad at him. *Damnit*.

Chapter Twenty-One

I put my nose back to the grindstone. I still had plenty of work to do between the retaining wall, my garden, and the four million little things I needed to do around the house. I preferred working outdoors though. Manual labor seemed to help ease the tension best. My physical experience of anxiety had become concerning over the last couple of months. My heart palpitated and I felt the need to check my blood pressure multiple times a day, but every time things checked out fine.

My heart rate was normal. Same with my blood pressure. My body was performing quite well really. I averaged about twelve to fourteen thousand steps a day and wasn't feeling any worse for the wear. Well, maybe a little achy, but not broken. I was getting a ton of good sleep. But even so, I was tired. Not body tired. More like worn-out at my core.

Since giving up social media for Lent, I hadn't picked the habit back up. But on the third Thursday of June, I decided to hop onto Facebook to wish my Aunt Barbara a happy birthday. That's when I saw my sister's post. She was in California. I had all but forgotten about the trip she had mentioned, the one she couldn't really talk about.

She had not specified when she was planning to travel, but I knew in my gut it would be for Father's Day weekend. I had even prophesied it to Bryan during one of my many "how could she do this to me?" rants. It made me both sad and angry to think about how awkward she had been about this trip. For whatever reason, she would not share this with me. I think it may have to do with whoever the "they" was that she was meeting up with. I guessed it was my stepmother and maybe her grandmother. I wished I had not seen the post. I wished I knew nothing about what she and "they" were doing. I could feel one doozy of an anxiety flare up coming on.

That next morning, I was in a mood. Struggling with deep emotional stuff and then still having to care for other people makes me beyond irritable. I mean, if I must pull it together from time to time, that's ok. But I'd been dealing with this for months and all the while being a mom, wife, and homemaker. I just wanted to stop the bus and get off for a minute to handle myself and this flood of feelings. And well, I was short with my kids that morning. Especially with Alex.

When I picked him up from school, I apologized. I said, "Hey dude, I'm sorry about how cranky I was this morning. I've just been having a real tough time with my family stuff… ya know, with my dad dying and now with Joni and Jennifer acting all weird."

I had been sharing some of what was unfolding with my kids. I didn't give them all the dirty details, because I still wasn't sure what I was going to do with these relationships. But I told them enough so that they would know why I was crying all the time.

I said, "Well, I made the mistake of looking at a Facebook post and it upset me, and I was just crabby. I'm sorry."

He said, "It's ok, mom." He paused and said, "I don't know how to say this. I don't want to be mean."

I said, "Just say it, son."

He said, "You need to get rid of those people." It startled me. "They don't care about you." I started to tear up.

He said, "I'm sorry, Mom. I didn't mean to upset you."

I said, "No no, I'm fine. I'm not crying because you hurt me. You are right about them, and that part hurts. But I'm touched that you cared enough to say something. Thanks."

Now, if I had any good sense, I would have stayed off social media, but I did not. For four days straight, my sister posted about her trip down memory lane. On Father's Day, she posted something that said, and I paraphrase, "I didn't mean to be in southern California on Father's Day, and I didn't mean to be on a mission to find the beach my dad took me to as a child, and I didn't mean to… *blah blah blah fuckin bullshit blah blah blah.*"

What is that garbage? She *did* mean to do all that stuff. What the hell was the point of all that? *Ugh, why did I have to look?* I knew I would be a mess on Father's Day weekend, well in advance. I should not have fed those demons. I knew better. I had even made a plan for dealing with grief on Father's Day that I thought would keep me emotionally sound. I was wrong.

My husband was out of town for the weekend, and I was going to surprise him by painting his office bathroom. During times when I was waiting for paint to dry, I'd stay busy organizing my craft room… or is it the guest room? Unfortunately, the number one thing it becomes is a storage closet. There was a ton of work there to distract myself with. The plan was fool proof… until it was not. I had failed to consider how full of memorabilia this room was... and it all started with the pictures.

As soon as I came across the first box, I knew it would be my undoing. But I could not stop. I began with the box of "mixed photos," ones that spanned my lifetime, and grabbed a handful to leaf through. There were shots from when I was very young. Times I could not remember. Pictures of my father as a long-haired hippy always made me happy. They were so contrary to the guy who ironed his jeans and wore loafers.

I paused at a picture of Jeff, Charlotte, and me. She was so pretty. Long, beautiful brown hair and a smile that lit up the room. She could have been a model. We looked happy. It is the only picture I have of her.

I wish that wasn't the case. Then there were pictures from Jeff and Joni's wedding of my father and grandmother dancing, and my father and me dancing. There were none of my stepmother from the wedding. In total I only found three pictures of her.

I had a ton of pictures of my sister though. I started to sort them out from the rest of the pictures. I don't know why. I didn't have a plan for them. It just felt like a symbolic way to weed her energy out of my life. I got the urge to do the same with any gift she'd given me, many of which were already in that room. Again, I did not have a plan for them. I just wanted them to be separated.

I thought, "I should do the same with anything Joni had given me too," and then it struck me. She had not given me anything for as long as I could remember. I mean, she helped with Christmas shopping for me as a kid, but since I had moved out of the house in 1992, she hadn't given me a single gift. I know I had given her gifts, gifts that she often did not acknowledge the receipt of, never mind thank me for. My dad sent me things now and then. But, as mentioned, since having children, I stopped receiving Christmas or Birthday gifts. I didn't believe that the same rule applied to my sister, not that I could prove it. And I know that Joni had mentioned sending gifts to her sister on more than one occasion. But she's never sent me anything. Alex was right. She didn't care about me. How had I not seen it before? I just thought that was how she was. *But, no.* That's just how she was to *me.*

I pictured Jeff sitting on my craft room futon in between two stacks of boxes and fabric. His gaze was lost in the chaos of the room. "Yeah, Beans, I'm trying to tell ya," he said, shaking his head. "There's nothing good there for you." Before I could ask the question, he looked straight at me and cut me off with, "There is no why, Beans. It just is." That was not what I wanted to hear, and he could tell. "What good would a 'why' do you anyway?" he asked.

I replied without thinking, "Because then I could fix it."

"Fix what?" he asked.

I started to cry. "Me," I said in a whisper, "I could fix me."

He waited until the crying passed. "There's nothing to fix," he said with as much empathy as he could muster. He knew that it was not what I wanted to hear either. "Look, it doesn't matter… the who, how, or why… it just doesn't matter. All that matters is what's happening now. You must deal with the fact that neither of them cares about you, and that is not your fault. It just is that way. Jennifer may care… some… but there are things that she wants more than having a relationship with you. She's made a choice. Now, you must choose as well."

The sudden sound of my ringtone made me jump. I looked down at the phone in my hand and saw my stepmother's name. I rejected the call and dropped my phone like it was covered in flesh-eating bacteria. "What the fuck does she want?" I snapped at Jeff. "She can't be for real. You just said she doesn't care and now she's calling me. What the fuck?"

He let out an amused snort and said, "It's for show. She wants it to look like she cares."

"To who?" I asked.

"I dunno. Everyone. Anyone," he said, rolling his eyes.

"Do you think she's with someone and is trying to convince them that she cares? Is she with Jennifer, or her mother?"

He just looked at me and said, "Would it surprise you?"

The answer was no. At this point, nothing surprised me. She didn't leave a message or send a text to say why she was calling, just like she had on my birthday.

My sister would post one last thing about her trip to California saying that she was headed to San Diego. Then, after four days of smearing her "pilgrimage" all over social media, she went silent. I'd have to guess that whoever she met in San Diego didn't want her posting about their good time. I was sure that it was my stepmother, but I could not be one hundred percent. And it didn't matter. One thing was sure, after this past weekend, I knew that I had to stay off social media. I couldn't help but look and there would never be anything good for me there.

It was July before I knew it. My garden, which had gotten a late start, was looking better than I would have predicted. Because I knew it was the grief of losing Jeff that had given me the energy to create the loveliest garden I'd ever created, I decided to dedicate it to him. I made a little memorial plaque and wanted to do some kind of inauguration ceremony, and the 23rd of July was the perfect day.

It's a date that held meaning to me for many years, for both reasons I loved and hated. I'll start with the latter. The 23rd of July was Jeff and Joni's wedding anniversary. This year would have marked thirty-nine years. I remember their wedding like it was yesterday. They hadn't been together, officially, for a year and I was already sad about this wedding occurring. Whereas I had looked forward to Jeff and Charlotte's wedding, on July 23rd, 1983, I was full of dread.

The 23rd of July is also the anniversary of Ginny, Jeff's mother's, death. Even though her passing was one of the most difficult losses of my life, having a day to remember and honor her brings me joy. The 23rd of each month is also a day of veneration for one of my favorite saints, St. George. While my father went by the name Jeff, his first name was George. It was a name that went back in his father's family for five generations. I've taken a liking to St. George over the last year or so and light a candle to celebrate him on each month's 23rd day.

My husband and kids were out of town for the weekend, and I had made plans to have a couple of friends visit, Runa and Tina. I met them both in 2020, on Instagram of all places. We have similar interests and common friends and would bump into each other on Instagram Lives. Then we all met in real life in 2021 and have been tight ever since.

Runa arrived early that day. She had a much longer trek than Tina. We set up camp at the dining table in my garden and kicked off the festivities with snacks and day drinking. Tina joined us a little past noon. The day was beautiful. Warm, just on the edge of hot but not quite. It wasn't breezy per se, but the movement in the air was fresh and pleasant.

When Tina arrived, she walked up to me, handed me a bottle in a bag, and said, "This is for you and Jeff."

I pulled the bottle from the bag. It was Port. I thought of my father. The last gift he had given Joni for Christmas, two days after he was already dead, was a bottle of Port. Many, many memories were made between him and I over glasses of Port. I choked on the tears that burst out of me. Once I could talk again, I asked, "Why did you pick Port?"

She said, "I don't know. Just came to mind, so I did it."

It felt like Jeff had reached right through Tina to give me that bottle. This garden dedication needed a little port. I was so grateful.

I asked Runa and Tina if it would be ok for me to do the ceremony part myself and they obliged. It was a simple little ritual, but I knew I'd be a mess and preferred to be alone. I had a huge planter in which I had placed a small breath mints tin of his cremains and planted three small rosemary shrubs on top. My father sure did love his rosemary. Then I placed a sign in it. The sign was painted with a guitar, wound around with vines of flowers. It had his name and the year of garden's establishment with the quote from Van's Marrison's "Fair Play."

I played the song from which that quote comes, "Fair Play" by Van Morrison, the song Jeff made his outro to. I walked around the circular path of my garden, at a slow and meditative pace, and imagined talking to Jeff.

"So, what do you think?" I asked. Here I was, seeking his approval again.

"I like it," he said. He was walking with me, but in the opposite direction around the circle. "You've done good work."

I snickered because I had just made my imaginary father compliment me. "Thanks," I said. "I'm glad you were with me. I wished we could have done this… ya know… before." I got teary.

"Yeah, wasn't gonna happen," he said with a nonchalant shrug.

"How come?" I asked, sounding a bit like a pouty child.

He said, "It just wasn't me. I mean, it was but… if I couldn't do it wearing khakis and loafers, then I kinda didn't wanna do it. I like inside plants. They're… more civilized." The look I gave him said that I wasn't fully buying that reason. Then, he said, "All right fine, I didn't like getting dirty. Maybe when I was young. But by the time you were into this gardening stuff, I was old and liked being clean…," his sentence drifted, and he appeared to be lost in a thought for a moment, then said, "next time, maybe."

"Sit with me," he said and motioned to the garden wall behind my tomato house. The little hoophouse sat in the middle of the garden and the space behind it was sheltered and private. The song that had been playing was over. He said, "Sit. Play that again. Let's listen." So, we sat, and I closed my eyes and listened.

The song starts with soft, sweet strums on an acoustic guitar. A couple measures in, and a gentle little up and down on the bass rolls you into a piano that sounds like rain falling and brushes on the drums that sound like leaves on a breeze.

"Fair play to you," Jeff began to sing. His voice emulating Van's perfectly. I close my eyes and am whisked away to somewhere hidden in my mind. I'm walking downhill on a tree-lined path. I look out over a hedge of boulders and bramble, past rolling hills of grass, down to a small village on the banks of an enormous sapphire lake. Beyond the lake, a group of green mountains dominated what was otherwise flat terrain as far as the eye could see. I could feel the mix of dirt and gravel under my feet. I heard it crunch with each step I took. I could smell a mix of petrichor and damp hay. I could feel the chill of morning and heat from the sun on the top of my head as it peaked above the tree line. Its light shined through holes in a dark and drizzling sky, making the droplets around me sparkle. These senses seemed all too familiar, like I had walked that path a million times, like I was home.

The entrance to the village was an iron gate just large enough to accommodate a horse and cart. It was cut into a thick stone wall covered in climbing roses. I passed through and as I reached the village side, I noted that the sun had broken fully through the clouds and rain. It was early morning, so it sat low on the horizon. Its warm rays, tinted with pink, illuminate a cobblestone road lined with small, tightly spaced, two- and three-story buildings. Each structure had oversized wooden doors and window shutters painted in bright, vibrant colors. Large ornate pots, overflowing with ferns, ornamental grass, and pothos, adorned the stoops of what looked like a mixture of shops and homes.

I was alone in what seemed like a sleeping town, as I continued down toward the dock at the end of the road. Then, I noticed in my periphery, doors opening as I walked past and people coming out to follow me. I couldn't see them in my direct sight, only on the edges of my vision.

I noticed the golden aura they held and began to feel the warmth of them on my back. I felt safer than I had ever felt in my life. Every step I took became surer, as more and more people stepped out and took their place in the march behind me. *Who were these people? Why were they getting behind me?*

Then it hit me. Like a freight train. These people are the reason I am here. They are the people that tie me to the moment of creation. They are every breath and drop of blood that was necessary in the culmination of my life. While I already knew that I carried traces of their trauma in my DNA, this was the first time that I had ever felt their strength. These people had endured and survived great suffering, but they were also brilliant, creative, skilled, passionate, and endlessly determined. These were formidable people. And they were there, for me, to give all they had learned so that I can heal and grow, and my children can thrive. So that all our children can thrive. I had work to do. They wanted me to do it, and they were there to protect, guide, love, and support me with all their might. *How could I deserve this?*

I stood there shaking, crying, and barely able to contain the emotions that welled in me. I burst into a sprint, so fast that I could barely feel the wood of the old dock beneath my feet. *Oh my god, what was I doing?* When I reached the end, I leapt with every ounce of strength I could muster, and for a moment I was flying. Soaring into some unknown fate that I had been destined for since the dawn of humankind. There was no stopping what was to come. There was no time for second-guessing and regret. Because I knew that there was only one way to go.

I slammed into the cold water and was shaken back to reality. Kind of. I was back in my garden, sitting behind my tomato house. Jeff was still there next to me. He was playing his guitar and singing along. He looked young and happy. The smile on his face said that all was well with the world, and there was no doubt that it would be that way forever. Jeff sang like that song was one of his oldest friends. He knew every nuance of it with every cell in his body.

Fair play to-ooo you-oooooo

That last line lingers as a measure of sweet little piano notes ends the song like a sigh of relief. It brought my father's last breath to mind.

"God, I love that song," he said with a sniffle.

I looked at Jeff. He sat with his arm draped over his guitar in a way I had seen hundreds of times. His gaze was soft and focused on the ground in front of him. He was smiling and I could see a glint of water trinkling down his cheek. "It was a good way to go… ya know… to this song. It was the perfect ending to an imperfect life." He looked at me and I saw another tear escape the corner of his eye, "Thanks, Beans...," his voice trailed off and he put his head down and sobbed a couple of times.

"You're welcome," my voice broke, "I wish I could have done more."

He said, "No, it was perfect." Then, he took a deep breath, sat up straight, gave one last sniffle and said, "Alright, enough of this crying business. You have friends over. Go hang with them. I'll be around."

I said, "Yeah, ok," took a good, cleansing breath, put my hands on my knees, pushed myself up, and wiped the tears off my face, "See ya later."

I started to walk off and he said, "Hey Beans." I stopped. He said, "Thanks for the garden."

I smiled, "Anytime, Papa."

I then had the honor of giving my friends, Runa and Tina, the first official tour of the "George Jeffrey Rafter Memorial Garden." I was so grateful that these ladies were with me. We share many of the same spiritual beliefs, and they knew how significant this moment was for me. And even though I knew this, there was a part of me that felt embarrassed and vulnerable. In my mind, I could see my stepmother and sister, both with sour and disapproving faces, saying, "Why does she have to be so dramatic? She just wants attention! She's always got to make it all about her."

I had to shake that off. That was not what was happening now. I did not want attention. I was not being dramatic. I loved my father, and it needed to be expressed, and my friends got it. In this moment, I was sharing my grief and my love with two people who got me. I ugly cried and laughed, and felt accepted, supported, and understood. There's a deep healing that occurs in safety and peace with good people.

The second highlight of the summer also happened at the end of July. My oldest son, William, announced his engagement to his girlfriend of five years, Josie. They had met in high school and started dating at the beginning of Junior year. At the time, William and I were going through some challenges. That is not a story I'll tell here, but I can say that I was grateful that he had Josie to love him during that time.

My reaction surprised me. Not only with its content, but also with its variety. I was happy, I like Josie and was very happy she was going to become family. I was just a little worried. Even though they had been together for five years and had been living together for almost three of those years, they were young. I knew that love wasn't lacking in their relationship, was maturity? But the feeling that caught me most off guard was the fear. I was afraid that I was going to lose my son. In my mind, I could hear some very familiar words, "He's going to choose her over you." I mean, of course she would be his priority moving forward, but deep in me I felt like I would no longer matter, just like when Jeff married Joni.

It was a sentiment deeply rooted in abandonment issues that predate my ability to recall, but my first memorable experience of feeling like someone had chosen someone else over me was when Jeff married Joni. I was triggered by Charlotte, too, but I think she countered those fears with her behavior. She expressed true love and concern for me. I was important to her. That was not the case with Joni.

From ten-year-old Korva's perspective, her father chose to marry and make a life with a woman who did not like her. He was choosing to subject her to that because this woman was more important to him, and Korva didn't matter. It reinforced the deep-seated thought that Korva was discardable. It made actual love bring out fear and desperation in her. She knew it would just be a matter of time before something better or more important would come along and she would be tossed aside.

Now, here I was having these thoughts and fears about my son. *No.* I didn't want to have to go through this ever, but especially not now. I was low on fortitude. Too many things were changing, and I was tired. This lingering anxiety was taking its toll on my body, and I felt like facing one more demon was going to knock me off my horse. But they don't call it divine timing because we get to choose it. Here it was. What was I going to do?

I've never done anything other than survive and respond. I don't know how to behave when I'm not doing that. But what I do know is that I'm not going to do what I've always done. I was not going to lose my son, and I wasn't going to be fearful or desperate about it. I was going to be something else. I'd find a way to love us both, him and I, without fear. I would love my new daughter-in-law, and the life they would create together, with everything I had. I'd do my best for us. It was all I could do.

I've got to laugh because those words make it sound so easy. Just think different thoughts and feel different feelings. "Do my best" and make that be enough just by saying so. Easy peasy, lemon squeezy, right? No. Nope. I'm sure I'll have to slay this beast a hundred times before I'm free of it, and it will be worth every ounce of effort.

Chapter Twenty-Two

August is one of my favorite months of the year. Not because it's all sun and fun, because I'm much more the gloom and doom type weather-wise. I love August because it is harvest time. All the work in my garden starts paying off. We have on-demand veggies, and this year my tomato crop was outstanding. The zucchini was not as abundant as normal, I think because I needed to do better crop rotation, but I had my first decent eggplant harvest ever.

I love being able to go out into my yard and pick food. In part, because I know that it is healthy, safe-to-eat food. But it's mostly because it appeals to my inner rebel. I love knowing that I can grow roughly thirty pounds of tomatoes for about what it would have cost to buy three pounds at the grocery store. I feel like I'm getting away with something, not just saving money. I also feel like I am taking my power back by growing food. I sleep better at night knowing that if I had the right set of circumstances, and some seeds, I could keep people alive. It's my superpower.

Well, all that serious business aside, my favorite garden creations to play with are the herbs I grow. I have an abundance of lavender, rosemary, and sage. All solid, useful herbal staples. Plus, some other self-seeding plants that grow wild in the garden now, like calendula, chamomile, and borage. I like to use these herbs to infuse oils for making soaps and lotions, as well as cooking oils. I also have a copper still that I use to extract essential oils. It does not produce that much oil, but it does create a fair bit of the by-product, hydrosol. The lavender variety makes one of my favorite pillow sprays.

I'm also glad to have all these potential projects for this time of year because they are all inside tasks. I do not do hot. I prefer seventy-five degrees or cooler. Anything above eighty degrees and I'm starting to wilt. Above ninety degrees means I will not see the outside world. This year, August had a lot of days over ninety degrees. I would get up before the sun to water my garden and then work on all the projects… indoors.

There had not been any new developments in the stepmother and *half*-sister saga since June. My stepmother had tried calling on Father's Day and I declined that call. She tried again about three weeks later. I didn't answer. What was I going to say? I couldn't have a regular conversation with her, and it wasn't time to address my issues with her. She didn't leave a message or send a text. Again.

My sister sent a text at the end of July,

> *Hey! Sorry I've been checked out this summer. I always think being home for the summer sounds good, but I need to accept that I need the structure. I'm either packed to the brim or spaced out on the couch. Let's check in soon!*

Uh-huh. At this point, I'm sure that she knew her mother had tried calling and I hadn't answered or returned her call, twice. She's a perceptive girl, so she knew when she and I got off our last call in May that something was amiss. And here she is sending me this innocuous note like she's just been too busy to reach out. I'm not buying it. I didn't respond. A couple of weeks later she sent:

> *Been thinking about you the last couple of days. Hope you're doing ok. I'm trying to admit to myself that I am not. Love you.*

Um really, you hope I'm ok? You're part of a group of people conspiring to withhold the truth from me and pulling some shady-looking shit, and you hope I'm ok? *Fuuuuck you.* And, trying to pull at my heartstrings will not work this time. It was reliable in the past, but your get-out-of-jail free cards were gone, gone, gone. *You love me?* How can you do what you're doing and say you are someone who loves me? *Um, nope. No.* I didn't respond. What was I supposed to say? "Oh, thanks! Sure, I'm great. Love you too?"

I wasn't ready to deal with this. I still didn't know what to do, or what to believe. And I was afraid. I had little to nothing left of my nuclear family of origin and I was afraid to lose it. Thinking it was still there gave me a sense of security, albeit a false one. It would appear that any real shred of security that was there for me left with Jeff. Knowing that didn't make it any easier to end this relationship. Jeff had asked me to wait a year. He had said time would make things clear. Well, since I still wasn't clear yet, I would keep my mouth shut and stay busy.

By the end of the month, I had hand-dipped somewhere near seventy-five pretty little tapered candles, mixed up forty bars of soap, herbal infused several oils for later use in lotions, concocted a few bath salts and foot soaks, and distilled a batch of lavender essential oil. It was work that had a luxurious quality that made it feel less laborious, and doing tests and trials was fun and relaxing. I needed it. I felt like my anxiety had aged me years in the months past Jeff's death.

By the beginning of September, my hair was coming out by the damn handfuls. It was the perfect storm of stress, perimenopause, and product changes. I didn't start off with a ton of hair and have been steadily losing it since I was twenty-five years old. It's something I've been aware of for a long time but found ways to hide. Though in the last few years, that has become more difficult to do. And this September's shed was a real bitch.

I had two things I had to deal with here. Number one, I had to address the stress. The anxiety I was feeling because of having unfinished business weighed heavy on me. I knew the stress was a product of the impulsive urgency I felt to "fix" things with my family. It's a product of trauma, abandonment, and anxious attachment. Yet knowing that didn't quell the urge. I know I said I would wait a year, but I wasn't sure that I could. I'd settle for waiting one more day and we'd see about the next day tomorrow.

Then, I had to choose a new direction to go in with my hair, change my mindset, or consider new solutions. I had tried so many goddamn hair products and I've sunk so much money into solutions that often bore no result, or if they did it was minimal and temporary. My updo slinky bun, which my youngest son nicknamed "The Bunion" back when he was around 3-and-a-half feet tall, no longer hid how fine and thin my hair was, and I had no idea what to do.

One morning, after dropping the kids at school, I decided to see if there was any other style I could pull off. I got out every curling device, styling product, and hair do-dad I owned. Two hours later, my hair was a hot mess, and my sense of hope was more deflated than Tom Brady's favorite football.

"Well feck," I said with a defeated sigh. I thought of Jeff and his hair, how he would rather have met the Grim Reaper wearing his hard rimmed Yankee's ball cap than let someone see his balding head. *I could relate.*

"I know you can," Jeff said, "It's a real son of a bitch, huh?" He was standing in front of the bedroom window, looking out at the treetops of my back yard. He stood in an at-ease military pose, feet spread hip width apart, and hands clasped behind him. The look on his face was surprisingly serious.

"Yeah. I'm so sick of it." I wanted to cry, but I was all out of tears for this matter. They did no good.

He turned to me, face still dead serious, and said, "You need to buy a wig."

"Whaaaat? Nooooo….," I whined. "Don't you have access to some kind of ancient, ghostly hair-growth secrets?"

"Nope," he said, "But I've got wisdom. Don't waste your time worrying about your hair."

I laughed, "You've got to be kidding me. This from a guy who wore a ballcap to his deathbed."

"Yeah, yeah, I know. But if I had to do it over….," he paused and gave me a poignant look, "I would not do it the same. My damn hair was my undoing. I would have traded my firstborn, no offense, for a full head of hair."

"Ummm, none taken?" I said, only half amused.

"Well, no, not really, Beans," he said in a way that acknowledged that that was a messed-up thing to say, considering that there were times in my life that I would have believed him. "But seriously, I wish I could get back all the energy that I lost worrying about my hair." He sighed. "Look, what's more embarrassing, and be honest, people seeing your hair thinning or people knowing that you're wearing a wig? I know you have thought this through."

"I have. And I do land on the side of wearing a wig being less embarrassing. But I tried a hairpiece once and it was awful."

"Yeah, but that was a long time ago. You see these wigs nowadays?" he asked, eyes wide with enthusiasm.

"Yeah, I know but… ugh. These things aren't cheap. I'll have to talk to Bryan about it. I don't wanna talk about it. I hate it," I said, stifling tears. No. I was done crying over this bullshit.

"Look, Beans… Bryan sees your hair and he doesn't care. He's here. And he supports the shit outta ya." His voice got caught in his throat as something occurred to him. He looked at me with a hint of tear forming, "I underestimated your husband. He's done a lot of work. I'm glad you two are well."

I smiled and laughed through teary eyes at the acknowledgement that my husband had indeed done a lot of work. And he did support the shit outta me. Everything that I've wanted to accomplish in the fifteen years we'd been married he was behind one hundred percent. We'd weathered many things, and I think we were both better for it.

"Yeah, I'll take a look-see and talk to Bryan," I said, still sniffling. I changed the subject with "Hey, I know I've already asked, but I'm asking again… got any new advice about Joni and Jennifer? I don't know what to do and I just can't do this anymore. It's killing me."

He gave me a flat, side-eyed glance, and made a closed mouthed "hmm" sound and said, "Look, you have one question to answer, do you want to continue to have a relationship with them? And, before you can say it… yes, it is that simple. Ask yourself, do you even like them? Are they the kind of people you want in your life? Can you ever trust or forgive them?"

I let out an audible, "haaaa." That wasn't what I wanted to hear. What I wanted were magic words. I took another deep breath in through my nose and did it again. "Haaaaaa," then said, "I guess I'm not ready. I just… I just don't know yet."

"Welp," he said, sounding like someone who wanted to get off the phone, "It's not been a year. You still have plenty of time." He turned to face me with a sympathetic smile, and said, "Chin up, kid. This won't go on forever and, really, you've been through much worse. You'll figure it out when you figure it out. In the meanwhile, I suggest you go look at some wigs."

I'd spend the next week or so doing two things. First, researching wigs. "Alternative hair" is the industry standard term for wigs, toppers, or hair pieces. I like it. It feels like a comfortable term to use for an uncomfortable matter. I spent at least half of my days reading about the different types of hair pieces, how they are made, and what they are made from. I also learned that the whole hair-loss industry is riddled with scam artists, in both the alternative hair market and the hair products market. Hair-loss is a vulnerable thing to experience, and bad people take advantage of it. So, to navigate these waters without the risk of running into sharks, I booked an appointment with a woman named Lacie Rodriguez for an Alternative Hair Consultation. Although I'd have to wait a few days to see her, I immediately felt a sense of relief about my hair having taken action.

The other thing I did was think about Joni and Jennifer. The thoughts were always the same, I was getting nowhere, and my patience was running out. I wanted to call them out and I was becoming less able to stop myself. To help let it out, every time I had something I wanted to say to either of them, I scripted a text and put it in a run-on note document on my phone. Getting it out of my head gave me temporary relief. It also helped me clarify my thoughts. This whole situation occurred to me as so complicated and confusing, but was it? My son had said months ago, "They don't care about you."

It rang true, and I didn't want it to. *Like my hair loss. I looked in the mirror. I really missed my old hair.* Nothing about the way they behaved looked like the way people who cared behaved. They lied to me, to my face. They conspired in the next room within hours, or at best days, of my father dying. That happened. Period. None of these things were ok. The only reason I would have tolerated any of this is because of some unhealthy sense of family obligation. My sister was family, but my stepmother wasn't. Joni and I have no shared ancestry. We weren't "blood related." We weren't even friends. But she had been there, in the forefront and then running in the background of my life for eighty percent of it. Forty years is a long time, and now I must decide: stay or leave.

What if I stayed? What would that look like? *What would I look like with alternative hair?* I guessed it would look more of the same. Except now I know the truth, and nothing would ever be the same. So, no, that wasn't a good choice.

I could maintain minimal contact, cash the checks for the kids on their birthdays and Christmas and watch us all make excuses for why we can't get together. I'll have to pretend that I don't know what's happening behind my back and being kept from me "for my own good". Or someone else's good. There will always be a reason to lie to me and make it okay. And that's not okay with me. Not anymore. So, nope. That won't do either.

I could cut ties with my stepmother and just have a relationship with my sister. *I could shave my head.* I guess she's been less shitty to me… I think. We will have calls similar to the last one we had for the next couple of years. At least until we get used to me not having a relationship with her mother. There would be whole areas of her life that she couldn't share with me, and it would feel forced and awkward. So, no thank you.

I could call them both on their lies and bullshit and hold my breath waiting for an apology. And then die of asphyxiation.

Or I could leave.

I could leave without a word. I could simply fall out of touch. I could miss calls and take forever to return them. I could switch to text-only communication and only on birthdays or special occasions. I could hide them on social media and make my posts unviewable to them. Then, little by little, I could extract myself until one day, like magic, I would stop occurring to them. After that, with any good luck, what's dead would stay dead.

Or… I could leave with a bang. I had this beautiful visual of throwing a loosely tied bag of angry snakes into a room with the two of them and slamming the door behind me. *I would rock a motherfucking hair piece.* I knew which exit strategy Joni would prefer, and I was not interested in giving it to her. Oh no, she would be getting exactly what she deserved.

I've never been much of a morning person, but my body chemistry was changing, and sleeping in, or even through the night, had become a thing of the past. Many of the people I know who are my age, especially women, express a similar sentiment. Since returning home in January, I have been in bed by 9:30 p.m. and up at 6 a.m., even on the damn weekends. Not my characteristic behavior. For the last couple of weeks, it had been worse. I was waking up at 4:30 and 5 a.m., angry from the jump and unable to go back to sleep.

One of these mornings I lay staring out my bedroom window. The shades were open, but the window was not. Every previous year, a couple of weeks into September, I would be able to open them to let in a cool, fresh breeze, and listen to the rain. But not this year. It had been hot and dry all summer and now add horrible air quality to the mix. Since 2017, the Pacific Northwest has been dealing with excessive smoke from wildfires. Areas west of the Cascade Mountains were experiencing the impact in a way I hadn't seen in the nearly 30 years I have been here. It sucked. It was scenery straight out of every dystopian, post-apocalyptic movie I've ever seen, but it most reminds me of the version of Earth in *Interstellar* - scorched, dusty, and dying. It affects me worse than the eight months of clouds and rain that cause annual depression for a huge portion of the Pacific Northwest population.

I watched the sunrise. It was the color of a blood orange from the smoke in the air, and the light that came through my window illuminated everything in a hazy peach glow. Too bad I couldn't appreciate it, knowing that the sky may be pretty but breathing the air gave me a headache.

Jeff stood at the window. "Goddamn, Beans, this is nuts." He shook his head in disbelief, staring at the bizarre atmospheric display outside.

"Yeah," I said, got up, closed the shade, and got back in bed. It was only 5:30 a.m. after all. "Hey Jeff, I think I'm done."

"Ya mean with those two?" he said with a raised brow.

"Yeah," I said.

"You sure? You've thought this through?" he asked.

"Yeah," I said again.

"Alright, well let's hear it then," he said with genuine curiosity. "What's the plan?" I gave a little laugh thinking of how many times in my life I'd heard my father ask, "What's the plan?"

"What do you mean?" I asked, feeling annoyed, realizing that being done with something was not a plan and that he was right to question me.

"Well, first, what does 'being done' look like?" he asked.

I mulled that over for a moment and said, "It looks like nothing. No contact. Done. Donezo. *Finito. No mas.*"

"So, no contact at all? Not even on holidays?" he asked. His tone suggested that he was testing me.

"No. Not ever."

"What about the money? What about the occasional checks for the kids? Gonna cash those?" he asked, again, sounding like he was testing me.

"Um, no. Nope. They're insulting. They aren't real expressions of caring. It's scraps off her table that she'll toss at us to assuage her guilt and not out of any kindness toward my kids. No. I'm not cashing those stupid checks."

"What about your inheritance?" he asked.

I laughed. "You gotta be shittin' me. If I'm not written out already, I will be. She won't need a reason. She'll just wait to spring it on me when she's dead. One last shot at me from the grave. Then she won't have to deal with it. She'll have Jennifer handle her mess. Again. I'm never seeing a dime of that money and that's fine by me."

He let a long deep exhale out of his nose, audibly, until his lungs emptied. He paused for a moment, drew his next breath deep into the bottom of his lung, and said with a heavy exhale, "You're not wrong." His tone was dark, defeated, and definite. "But if there's an off chance, is it worth risking?" I could hear by his tone that not even he thought that likely.

"I'd rather starve to death than take the scraps off of her table for the rest of her life in the hopes that I might get money from our family estate." Saying the word "family" left a bad taste in my mouth. *Some family I had. I was like a rabbit raised by wolves for slaughter.*

"Ok, so you don't care about the money. What are the other costs of leaving?" he asked. He was doing his due diligence and making sure that I thought this through.

I took a deep breath and let out a loud *haaaaaaa*, trying to soften the locked down feeling in my chest. "Well, there isn't much there to lose, except maybe Jennifer." I held back tears. "She's my sister. My *half*-sister anyway. This wasn't supposed to happen. I thought we were for real, like we'd be family no matter what. We'd be old together."

He looked at me with sadness, "I know you did, Beans. I know you thought that, but it was only because you saw what you wanted to see." He looked down, his expression a mix of guilt and frustration. He whispered "*Shit*," under his breath, shook his head, raised his shoulders, and said, "I tried to warn you, but what was I gonna say?"

It took me a moment to process what he had said. While I still wasn't sure what he meant, I instinctively felt pissed.

"Um, you wanna say what? You tried to do what? Wait. What?"

"Gah, shit… Look…" He was clearly flustered, knowing he had made a complicated situation for himself. He paused to formulate his next words. "Remember when you and your sister came to visit? It was the summer after I was diagnosed, so… uh… 2019."

"Yeah sure, you mean the time I cancelled my direct flight to Boston with two days' notice and instead flew to Indianapolis so that I could drive to Boston with my sister because she was afraid to get on a fucking plane? You mean that time? When you and her mother all but mocked her for being a chicken shit but I did my best to support her? You mean that fucking time?" There would have been cartoon steam streaming out of my ears if I were a looney tune.

"Um… yeah, that time," he said, looking sorry for having brought it up. "Anyway, remember when the three of us were sitting on the porch, just the three of us?" He paused but not long enough for me to answer. "Ya remember when Jennifer got up and went back inside because she hates sitting in silence. You said to me, 'Jeff, I'm grateful for my sister. I love her and I'm grateful for our relationship.' Something like that. Do you remember that?"

"Yeah," I said feeling irritated, "And I remember that your response was… weird. Like, you just said, 'hmph'. At that moment I read it like you doubted my sincerity. I even asked you what you meant by it, like why wouldn't you believe me. You said, 'oh yeah, of course I believe you' and changed the subject."

"Yep, that's right. I almost told you then," he said.

"Told me what?" I asked. My tone suggested that I was running out of patience.

He sat silently. I could see him working hard to find the right words. "Look, things were not the way you thought they were. Your sister… was not who you thought she was. It started around the time she was with her ex-husband." He paused and looked at me. He could see I was still processing what he just said.

"It started when she was with Chad?" They were married briefly in their early- to mid-twenties.

"Mmm hmmm," he said. "Think about it. She was young. She went away to college but struggled with that and had to move back home to go to school. She did a brief stint in the military, dated her recruiter, got pregnant, and chaptered out. She was feeling… insecure. She wanted our approval. And she figured out then that as long as you looked bad, she looked better."

I thought back. Even though privately she and I got along fine, in front of our parents it was a different story. During the time Jeff referenced, anytime there was a subject to debate she hopped on the gang-up on Korva bandwagon without hesitation. Less so in recent years, especially since marrying Josh. Her opinions began to align more with mine, but back when she was with Chad, they did not. Looking back, I remember wondering at times if she even liked me. Once, sometime in 2014, she started a Pinterest board titled, "For Korva, because I can make you mad, and you still have to love me." It was full of memes chastising people for making political posts on social media. It was meant to insult me. It was just… shitty.

As if he could see an awareness growing in me, he said, "Yeah, Beans. I'm sorry. She was not your friend. Not really. Maybe part of her loved you or wanted to love you. But her insecurity… her need to be superior to you… it would not allow it." He paused and sighed in a way that felt heavy with disappointment and went on. "After that whole Thanksgiving debacle, she solidified herself as your 'handler.' Any time you needed to be dealt with, your sister would do it. Not always without complaint, but never with hesitation. She did it to keep herself in the loop… and you out of it."

"Of course, she did. Well, that's just fuckin grand."

I wanted to cry but I was too angry. How had I been so naive that I let her manipulate me like that? What else had I missed? How deep was her deception? Now my mind was reeling, and I needed to get out of bed and start moving. I got up and wandered into the kitchen to make some coffee.

It was still early. The sun was just barely above the tree line, which meant it was high enough on the horizon to hit the prism that hung in the window above my kitchen sink. A hundred little rainbows lit up the room. It was one of my favorite things. It's hard to be upset in a room full of rainbows.

I placed my cup where a ray of the prism light would hit it right in the middle. I stirred slowly, clockwise, and sang the pick me up and lift me up lyrics of Dave Matthews Band's "Everyday" over my coffee. I needed something to lighten my load. I was tired of being

angry and this conversation with my father was not helping. At the same time, I knew these were things I needed to be honest with myself about.

"How much did she know? About this property purchase bullshit. How much?" I asked. I was fighting off flying into a fit of rage. It caused little quakes of tension to roll over my body.

He looked at me. I could tell that he didn't want to have this conversation. I could sense the discomfort he was experiencing in not being able to say more. Whatever sense of allegiance he had to Joni and Jennifer, silenced him of certain matters. "All I can say is that she's not who you thought she was."

To which I responded, "Well then, that answers that. I've got nothing to lose."

Chapter Twenty-Three

It was Sunday, September 11th, when I got to work on the message I would send to end my relationship with my family. I couldn't help but think breakup by text was a cowardly means, but no other option looked good. If I spoke with them, they'd just stonewall or gaslight me. I didn't think anyone was going to come clean, and if they did it wouldn't be the whole story.

I wrestled with the choice of which voice to use in the message. The one of the ten-year-old girl that just wanted a family to belong to, or the one of the fifty-year-old woman who was no longer going to accept their bullshit.

I decided that I would just let it out. It would be a little of both Korvas; a little "how could you?" from the young girl who couldn't defend herself, and a little "how dare you?" from the now grown woman who is no longer begging for their leftovers. I am eating nutrient-rich meals now. They could keep their scraps.

Two days later, that message saw more edits than the King James Bible. I gave it to Bryan to read.

"It's good," he said. I could tell there was more to that story.

"Yeah, and…?" I prodded.

"No, it's good. It starts off strong but…," his voice trailed. I got the impression that his hesitance was from his desire not to hurt me. He continued anyway, "um, it's just… whiney."

Ouch. That hurt. And he could tell.

"Ok, not whiney. It just sounds like the words of a hurt child," he said in the hopes of clarifying his meaning.

"I know! Those are the words of a hurt child! She deserves a voice!" I said, feeling protective.

"Of course she does," he said with a tone of empathy, trying to lower my defenses. "But Korva, that's not who you are now. You're a strong, kick-ass woman. That's you. You're not a little girl anymore."

Dammit, he was right. I was eating meals!

There was something behind the words I wrote, but I would not call it "whiney." I was, however, trying to garner sympathy. Part of me wanted to believe that if they understood the impact they were having on me, they would change. But that was a fool's errand. They knew exactly what they were doing to me and nothing I said would change them.

Several hours later, I brought a new draft to Bryan. He read it.

"Well, it's certainly not whiney," he said. He looked at me for a long moment. It appeared that he was searching my face for something. "You sure you want to do this, Korva? There's no coming back from this."

"Yes, I'm sure," I said, firm in my stance. "I'm done."

"And what if they want to make amends? What if your sister wants to work this out? What then?" he asked. I could practically hear my father speaking, testing my resolve.

"No, Bryan, I am done. I do not want to come back from this."

"And there's no other way?" he asked, still testing my commitment.

"No, there's no other way. I know Joni would want me to bow out in the least impactful way possible, and there's no way in Sam Hill fuck she's gonna get that. Nope, I'm throwing a bag of angry snakes in that room and slamming the door behind me. She can clean up whatever mess is left," I said with as much venom as said sack of vipers.

Bryan took a deep breath, and said, "Ok, but I have one request. Sleep on it."

"Ok. I will," I agreed but I did not want to. I knew damn well there would be no change of heart, but I could wait one more day.

Friday the 16th of September looked like any other Friday. I shuttled the kids to and from school. I cooked and cleaned. I gardened a little and took the dogs for a walk with Bryan. But on this Friday evening, I was going to do something that would forever change my life. As confident as I felt the night before, pressing send on that text was much harder than I would have guessed. I mean, this was a big deal. I was about to cut ties, not only with my stepmother and sister but also with a huge portion of my life. With my entire childhood. And there was no coming back.

At the same time, there was a part of me that looked forward to experiencing life without them. It's been burdensome being our family's scapegoat, and for the first time in my life, it occurred to me that I could quit that job. I never applied for the part, I didn't mean to play it, and now I don't want it. It was time for me to move on to the next act. One where I'm not cast as the fat daughter, or the reckless child, or the reason for all the bad things. I could… quit.

I sent the following message that evening:

I've included James as a recipient of this text because I don't trust that history will be recounted to him accurately.

To catch up, the last time I spoke with Joni was at the beginning of May, when she informed me that she'd chosen to move to Indiana and had purchased 30 acres of property. She then attempted to call me on Father's Day and then again, a couple weeks later. I didn't answer. She didn't leave a message or send a text.

The last I spoke to Jennifer was just after her birthday. She texted at the end of July and again a couple of weeks later. I did not respond to either text.

Since then, neither of you has reached out to ask why I wasn't responding or express any concern for the uncharacteristic behavior of non-response. I could speculate as to why, but it simply reads like you just don't care. You already know why and just don't want to face it.

Care or not, like it or not, here it is. I haven't responded because I'm furious with you, Joni and Jennifer. You lied to me. Again. When I picked Jennifer up from the airport the day Jeff died, on the ride back to Boxborough I asked what she thought Joni would do now and she said "Oh, I don't know," like she had not even consider it. That was a lie. And then days after Jeff died, when I asked Joni what she wanted to do now that he had passed, she also lied by feigning she didn't know.

Truth is, 20 acres of property were purchased in Indiana in June of 2021, nearly a year before you delivered your "big news" to me. Other people knew. Jennifer knew, and I'm sure Joni's friends and family knew. Greg knew. Who didn't know? Why lie? The only reason to lie about such a thing is to manipulate someone's sense of reality to control their behavior.

But the best part is the plot twist that would make millions.... The second property purchase. Ten acres with a barn adjacent to the property purchased in 2021. After being on the market for many months, an offer was placed to purchase it the day after Jeff was put in hospice care. (Or at least the day after I was told he was put in hospice care. That could be another lie) The offer on the 22nd was rescinded, my guess was to avoid paying 2021 taxes on it or something like it, and then the property was relisted and was purchased by Joni on or about January 10, 2022.

Why wait to buy this property? Why not buy both properties at the same time? I'm sure you have a slick answer to that, but I won't believe it. I can't ever believe either of you. My gut tells me it's because Jeff said no. You didn't need it. That 10 acres with a barn is for Jennifer, and he didn't support that. Why else wait? While I can't prove that or that the offer made on 12/22 was you, every bone in my body says they're both true.

Either way, you two were in the next room scheming about this purchase within days or maybe even hours of my father dying. Likely before he died. What kind of people do that?

You lied to me because you knew what you were doing was wrong. Jennifer gets $218k worth of property (and likely more) and I get nothing and y'all know that's wrong. And it's not about the money, it's about equality. Jennifer isn't more deserving of receiving benefits from the Rafter family estate than I am. But she will. I accept that there is nothing I can do about it, and I honestly don't care. There's no amount of money on earth worth selling myself out or kissing your ass for. And I'm not going to watch the indecency unfold or be lied to about what is happening.

I'm done. I forgive myself for having wanted a family so badly that I allowed myself to be fooled by the two of you. Joni, I knew who you were 30 years ago when you told me that you "just didn't like" me. That never changed and I wish I saw it sooner. If you held an ounce of care or respect for me, you would never have done this, especially so close to losing Jeff. There's just no decency there and I think it's pathetic and disgusting. Jennifer, I've barely begun to process my thoughts or feelings about your role here, but I can say that's some fucked up shit you did, and you ought to be ashamed.

I hope you both get what you deserve. I know that you both find comfort in your wealth. Don't take it for granted. The universe giveth and the universe taketh.

If your response is anything other than fuck you, don't bother. I won't believe you. And really, you should save your fuck yous because this relationship is over.

James, I'm sorry we never had the chance to develop a relationship. I think that was probably by design. I also think that Jeff wanted us to connect, which is why he made the efforts he did in his last days. I know that it would be difficult to have a relationship with me so I don't expect it but know I'm family and here if you need me. I promise not to lie to you.

Was it perfect? Nope. Did I feel bad for being mean? A little. Did I regret it? Nope. I expected to feel more anxious after sending that message or to be worried about the backlash I could potentially receive. But I felt none of it. I was done.

That night, I had a dream about them. I dreamt that Joni, James, Jennifer, and her family flew in to spend the weekend with me. I chose the first night they were here to send them that message. The dream begins with me waking up the morning after sending the message and realizing, "Shit, I gotta look these people in the face."

In my dream, I came downstairs to see my stepmother standing by my front door. She was seething with anger. I noticed Jennifer scurrying around packing and gathering her kids. I said to my stepmother, "So, ya leavin'?"

Without looking at me, she replied, "Yep." Her nostrils flared.

"Ok," I said with as much nonchalance as I could manage. Then, I turned to my sister and said, "You got a minute?"

She said, "Yes," and I motioned for her to follow me into the downstairs restroom.

I said, "Um, so is she pissed?"

"Ah, yeah," she said in the same way you would say, "Well, duh." "Didn't you hear her? She got up in the middle of the night and walked to her mother's house."

"Holy shit," I said, being lucid about the fact that her mother lived in Nevada, which was definitely not within walking distance.

She said, "Look, I gotta go." She turned to walk out the door.

I said, "Yeah," my tone acknowledging how awkward I made things. "But wait, before you go…. Was I right?"

She stopped mid-step, thought for a moment, and said, "Mostly. You got a couple of details wrong, but the sentiment was dead on." She then hurried out my front door to catch up with her mother who stormed off with her nose in the air.

As they were leaving, I noticed my father approaching from behind me, preparing to follow them. *Where did he come from?* I hadn't realized he was there. I felt a wave of guilt. I said, "I'm sorry, Jeff. I just couldn't keep doing this."

"Don't be sorry," he said. "Look, I gotta go clean up this mess. I'll see ya later, Beans." For a moment I felt bowled over by a wave of terror. *He was leaving me again. He was choosing her over me.* He stopped, paused for a moment, and turned his head over his shoulder. "I'll be back. Settle down over there," he said with a grin. He gave me a nod and winked, and the dream faded.

Chapter Twenty-Four

I woke up the next morning, again, with the sun streaming peach-colored light across my room. The shade and hue were getting darker with each passing day, as local wildfires burned out of control. My routine of recalling reality looked different this morning. "What day is it? Am I supposed to be doing something? What's up with this peach light? Jeff's not here anymore. Oh yeah, I'm done with Joni and Jennifer."

I expected to feel anxious or guilty, but I didn't. I felt relieved. The list of things that I would never have to experience again was long and lovely. I'd never be lied to, or excluded, or blamed, or gaslit, or stonewalled by those people again. I quit the shittiest job ever, and it felt amazing. I took a deep, satisfying breath, and let it out with an "ahhhhhhh."

"Yeah, well, you better keep that door shut, Beans," Jeff said. His voice broke the silence of morning. He stood looking out the bedroom window with an expression of concern. I wasn't sure if it was for me, or for the scene outside.

"Yeah, I know," I said, feeling a little annoyed for having lost the contentment of the moment.

"Do ya? Because I don't think you know what that's going to take." His voice was both stern and caring. "You can't open that door back up. Ya got me?"

"Shit, Jeff. I just woke up. Give a girl a break," I said, sitting myself up and rubbing my eyes.

"There won't be any breaks for you this weekend, Korva," he said very seriously. "Things are happening, and this is not done. She is beside herself livid with you. I'm talking about nuclear mad, Beans. Even if she doesn't reach out to talk to you, you be on guard because her thoughts are like a thousand daggers headed this way. Watch yourself, and your step. You're going to have to be ready to keep that damn door shut," he said, sounding like a drill sergeant. "Now, get up, get yourself some coffee, and get the ol' blood flowing. *Andale!*"

I got up and fixed some joe. Light and sweet. I took it outside with me to check on the garden. The morning dew kept the low-lying air somewhat clear, but I could tell the smoke was winning that battle by the itchiness of my eyes. Most everything in the garden was harvested. I was still picking a couple of tomatoes each day but had finished watering them for the year. There wasn't much to do but wander and observe.

While I strolled through my garden, taking note of what went well this year and what hadn't, and planning for next year, texts from friends started rolling in. "Hey honey, how are you this morning?" "Any word from those two?" "We're here if you need us?" "We're proud of you" and so on. It felt good to feel so supported. It would make keeping that door shut a little bit easier. Each message that rolled in and each minute that rolled by left me feeling better and better.

Until just after noon when I noticed the text from my sister. I felt an immediate shift in energy. My heart skipped a beat and started back up fast and heavy. This wave of anxiety was all too familiar. Yet, I noticed it more now since experiencing a brief break from it. I took a deep breath and debated whether I should read this message or just delete it without opening it. I should have chosen the latter, but reflex took over. I opened it and was reading before I could even finish my contemplation.

> *I have a few things to say that you can choose to consider them or not, but I deserve to have my say if that's how you are going to speak to me.*

First of all, it's not my responsibility to chase your responses. Silence is an answer, and I respect it. I don't read between the lines anymore.

Next, you're right to be mad at Jeff and Joni. What they did was bullshit. I told them as much and told them (my mom, at least because I barely spoke to dad) repeatedly to tell you or this would happen- because it should. You should be mad. The way they handle shit is insane. But here's the thing: I chose to stay out of it. I'm not taking responsibility for shit that's not mine anymore. You may think that was the wrong thing for me to do, and I do see where it looks from your perspective like I was on "their side." I just won't engage in this dysfunction anymore. That was between you and them, and I wanted nothing to do with it. And they let it get completely out of control. It put me in a terrible position, and I have my own repair work now to do with my mom if her choices have now hurt our relationship.

I can't control how you want to feel about me in all this. That said, the way you're choosing to handle it is disrespectful to me and you're trying to glorify Jeff, and you and I both know that's not true. I'll leave the details of the property to my mom if you want them because once again, they're not my responsibility to deal with, but no one's giving me any land, so dad didn't intervene on anyone's behalf. Last I asked, the will was still going 3 way and I'm getting literally nothing from the estate until my mom is gone. You should try asking rather than filling in the blanks that fit your narrative.

It's a shame if you want nothing to do with me because of their dysfunction, but once again, I'm going to respect whatever boundary you set. I'm open to talking through text or call, but that's your decision. I'm truly sorry for the way they treated you.

I just hope we can all step out of the dysfunctional roles we've been given.

Oh boy, oh boy. For a moment, it worked. For a moment, I thought she was right. I did. That all sounded so rational, so practical, so confident.

"Read it again," Jeff said, startling me. He sat in the chair in front of my living room window looking out, watching my chickens scratch and peck around. He glanced at me from the corner of his eye and said, "Read it again." I read it again. "What do you see?" he asked.

"Well, she's pissed. That's clear. The way I'm handing this is 'disrespectful to her?' Is she fucking serious? Why would I be respectful to her?"

"Yeah, right? What else do you see? Read it again." So, I did.

"Um, she feels justified in her behavior. Like she had no other choice… maybe?" I said with uncertainty.

"Uh-huh, what else?" he asked. I couldn't help but think there was a point to all of this that I wanted him to get to, but I played along and looked over the message yet again.

"I don't know, there's something there, but I can't pinpoint it," I said feeling frustrated.

He took a deep, nostril flaring breath in and let it out hard. "You'll see it. Just give it time." He furrowed his brow and said, "Is it true, the contents of this message… I don't mean, is she lying? I mean, is it true, what she's saying?"

I opened my mouth to respond, and nothing came out. I didn't have an answer because it was a question I'd ever pondered. *"Is it true?"* I mulled over in my head and joined Jeff in watching the chickens. It took a surprisingly long time to come up with an answer.

"It's true… to her… I guess." I was not confident that was right. It was the only answer I could arrive at, and it seemed too simple. "I mean, I guess in her story it's true."

He snapped his fingers and pointed to his nose. "Bingo," he said with a smile, sitting up in his chair. "In her story it's true. What's your story, Beans? And here's some advice… keep it simple."

"Um…. Well, in my story she made a choice. As soon as her mother let her in on that secret, she no longer had the option to stay out of it. I'm sorry that the choice was made for her, but she was involved. Then, she kept quiet because it benefited her. She watched as people took action that would hurt me and did nothing. And then she lied and schemed in the next fuckin room the day after you died. That's my story. She had choices and the ones she made crossed my boundaries."

"Well first of all, Bravo! It's about damn time you erected some boundaries." He clamped loud and proud. "Now answer me this, is *that* true?" he asked, obviously trying to make a point.

"Well, it's true to me."

"And that's exactly so, Beans. We are all the center of our own stories, like the nucleus of an atom." He spoke with enthusiasm I hadn't seen in him in decades. "When we combine our stories with other people's stories we create versions of reality. It is very much like how atoms combine to become molecules, then cells, then tissue and so on…. Ya with me?"

I nodded.

"Reality is effectively a collection of stories, the same way an organism is a collection of atoms. But sometimes, our stories don't align, and it causes dysfunction. In organisms, that shows up as cancer. For people, it's strife, intolerance, hate, and suffering." he paused a minute to let me take that in. "Who you are in their story, does not align with who you are in your own story. And vice versa. It's not about who's right or wrong, it just doesn't align and as a result is unhealthy. And I'm sorry, but it's unlikely to ever be healthy. I think you've known that for a long time."

"Yeah…," I said and started to cry. I cried because I wasted so much time holding onto the hope that I'd someday find what I was seeking with them. And even as detrimental as that was, the loss of hope still occurred as sad to me.

"You've chosen to stop being in their story, so now your sister's truth is just that, hers. You don't have to settle for her reality. You don't have to agree or disagree. You don't have to keep trying to make it work," he said and gave me an empathetic smile.

We sat in silence and watched the chickens. I allowed these thoughts to sink in. I began to feel more confident that I made the right decision. I quit my shitty scapegoat job. I tend to stay in unhealthy situations too long and make a mess when leaving them. With this new understanding, I'm hoping in the future I will quit sooner and make fewer messes.

I read Jennifer's message several more times but still couldn't put my finger on what I was missing. I let it go. I had closed the door, and I could not let this message open it up again. I spend the remainder of the day chatting with my friends and indulging in a variety of self-care activities. By bedtime, I was back to feeling well, at peace, and ready for a good night's sleep.

The next morning, I woke up early, still feeling good. I made myself some coffee and got cozy on the couch to check my emails, etc. That's when I saw another text from my sister.

It might also be pertinent to that you know I have heard nothing from my mom since you sent that text. Not a single check in for putting me in this position after I very clearly said that's how this would go. Not a sign of worry that my sister intends not to continue a relationship with me. There's a lot more than just land I don't get. That we've never gotten. To tell me to be ashamed of myself and wish upon me what I deserve...? How misguided and hurtful. You're not the only victim of this family, so please don't paint me as the villain.

I checked the time stamp. It was sent after midnight, her time. She wasn't one to stay up late. I felt another familiar wave of anxiety roll over me.

"Don't do it, Beans," Jeff said from his favorite chair. He sat sideways with his legs over the arm of the chair so he could get a better view of the chickens.

"Don't do what?" I said, knowing damn well what he meant. The look he gave me told me that he knew that as well.

"Don't call Jennifer," he said.

I rolled my eyes and let out a heavy sigh to try to lessen the renewed tension in my chest. "What am I supposed to do? She's my sister," I said.

"Look, I don't expect you to listen to me on this one, but I'll say it again... don't do it. You won't get what you want," he said.

"Yeah, I know. But what if what she's saying is true?... Damn, that's messed up." I paused, thinking about what she said about me wishing she would get what she deserves, and saying it was 'hurtful and misguided.' "She's right. I think I took too much aim at her. I mean, I'm friggin livid with her, but she didn't deserve it the same way Joni did."

"How do you know that?" he said with narrowed eyes.

"I don't. I don't know anything anymore… and I don't need to." I took a deep breath and said with resolve, "I know I shouldn't, but I'm going to talk to her. I made a wee mess. I should clean it up."

"Alright," he said with cynicism. "Just promise me something." He paused to make sure I was listening closely. "Don't get sucked in. Figure out what you need to say to leave on a better note. That's it. Don't let it get away from you. Ok?"

"Ok."

I went downstairs to Bryan's office and said, "Guess who sent me a text?"

He slumped a little in his chair and looked at me with the same expression of resignation that Jeff had. He knew who sent the text and he knew what I was going to do.

"Your sister?" he asked.

"Yep," I said, handing him the phone. He read her message and slumped a little further into his chair.

"Korva, don't do it," he said like he was trying to appeal to something in me and knew it was a pointless effort. "You aren't going to get what you want out of this."

I felt like I was hearing an echo. *Were he and Jeff in cahoots on this or what?* I saw a brief snippet of Jeff in my mind, shrugging with a grin.

"I don't want anything out of this. I just don't feel right about the way I ended it with her." Even I could hear the child in me justifying herself in my words.

"No, Korva… there's something else you want. I don't know what it is, but I know you won't get it. Why open that door back up? I mean, didn't you just throw a bag of snakes in there?" That made me chuckle, and I needed that. I was feeling all too serious and the levity was like fresh air.

"Bryan, I know I shouldn't do it, but I have to."

He gave me a hug and said, "You do what you have to do. I'll support you either way." Then he laughed and said, "I won't even say I told you so."

I gave him a playful shove and laughed. "Whatever. Jerk," and walked away.

I sent her the following text around 8am.

> *I can talk a little later this morning, but I have some parameters. It's got to be on FaceTime, and I get the first 5 minutes. I promise to be respectful and keep chill. I ask that in conversation if there is something you have to lie to me about, that you tell me that rather than lie. I can then choose whether to accept that and continue our conversation. Would you still wish to talk?*

To which she responded:

> *It's Josh's birthday so the only time I have to talk today is while I drive to run some errands. We have plans for the rest of the day, so if you want to FaceTime it would have to be another day. You're welcome to take as much time as you'd like, but that means I get the same if I feel it necessary to make my own point. I am going to put out there though that I've stayed out of the middle of this intentionally and that's what I intend to continue to do, so if you ask me for details on anything our parents did, I'm going to tell you to ask her. There's lots I don't know and none of it is my*

responsibility to mediate. I won't be repeating our conversation to her and won't repeat hers with you.

Sure she wasn't going to repeat our conversation. I already regretted opening the door again.

"Yep… ahhh… I… um… told ya so," said Jeff from his chair. His gaze never broke from the chickens he was so content in observing. "Hey, I never promised not to say it. What did you expect, Korva? She's pissed."

"She's pissed? Fuck her!! She's mad at me for being mad at her?" I was fuming.

"Yeah, I get it," he said, "From your perspective she has no right, but she doesn't see it the way you do. She thinks she got screwed. Well, at least that's what she's convinced herself of."

"Well, I don't disagree there. She did get screwed. But not by me. And in my book, she made a choice. As soon as her mother let her in on the big secret, there was no such thing as staying out of it. Her mother took away her choice of neutrality, forcing her to choose. And she chose."

"Again, that's your story," he said before I could even finish the last syllable. "And… you'll never get her to buy into your story. So don't bother."

I sat with those words, and they didn't want to sink in. How could she not see what she had done? I just couldn't get it.

"Look, Korva, in her story, she's the victim. So are you, to a certain extent, but she thinks you asked for it. I mean, she isn't wrong."

"Excuse me, what did you just say?" I said, shooting him a look that suggested that I needed him to defend that statement before I released the Kraken.

"I'm not saying that it's your fault, but you have fed into every narrative of you that has ever been written. So, from her perspective, you were fulfilling the prophecies and getting what you deserved."

"So, she doesn't feel bad at all. She really thinks she was minding her own business?" I asked.

"Well, I didn't say that. But she can't accept any other reality right now. And really, Beans, what she thinks and feels is none of your business. How do you feel? What do you think?"

"I told you already," I said, not wanting to repeat words I was getting sick of hearing myself say.

"Well, there it is." He looked at me with a cocked head and squinted eyes and asked, "You still going to talk to her?"

"Well, if I had any respect for my own boundaries, I'd wait until later this week when she can facetime but.....," I said, hesitating to finish my sentence.

"Everything before *but* is bullshit, so what's the truth?"

"I don't have the patience to wait. I want this over with. I know that I am once again bailing on my boundaries but… that's ok. I just need this to be over."

"I get it. And that's ok. But moving forward, let's work on that. It would behoove you to leave people hanging a little bit longer and a little more often."

He wasn't wrong. Silence and patience have never been my strongest suits. That said, it doesn't mean they can't ever be.

Against my own better judgment, I sent her a text agreeing to her terms. We would talk while she was running errands and not over facetime. I'll admit, I felt suspicious and wondered if there would be someone in the car with her but chose to overlook it. I wasn't going to say anything that I didn't want repeated. On the contrary, I was so full of righteous indignation I would happily rant to a car full of witnesses, friend or foe mattered not.

We worked out a time to talk. She could squeeze me in between errands and kid's softball. She had said that if I wanted more time, we could wait until later in the week, but, again, I wanted this over with. I had about two hours to kill and decided to use that time getting myself clear on what I wanted to say. I sat at my outdoor dining table, writing notes and organizing thoughts. Bryan came out to check on me and asked what I was up to.

"I'm getting my thoughts together before this call. I want to make sure I get a couple of points across."

He chuckled and said, "You realize that as soon as you start talking, all those notes may as well get tossed out the window."

"Nuh-uh," I said like a ten-year-old kid. But then laughed and admitted, "Yeah, you're right. Conversations never go how we plan them in our heads."

"Nope," he said. "What did you say your commitment was? To end things on a better note?"

"Yeah."

"Remember that. Don't get sucked in," he said, once again reiterating everything my father had said.

"I will. And I won't."

The phone rang a few minutes late. Felt like a power play but maybe not. "Hello," I said, sounding hesitant.

"Hey," she said. Her tone sounded curt and annoyed, as if to relay that she did not appreciate having to deal with this.

I said, "So, should we get right to this?"

"Might as well," she said.

"First, I want to apologize," I said. I had my notes in front of me and I was sure that this time I'd make a conversation work out as desired. I spoke slowly and intentionally. "You're right. It was unfair of me to take out my anger on you and your mother equally. While most of that hatred was aimed toward your mother, you didn't deserve to experience the full one hundred percent of it. It's more of a seventy-thirty split."

She made a "hmmph" sound that suggested she had her own thoughts about my assessment, but since the agreement was that I had the floor, she kept her mouth shut.

I continued, "Listen, as far as me wishing for you and your mother to get what you deserve… I picked those words for a reason. You see, I want you to deserve good things. But now, I don't know who you are or what to believe about you. You're saying that you're innocent, but the bottom line is now I can't trust you, so I don't believe you. And if you are doin' me dirty, I have no problem with the universe teaching you a lesson for it. But that isn't what I want. I want good things for you. At least the person who I thought you were."

I could feel the tension mounting in me. I was losing my grasp on whatever cool I might have had. Even though I couldn't see her, I felt like she wasn't listening to me and that she was just waiting for her turn to talk. I supposed that it didn't matter whether she was listening or not. I was saying these words for myself, if she didn't hear them, that's on her.

I took a deep breath and let it out with an audible sigh, "Ya know, I hear you when you say I'm not the only victim. I know you're a victim, too. You got put in a fucked-up position and I'm sorry for that. It never should have happened, but you gotta own that you made a choice. You lied to me, and you chose that course of action. And I hear you when you say that you were just 'staying out of it,' but ya know… I don't think that's a thing. As soon as you knew anything about what was going on, there was no staying out of it. You were in it."

I took a deep breath to help temper my anger and continued, "Jennifer, I don't want people in my life that 'stay out of it' when they see other people hurting me. I want people in my life that have my back, and I don't think you do." I could hear impatience and agitation in her breathing and the noises she made but continued.

"Listen, I don't care anymore about who did what, when, where, how, or whatever bullshit. All that matters now is that I don't trust you, and I sure as shit don't trust your mother, and from that perspective I can't have a relationship with y'all. I wish that wasn't the case, but here we are."

I paused for about 10 seconds, not knowing what to say next. I had a whole list written out in front of me, but now none of it seemed necessary.

"Are you done?" she asked without hesitation.

I fought with the notion that I should use the full five minutes that I asked for, but I didn't have anything left to say. I said with reluctance, "Yeah, I guess so."

"Ok," she said, and I had the sensation that I should put on a seat belt because she was about to take me for a ride. "First of all, I want you to know that I agree with how you are treating my mother about this. It's fucked up what they did to you, and you should be mad. I would be too. But…," she paused, and I remembered what Jeff said about everything before *but* being bullshit. "…you had no right to go off on me like that.

I'm just as much a victim in this as you are. How dare you come at me like this is my fault. I just… "

I cut her off, "I've already apologized for this. I'm not going to apologize again."

"Oh, well, yeah…," she said, sounding thrown off. I'm sure she had her own list of talking points that just got tossed out the window. "Well, I don't know what you expected me to do. After that whole Thanksgiving drama, when I had to handle their bullshit and clean up their mess, I told them to keep me out of it."

So, I was right, she had been sent to handle me after that incident. She called acting like my sister but was in fact an operative. I didn't say anything, and she kept going.

"I mean, I told them this exact thing would happen, but they didn't listen to me." Her smug self-righteousness disgusted me. All this told me was that she was more interested in being right than protecting me or my feelings. I kept that to myself. "Oh, and as for the property with the barn. That's not mine. Nobody bought me any properties."

"I know it's not in your name, it's in the family trust, but it's for you. Why would your mother need an extra ten acres of land and what would she do with a barn? You're the one with the horse. That barn is for you. I mean, duh, come on now…" She knew by my tone that I was not buying any brand of her bullshit.

She said, "Yeah well, have you seen the barn?" insinuating that it was in bad condition. However, her statement acknowledged to me that I was right.

"Still nicer than my barn," I said with a good eye roll. "This isn't the point. It's not about the goddamn barn. It's about fairness. Your rich mother, who got rich in large part from the labors of *our* father, is about to move into the same town as you and you are going to benefit from it. A lot. And you know it. I don't begrudge you that. I never have begrudged any of the things you got that I never had. I want you to get good things and have a good life. But it's not fair and I can't keep watching it happen. It hurts and I'm tired of it. I'm tired of being treated as less than. And I can't keep being lied to when y'all try to cover it up."

She stumbled over her words a bit "Yeah, I get it. And uhhh… well, we'll see." Then with regained clarity, she said, "But I'm not talking about the properties anymore. If you need to know anything about it, you'll have to ask my mom."

"Yeah, nope. I'm never talking to your mother again. Ever. She has told me one too many lies. Whatever is up with these properties doesn't matter. It looks shady and I'll never trust being told otherwise."

"Jeff lied to you, too, ya know. He's just as much to blame," she said spitefully.

"Yeah, well he's dead." I spat back.

"I know he's dead. You aren't the only one who lost someone. I lost my father too."

"Yeah, I know. But I didn't betray you in the process," I said and started to cry. "My father had just died, and you were lying to my face. And your entire demeanor toward me changed, like, the next day and I had no idea what the fuck what was happening and…"

She cut me off, "My demeanor changed!? You were the one that started acting weird!" Her pitch was reaching a level I'd never heard from her. Was this how she argued with people? I'd never heard her like this.

"What are you talking about?"

"You know exactly what I'm talking about," she shouted.

"Um, no, I don't. I was just responding to what I saw in you. You two were acting all weird. And now I know why."

"You don't know anything. If you thought something was off, you should have just asked." Jennifer said sharply.

"Bullshit. I did ask. And you lied. You were already fucking lying to me… and your solution for my upset is for me to ask you for the truth?" Now I was mad. I took a deep breath and found a sliver of calm. "From my perspective, from the moment Jeff died, you occurred as though you were mad at me. You ghosted me. You avoided topics. You were just overall weird. And then, neither of you two reached out to me on his birthday. That really hurt. I felt so alone."

"Well, you could have reached out to us! Why is everything on us?!" she shouted angrily at me.

"Because I couldn't. You two were together and had each other, and I had already told you how insecure I felt. You know, like I did not belong. I guess I hoped you'd prove me wrong."

"Your feelings aren't my responsibility, Korva! If you wanted to connect you should have reached out. It's a self-fulfilling prophecy. You think you don't fit in, so you act like you don't, and then you don't!"

"Oh my god, stop gaslighting me," I said in disgust.

"Pftt, whatever… You're just looking for ways to feed your narrative. You are the one that has been manipulating us. Trying to see how we'll act is manipulation!!" she was still shouting and now was in a complete tizzy.

"Look, I don't know… maybe it was manipulative… but that wasn't the intention…"

"See?? You were manipulating us!! You just…."

She was about to go off on that tangent when I said, "Perhaps so… I never did know how I was supposed to behave in that environment." Something about that must have hit close to home because it stopped her in her tracks.

"Well, yeah…," her voice softened.

"Look, we're never going to see eye to eye on this. Who's the victim and who's not. You vilify him and I vilify her. Over and over. Never agreeing. Again, Jennifer, none of this matters to me. All that matters is that there's no coming back from this. I'll never have a relationship with your mother again. Ever. And because you are a link to her, and because I can't trust you now, I can't have a relationship with you either. I wanted to talk to apologize for having gone off halfcocked on you, but I don't think there's anything left to say. Maybe we can try again down the road. Maybe not. I don't know."

We sat for a moment in awkward silence before I continued. "As for your hope of us all stepping out of our given dysfunctional roles," I said, having to restrain myself from making any statements about who I think gave us those roles, "I've already stepped out of mine. I quit that job. I mean, I know I'll keep being scapegoated, for years to come, but it won't affect me. It can't touch me. Y'all can throw me under a million buses, and I won't feel it." *Good lord, that felt good.*

Having had my share of discomfort for the day, I said, "I don't think there's anything else to say. I hope for good things for you and your family. And maybe we'll be able to reconnect down the line. Maybe when you're able to be honest with me..."

"… Or when you're willing to trust me," she said.

"Yeah. Well… take care."

"You too," she said. Her tone was awkward and unsure. "Love you."

"Love you too," I said in a mirrored tone.

I hung up and let out a huge sigh of relief. I was done. That was it.

Wait, that was it? It felt all too anticlimactic, like I'd expected fireworks or something. But no. I sat in silence in my greenhouse, all alone, for what was one of the most significant and impactful conversations of my whole life. On September 18, 2022, I left the matrix of dysfunction that had programmed me as scapegoat for the last forty years, being fed garbage and convinced it was a square meal. Now that I could see it and I would never again be blind. My life, my real life, begins now.

Chapter Twenty-Five

Monday, September 19, 2022, the first day of my new life, looked like any given Monday morning. I expected to feel like the newly-reborn-from-my-ashes phoenix that I thought myself to be. But no. Up at 6:27 a.m. to take the kids to their respective schools. Starting with my daughter.

I enjoyed these early morning rides to school with Annie. We're either recounting our dreams from the night before or just being goofy morning people. But this morning I was caught up in my head thinking about my conversation with my sister and the list of things I hadn't gotten to say. After I dropped Annie off, I started thinking of the text I wanted to send her later. I intended to specifically warn her about the newly opened job of scapegoat. If I was right, it would be a position given to her husband next, or maybe her son.

An image of Jeff entered my mind. He was in the passenger's seat. And he was angry.

"Are you mad at me?" I said with a tone of "how dare you?"

"Yep," he said.

"What!? What the hell are you mad at me for?" I said with genuine shock.

"Because, you need to keep that damn door shut, Korva. It's done. You got your pound of flesh, now move the hell on."

"I know, but there's one more thing that-"

He cut me off. "What did I say about 'but?' And there's always one more thing." He took a deep breath and calmed down as best he could. "Listen to me, leave it alone. You're done. Stay done."

I let out a sigh, "Ok."

"I'm serious. You need to cut yourself off. Unfriend, block, and delete every tie you have to them. Facebook, gone. That Pinterest App, delete it. Don't look. It won't make you happy. Just stay done."

"Ok, ok. I will."

I considered what he said, and the words "pound of flesh" stood out to me. Is that what I had done? I mean, I had thought that this lashing of truth and honesty was righting a wrong, but it was more than that. I was hurt, and I wanted them to hurt too. How many times had I done that? And if I had taken a pound of flesh, had I fully paid for it?

"One more thing," he said, his tone less harsh.

"Oh wait, you get one more thing?" I said with a chuckle, trying to further diffuse the tension.

"Yeah yeah, Wise Guy. Anyway, have you seen it yet?" he asked. I had to think for a moment to get his meaning.

"You mean whatever it was that I was supposed to see in Jennifer's text message?"

"Yeah," he said.

"I'm not sure. I can see that there's no way we'll ever find agreement. But…," my voice trailed off. "Gimme a hint,"

"What's missing?" he asked.

I could tell him what I could see – anger, denial, blame, frustration. *What was missing?* Then it hit me.

"Sadness. She wasn't sad. She didn't cry or express regret. She wasn't… sad. She did not hurt. She… didn't see this as a loss." It was so clear that I could not believe it took me this long to see it. "She doesn't care." I heard my own son say the words to me months ago, but it wasn't until this moment that I felt the truth of it. I understood it with clarity and detachment. She did not care.

"Bingo! She isn't being affected. She will be… one day. But for now, she's fine. It's all business as usual. She doesn't care. I'd say that I'm sorry about it, but it's not a loss to you. You'll get that someday."

"Yeah, I think I may already be getting that now," I said feeling a little surprised by how okay I felt.

"Go easy on yourself, Beans. It's gonna be a rough couple of days. But you're almost out of the woods."

He wasn't wrong. The next couple of days would prove to be a real challenge. There was indeed a price to pay for that pound of flesh. Some folks refer to it as the three-fold law. For everything you put out into the universe, it comes back in threes. I had three truths of my own to face, and God or Spirit or the Universe or whatever you call it, conspired to force me to confront them.

While they were all truths that related to my own nuclear family, only one of them is mine to share. My husband accidentally let it slip to my daughter that *mom smokes weed.* She and I had to have a rather long and uncomfortable conversation. I had to answer questions I didn't want to answer, and those answers led to more revelations. In the end, I'm glad that it happened. I'm also grateful for the other two truths that were revealed, because it created an opportunity for vulnerability and growth.

Monday night, one night after my departure from the matrix, sleep was still hard to come by. I had counted three payments of that law and wondered if there would be more. What other things out there do I need to be accountable for? The minutes of lying around restless turned to hours, as I felt an increasing sense of anxiety and impending doom.

"Oh my god, Beans. You gotta settle down over there. You're done. It's all good," Jeff said. It was sometime after 1:30 in the morning.

"You sure?" I asked. My voice was small and cracked with fear.

"Yes. Just had to make sure you would walk the walk. Ya know, like you're not living in a glass house."

"Um, excuse me. You wanna say what? Did you drop all those truth bombs? Were you testing me?" I said, feeling a little torqued. I was tired. I did not need any more damn testing.

"Yeah," he said, shrugging. "I mean, if ya talk the talk, Beans…"

I let out a sigh, rolled my eyes, and said, "Fair enough. But listen, this is done, yeah?"

"As long as you keep that door shut," he said with emphasis on the word shut. "You open that shit back up, and there won't be anything I can do for you. But as long as you keep the past in the past, that's where it will stay." That must have done the trick because it was the last thing I remember before drifting off.

Midway through the day on Tuesday, September 20th, I realized that I hadn't cried since Sunday afternoon. For the first time since… well… sometime last December, I went a whole day without crying. I also had something fun to look forward to, I was meeting with Lacie Rodriguez to do my alternative hair consultation. I was both terrified and excited, but relieved that I was taking what felt like an empowering step in my hair loss journey.

She started our zoom call with, "So, tell me about your hair loss. Where are you in the process?"

"Well, I started losing my hair when I was twenty-five." I laughed and said, "In hindsight, I feel the same way about my hair as I do about my weight… I wish I was as fat as I was back when I first thought I was fat. In other words, I wish I hadn't wasted so much time stressing about my hair at twenty-five, because as time would prove true, it coulda been worse."

"I know exactly what you mean," she said, and I knew she meant it.

Being able to talk to someone about this, without fear of judgment or pity, was so refreshing. I mean, I have discussed it with close friends, but they just don't get it. They have plenty of hair. And, while I know they want to say nice things or give endless suggestions to be helpful and kind, oftentimes it falls flat. But Lacie got it.

"Since then, I've been on the roller coaster of hair loss. It comes and goes. But the trend is downward. I've been wearing my hair in a high messy bun-ish thing for years. And now, it's not even concealing the loss." I had to pause to choke back some tears. She understood.

"Here's how I see it. I'm going to be uncomfortable going bald, and I'll likely be uncomfortable wearing a hair piece. But at least with alternative hair, I'll have more fun."

"Well, and there's ways to be covert about it," she said with enthusiasm, but I cut her off.

"I don't need to be covert. I don't care. If it's obvious that it's not my hair, that's fine. I mean, one day someone has no boobs, the next day they do. People talk and then they get over it." I let out a sigh of both relief and resignation and said, "Look, even if I stopped losing hair, I'll never have the hair I've always wanted. That's just the reality of it. If this is how I can finally have fun hair, then so be it."

She said, "You sound like you're in a good place."

I said, "Yeah, I'm ready for what's next."

She smiled and said, "You sure are."

Lacie gave me the complete run down on the different types of alternative hair and their respective pros and cons. We discussed what I was looking for in length, color, and style. Later that afternoon I received an email with suggestions of three different toppers that would fit my criteria. She also suggested not waiting to make a choice as these hair pieces move fast. That night, I picked one out and paid more than I care to admit to have it sent two-day express.

I had only three days to decide whether I would keep the piece I had chosen. I was investing quite a bit of money into this piece and I wanted to be certain that it was worth it. I wore my topper as much as I could over those three days and tried to go about life in a business-as-usual kinda way, but it was odd.

First of all, it's hot and heavy. I'm not used to having that much insulation on my head. I'm also not used to seeing myself with a ton of hair. I felt more comfortable about it when I was out in public, alone, because no one knew what I was supposed to look like. I did, however, feel a little insecure around people that knew me well. I figured that was a sensation that would pass. All that said, I did know after three days that while I wanted to keep the topper, I would likely not wear it daily or even regularly. If I was dressing up for a special occasion, then I would. Or maybe I needed the insurance of having it. If I lost more hair, I would have an immediate solution. It was relieving and liberating and, dare I say, a little exciting.

By Wednesday morning, I was feeling good. For the first time in months, I didn't feel burdened by unfinished business. All I had to do now was heal. I had two whole days without crying, and this morning my first thought wasn't "oh yea, my dad is dead" followed closely by "oh yeah, my stepmother and sister are treacherous bitches." Thankfully, there was none of that this morning. I felt lighter.

It was another average weekday. Up early, driving the kids to school, feeding my chickens, tending to any necessary gardening, dishes, and other household chores. Nothing unusual, but it felt like a fresh new day. At lunch time I sat down to eat some leftover chicken and dumplings and watch a little *Supernatural* on TNT. All was well with the world. And then it happened.

Pah-ting My phone chimed the familiar noise of someone messaging. I thought it was the group chat with Toni, Runa, Susan, and Tina. That message thread *Pah-ting*s many times a day. But nope. This message was from no friend of mine. It was from Joni.

My gut dropped, my chest tightened, and my stomach considered sending those few delicious bites of leftovers back to the chef. "Fuck," I said out loud. My dogs looked at me with concern. "Fuck fuck fuck fuck fuck." I stared at the phone in my now sweating hand. "What the fuck does she want?"

I went straight to Bryan's office, handed him the phone and said, "Read this. Tell me if this is worth me reading."

My hands shook as I handed the phone to him. I couldn't believe how quickly I had gone from a state of calm and content to wanting to vomit. It was faster than a sprint car, like zero to sixty in 2.2 seconds. Dammit, I hated how much power she had over me.

He read it, expressionless, while I paced back and forth in his office. When he was done, he sighed and said, "Shit."

"Shit what!? What do you mean shit!?," I asked. I was ready to explode with anxiety.

He paused and narrowed his eyes on something only he could see. I tapped my foot, squirmed, and paced, trying my best to contain my angst.

"Well, it's just… She's just… so… practical," he said trying to express something he couldn't quite put his finger on.

"What the fuck do you mean?" I said, wanting him to get to the damn point.

"I don't know. I guess she… um… seems rational. It's just the facts ma'am. She's not angry or emotional. She's just spelling it out," he said, and gave me a look of concern. "Shit, maybe I shouldn't have encouraged you to end things, Korva."

"You wanna say what? Look, should I read the message or not?" I was pissed. Given the tone of my voice and the palpable tension that rippled off my body, Bryan could tell. He took a step back. *How could he doubt his support of my choice to ditch these people?*

"I guess you can," he said, "there's nothing bad about it."

I snatched the phone out of his hand and started reading.

Obviously, I think there are a few issues that we need to discuss. First, however, I do want to apologize for not having spoken with you sooner about the plans to move to Indiana. Jeff and I contemplated different options to take after his retirement. Indiana was the best choice to cover concerns that we had, and we decided to go ahead with that plan. We did not want anyone to know about the plans until we purchased land and had a chance to talk with James. Having said that we should have let you know once the land was purchased. Again, I apologize that you weren't informed.

In August we bought the 20-acre parcel. We didn't want the 10-acre pasture at that time but we also didn't want anyone else to buy it and build on it. So, we set up a First Right of Refusal on that parcel. On December 22nd a Purchase Agreement was signed by two couples with the intent of building on the lot. That Agreement plus a letter from the owner was overnighted to us. With everything that was happening and the fact that it was a holiday weekend, I did not check the mailbox until the following week. In keeping with the First Right of Refusal, we were informed that we had 30 days from December 22 to purchase the land or forfeit it. Since I still didn't want anyone to build on the land I went ahead and purchased it in January.

Again, I'm sorry that neither Jeff nor I told you when we purchased the land. It is unfortunate that Jennifer has been caught in the middle as she said more than once that you needed to know. Let me know where you want to go from here. I think everything else is something that needs a phone conversation.

"Fuck," I said out loud to myself, realizing what Bryan meant. Her message made me doubt myself too. I guess all that added up. Maybe I had made a huge mistake. I spun around and left the room. I needed to get some space to move and work this out. I ended up pacing the upstairs hall. "Shit, what have I done?" I thought.

"Read it again," Jeff said, his voice breaking through the tension that was building up in the space between my ears. "I feel like a broken record over here, Beans. Breathe first… and then read that again." So, I did. I paced back and forth, up and down my hallway, reading that text message over and over until I saw it.

In between the lines, hidden behind layers of psychological coding and years of Pavlovian training, I could see it. After forty long years, I could see it. There was something she did - she had always done - and I could finally distinguish it. First, I could see that every single one of those words was chosen with the purpose of making her look sane and me look insane. Her words were mostly true, at least enough to float, but they weren't the whole truth. And none of these so-called facts were verifiable. Jeff was dead so he had no say. And what was I supposed to do, ask her for documented proof? I had to take her word, the word of a known liar, that this well-crafted text message was the truth.

"She's lying," I said with certainty. "She's giving the closing dates on the property purchases to look better because the actual offer was put in at least 6 weeks earlier. Jesus, she must think I'm stupid." I read the message again. "And does she expect me to believe that after being on the market for over 15 months, someone just happened to make an offer on this property the day after you were put in hospice care, and the goddamn day before you died. I mean, what are the odds? Somebody get me a damn mathematician because those odds are wild."

But as assured as I felt, in the next breath I felt a pang of doubt. It was ingrained in me to doubt myself, yet I knew I couldn't believe a word she said. This gaslighting was working well, and right as I started to get worked up again, I caught myself.

I took a deep breath and blew it out hard. "Shit. Maybe it is true. Maybe it isn't. But it doesn't matter. It doesn't change whether or not I want her in my life. I don't. That's not changing. I've never been more sure of anything. Ever."

"No, it doesn't matter, and I'm glad you can see that," Jeff said, sounding relieved.

"She sure threw you under a bus or two," I said, acknowledging that her message put quite a bit of responsibility in Jeff's lap, which I thought was unfair. "I mean, she can't expect me to think that you were the mastermind behind this," I said with a little chuckle.

"Yeah, no, not the mastermind. God knows that would have been too much work for me," he said, returning the chuckle. Even in life, he was too quick to be self-damning. It was a thought that caused passing sadness. "But seriously, Beans, I shouldn't have gone along with it. And I have no good excuse for that."

"No, you don't," I said in a tone of reprimand but then lightened. "You've said sorry, and I've forgiven you." I felt content knowing that was true. "Her on the other hand… um… nope. Nuh-uh. That was the most pathetic excuse of an apology I have ever heard. In my life. She says she's sorry she didn't tell me sooner. She should be sorry that she *lied* to me. And she's not sorry. She's just sorry she got caught and now Jennifer is pissed at her… allegedly. She's deflecting and hoping that her manipulation works with me, again, so that we can go back to whatever bullshit we had before just so her daughter will stop holding this against her or whatever. Um. No thanks. Hard Pass. Not today, Satan."

I returned to Bryan's office a different person than the one who had walked out just ten minutes ago. "Um yeah, this is gaslighting. Or stonewalling. Or well…both," I said as he looked up from his computer curiously. "It's what she does. She acts all nonchalant about whatever has happened, seeming rational to make me look like a nut case. It's gaslighting. It makes people doubt me. It makes me doubt myself." I looked over the rim of my glasses and said, "But you know what I don't doubt? That she's both pissed as hell and anxious. She ain't as cool as this message would lead you to believe. No way."

I let him take that in for a second and continued before he could respond. "Also, all of those words are equally true and untrue. True enough to pass a lie detector, maybe, but they don't paint the whole picture. It's a tactic. She's probably stewed on these words for the last few days, finding the perfect ones to fulfill whatever selfish goals she has. She wants to make me happy enough to have a relationship with Jennifer, so she's off that hook. But she has no intention of ever being honest with me or showing me any respect. But hey, that gaslight worked didn't it? At least for a minute."

"Yeah, it did," he said and went silent for a moment. "Ya know, Korva, I'm always impressed by your ability to change. To change your perspective, your direction, your goals, your focus. I just…," he stopped to think. "I'm just impressed that you have made this whole thing with your parents, all this bullshit this year, work for you. Like, I can see that… you're better for it."

I started to cry, and he gave me a good hug. "Thanks, Bryan," I said sniffling. "You know what's great? It doesn't matter to me anymore." I backed away so I could see his face again. "For a brief moment, I felt doubt. I felt shameful and embarrassed for having overreacted. I felt regret. But only for a moment. That relationship needed to end, and it doesn't matter what made it happen or how it happened. And those things I felt for a second back there, I don't have to feel them anymore. It doesn't matter."

The anxiety I had felt when I had first saw her message was gone and I had returned to the same state of calm I had started in. In the past, it would take hours, or sometimes days, to feel relieved from the anxiety symptoms I experienced after parent triggers. But now, less than fifteen minutes and I'm good, feeling grounded and sure. I did the right thing. Had I done a neat and tidy job of it? No. Was I right about everything? No. Would I do it again? Hell yes, I would.

This state felt like closure. A simple "hell yes, I would do that again" was what I needed to start packing that world up and leaving it behind me. I knew I wasn't done returning things to the past, but the grounds I had gained were remarkable. And better yet, I knew that I would keep gaining ground. I would continue to erect boundaries, and I would protect them with vigor.

The parts of me that have felt less than or unworthy were healing in a tangible way; I was no longer willing to engage in unhealthy or abusive relationships. For so long I had settled for what I could get because I didn't feel worthy of anything else. But no more. I couldn't begin to imagine how this would alter the trajectory of my life, but I was excited to find out.

No Mas

Chapter Twenty-Six

The remainder of the year, while less eventful, certainly was not easy. I still had to get through the rest of "Smoke Season" (blech), a couple of the year's most significant and sentimental holidays, and a surprising amount of residual psychological baggage before I hit the one-year anniversary of Jeff's passing.

This year, there were several fires feeding smoke into the air currents that passed by my home. The Bolt Creek fire was the closest, at about forty-five to fifty miles away. It started on September 9th and burned until October 21st. Usually by the end of September the moss is starting to take over my lawn again, but my grass was still dead brown and crunchy dry. It was hot, and I am talking summertime hot, in October. Which I suppose would have been lovely except the air was unbreathable. Our Air Quality Index or AQI, which is the measurement of particulate matter in the air, is normally excellent or good with an AQI of less than 20pm. On October 20th, the AQI peaked at 357pm, which is considered hazardous to breathe.

I didn't go outside. I couldn't. It hurt my throat and made my eyes burn within just a few minutes of being outdoors. I was grateful there wasn't much to do besides picking the last of the ripened tomatoes. Even then I would wear a mask. If I wanted to see a bright side to all this prolonged heat, every tomato I grew in 2022 ripened on the vine. It was a first and certainly a phenomenon for the Pacific Northwest. And something I could live without if it means more smoke seasons. No thanks. *I pray this is not the future of our climate.*

By the end of October, at long last, the rain returned. It would be an abbreviated season of fun harvest-time festivities. Which was fine because my normal enthusiasm for Halloween was missing. This year there were no parties to attend, and my kids had made plans with their friends. While I love costumes, there was no reason to dress up. This year's annual observation of honoring my ancestors would look very different, too. Now, I would be adding my father to the list of ancestors I remember on this day.

During our kitchen remodel, I had converted our old china hutch into an indoor greenhouse. It was now brimming with plants, many of which had been Jeff's. On Samhain (pronounced Sow-in, aka Halloween), I added photos of my departed loved ones. I put up pictures of Jeff, my mother, my grandparents, my Aunt Lizza, my good friend Melody, and my cat Autumn. I added my mother's rosary beads, my grandmother's grandmother ring, and my dad's old zippo. This hutch was now my ancestral altar, and it was really blossoming into this repurposed job. To think, last fall I had considered getting rid of it.

That night I had a dream that was truly worthy of Halloween night… and it shook me. I dreamt that I lived on the top floor of a three-story apartment building that looked to have been built in the early 1900s. It was made from tan masonry, and had ornate architectural accents painted in blue and burgundy. It reminded me very much of the Chelsea Apartments on Queen Anne in Seattle, where I had lived from 1996 to 1998. But the building in my dreams wasn't in the city. It stood alone in the middle of a forest.

I was in a small bathroom, just large enough for a pedestal sink, toilet, and tub/shower combo. The floor and walls were covered in mint green tile. Up high on the longest wall of the tub enclosure was a small rectangular window. Its purpose was primarily for ventilation, with natural light a secondary goal. In other words, it was small.

I was standing at the sink, looking into the mirror of an old school medicine cabinet, when I caught movement out of the corner of my eye. There was something coming in through the tiny shower window. I turned quickly to see what it was. Oh my god, it was a woman. *I think*. She moved like an octopus through the window. Her body seemed to collapse into itself to allow her to get through such a tight space. Her hair was long, black, and oily. It was strung across and stuck to her face. Her skin was gray and dirty cloth, which had once been white, hung loosely from her bony skeleton.

She lunged at me. In a flash, I remembered that my nightstand was just outside the door and that there was a revolver on it. I missed her grasp by a hair, grabbed the gun, and started shooting. I blew off at least four rounds, each hitting her squarely. She did not flinch and kept coming at me. When she was too close for me to shoot, I hit her with the butt of the gun, over and over, at least a dozen times. No effect. I stopped, looked her in the face, and with as much lunacy and rage as I could conjure screamed, *"Get the fuck out!"* with enough force to redden my face and burn my throat.

My voice boomed. The percussion of my words knocked her backward into the wall. From there I was able to grab her, ball her up like a dirty old rag, and toss her out the window. I slammed it shut and locked it. She looked back at me through the window, and I watched her mouth contort into a devious grin. I realized that we, because my family was with me, were still very much in danger.

I knew how this thing had gotten into my third-floor apartment. There was a ledge outside the entire third floor meant for maintenance access. She could still be on it and trying to get in. I raced around and locked all the windows, as well as the door to our outdoor patio. Even though I had done everything I could do, I still didn't feel safe. She was still out there. On the ledge outside my house. I had to put an end to this.

I stormed out onto my balcony to access the ledge and told my kids to lock the door behind me. I needed to make sure she wasn't still up there. As I crossed the balcony, I had a flash. I remembered that there had been unexplained disturbances on that patio, as well as in the woods by my house. This *thing* had been the source of them. It had always been there, stalking me and my family. Now, I was even more determined to put an end to it.

I made my way out onto the ledge, unphased by the heights, which came as a surprise given my real-life fear of it. I started searching around the perimeter of the top floor. All the while, screaming at the top of my lungs in the direction of the woods, "I'm going to fucking find you!! I'm going to find you and I'm going to fucking end you!!" I mean, I was losing it. Growling like a wild animal, wide-eyed and foaming at the damn mouth.

I came to the ladder that allowed access to and from the ledge from the ground level. There were two maintenance men working on something I couldn't see. I, in my frenzied state, informed them that a crazy woman living in the woods had attempted to gain access to my apartment. They told me to go to the office in the lobby. They would check things out and meet me there. Of course, I'm still screaming at the woods, to this boogeywoman, that I'm going to get her. I had just told those two men to look out for a crazy person, and I was sure they walked away thinking I was referring to myself.

I made my way down the ladder, around through the front door of the building, and into the lobby. There was a long line of people waiting to speak to the manager. As I was making my way to the front of the line, I passed a bank of elevators. One of the doors opens and out walks a giant lion, directly in my path. I stopped, strangely unconcerned. It bumps its gigantic head into my arm like a domestic cat would give a loving head bump to its human.

As if by the snap of a finger, I am brought back to calm. I remembered that my next-door neighbor had exotic animals and decided that rather than pursue this monster lady in the woods, I should return this cat to its owner. As I'm getting on the elevator, another lion enters with us. I pressed the number three button, the doors closed, and I woke up.

The next morning, I recounted the dream to Bryan. "Well, you don't need a psychologist to tell you that the monster thing is Joni, but I wonder about the rest of it," he said.

I agreed and wondered the same, so I consulted with my friend and favorite dream interpreter, Runa Troy. She also agreed that the monster figure was likely my stepmother and was able to add clarity to some of the other features.

First, the ledge around the upper floor of my apartment represented my boundaries. They start off being weak and were letting in the literal boogeywoman, but by the end of the dream I'm defending them with all I have. The flashbacks represent my new understanding of all the ways my stepmother had shaped my behavior and subconscious. And the lions represented my strength to overcome this monster, as well as the protection I'm being granted by my ancestors and guides.

This dream seemed to dislodge a few nasty psychological bits. Even though I was feeling less and less phased by my family-of-origin issues, it seemed that every other insecurity I had in my current life was prime for triggering. I spent the next month having to convince myself that my children weren't going to reject and leave me as soon as they are able, that I'm not a complete burden to all my family and friends, and that there are people who do like me, and it's ok if there's only like ten people, as long as they're good. I could go on and on, but the point is that I was seeing deep into the programming. *November was heavy.*

My oldest son's birthday is at the beginning of November. Although I didn't expect to hear from Jennifer or Joni, I wondered whether either would send cards for him. My stepmother may not have done anything to have a relationship with my kids, but she always sent the checks… Oh, I mean guilt money… Whoops, I mean cards. But not this year. I thought, "Phew, I guess I've heard the last of them." But that's not how things would go.

In mid-November, my friend Katrina and I took a weekend trip to the Olympic Peninsula, to stay at Katrina's parents' home. They were off snow-birding in Arizona. Their home, nestled in the woods above a golf fairway that you can only see a sliver of when the trees are bare, was like a magical treehouse. Katrina's mother, Kate, had decorated for Christmas prior to leaving for Arizona. The lofted ceiling provided ample space for a tree that stood tall and slender in the corner of two walls of windows. The lights on the tree reflected off the windows in a way that mirrored and multiplied the golden sparkles. They seemed to go on forever. The tree's decorations' style matched the home's mid-century modern décor. It was simple, tasteful, and added to the already fairytale feel of this home in the trees.

It wasn't an eventful weekend. As a matter of fact, we didn't leave the house once. We had brought all we needed. We cooked and ate delicious food, engaged in self-care-oriented pampering, and gabbed about all the things. At one point Katrina asked about Joni and Jennifer.

"So, you're never talking to them again? Aren't you curious about what they're going to do?" she asked.

"I mean, yeah, I'm curious. But I don't want to know. I'm not in a place where I'd be happy for them, but I also don't wish them harm," I said, then shrugged and grinned. "...mostly."

"Well, I do. I wish them… not well," she said and tried to mask her dark side with a little *teehee*. But I knew better.

"Yeah, it's hard not to. I do have a little revenge fantasy that I whisper into the candles every now and then." There was a devilish glint in my eye.

"Oh yeah, girl… Spill it," Katrina said.

"Ok, here it is. My hope is that Joni falls in love."

Katrina cut me off, "So far, you're bad at this."

I laughed. "Hear me out. I want her to fall in real love. Like cuckoo for cocoa puffs love. I want him to be the whole package. Rich, handsome, smart, romantic. All the things. And… I want him to have a daughter."

"Okaaaay…" she said, catching a glimpse of revenge potential.

"I want his daughter to also be the whole package. Educated, successful, beautiful, slender, flawless, well loved by all the creatures of the land. I want her to be an only child and the apple of her father's eye. She's married to a handsome and successful man and has a gaggle of gorgeous children that Grandpa dotes on. He never misses a soccer game or play."

"Okaaaaaaaaay…" she said, clearly wanting to know the hitch.

"And daddy's sweet baby girl… does not like Joni. And after years of turmoil, Joni gets dumped by the man she loves because he chooses his daughter over her."

"Ahhhhh, I see what you did there."

"Yeah, and Jennifer will be triggered to compete with Loverboy's daughter, so it'll be like a two-fer."

"Oh yeah, I hadn't gotten there yet. Love it."

"Heh, yeah. I read somewhere that entertaining revenge fantasies is just a sign that you still haven't healed." Being vindictive wasn't in my nature and made me uncomfortable.

"And why would you be healed? Give yourself a break, Korva. I mean, I hope one day you don't think about them at all, but if today you need a good karmic fantasy, then that's ok." She was right.

I was glad to have had that little getaway with her. Having these few days of respite made a huge difference for the state of my mental health. I still wasn't out of the woods where grief was concerned. I had two firsts without Jeff that were fast approaching, Thanksgiving and Christmas. I would also be experiencing the first anniversary of his passing. I could sense the oncoming tsunami of emotion en route, and I wasn't looking forward to it. At least now, I felt rested, stronger, and more prepared for what was to come.

My youngest son's birthday is around Thanksgiving. When the actual date came and went, and I saw nothing from my stepmother, I thought I was in the clear. Not so lucky. It was Thanksgiving's Eve. I was in the kitchen chopping onions for my stuffing. Bryan came inside from getting the mail.

"Korva," he said in a sharp and serious tone. It made me feel like a kid who had forgotten to do her chores.

"Um, yeah?" I said nervously, worried about what could have caused his stern demeanor.

"A card came from Joni today. It's for Alex." I felt like this was the version of Bryan that the people at work talk to.

"Well, shit," I said in my best fake southern accent. I stopped chopping and put my knife down. I felt a brief pang of anxiety, but it was gone in a flash without effort.

"What should we do with it?" Again, he spoke with such seriousness.

"Shit, I dunno. I wudn't expectin' this," still with the bogus southern accent. And that was the truth, I didn't expect this. She hadn't sent anything to William and now I wondered why. Maybe because he was twenty-two, he had aged out of receiving birthday cards? I mean, that sounded like some bullshit she'd pull and not explain herself.

"Well, we need to make a choice here. If we don't intend to have a relationship with her, there's no integrity in taking her money," he said.

"Oh yeah, I agree one hundred percent," I said, gaining greater focus and losing the accent. "I never intended to cash her checks or whatever. I'm just wondering what I should do… should we open it? Send it back "Return to Sender" or burn it or what?"

"Well, let's get the kids in on this discussion. Ya know, this card isn't addressed to us," he said and called Annie and Alex into the living room.

The kids had been kept up to speed on what was happening. I didn't think that there was any good reason to keep it from them, so Alex was able to make his own informed choice.

Bryan showed Alex the card and said, "So this is from… Mimi. It's likely a birthday card and there's probably a check in here. Alex, it's your choice, but Mom and I think that if we aren't having any real relationship with… Joni, then we shouldn't take her money. What do you think?"

Alex responded without hesitation, "Yeah, send it back."

Annie chimed in with, "Wait, whaaat? We should take her money!"

I shot her a look of astonishment and surprise but not anger.

She said with a laugh, "What? – heheheh – I like money. I mean, who doesn't? And, if she's going to act the way she is, shouldn't it cost her?" I had to laugh because she wasn't wrong. "But seriously," she said, no longer teehee-ing quite as hard, "I would send it back, too."

Later we talked with William, and he'd agree as well. I still didn't know what I was going to do though. Open it, return it, or burn it? In the meanwhile, I kept the unopened card under a pile of garlic to keep the soul-sucking vibes at bay.

I hosted a low-key Thanksgiving. Bryan's sisters came over for an early dinner, and William and Josie came over for dessert. To my own surprise, I didn't experience any triggers. I think that it's because I didn't have many sentimental Thanksgiving memories of my father or my childhood family. The only memorable Thanksgiving was the one I didn't get invited to. I was thankful to find that this memory no longer upset me.

December was an emotional rollercoaster. I had expected to be triggered by the anniversary of Jeff's passing, but the anniversaries of him dying hit harder than his actual death. On December 13th, I remembered it was a year ago that day that I got the call from Joni telling me that Jeff had been hospitalized. And each day between then and the 23rd, I'd think about how Jeff's days, just one short year ago, may have looked. I wished I could have been there. I wished I could have helped. I wished I could have made him feel loved and cared for. It will be a long time before I forgive both him and my stepmother for having taken that from me. And myself for letting them.

Chapter Twenty-Seven

On the morning of the 23rd, the anniversary of Jeff's passing, I woke up to a world froze over. It had been snowing off and on since the 19th. We had about four inches of accumulation overnight on the 22nd. Then on the 23rd, we had freezing rain on top of it. There was a thick layer of ice covering everything the eye could see. The world outside shut down, as evidenced by the eerie silence of complete inactivity.

It was perfect for me though. I needed the excuse to be still on this day, and nature helped make it happen. I had planned to spend the day cooking, cleaning, and preparing for Christmas, but now we had to reconsider our plans. Christmas was going to be similar to Thanksgiving, Bryan's sisters would come for early dinner, and William and Josie for dessert. However, his sisters lived far enough away so that travel would be adversely affected by this whole weather situation. Rather than busting my ass to get ready for Christmas, only to cancel last minute, we chose to reschedule for the next weekend. My day, as if by magic, opened up.

I enjoyed a leisurely cup of coffee and watched the frozen wonder out my front window. That's when I noticed the family of four small dark-eyed juncos flitting about in the Japanese maple just outside. I thought, "Oh no, poor little birdies must be freezing… and hungry." Well, that put me on the mission.

First, I refilled the bird feeder that we have hanging in our dining room window, as well as the hummingbird feeder on the back deck. I found a heat lamp for the hummingbird food to ensure it wouldn't freeze. I also put out solid, black plant trays full of bird seed in several locations in my front yard. I then resumed my coffee drinking, cozy on the couch, and watched with curiosity what would come of my efforts.

The juncos found the trays first. Little by little, four tiny birds turned into sixteen birds, including small birds of mixed species, plus a couple of crested jays, also known as Steller's Jays. Within an hour, there were so many I couldn't count them. The ground seemed to crawl with birds flitting to and fro.

"I always loved watching birds," Jeff said from his favorite living room chair. "They fascinated me. And...," he paused and narrowed his eyes in concentration, "I envied them."

I could tell Jeff was formulating an explanation of what that meant. We sat quietly for several minutes as I watched him focused intensely on something I couldn't see. He then pursed his lips, drew in a deep, audible breath in and out through his nose, and continued.

"I didn't care much for being human." He paused and looked at me out of the corner of his eye. I think he wanted to be sure that I wasn't upset by what he had said. When he saw no sign of discord, he moved on. "It was boring."

He turned to me with a pleading look on his face. "And, ya know, don't take that personally. You weren't boring." He stopped to laugh. "You, Beans, are anything but boring." He returned to a more serious demeanor and continued. "No, being human was boring. I mean, at least the way it's being done. I hated my fuckin job… but I also hated being broke. I hated pretending and lying and all the bullshit complications. I hated explaining myself. Oh my god, I think I hated that the most."

I thought back to how much I had wanted to understand him and how many times I wanted him to explain himself to me. I should have known how much it would bother him. No one with an Aquarius sun and Mercury wants to explain themselves, because even if they did, they wouldn't feel understood.

"No," he said, his tone grave. "No. Dying of cancer was what I hated the most." He shook his head and let out a heavy sigh. "I was glad it was over. I mean, I'm sorry that it hurt, Beans, but I wanted it to end. I still appreciate the outro you gave me though. I couldn't have asked for a better way to go."

"So, what's it like… ya know… being dead?" I asked, feeling awkward. I mean, what's a tactful way to ask that?

"It's… busy. Look, Beans, whatever you do, keep your unfinished business to a minimum. The postmortem clean-up is a bitch. You aren't the only one I've got my eye on, ya know. Plus, there's all the karmic shit. It's wild." Then he smiled, with raised brow and a grin, and said, "But it's definitely not boring."

"So, what is our unfinished business?" I asked, not knowing if I really wanted to know.

"Well, that's a lot to unpack, Beans, and not for today. But my first order of business was to get you outta that situation." He locked eyes with me, and I could tell he wanted me to get what he was about to say. "Look, Korva… You don't belong there. You hear me? You are not one of them." His face was stern but then softened. "And I'm glad for that. Just… stay away from them, Beans. I'm tellin' ya, there's nothing good for you there. I want you to keep that door closed like it's the most important thing you have to do."

"Yeah, I will," I said with confidence.

"It may not be so easy. They are committed to making you the bad guy, Korva. For your own sanity, you need to start being ok with it. Embrace it even. You can't stop or fix it, so don't even try." He gave me a look that reiterated that last sentence, knowing that it's hard for me to leave things alone. He furrowed his brow and continued, "Listen," he sighed, "people who are trying to cling to their narratives will do and say the shittiest things. Be ready for that."

"Yes, I'm half expecting to hear all about how you didn't love me." I had already walked through the exercise of hearing that several times. Plus, I had already gone through that after my mother died.

"It's quite possible you will hear that, or something like it. And I'm sorry for it. I gave them plenty of ammunition to use against you…and me."

For a moment I felt a familiar wave of anger and pain, but it drifted. "Yeah, I know. It's ok." I thought about that for a second and said, "Correction. It's not ok. And I forgive you. *No mas* with that bullshit though. No more scraps off the table. No more swimming across an ocean for someone who won't jump a puddle for me. *No. Mas.*"

"*No mas* is right, Beans."

"So, what now? I mean, I think that part of our business is finished," I said with a sudden sensation of fear. I wondered if he'd leave me now.

As if reading my mind, he said, "I'll be around. Ya know... if ya need me. But you seem to have things squared away. Plus, I've got some other unfinished business to attend to."

"Yeah, well… good luck with that," I said, trying to hide my disdain.

"Heh, yeah," he said and got lost in thought for a second until he seemed to remember something. "Oh hey," he said, "Little change of subject… Listen, the plants are all looking pretty good. Thanks for keeping them alive. I appreciate it. But... um… I noticed a couple of my orchids are lookin' a little rough. Can ya give 'em some love?"

"Yeah… no."

"What??!!," he said with astonishment.

"Sorry. They're too much work and not enough pay-off. I mean, I know they're important to you, but… I'm a little too busy right now for finicky plants."

"Huh, I can't believe you just said no to me." He said with genuine surprise but laughed it off. In his defense, it wasn't something I had done… like… ever.

"Yeah, well… I say no to things now," I said with a smile and a wink.

"Fair enough," he said. "I suppose you do have a lot going on." He looked around my living room. "You've made a good life for yourself, Beans. It really is… beautiful. The home you've made is vibrant and warm. It does feel good to be here. And your kids…," he stopped, shook his head, and smile as his eyes welled with tears. "I wish you and I had what you and your kids have. Your relationship with them is true and real. I know you do your best and I'm so proud of you. Our day will come, you and me. Next time, Beans. Next time,"

December 23, 2022, in addition to being the anniversary of Jeff's passing, was also the Capricorn new moon. I thought back to the last one, which happened on January 2nd of the same year. I was with Toni. I considered the new moon wishes I had made and how they had manifested.

1. *I want to easily find myself in a new and healing relationship with my father.* Well, I could put a big check mark next to this one. While I was still on the fence as to the nature of the relationship, it felt "new and healing."

2. *I want to easily find myself listening to and expressing my own inner authority.* I'll call this my second check mark. I had put an end to accepting scraps. I had created new boundaries and was learning how to keep them. I had learned to have more faith and trust in my own intuition and rely less on the thoughts of others.

3. *I want to talk to Dave Matthews.* I'm still working on this one.

I'd made a lot of progress since the days following Jeff's passing, and I still had a long way to go. I look forward to the day that I no longer consider what could have or should have happened. I know there will come a time when I don't even think of Joni and Jennifer. I look forward to that as well. In the meantime, I'll be kind to myself, call on my father when needed, and tend to what's left of Jeff's plants.

I Hear You Singing to Me Still

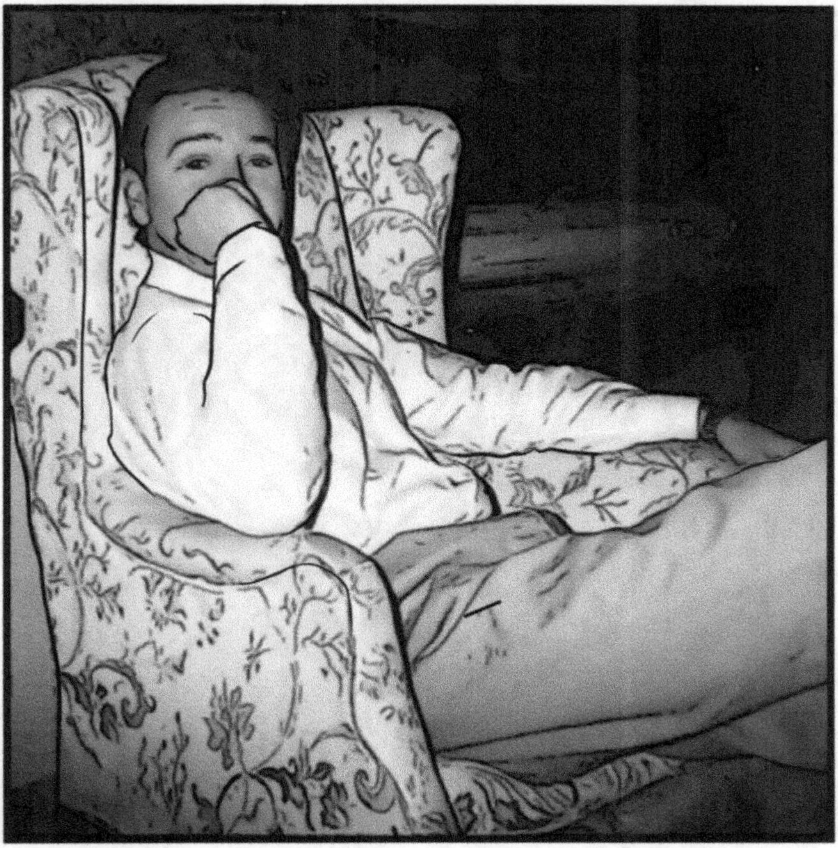

Epilogue

He was right when he said that I would have to be intentional about keeping that door closed. In the week between Christmas and New Year's Eve I would receive packages from both my stepmother and half-sister. My stepmother sent her usual manilla envelope addressed to me. I knew that there would be cards for each of the kids, but not for Bryan and myself. I didn't open it this time, because I didn't want to know whether she had cut William off. I didn't need any more reason to be mad at her.

My sister also sent an envelope addressed to me. I did open hers. Just cards for the kids. We, as a family, had already determined that we weren't going to pursue a relationship with these people. As per this agreement, we would not be accepting the gifts. After the holidays had passed, I sent them back. No explanation. I don't need to justify myself.

The middle of the following week, Bryan and I were sitting on the couch watching TV when I received this text from my sister.

Hey Korva. I hope you guys had a good Christmas. I got the package with the cards I sent for the kids. If I'm completely honest, it was hurtful, and I didn't feel I deserved it. I sent those because no one's children did anything in this situation, and it was a genuine attempt to be kind in spite of everything going on. I will continue to send them just as I have in the past, and you will be welcome to return or discard them.

I look forward to a time when we're able to work to repair a relationship but will continue to maintain the boundaries I've worked hard to learn and allow me to be healthy, which for me looks like not trying to fix situations I did not create and are not mine to resolve. I hope you're able to find what brings you peace as well. I love you.

"Well, there it is," I said and looked over at him. "I just got a text from my sister. Wanna know what she said?" I asked, sounding bored.

"Yeah, sure?" he said, his eyes wide with confusion.

"Ah, let's see…. I'm a big meany for sending her stuff back… umm… She was just trying to be nice since the kids shouldn't have to suffer because of our drama…. Ah… bullshit, bullshit, bullshit… and… uh….," I looked down and scanned the message and said, "Oh yeah, she doesn't think she deserves this because she didn't do anything wrong." I turned off the phone screen, put it down, and went back to watching *Modern Family*.

"Huh. Are you surprised?" he asked.

"Nope."

We watched TV for another few minutes until the next commercial break. "So, what do you think they'll do now?" Bryan asked.

"Those two? I dunno. Life goes on, yeah? I mean, they'll keep scapegoating me for, like, ever. But you know what's awesome?" I said with a tone of amusement as a thought came to me.

"What?" Bryan asked.

"They'll use me as something to power struggle over, and by doing so they will fight my fight for me."

"I'm sorry, what?" Bryan asked and straightened up a little, as if sitting taller would help him understand.

"Well, Jennifer will hold the fact that I don't have a relationship with her against her mom. She'll use it as leverage. And I can't blame her.

It'll be one of the only power tools she has. And then, Joni will call Jennifer out on her bullshit, reminding her of the fact that she made a choice AND benefited from it. They will fight my fight for me. I don't even need to be there. It's beautiful," I said, pleased with myself and my likely-to-happen revenge fantasy scenario.

"Heh, that's probably pretty accurate." He said and settled back into his seat. "You gonna respond to Jennifer?" he asked with his eyes back on the TV.

"Nope."